CONNOR

THE BILLIONAIRES OF WHISPERS
BOOK 3

SAMANTHA SKYE

EBOOK ISBN: 978-1-923258-10-5

PAPERBACK ISBN: 978-1-923258-11-2

ALT PAPERBACK ISBN: 978-1-923258-12-9

Cover Design: Angela Haddon

Editor: Nice Girl Naughty Edits

Proofreading: Kimberly Dawn

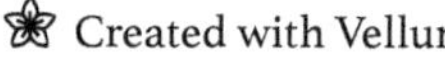 Created with Vellum

1

DAISY BECKETT

I fold the bed linen just the way I like it before looking around the room.

"Was there any other special requirement?" I call out to my mom. The two of us are the only ones here at the moment, a small reprieve from the long line of clients we've had all day.

"What's that, dear?" Mom asks, her voice serene, even when she's raising it.

I ensure the essential oils are tidy and light a few candles. Our Sunshine Space Wellness Clinic is one of the most tranquil places in all of New York. Somewhat of an institution, it's where I've worked and trained with my mom since I left high school. Sure, the place is pretty old now and needs a total refurbishment, and Mom hasn't invested in any of the modern technological upgrades. Her life of natural well-being is something she was born with, and it remains to this day.

"I said, did they require anything else with this couples' booking?" I take one last look around and walk out of the special treatment room, heading toward our tiny kitchen. Mom has a few jars of mung beans on the small window ledge, as well as our herbal tea collection, one we developed ourselves. She keeps our cupboards full of remedies for everything from insomnia to sexual appetite.

"They? Oh no, sorry, honey, I must've forgotten to tell you in between the shiatsu treatment I did this morning and the acupuncture treatment I had straight after it..." She looks a little flustered as she steeps some of our homemade herbs in some hot water to make a tea concoction.

"Forgot to tell me what?" I ask, puzzled, watching what she's doing.

"There's only one person coming today. They had to cancel the duo. Can you still do it, though? My hands are aching," she asks, and I frown as I look at her hands. She seems too young for arthritis, but it's starting to riddle her joints, especially in her hands and wrists. Her knuckles are getting a little larger, creating some disproportion to her fingers.

"Sure. It's not like I have a hot date or anything," I murmur, only half joking. It's Friday, and while most girls my age are heading out for afterwork drinks, maybe at a nice bar in Manhattan, where they'll flirt with the bartender or a businessman, having the time of their lives, I'm here.

"Oh, have you met any interesting men lately?" she asks, looking hopeful, clearly interested in an update to my very sad love life. I roll my eyes.

"None who like a girl like me." I pull at my top, glad I

chose the flowing tunic today. It hides my rolls and curves a little better.

Her lips pinch as she notices my body language. "There's nothing wrong with you. You're beautiful, inside and out."

I give her a tight smile as I play with the Daisy chain necklace she gave me when I turned twenty-one a few years ago. Something she made when she was young, now handed down to me.

"You're my mom, you're supposed to say that," I tell her, appreciating her love. Unfortunately, though, the majority of men in this city don't share her views. I haven't been on a date in months. The last guy took one look at me and told me he "wasn't really feeling it," then made a quick exit. We barely even spoke, and the embarrassment of that night still stings, my confidence in dating now at an all-time low. Humiliation is a constant feeling for me when it comes to the opposite sex. Has been even since school. I was always picked on for my weight, and even now, being plus-size doesn't really sit on the majority of men's wish lists.

"Soooo, have you thought about that new booking system I was telling you about?" I ask tentatively. While Sunshine is amazing on the wellness front, we severely lack any type of business support, policies, or growth plans, but my mom doesn't have an eye on the future.

"I don't think we need anything like that," she says in a tone that I know too well. The one where I know she hasn't even looked at my proposal to invest in some computers, along with a new software that will book, rebook, and do direct messaging to clients to ensure they're continually provided information about new products and treatments, making it easier to progress our business.

My passion for business isn't something that I studied or had any desire for when I was younger. Now, after a few years here, my interest has grown, and I really want to take Sunshine to the next level.

"But Mom, I really think that—" I start to say.

"Honey, computers have too many electromagnetic fields to combat; I've told you that." Still smiling like she doesn't have a care in the world, she waves off the idea. I, on the other hand, feel my once relaxed shoulders now up around my ears. It isn't like this is my first time suggesting business growth to Mom. Last month, I tried to discuss commercializing our tea into a brand that we sell online or through other spa sanctuaries and wellness businesses. The month before, I tried to talk to her about my biggest passion, yoga, and offering yoga classes online via a membership subscription. But again, she didn't like that idea either.

"I understand, but there's just so much potential at Sunshine," I tell her, hoping she can see it too, but as she gives me her small smile, I know she doesn't. A hippie, through and through, not interested in anything that remotely sounds like commercialism. I commend her for her steadfast approach to staying true to her roots. I mean, that's what makes Sunshine different. But the world is changing, and I want to be a part of it. When she doesn't answer me, I decide to drop it for now.

"Are you making some tea for your circulation?" I ask, changing the topic. I grab her favorite teacup from the cupboard for her, the one she's started to have trouble clasping. I smell the herbs, taking a deep breath in, visualizing them coating my insides as my mom hums, the mood around me relaxing again.

"No... I'm just making this up so it's ready for our next guest. A little afternoon pick-me-up." There's a weird look on her face when she glances at me, one I can't place.

"Are you feeling alright?" I ask her, looking over her body. Her hands are obviously bothering her a lot. But other than that, Rainbow Waterfall Beckett looks exactly how you would imagine. The commune life she grew up in lingers in her appearance, as all these years later, her hair is still long with a few purple streaks, her skin is free from makeup, and her aura is perfectly balanced. My dad, an accountant, is the complete opposite.

"Oh, fine, dear. Just a little tired. Don't forget, it's a full moon tonight," she explains, and I nod, making a mental note to clean my crystals, knowing that's what she's talking about.

I sit at our small table, watching her with the tea. I have a few more minutes before the next client arrives, so I might as well take a load off.

"You know, we should really be doing a full moon meditation online, or at least a big sale on crystals each full moon or something..." I murmur to her, my mind buzzing with new business ideas, yet fully aware she won't appreciate my business talk because, apparently, she's allergic to it.

She sighs, like I'm annoying her, and gives me a look. "Sunshine is fine the way it is, honey. I like simple. I like natural."

I mean, I love yoga, meditation, and natural remedies, too. I try to salute the sun every morning, and I consult the crystals. But I'm my father's daughter and, clearly, I got my business brain from him.

"Sure, Mom... whatever you say," I agree with her, albeit halfheartedly, biting my bottom lip as frustration nips at my skin. Sunshine Space Wellness Clinic is all I've ever known. We have great clients, but I've reviewed our paperwork. We're not growing. In fact, we're going backward. We aren't getting new people in the doors. We haven't moved with the times at all. And I ache for it. I want to push, I want to grow, I want to build something.

Starting something new, that's just mine, would be a dream come true, especially in the yoga space, but it would probably break my mom's heart and would also require financial investment, so that isn't going to happen either. So, until I win the lottery, I'm here, every day, all day.

"I can see you thinking, Daisy. Leave it to the universe; it will make the decision for us," she says, smiling. Only my mother can take what I think are crucial business decisions and hand them over to the universe for answers.

I nod, taking a few deep breaths. "So what am I doing this afternoon?" I ask her as I try to get my mind on the task at hand, now that I'm in charge of our last client.

"It's a sound therapy and then yoga flow," my mom says. I frown. It's odd; I never do personal yoga flows. I usually just run classes, which is another thing I've been meaning to discuss with her.

"Is it a friend of yours?" I ask her, assuming it is.

"No..."

I don't know how I know, but I feel like she's not telling me something.

The windchimes connected to our front door tickle through the place, indicating someone has arrived.

"Oh, that will be him now." Her eyes glisten as she grabs the tea, pouring it into a cup. For someone who's too tired to do the treatment, she's certainly quick to get to the door.

"Him? I thought I had a female for this treatment?" I confirm with her before she exits the kitchen, stopping at the door, looking back and giving me her smile.

"Oh... no, darling. It's a male, and his name is Connor. Let me go check him in." Then she's floating down the small hallway, her long purple dress flowing behind her, and I sigh.

Is this really all I'm going to do with my life?

Maybe Mom is right. Maybe the universe will decide for me.

2

———

CONNOR WHITEMAN

This is the last thing I have time for. Yet here I am. If Lacy wasn't my best staff member and Hudson wasn't one of my best friends, then there's no way I would put my hand up for this shit. Hopefully, they enjoy their private time in New York, and we can all move on with bringing the Whiteman's Distillery Spa to fruition.

It will be a game changer. I can feel it. All the wives and girlfriends who accompany their partners to our small town to drink our whiskey need something to do if they don't like our liquor. And a wellness retreat is the perfect thing. It'll complement our nearby mineral springs, and while Lacy and Victoria are in charge of this research trip, they both had to leave early. Since I was coming to the city to watch the Jets this weekend anyway, I was lumped with testing the final treatments they had lined up. The plus side to it all is now Hudson owes me. Big-time.

"Shall I wait, sir?" my driver asks as we pull up to the

side of the street, having reached our destination. I look out the window and frown. He's clearly unsure if we should even be here on this side of town, let alone getting out of the car and going inside this shanty.

"Might be a good idea..." I murmur to him as he steps out and holds my door open and I meet him on the side-walk. I glance up and down quickly. The street is pretty quiet, all the shops a little nondescript. There's a small café next door, which is already closed, a children's clothes shop a farther up, and I think I see a convenience store at the end of the block.

It's a standard New York street on the edge of the city, and I have no idea why the girls chose this place to research treatments. I thought for sure I would be going to the spa at The Plaza or something.

Dressed in my gym shorts and a t-shirt, having no idea what to wear to a fucking spa treatment, I look back at the door. Sunshine Space Wellness Clinic is written in chipped yellow paint on the glass panel of the door. The timber doorframe is a muddy red color, flaking in the corners. It's clearly been here for some time.

I grit my teeth, a little frustrated, because I've a million other things to do today, preferring to meet up with Sawyer at the bar near our office to talk business, rather than be here, doing whatever treatment Lacy and Victoria have picked.

"If I'm not out in an hour, you better call 9-1-1," I tell him, only half joking.

"I will wait right here, sir," my driver says, and I nod, striding forward, wanting to get this over with.

I walk up to the door and push it open wide. Some

type of wind chime announces my arrival, and as I step inside, the smell hits me.

It's like someone is smoking weed. I breathe in and start to cough, my throat drying almost instantly. Yep, some asshole is in here smoking weed, I'm sure of it.

"Oh, that's our incense. It can tickle the throat if you're not used to it. Welcome to the Sunshine Space," an older woman greets me. She looks like a witch. Not an evil witch, just a normal witch, if there's such a thing. Her long black hair has a few purple streaks in it and a sprinkle of gray throughout. Her skin is pale and wrinkled with age. She's even wearing what I imagine to be witch clothes, a long, flowing dress that falls to the floor, again in black and purple, and I'm sensing a theme. I quickly look around, spotting incense burning, candles, teas, crystals, and all sorts of potions, and I wonder if the girls have sent me to have some sort of satanic seance or something.

"You must be Connor. Please, come in," she encourages me, and I blink. Should I really go any farther into this place? I can't see anyone else here, and I roll my shoulders a little. I could take her down if I needed to, right? As long as she doesn't tie me to the bed or anything.

"Ahhh. Thank you, ma'am." My voice comes out a little rough and reserved, my country accent peeking through and sounding nothing at all like her voice, which is very deliberate, melodious, and suspiciously calming.

"I've made you a beautiful welcome tea. Something to soothe your worries from the day before you begin your treatment with us." Thrusting a white teacup with daisies painted on it into my hands, I take it, the cup looking comically small in my large grip. It's cute, though, like it has meaning.

"I appreciate it," I say, still hesitant. I take another quick look around, noticing colorful throw rugs and blankets.

"My name is Rainbow. I'll need you to complete a new client form, and then we can begin. Please, take a seat. Relax. We like to leave all our stress at the door and come into Sunshine with an open mind." Passing me a clipboard, I feel like her voice would be ideal as background music in my new spa, maybe even for elevator music. It's very soothing.

"Of course," I say, sitting in a wicker chair that creaks under me. I take after my dad in my physical appearance. I'm tall, broad, large, and heavy. And I swear to God, if this chair breaks under my weight, I'm never talking to Hudson again.

I haven't completed a paper form like this in years. Usually, it's done electronically, and I look up, the woman getting busy behind the reception desk. I notice no computer, no screen, and I'm starting to think I'm in the twilight zone or something.

I look back at the form and fill in my details, mindful to leave the number to the distillery rather than my personal cell. I may be waiting for my death in this place, but I'm not stupid. Data theft is a real crime. Who knows what Rainfall or Rainbow, or whatever the fuck her name is, is capable of.

I finish the form and throw back the tea without thinking. The warm liquid hits the back of my throat before it nearly comes right back out. It tastes like shit, and my cheeks puff with the need to spit it out, but I look around, and there isn't a trash bin in sight. So, I gulp and immediately grimace as the earthy taste slides down my throat. I close my eyes, hoping it doesn't kill me so she can harvest my kidneys or something.

"So what treatment am I in for today?" I ask, having no idea and not a lot of patience for this kind of thing. I'm expecting a relaxation massage. I've had one of those before a few years ago, and it wasn't bad. I'm not really a spa kinda guy, though, and this whole situation makes me itch. *Or is that the tea?*

"We have you booked in for a sound healing massage and private yoga flow," she says, and I'm glad I have finished my tea, because I would have spit it out in shock. Sound healing? Yoga flow? I'm going to kill those girls for leaving this part of our spa research to me.

"I'll tell your therapist you're here." Her voice lowers an octave that decreases my stress a little. I clear my throat again. That incense feels like it's drying it out completely. I watch her walk down the hall, presumably to get my therapist. I'm bracing myself, thoughts churning about if the witch has a wizard, and if they're going to lead me to their cauldron.

But she comes back alone, a warm smile on her face. "Daisy will be with you in a moment," she says, nodding, and I reflect the motion, nodding back. Should I just cut my losses and walk the fuck out now? I have no idea who Daisy will be and what special type of hell I'm in for. I look back at the front door, seeing my trusty driver through the dirty glass panel, standing at the car, waiting.

"Hi, I'm Daisy, I'll be your therapist today," a soft voice says, one that has my immediate attention. My head swivels back around, and I lock eyes with her. Vibrant blue shines back at me, and my shoulders lower instantly. I'm not sure if it's the tea or if it's the fact that she's fucking beautiful. Her smile is small but welcoming, her lower lip slightly plumper than her top, giving her the perfect Cupid's bow that has me staring. She isn't like the other women I tend to see around the city, and although she's in a uniform of sorts, I can tell that she's a curvy goddess underneath.

"Connor," I grit out and give her a sharp nod, then immediately clear my throat. *That fucking incense.*

"Welcome, Connor. Just this way." When she turns, I get to appreciate her from behind. I usually don't stare at women. I mean, I look, I'm a hot-blooded male, after all, but as I stand where I am, watching her retreat, my eyes slowly run down and up over her frame again in appreciation. Her long, thick red hair trails down her back, almost touching her beautiful round ass, hips swaying with every step and putting me in a trance.

"You better follow. She can't do the treatment without you," Rainbow says from the reception desk, and I look at her quickly, seeing a smirk on her face at catching me clearly checking out the therapist.

"Thank you," I tell her gruffly and step forward, past a beaded door curtain that clatters against the timber doorframe as I move through, interrupting the otherwise peaceful sounds of what I think is waves crashing with windpipes, a sound I never hear in Whispers.

I duck a little, my tall frame almost too much for this

small hallway, and as the floorboards creak under my weight, I wonder briefly if I'm about to fall through them completely. This place looks so old, I wouldn't be surprised. The hallway is dark, the windpipes haunting melody tracking me the entire way. The only thing I take comfort in is her red hair as it moves as she walks, almost in time to those waves crashing in my ears. When we reach a room at the end, the windows let in more light, the ceilings higher, so I can stand tall and the air isn't as thick with incense.

"Okay, so we're going to start in this room today for the sound healing massage," she says, and I whip off my top.

"Ahhh, what are you doing?" She takes a step back, looking stricken. Her eyes dart around the room, at every-thing but me.

"Getting ready for the massage," I say as my thumbs hook into the waistband of my shorts. Sure, I'll keep my boxers on underneath, but I've had a massage before, and this is what they usually require. Just as I start to lower my shorts, she shrieks.

"No! Stop!" Her hand slaps across her eyes, shielding her sight from me. I pause, my shorts wrapped around my thick thighs, my clean white tight boxers protecting my manhood as I frown. That hasn't happened before. I work out, I'm in shape, and most women are in a hurry to take my clothes off. I've never had one who's hidden her eyes from me. I stop what I'm doing and look at her blankly.

"What's the problem?" I ask, confused, as her eyes remain hidden.

"This is a *sound healing* massage!" she blurts, her cheeks blooming to a vibrant pink, which is in complete conflict with her red hair, and I still.

"What?" I start to pull my shorts back up, feeling like I've committed a faux pas.

"It's a fully clothed treatment. I need you to put your clothes back on," she tells me, her hand not moving from her face, still not taking a peek at my nearly naked frame.

"Oh shit," I mutter, my shorts now back in place as I grab my top and put that back on as well. She remains rooted to the ground. Hasn't moved an inch. I stand quietly, watching her. Her large round breasts lift and fall quickly, but her hand remains glued across her eyes.

She's the first woman I can't take my eyes off, and she doesn't even want to look at me.

3

DAISY

I'm mortified and too scared to remove my hand from my eyes as I squeeze them together tighter. The vision of his very chiseled chest is now imprinted on the back of my eyelids and the only thing that I can see.

Sculpted doesn't come close to describing the chest that I just saw. Broad muscles, a scattering of hair that almost makes me want to reach out and touch him. He's an Adonis. My heart thuds. Like it does when I climb too many steps or hold a yoga pose for a long time. Not rushed, just hard, heavy, deep thuds, and I wonder if he can see my chest pulsing.

It's been a long time since I saw a naked man. It was one night maybe a year ago, when my roommate, Trisha, forced me to go on a double date with her. I didn't want to go, preferring to do anything else, but it was eighties night, and I love to dance, and I'm nothing if not a supportive friend. So I went, and the blind date I met up with was nice, and we unexpectedly had a good night.

The man was gone when I woke, and while I enjoyed it, I've never double-dated again. I'd rather dance in my room alone.

"I need you to please put your clothes back on," I say with some urgency.

I'm a professional, and I need to pull it together. I conduct wellness therapy services on men all the time. But it's usually Arlo, my mom's yoga coach, or Soren, the guy Mom buys her crystals from, who comes by every couple of months. But this guy? This guy is so far from the normal man I would even meet, let alone consult, it's making my brain short-circuit.

Most people who come here know what treatments they're booking for and know what that requires. Apparently, he doesn't. We don't actually do any treatments that require partial nudity outside of cupping and acupuncture. We have such a litigious culture at the moment, so we prefer not to open ourselves up to any issues that may arise from miscommunication. Like today.

"You can look now." His deep tone is a little sheepish, and I keep my hand where it is, splitting my fingers wider to create a peephole to check before lowering it completely.

"Where shall I put this?" he asks, lifting the teacup, which I notice is empty. I look at the cup in his abnormally large hands as I try to cool my body temperature.

"I can take it." Grabbing the cup from him, I move to place it on the cupboard. I frown, wondering why my mother gave him tea in her favorite cup. The little white teacup that I made in preschool with daisies painted on it, each petal my child-size fingerprint. I get a whiff of the elixir she made him and inhale the slight aroma of Maca, freezing as I remember the herb concoction she was steeping earlier. *I'm going to kill her.* She gave him tea to promote sexual arousal. Our aphrodisiac tea. No wonder she was smiling at me weirdly. I clear my throat, putting that to the back of my mind to talk to her about later.

"If you would like to lie down on the bed, we can start," I tell him, turning my back to him so I can take a few seconds to get my head right. I hear him shuffling around, the bed creaking under his weight, and I look up to the ceiling, praying the old bed holds steady. He's a big man, and if it doesn't hold, I'll be mortified. I had put a proposal forward six months ago to Mom for us to invest in new beds, the ones that I could mechanically raise and lower with a foot pedal so that I didn't have to lean over so much when doing treatments, but again, she wasn't interested. So, these old, timber-legged beds remain here, squeaking every time someone lies on them.

I gulp as he settles, hearing him take a deep inhale. My shoulders lower with the sound, my breath following his. I spot my tools for this treatment, grabbing my singing bowls of various sizes and my favorite mallet. I'm now ready.

He's silent as I walk back to the bed. His hands are joined and rest on his chest, his eyes closed like he's in a state of relaxation, and I run my eyes from the top of his head to the bottom of his feet. He has a full head of hair and is extremely handsome in a rugged, manly kind of way. He has a full beard like he works in the country, but I can already tell he isn't a lumberjack, although I got a hint of a Southern accent when he spoke. My eyes lower, taking in his thick thighs and sculpted legs, all the way to his feet, him being so tall they hang off the end of the bed.

"Are you just going to look, or is something else going to happen?" he murmurs in a lower, sultry tone that shouldn't sound as sexy as it does. I blush *again* but roll my shoulders and get started.

"I'm just getting ready," I say as I take a look at his client form in case there's anything I've missed. He's fit, healthy, a non-smoker. I notice he's from a town called Whispers, and his date of birth puts him at thirty-five, just over a decade older than me. I run through any known ailments, and then I'm all set.

"As you lie on the bed, I'll place various bowls on your body, in alignment with your chakras," I tell him, my inside meditation voice now apparent.

"My what?" he asks, and I roll my lips so I don't laugh. This guy is so far out of his element, it's almost comical.

"Chakras, they are the different energy points in your body," I say smoothly to try to help him relax. The sound pipes meditation music infiltrates into the room, and we're quiet as I get into my flow state. I've been practicing yoga, meditation, and sound healing for years now, and I love it. I enjoy treating people, having them leave the clinic more energized and aligned than when they arrived. I'm also an herbalist, the tea making Mom and I do my other secret passion.

He hums as I place the bowls onto his body, paying absolutely no attention to his amazing physique.

"The sounds of the bowls, along with the vibrations, will run through your body, creating a sense of wellness and calm." I tap onto one of the bowls near his feet. "You will experience inner harmony, and it will induce a feeling of very deep relaxation."

"Whatever you say, Daisy." He grumbles my name in what appears to be a half-asleep state. His slight Southern accent comes through again, saying the *I* in Daisy a little higher in his pronunciation, which does something to my insides, and the vibrations around my body start just by the sound of hearing it. I push that to the back of my mind and concentrate.

As I tap the bowls and get into a rhythm, I quietly move from his feet to the lower thighs, near his knees. His legs are more toned and tanned than most of the men we have come in here. I run the mallet around the bowl, trying to concentrate on the vibrations rather than his physique. Then I move to hit a bowl placed on his torso. He's so toned, the bowl doesn't move, and I can make out the ridges of muscle that I glimpsed earlier underneath his t-shirt. I find with other clients, the bowl can wobble because the foundation it sits on is usually uneven. Breasts in women, rolls of belly, or just normal stomach curves can make the bowl on the torso one of the harder ones to keep in place.

But not Connor. No, his torso is flat, tight, and the bowl sits completely flush against his body. I take a breath in, feeling my own bloated stomach tighten before I exhale, knowing it's futile. My stomach is squishy, and I let it go. When I look up to his face briefly, his features are soft, relaxed, half-covered by his beard that's well-trimmed and suits him. I spot his lips, the perfect shape.

That always happens. Men always get long lashes and great lips.

I refocus my mind, giving him my energy, soaking up his stress and worries, and after a while, I hear him dozing. Small tufts of air puff out his lips, and he looks peaceful. It happens sometimes and, clearly, he's either exhausted, or the sound healing is doing exactly what it's supposed to. I'm proud to have this effect on him and many of my other clients. It takes a lot for people in this city to truly relax and feel safe enough with me that they sleep with me standing over them. Given that this is Connor's first time here, it's even more surprising.

I continue on, quietly chanting my own meditative words to him, instilling energy, calm, and resilience into every tap of my mallet and every spoken word until the treatment is complete. Quietly, I remove each bowl and put them back, then turn to look at him, watching his chest rise and fall heavily in slow, rhythmic beats, him now in a full state of sleep and one I'm hesitant to wake him from.

So, I don't. I pull a light blanket over him and leave him in the room to relax as I tiptoe out. He'll wake up soon. His body will know when it's time. On light steps, I walk to the kitchen for a glass of water to replenish before I go in search of my mother, who kindly gave him our aphrodisiac tea.

She has some explaining to do.

4

CONNOR

I wake up feeling like I slept for days, except my throat is dry like I went on a bender last night. I can't remember the last time I smoked weed, but it's been a while.

Rubbing my eyes, I roll to my side, then stop, something amiss. The bed feels different, and I open my eyes and get my bearings.

I'm in a large white room. I spot bowls on the floor, the haunting melody of pipes coming through the speaker at the side, and my memory kicks back in.

I groan as I sit up, looking around the room for Daisy, the curvy redhead, who not only didn't look at me, but also didn't touch me. The sound healing treatment is something I've never heard of, but after about five minutes, it had me out like a light, so I guess they get a big check for relaxation, even if her hands didn't make contact with my body.

As I wake fully, I roll my shoulders, feeling less tightness than I usually do and the familiar ache in my back now gone. Pain relief, stress relief, and relaxation, all things I want for the distillery spa. I'm impressed.

Voices are murmuring from down the hallway as I sit up, so I grab my things and walk back toward the reception area.

"I need to go. You need to lock up," one woman says, whom I recognize as Rainbow, the witchy lady from earlier.

"Seriously? You're just going to leave me here with him?" Daisy says, and I balk. Clearly, she doesn't like me. My ego is getting more bruised by the second with this woman.

"Well, you're the one with magic hands," Rainbow says, and I begin to feel like a creeper just standing in the shadows of the hallway listening. But I'm not sure if I should retreat or walk out to meet them. Not wanting to interrupt, I remain rooted to the floorboards, scared to move in case they creak and give away my position.

"You gave him ginseng and ginkgo. You gave him our *tea!*" Daisy exclaims.

I frown as I swallow past the dryness in my throat again. That tea was pretty awful I have no idea what ginkgo and ginseng are, but I hope they didn't drug me. I lift my hand in front of my face, and I see it clearly, my vision not blurry, and I feel alright. Actually, I feel great. More energized than when I arrived here, that's for sure. I don't know how long I've been out for, but I feel like I've slept for days.

"So? I give it to your father almost every night, and he doesn't complain," Rainbow says, and I raise my eyebrows. Father? Is Rainbow Daisy's mother? And is she drugging her father every night, or is it some type of health elixir that they've given me?

"Oh my God, my ears!" Daisy groans, covering her ears. And I wonder why she continues to cover her face so much when she's so beautiful.

"He could be an axe murderer, for all I know, and you're leaving your only child here like a lamb to the slaughter."

I'm starting to see the family dynamic, and now as I watch them, they do look alike a little. I decide then to step out, because I don't want either of them to be afraid of me.

"Not an axe murder," I say, stepping out from the beaded curtain, putting my hands up like they're holding a gun to my chest. Daisy is odd. She doesn't want to see me, barely touches me, and now doesn't want to be alone with me.

"Sorry. I didn't mean..." She stumbles over her words, rubbing her face, looking flustered and remorseful.

"I need to go. Daisy will take care of things for you." Rainbow, who I now know is her mother, says, before she glides from the reception desk and out the door like she's floating on air. Maybe she is a witch. I look out the door after her, seeing my trusty driver still waiting outside.

"How long was I out for?" I ask and cringe, my voice rougher than usual, a clear indication my sleep was deep.

"Only about half an hour, but unfortunately, we need to reschedule the remaining treatment," Daisy says.

"Remaining treatment?" I question, because I thought that was the treatment.

"You and your wife were initially scheduled for sound

healing *and* a yoga flow. We'll need to reschedule the yoga flow. Perhaps next time she'll be able to make it?" she asks, looking up at me with those damn big blue eyes that do something to my insides.

"No wife. Just me," I confirm firmly so she really understands my meaning.

"Oh, it's just that today's booking was for two. A couples' treatment." Looking back at her booking diary, she frowns in confusion. Again, no computer to be seen.

"My staff were meant to come, but they got held up, so I'm here in their place. I own a whiskey distillery a few states over, and we're putting in our own wellness spa," I tell her honestly, waiting to see the penny drop of exactly who I am, but it doesn't.

"So you're spying?" Her hands find her hips in a defensive stance. My eyes narrow on the movement. She seems a bit feisty, I'll give her that.

"No. Researching," I clarify, sounding cocky, and her stance doesn't soften.

"Potato, potahto." She shakes her head.

"It isn't like we'll be taking any of your business," I murmur sarcastically, looking around the room again. It needs remodeling, badly. She inhales in a sharp breath at my comment. Maybe I stepped over the line too far by insulting her clinic, but I'm a businessman, a successful one, and I certainly don't need whatever lack of business sense they have here, regardless of how amazing that treatment was or how captivatingly beautiful the voluptuous woman standing right in front of me is.

"Oh, well, please enlighten me and tell me what you really think?" she retorts, crossing her arms over her chest. This conversation is moving into an area that wasn't my intention. But I'm honest to a fault, so I look around again, before my eyes land firmly back on hers.

"This space needs remodeling," I start, and her expression only hardens. "You need to introduce some technology for efficiency..." I add, thinking back to my form I manually completed. As I do, I swallow, my throat drying up from the incense again, and I cough. "And new scents are required, ones that don't make you feel like you've swallowed sandpaper."

"I just don't know how I haven't noticed all that before. You're obviously a very smart businessman." Her tone is full of sarcasm and sass, and I clench my jaw. *Yep, I overstepped.* "There must be something good here at Sunshine to make you come all the way here?" She asks a valid question that I still don't know the answer to.

"Clearly, it isn't the customer service." Apparently, I can't keep my mouth shut, and I see her mouth open in shock at me calling her out, her eyes burning holes into me, before her mouth closes and she takes another deep breath, like she's steeling herself.

"Fine. Okay. Well then... did you have any questions? About the treatment or anything? Perhaps I can give you my expertise for free so you can create your own amazing wellness center based on my experience and knowledge. You know... one that has a newer fit-out and a computer to do half the work for you?"

I'm not used to people taking this tone with me. Probably because I'm usually not such an asshole that I would step into someone else's business and verbally tear it down like I just did. Maybe that witch did drug me...?

As I look at her, I see no dollar signs reflected in her eyes, and she didn't offer any flirtatious remarks. In fact, it's the complete opposite. She's visibly annoyed, and perhaps when we booked, we should've been more transparent about our trip being for research. But most people I speak to jump at the word "distillery." Women, in particular, want to know all about it. And I know she saw my name on the client form, yet Daisy doesn't seem to care.

"I don't normally sleep when I have a massage," I grumble, not that I really know. I don't make a habit of taking time for massages, having only had one before, but I never was able to get my mind to fully relax, not like today.

"Is that a question or a statement?" she asks, eyebrows raised, and I bite my tongue. I should've expected that. She's quick. Calling me out. I clear my throat from the incense and try again.

"Can you explain sound therapy to me?" I ask a clearer question, something I'm not used to doing. I rarely repeat myself. Calm, confident, concise are all words that people use to describe me. Those attributes have all left me today.

"Sound therapy is good for relaxation. It taps into the inner body, sending vibrations through your cells and connecting those frequencies."

I nod, taking in the information and appreciating her words, yet having no real idea what she's talking about. She seems to see my confusion, and this time when she takes in a deep breath, her shoulders lower, more resigned to talk than wanting to.

"In basic terms, I think the sounds lulled your body

and mind to sleep," she says, smiling a little, that Cupid's bow now in full effect. I force my lips to stay level and not curve at the ends like they're wanting to. "That, or maybe you've just been tired and stressed lately and needed an hour of me-time."

There's been a lot going on. We're expanding the distillery, so work is busier than ever. Hudson is back in town, so I'm spending more time with him. Dad and Victoria are starting to settle into their new routine, and having a new person, especially a woman, in the family brings a new dynamic. Not to mention, her fucking goats.

"Tired and stressed sounds about right. You didn't use any oils or products, is that a usual thing?" I ask. From a pure financial point of view, the less products we use, the better for our bottom line. It also means less storage, less waste, and less opportunity for damaged products, so overall a better investment. Her eyes narrow on me, like she's seeing through me, like she's deciding how much information to offer.

"There are treatments where products are used, like a little oil during cupping, for example, and obviously needles during acupuncture and things like that, but what I do is work with the body for it to find its own natural rhythm. Mud wraps and body scrubs are all a bit of fun and topically relaxing, but they don't provide any harmony within the body for overall well-being and alignment. They also require a higher usage of water, more product, towels, heavier cleaning in the rooms between clients. They're a bigger burden on the environment, the staff, and so they eat into the profit more."

I raise my eyebrows. She clearly knows a lot about it,

and I have the feeling I severely underestimated her. I'm more about the dollars and cents, always looking at the bottom line, so it's interesting to hear her speak about it all.

"But... we do have after-treatment products, because with only two of us here, that creates an income ceiling, so in order to make money, retail is really where we need to focus." She walks over to the shelves in the small waiting area that I spotted earlier. "We develop our own teas, which are elixirs for a variety of symptoms, as well as build our own natural oils and blends for burning or massage. We also have crystals, which are not for everyone, but they do help bring a sense of natural energy to your body and your environment." As she showcases the products on the shelf, I feel like I may have been too flippant when I entered before, because Daisy is passionate and clearly intelligent about all this.

"Do you have an issue with dead stock? Or stock that goes off and needs to be thrown away?" I ask as I pick up a small box of tea. Their branding is cute. Of course, it has a sun on it, the bright yellow making me feel energized just from looking at it. I turn the box, reading the all-natural ingredients, of which there are only a few, all easy-to-pronounce herbs or plants of some kind. I wonder what their shelf life is. She has a lot of them, seemingly something for every ailment you can think of.

"No, not really. The tea is obviously dried and so that lasts a while. We box our tea, because the packaging is recyclable. As far as the oils are concerned, they don't really go bad. But I think the key with the wellness treatments we do is that it's less about general retail to make a buck and more about prescription."

"Can you explain that?" I ask, very interested, but I have no idea what she's getting at. If we can hold stock that doesn't spoil, I'm seeing a lot of savings with having wellness as a focus as opposed to having mud wraps and creams everywhere. I see her tone change, her body now more at ease as her face lights up. She enjoys talking about this, the business side.

"I like to think of us as wellness doctors in a way. We treat people for a variety of ailments, or just for general well-being, and as such, they'll usually be prescribed a tea or an oil that they can take home with them to use and order more regularly or come back for a reassessment. So it's less about pushing the nice teas or candles, and more about prescribing a healing tonic that's going to give them at-home care they can do on their own."

"So let me get this straight. You treat people without the need for a lot of product usage, therefore limiting breakage and spoiling and storage. You then have long-life products available that, from what I can see, are easy to store and that last months, perhaps even years, in some cases. Meaning that your overhead must be..." I say, thinking about it.

"Low. One of the lowest in the health industry," she says, nodding, and as the CFO of Whiteman's Whiskey, my radar for financial success is strong. I admire Daisy's passion. Beautiful and smart, it's a deadly combination.

"You sure run a pretty tight ship here. Very knowledgeable about it all."

"Oh sorry, are you talking about me? Here? In this

run-down clinic without any technology and incense that makes you cough?" she sasses, and my eyes narrow as my mind runs wild with an idea.

"I want you to come and work for me," I state, and she stills. The words leave me before I really thought about them, but when I get a gut feeling about something, I usually just go for it. My gut is telling me that Whiteman's needs someone to consult on the spa to bring it to life and that someone is Daisy.

"Excuse me?" She's looking at me like I'm crazy, but I ignore her and keep talking.

"As I said, I'm opening a spa at my distillery, one that I thought would consist of mud wraps and massages and facials, but now I see a different vision. A vision that I think could be brought to life with your expertise," I tell her, wondering if I can get her over the line.

"Oh, wellness and whiskey... they go so well together..." There's that sarcasm again. I frown but continue.

"Come on as a consultant, for a month or two... maybe three. Come to Whispers, the small town where we're situated. I'll fly you in, organize accommodations for you, you can meet the team, work with my colleagues, Victoria and Lacy, to get the spa off the ground." I give myself a mental pat on the back, because this is a fucking brilliant idea, and I'm not sure why none of us thought of it earlier. A consultant who can bring it all together is perfect. I know a good opportunity when I see it.

When she doesn't respond, I hand her my card. "Here's my card. Take the weekend to think about it." Giving her no other option than to take it, her fingers almost touch my own, and I feel a buzz ripple up my hand. It must be all those vibrations she was talking about.

"Wow, I wonder how many trees died for this beauty to be made." Looking at my thick, glossy card, she shakes her head, and I cut in again, not a man who takes no for an answer in the business world.

"I expect a call from you on Monday," I tell her.

"You expect?" There's fire in her eyes as she looks at me.

"I have a business to run. I don't like to wait." I'm really going for the asshole of the year award today.

"Ah, I see, but you know what? Hmm... I can't. I'm washing my hair on Monday." She gives me the biggest, most blinding smart-ass grin, and I grit my teeth. She really doesn't like me.

"I'll pay you much more than you make here, I can assure you that," I say, sounding more and more arrogant than ever, and I wish I could just rein it in, but it's too late.

"Yes, that's right, because I'm poor too. Thanks so much for that reminder. Just so you know, money isn't everything."

With a sigh, I pocket my hands and look over the space again. "Clearly... but this is a good opportunity."

"For whom?" she asks, and damn, she's quick.

"For both of us." I appreciate her negotiation and tenacity. It wasn't what I expected from someone who works in a place called Sunshine, which looks like a small breeze could knock it over.

"My answer is still no—" she starts to say, her hand pushing my business card back to me, but I cut her off again.

"Think about it. Call me on Monday, Daisy. Now, what do I owe you?" I ask, grabbing my wallet from my pocket, ignoring my business card in her hand that she still holds in front of my chest.

"It's fine. We're all good. But my answer will be the same on Monday as it is now... Mr.... Connor Whiteman." She takes a longer look at my business card, like she's reading my name for the first time, before looking back at me without an ounce of recognition or care. Then she throws my business card on the desk behind her like it's a piece of rubbish, and I have to hold back a groan of exasperation, even though the move makes me want her even more.

"I'll speak to you on Monday," I reiterate, my Southern accent seeping out a little more, probably because I'm agitated, and she swallows audibly. I should leave, but my feet feel heavy, like they're glued to the ground. I don't feel like I have her over the line yet. In fact, I know that I don't. I want to go back in time ten minutes to when I felt extremely relaxed after my treatment and hearing her kind voice, rather than the sassy one I'm getting now. She's different.

"Did you need anything else?" she asks, her hand moving to her hip, and I shake my head, taking that as my cue to move my ass out of this shanty.

"I'll see you around, Daisy," I say, liking her name on my lips, and she looks up at me, giving me a smile that's probably forced, but it still looks sweet as honey. Those vibrations she spoke about earlier are now moving around my body at the motion. Straight down to my dick. When I grab the door, the wind chimes tinkle loudly, and

I step outside. The cool air hits me, clearing my mind instantly as I step across the sidewalk to my waiting town car.

"Everything alright, sir?" my driver asks as I stall on the sidewalk at the open car door and look back. Sure, the peeling paint and the rustic signage are still there, but it gives it a more homey edge than the shithole I was expecting earlier.

"Everything's fine. Straight to the penthouse, please," I tell him, needing to go to my place to shower and change, as I have a business dinner to get to before my day is officially over.

As the car moves from the curb, I look back at the Sunshine Clinic and feel my excitement bubble. This is going to be a smart business move, and not just because of the voluptuous redheaded beauty I just met.

Now all she needs to do is accept.

5

DAISY

I jiggle my key in the lock and push through the door.

"I want pizza. Do you want pizza?" my roommate, Trisha, yells the minute I get inside. I ignore her and make a beeline for our tiny well-worn sofa, face-planting onto it. What a day. I'm exhausted, yet the entire time home on the subway, my thoughts were consumed with one thing and one thing only. Him.

"Pizza?" she yells again before I hear her steps coming from her bedroom to the living room in our tiny, two-bedroom Brooklyn abode. Situated on top of the local dry cleaners that is run by a lovely lady named Anna, which we secretly think might be a front of the mafia's, our space is nothing special, but it's our home and has been for the last two years.

"Hello to you too," I murmur, feeling tired. I always get tired after doing treatments. I give so much of my own energy to my clients and it makes me lethargic.

"Pepperoni?" she pushes, barreling into the living room.

"You seriously want pizza?" I ask, although at the thought, my mouth waters. I usually try to eat healthy, but despite my mom's continued harassment, I'm not vegan and am partial to pizza on a Friday night.

"Yes. I need that gooey, oily cheese in my arteries, like, now!" She flops onto the armchair opposite me, and I roll over to look at her. Trisha and I met through a roommate matching service a few years ago and instantly hit it off. She needed someone to help pay the rent on this place, and I needed to try to be a little more independent from my parents. She's also a casual waitress at Joe's Pizza restaurant down the street, as well as a myriad of other jobs.

"How can you feel like pizza for dinner when you work with it all day?" I ask her, not for the first time. This is our usual Friday night. I walk in exhausted, and we then order pizza. Not my finest meal of the week, but I'm only human.

"Because I get twenty-five percent off any orders. Staff discount. So unless you suddenly won the lottery, we can't afford anything else today."

I groan again. I love my job, and I love working with Mom, but I don't make a lot.

"Nope. No millions to my name today," I tell her, and she smiles.

"That reminds me, the heating bill came in today."

"Is it bad?" I cringe. I barely have a dime to my name, yet another reason I want to get Sunshine more advanced because, at this point, I'm struggling to pay my bills.

"Yeah, I think we'll have to eat rice and beans for a week or two," she admits. "But tonight, let's have pizza. I'll buy. My treat."

I raise my eyebrows. "Really? Are we celebrating?" I ask as she texts in our order directly to Joe, who we know will throw in an extra garlic bread because he's secretly in love with her. Or not so secretly, yet she doesn't appear interested.

"I met the man I'm going to marry today," she states, and I balk. My mind immediately flows back to Connor today and his job offer. He may be incredibly handsome, but he's arrogant and clearly inept at hearing the word no when it comes to business. I kinda admire that, actually, even though it's also incredibly frustrating.

"Really? Do tell." I say as I get cozy on the sofa, waiting for her latest dating news. I live vicariously through her. I hear her ups and downs with men, offering a shoulder if she needs it or cab fare if she's running short. At least one of us gets the male gaze.

"First, tell me about your day," she says, putting her cell down and looking at me. She usually lets me go first, because she will talk all night about her dates and knows full well I don't have much to offer her in that regard, but this afternoon was a little different for me.

"A new guy came in today," I tell her, shrugging like it's no big deal, yet it's the only thing I've been thinking about since.

"Well... was he cute?" she asks cautiously, immediately grinning, and I smile. I never do this, talk about a guy, let alone a client, yet here I am.

"Nooo, cute isn't the word I would use." He left me

feeling very frustrated, mainly because everything he said was correct. We do need to remodel; we do need a computer system, and I've been telling my mom for months to change the incense that she burns, but she doesn't agree, and it's her business, not mine.

"Good-looking? Easy on the eye? Hunk of spunk?" As she wiggles her eyebrows, I think about his kind eyes, his broad shoulders, and his chiseled torso that looked like I could bounce a coin off it.

"He was handsome, in a rugged, manly kinda way. He was a man. Like, a giant man," I say, nodding, happy with that assessment, which I know is accurate. Every time I blink, I still see his half-naked body from earlier.

"Man?" Trisha's interest has now piqued.

"Yes, not a boy, but a man. Tall, broad, big hands, beard, like a lumberjack," I tell her.

"Big hands, eh?" she says teasingly, and I groan, remorseful for sharing already.

"Oh my gosh, stop."

"So when are you seeing him again?" If it was Trisha who met him, she would have a date lined up already.

"I said good-looking, but then he opened his mouth," I say with a smirk.

"Oh God, a good-looking asshole. I hate them the most." She rolls her eyes.

"Not an asshole, exactly..." I say, because that sounds too harsh a word.

"A dumb idiot?" she counters.

"No, he's smart, very smart. Tenacious? A little arrogant, maybe?" I say, thinking about him.

"Hmmm, so smart, arrogant, good-looking...?"

"And frustrating. Like, really frustrating. Do you know he had the audacity to insult the business entirely before he had the balls to offer me a job?" I tell her, because that does take some balls. Regardless of whether my mom owns the business or not.

"Hmmm, smart, arrogant, good-looking, has big balls...?" she repeats, but I don't really hear her, my mind now spinning.

"He actually wants me to move to some small town in the middle of nowhere to work in some distillery. He makes whiskey, Trisha. I barely even drink alcohol," I tell her, like it's the stupidest thing I've ever heard.

"What kind of job?" Trisha crosses her legs on the sofa, and I know she's invested in this conversation now.

"They're opening a health retreat or something, and get this... he wants me to consult. Help them bring it to life," I tell her, snorting at the ridiculousness of it all.

"What the hell does a distillery want to open a spa for? Sounds a bit suss to me." Her eyes narrow, sensing something isn't right.

"Well, I haven't really looked into it, but I did look up Whispers, and it's a small town a few hours' flight away. Looks really pretty."

"What's the name of the distillery?" she asks, grabbing her phone again. "We need to stalk him on social media."

"We are not stalking him," I groan, but she ignores me.

"Whoops, my fingers have already moved."

"It's called Whiteman's." She'll find him online, no matter what I say. I know the name because I've done nothing but look at his business card for the last hour straight. I should have thrown it in the trash like I was going to, but I didn't. It's still burning a hole in my pocket.

"Whiteman's Whiskey. I've heard of them. It's like super expensive shit. Is this the guy?" she asks, thrusting her phone toward me, and I lean forward to see a very attractive older man's profile image staring back at me.

"Nope, the guy I saw today was named Connor," I tell her, and she looks back at her phone.

"Oh... Ooohhhhh..." Her eyes bug out. "Look at that! He's..." she trails off, lost for words, as she shows me an image on her small screen of the man I saw half-naked this afternoon. He's in suit that's tailored to his perfect body, and I swallow.

"Let me see!" I say, jumping off the sofa and moving to her, sitting on the arm of the chair to look over her shoulder.

"So, this is him?" she confirms, and I grab her phone. My gasp is audible, and my mouth immediately dries up.

"Yep..." The word comes out as a squeak as I look at the man who hasn't left my mind. I read the words under his headshot.

"Let me read," Trisha says, snatching the phone back while I sit in shock. I mean, I saw him in the flesh, so I shouldn't be surprised, but in that photo, he's in a suit and, damn, he looks good.

"Says here that he and his father, Tanner, own White-man's Whiskey, the most sought-after whiskey in the country. Let me search some more... 'cause websites can be fake," she says, her eyebrows pinching as she gets into detective mode and I go sit back down on the sofa, my nerves now a little frayed.

"Oh shit, he's like a gazillionaire… Says here he's best friends with the president," Trisha says.

"What?" I think I'm going to faint. How can such an arrogant, egotistical man be friends with the president? I love our president, everybody does, and his first lady is awesome too.

"Apparently, they went to college together. Oh, and he's single," she teases, and I roll my eyes.

"C'mon, Daisy, I've barely known you to date. Maybe a few guys from the apps, but you never put yourself out there," Trisha says, and she's right.

"Yeah, well, I'm a professional. I can't go hitting on the clients that come into Sunshine. I'm also not going to date a man who is such a…"

"Good-looking, rich, smart go-getter with big balls… Gee, Daisy, they all sound like pretty good qualities to me. Besides, there's nothing wrong with getting to know your clients. I hit on our patrons all the time."

"Well… for starters… it's unprofessional. People come to forget about their worries and to relax and relieve their stress."

"I bet this guy Connor would luuuurrrrve for you to relieve his stress," she murmurs.

"Trisha!" I admonish, throwing our lumpy cushion at her head, but she catches it in time.

"He's a client, not to mention, just offered me a job. There's no dating in that equation," I tell her, and she thinks about that.

"Hmmm, so you're actually thinking about taking the job, then?" she asks, and I swallow. It's all I have thought about since he left. He's clearly used to getting his own way, but I did enjoy talking about business. I enjoyed the fact he listened to my thoughts and ideas even more. But I couldn't leave my mom all alone to manage Sunshine.

"I'm not sure I could handle him being my boss," I tell her, not admitting that the desire to give the job a go is actually growing. I push that feeling down. Not going to happen. It can't happen.

"He wouldn't technically be your boss. You would be a consultant, which means you're not on his staff, just merely an expert hired to tell them what they need to do. Which you would be more than qualified for, I might add."

I take a deep breath, it all feeling a little too surreal.

"So, what are you going to do?" Trisha asks as she flicks through image after image, showing them to me and each one looking better than the last. He's in a suit, then in jeans and a button-down shirt, has a backward cap on in another, then I see all the ones with his various girlfriends. A lot of different ones. All the same type. Blond, skinny, tall, luxurious. He clearly has a type, and it's the complete opposite of me.

"I already told him no. Although, he's not really taking that as an answer. Told me to think about it and call him on Monday. But I can't leave Mom."

"Of course you can. She's holding you back. Not on purpose. You know I love your mom. But the two of you are just not aligned on the business. You're young, hungry for more, and she's close to retiring, wanting a simpler life. Besides, it's only for a month or two, and then you'll come back," Trisha says, putting it all into perspective.

"I can't bring wellness to a whiskey distillery. The two

don't even work together very well," I murmur. I mean, I've never had a glass of whiskey, but I know it has a high proof.

Alcohol generally isn't great. It's a toxin in the body, but I do know that whiskey temporarily widens blood vessels and can clear mucus congestion in your chest and nose, which is why so many people often take a nip of whiskey when they have a cold or flu. It's something my father swears by. While it isn't good in large amounts, in small amounts, it can be somewhat beneficial. I would probably steep eucalyptus or tea tree oils and do a steam bath when sick, a nip of whiskey probably does have its place.

"Whispers is about eight hundred and fifty miles from New York. Talk about getting out of the city." Trisha's not a fan of country living.

"See, too far away," I say, like that's my deciding factor, when, in reality, getting out of the city might be good for a while.

"At least we know he isn't a serial killer or anything, so that's a plus. And if you don't take his job offer, you still have his number, so you should ask him out."

I'm already shaking my head. "Not happening."

"Don't give me any of that bullshit about your size. Men love voluptuous women."

"I'm bigger than most." I sink into the sofa, feeling my rolls at my waist that are more pronounced now that I'm sitting. I never used to care. I'm usually happy in my body. I flaunt my assets, never hide. But things changed a few months ago.

"You're plus-size, so what? Most girls are!" Trisha is great for my confidence.

"But I'm not exactly what men are looking for." Not that I'm sad about that fact. I am who I am. Most people prefer beautiful skinny blond women. Trisha's looks fall into that category as well.

"That guy. I blame that guy about three months ago. Since then, you've been against dating." She jumps up, now pacing around the living room. She's right. He knocked my confidence big-time. Now I can't get past my size when I think about dating again.

"What guy?" I ask her, knowing exactly who she's talking about.

"Mr. *I'm Not Really Feeling It*. That asshole took one look at you and walked away. He didn't even talk to you and get to know you. He judged you solely on your looks, and let's be honest, he needs glasses because you, my friend, are beautiful."

I give her a smile. "Thanks, Trisha. But I'm fine. Mr. Right will come along one day." I tell her the words that no longer feel like they will come true, and she stops and sighs.

"You should call him. Meet him this weekend for brunch or something while he's in the city. Talk about the *job offer*." She makes a last-ditch attempt, which she already knows is futile.

"Can't. Mom's making me dahl," I tell her, my tone ending the conversation.

"Yum, bring some home." Her love for my mom's dahl is not to be underestimated. "Sooooo... I need to ask you a favor..."

"I knew it. That's why you're offering to pay for dinner."

"Yes, I need something from you." She sits up straighter, like it's of utmost importance. So I do the same.

"Okay, what is it?" I ask, ready for the onslaught, wondering what she needs this time.

"I need you to cover for me tomorrow night at the stadium." She says the words so quickly that they run into each other, and I slump.

"What?" I moan, already knowing that I don't want to. I've only done it once before, and it was a nightmare.

"Please? I have a date with Tom," she says with a bright smile.

"Tom? Who the hell is Tom?" I ask, wishing I could rewind the clock and go back to my last appointment at Sunshine, so I don't have to pretend to be a server at the stadium where she works casually on the weekends.

"The guy I met online today, the one I'm going to marry. He's super sweet, caring, and so funny. Look..." she says, thrusting her phone in my face so I can see his picture, and I cringe. He looks small, thin, and like he couldn't even hold my hand, let alone my weight.

"He's good-looking, right?" She sounds hopeful, and I give her a small smile.

"Yeah, sure. I mean, not really my type." I wasn't sure I had a type. Until today.

"So, please, can you cover my shift?" she begs, looking at me with those puppy dog eyes she gets. I sigh, and she grins, knowing that I will.

"What's on?" I ask, hoping it's something low-key, although I think it's mainly sports played there.

"Ahhh, well, it's Saturday night football," she says hesitantly, watching me carefully.

"Football? Really?" I groan again. I'm not a sporty girl myself, and I have even less of an appetite to be serving hot dogs to groups of men who yell and scream over other men who run around a field with a ball.

"Yeah, but it'll be way better than last time," she assures me, knowing that she really has to sell this to me.

"Different how?" I ask, not believing a word she is saying.

"Well, I was promoted, so now I look after a corporate suite. I've only ever done it once, and it was full of suited-up businessmen. You'll be fine."

That sounds a little better. Maybe only ten or twenty men, instead of the hundreds who usually come to the hot dog stand.

"What's the corporation?" I ask, not sure why, as I don't really care. But if they own a petroleum company or are killing off the rainforest or something, I might not be the best fit.

"The what?" She frowns, like the question I'm asking is odd.

"Who owns the suite? What kind of company?" I clarify.

"Oh, I don't know. I don't pay attention to that kind of detail," she murmurs, not really into it either. "Please, if Tom and I get married and have a baby, we'll name it after you."

"Really? You'll name your daughter Daisy?" I ask,

knowing that she hates flowers, and Daisy wouldn't be at the top of her list of names.

"Well, no. Maybe your middle name, though."

I laugh and roll my eyes. Daisy was Mom's choice, and my middle name was Dad's.

"You'll call your child Adeline?" I ask.

"Yes, hand on heart, when Tom and I decide to have babies, I'll call it Adeline," she says, holding her hand up like she's pledging.

"Please, you know I have to go. It's been such a long time since I have found a guy I really like online."

"What about Graham from last week?" I ask, thinking back to last Friday night's conversation about the man she met online and was going to marry then.

"Bluuurgh," is her only response.

"What about Christian from the week before?" I ask. We have this conversation every week.

"Bi," she states, and I raise my eyebrows.

"Really?" I didn't expect that.

"Yep, wanted a three-way with another guy, so I threw my drink in his face. I don't share, you know that."

I smirk before I breathe out a resigned sigh.

"Okay, fine. I'll cover it. But I need a uniform," I tell her, because we won't let her manager know. I'll just slip in, pretend I'm her for the night, and slip out. It worked last time, and I can't be bothered filling out any paperwork or employment details.

"I'll organize everything. Thank you!" she squeals, jumping up from the armchair and clapping before she grabs her phone and starts texting, clearly confirming things with Tom.

I sit watching her, wondering if I'll ever get that feeling. The giddy emotion of being so into a guy and waiting for their call. I think about Connor again, the man and the job offer. This could be something, or it could be nothing, but regardless, I need to think about my future. I need a change that brings me more joy. I need a challenge.

6

CONNOR

"So... I saw you in the newspaper this week with President Rothschild..." Bethany says, and I try not to roll my eyes. This is me doing yet another favor for my friends. Sawyer, this time, who needed Bethany off his back after taking her out during the week.

Last night at drinks, she turned up unannounced, and he pushed her on to me. After a few whiskeys, I invited her to the game tonight to try to get her off Sawyer's back. Apparently, all that did is have her clench on to me. I blame the stupid sound healing. I was feeling too relaxed after my treatment. Now, even though I'm with her on this stupid half-assed date as a favor to Sawyer, I'm still imagining her hair is red instead of box blond.

"He's a friend." I confirm the only thing I'm willing to tell anyone and hit the elevator button. The noise in the stadium is already loud, and I feel the excitement buzzing around my body. I'm looking forward to relaxing and watching my favorite football team play from my corporate suite.

"It must be nice having friends in high places," she says, looking up at me. I think she's batting her lashes, I can't be sure. She's wearing those fake ones that make her eyes look too black and overwhelm her face. Again, I think of those sparkling blue eyes I saw yesterday, the big, clear, vibrant ones that are unlike any I've seen before.

"It's nice to have a lot of friends." I keep my answers pretty vague as the elevator bell rings and the doors open to the much quieter level of corporate suites, where Whiteman's Whiskey holds the largest and best-positioned suite in the entire stadium. We walk out together, and I'm already regretting having her by my side. She's a bit shallow, comments on others too much, and seems like a bit of a mean girl with the way she acts. Sawyer owes me big-time. I hear my father's voice in my head, that I always date women who have no potential. But I like it that way. I don't get attached, and they don't get attached. It's a win-win.

As we walk to my suite, I look around. It was expensive, but everything that's worth it usually is. While I would like to use it more than I do, I try to get to New York every month or two, but I miss Whispers too much. The small town I grew up in now gives a better pace to my life, as the older I get, the more I appreciate the simple life, something as a kid I couldn't wait to get away from. Funny how things change like that.

"I never thought I would ever say that the president is a friend." She giggles as I reach the suite door and push through, ignoring her comment. If she's assuming

Harrison Rothschild, my best friend from college and now president of the country, is a friend of hers by association, she's delusional. If anything, Harrison's circle of friends has decreased, not only because he lacks the time to invest in many personal connections these days, but also his security is tight and there are only a few of us who have his personal number and that of his wife and the first lady.

"Oh wow, this is really amazing. Does my hair look okay?" she asks for what I feel like is the hundredth time as I watch her get out her cell and put it in front of her face. She pulls at her hair a bit, then pouts, and my shoulders feel tight with regret as I walk into the suite and leave her at the door, looking at herself. Am I being an asshole? Probably, but I should've known better than to bring her. I'm not sure what I was thinking, other than the stupid sound therapy massage I had with Daisy yesterday, and the fact that I'm now more excited about this spa development than ever before. It must have totally thrown me off my game and left my head in a fuzz.

I stand at the edge of the suite balcony, looking out over the crowd and the field. The teams warm up, people swarming everywhere, and the music is pumping. I love football. I've never played it, but I enjoy watching it. Especially from up here. I pay little attention to the staff flitting around at the back of the suite. They'll bring me my whiskey soon enough, so I stand there and take a breath. The stadium is packed to the rafters tonight. The game is one of the most anticipated of the season. There's a good feeling in the air.

"Oh my God, oh my God, will we get on TV?" Bethany

asks from where she steps up next to me, and I try not to roll my eyes. Being in the media is not my favorite thing, but it happens from time to time, especially when I'm in New York. The paparazzi here are always intense, and probably because I live in Whispers, I'm less accessible than most businessmen, so it's a novelty to catch me, and it makes the price of photos higher for them. I look to the suite to the left of me and spot a few familiar faces, and I give a wave and a nod in greeting. I turn to look at the other side and frown.

"Well, if it isn't the whiskey kid," a man old enough to be my grandpa says, and I walk over to shake his hand.

"Andre," I say, nodding to him. He might be pushing seventy, but his handshake is still firm as he grips my hand tight. "Got yourself a suite too, I see?" I ask him, because I haven't noticed him before.

"Ahh, it isn't the best sport in the world, but it will do," he mocks in his slight French accent. The hotelier legend is well known, grew up in France, probably picking grapes when he was still in diapers. He now owns and runs the largest hotelier group in Europe and his foothold here in the United States is growing.

"Probably should go back to Europe then and watch your soccer?" I suggest, knowing that's his comparison.

"Hmmm, maybe. But Tyler is here," he says, mentioning his eldest son, who runs his hotels around the world. I've met him a few times. He's a great guy, one who has good business sense, and I know the business has grown exponentially under his management. Andre's eyes flick to beside me to take in the perky blond date I brought.

"And… I like the landscape here an awful lot." His eyes run down my date and back up again. I look down at her, because even though I know we won't see each other again after tonight, I'm not going to make her feel uncomfortable. But she's grinning at him, biting her bottom lip in a flirty manner, and I rub my face. She can clearly smell money, and this old guy has buckets of it.

"Enjoy the game, then. We need to take our seats." I turn and start to walk to my seat, needing my whiskey now more than ever.

"Whiskey, sir?" a female voice asks from my other side, and I smile at the soothing sound before I turn and look at the woman who's working my suite tonight.

"Daisy?" I ask, surprised, almost tripping over my own feet.

"Seriouslyyy?" she moans, like the world has done her dirty, her face scrunching at just the sight of me. I'm glad I'm not easily offended, because this woman clearly doesn't like me. Although I can't blame her. In hindsight, I know my tone and words to her yesterday were out of line and something I should apologize for. I again wonder if the incense was actually weed and that's what made me such an asshole.

She clears her throat, rolling her shoulders like she's putting on an act of professionalism. "Whiskey?" she asks again, and I nod, taking the glass from her tray. She delivers it just how I like it. Neat, heavy glass, two fingers.

"What're you doing here?" I ask. I thought she was a wellness practitioner.

"Oh, you know, I can't stay in that crumbling place called Sunshine all day and all night. Heaven forbid if the smell of that incense actually suffocates me," she says, and I almost grin, appreciating her sass sprinkled with humor. Her face is softer, more relaxed now. She goes to say something else before she gets interrupted.

"I'll have a cosmopolitan," Bethany barks at her before she steps in front of me, marking her territory that isn't hers to mark. I internally cringe. I forgot all about her, and now I really wish I hadn't brought her along.

Daisy looks from me to my date, and her body visibly hardens as she pulls at her shirt a little.

"Certainly, ma'am," Daisy says in her professional tone before she turns and walks away, and my brow furrows. She hasn't been here before; otherwise, I would've recognized her. She's hard to miss. Short, voluptuous, that red hair, and those damn blue eyes. Those blue eyes were in my dreams last night. I rub my own, trying to erase the thoughts. I usually don't think about women after I meet them, and I've never dreamed about their fucking eyes like I did last night.

"Pfft. You would think they'd bring both drinks at the same time. It's a wonder she can even fit in here," she says, and out of my peripheral, I see Daisy balk, and I hold my breath. She clearly heard the remark, but after a brief pause, she continues on to the bar at the back of the suite, and I look at my date as she sits down in my seat. It isn't named, but it's big, plush, and in the center of the space, giving me the perfect view.

"Your meaning?" I grit out, this night turning tumultuous instantly.

"I just mean that... It's nothing. Forget I said anything." She smiles, sensing I'm agitated with her.

"Can you move over one, please?" I ask her, and she huffs but then gets up and moves over one seat, and I sit down. My date grabs a lip gloss from her tiny purse and starts reapplying as I crack my knuckles. I feel on edge now. Daisy didn't jump at my job offer yesterday like I thought she would, and she still hasn't called me to take me up on it. From what I saw yesterday, she probably threw my business card in the trash.

The whole situation leaves a bad taste in my mouth. I run my hand over my beard, wanting to go and talk with her, to get her on board with my vision. I see it clearly: her in Whispers, building this spa business alongside me. I know she has both the experience and the business mind, two things that are not always easy to find in a person. Plus, we're on a timeline. We're ready to go and need someone like Daisy to start almost immediately. But movement at my side keeps me from running to the back of the room to speak to her. I have a fucking date. I have a date I don't want here and a woman at the back of the suite I would rather talk to. No *need* to talk to. It's business, not personal.

"Here is your cosmopolitan, ma'am," Daisy says in a tone that's way too sweet and glides down my spine, making my body relax. I have no idea how she does it. Maybe she put something in my whiskey—that elixir her mother gave me yesterday, maybe—I'm not sure, but my whiskey has never tasted as good as it does after she made it for me.

She leans over, placing the cocktail on a small side table, and I take the opportunity to look at her. Her round, full breasts are barely contained in the tight white shirt she's wearing, and I bite the inside of my cheek as I salivate. I'm a breast man. I love a feminine body, with curves and softness. I scrub my eyes, trying not to gape at her. Nope. I can't be interested in a woman I don't even know, especially one who clearly doesn't like me. Plus, I just offered her a fucking job, and I can't be looking at my colleagues in any way that isn't professional. I force my gaze back at the field to the game and sip my whiskey, swallowing down the burn, my eyes not moving from looking straight ahead.

"Can I get you two lovebirds anything else at the moment?" she asks, her tone dripping with fake sweetness and her familiar tone of sarcasm, and at least I know she can be professional while also clearly still not happy with my arrogance from when we were at Sunshine yesterday.

"Oh, you're too kind," Bethany gushes, which I know is fake as well.

"I can take a photo of the two of you, if you like? Something to remember the night by?" Daisy offers, and my teeth are gritting together so hard I feel a headache coming.

"Oh, yes, please!" My date jumps up excitedly, and I rub my eyes.

"No photos," I say, remaining in my seat, putting an end to this charade.

"But you and your wife look so good together," Daisy pushes, and I look at her with narrowed eyes. She quirks an eyebrow right back. She knows I'm not married, so she's teasing my terrible date, who practically beams at the comment.

"We do look good together, don't we, sweetie?" Bethany says, looking at me with big eyes, and I see Daisy roll her own behind her. I don't blame her; she heard her remark from earlier, I just know it.

"Yeah, sweetie, just one photo," Daisy baits me.

"Not happening," I say, looking straight at Daisy.

"Hmmm, a bit like your job offer..." she says, and I can't help but smirk. I'm going to take it as a good sign that she's even bringing it up.

"It's a good deal, Daisy, probably the only one you're going to get." I know it isn't. If I find her brilliant, then someone else will, and as I think about it, I grip my whiskey a little tighter, not liking the thought of anyone else having her.

"You think so little of me, Connor," she calls my bluff. I'm starting to like this frustrating little game of cat and mouse.

"Ahhh, am I missing something here?" Bethany asks, but we both ignore her.

"Six figures is not so little..." I tell her, giving her an amount to think about. I see when it registers, and she almost trips a little.

"I told you, money isn't everything."

The fact that she has a second job tells me that she is, in fact, in need of some money. I appreciate her sticking to her morals, even if they're totally ridiculous in regard to my offer.

"It sure makes the world a little easier, sweetheart," I murmur to her, my Southern accent making the endearment sound more condescending than I had intended, and I watch her swallow roughly. She has no comeback for me, and my thoughts on her needing the money seem to have hit a nerve.

"Will there be anything else here for the lovebirds?" she asks, looking between me and my date and effectively ending the conversation.

"We're all fine for now," I tell her, and she spins on her heel and walks back to the bar.

Bethany huffs, clearly not happy and feeling left out. "God, you really would think they could get skinnier waitstaff," Bethany pitches, loud enough for Daisy to hear, and I almost choke on my whiskey.

"What the hell did you just say?" My anger is instant, and she obviously knows she's said the wrong thing again. Whether it was Daisy or someone else, that kind of commentary on other's bodies is so unbecoming. I let her earlier remark fly past, but not this one.

"Sorry, it's just that the uniform obviously doesn't fit her very well. It's unprofessional and distracting," she murmurs, and I frown.

"You need to leave," I tell her, my anger rising to a level that isn't sociable. She rears back, jaw dropping as she stares at me.

"Leave?" she asks with the audacity to look at me like I'm the problem.

"I don't take kindly to people who treat others with disrespect, especially when those people are working for *me* in *my* suite." I want her to know that this is my house and my rules, and I won't have anyone in here who treats people as less than.

"Are you serious right now?" I notice her gulp the cocktail again, clearly wanting to get the free drink in before she leaves. She knows she overstepped, and there's no coming back from it.

"My car and driver are downstairs, and he can take you anywhere you need to go," I tell her, wanting this date over with. My shoulders are stiff with tension. I should be concentrating on the game I love so much. But I can't. I internally curse myself. I should've just told Sawyer no instead of trying to be a good friend. Another asshole who now owes me big-time.

"I can't believe you. Who the hell do you think you are?" she says, her voice rising, and I'm glad the game is loud; otherwise, we'd be getting some looks. She's acting like we're a couple, not merely acquaintances who've known each other for twenty-four hours. My stare on her doesn't waver, so she knows I mean business.

"What a joke." She takes the last long sip from her cocktail and slams the empty glass on the table before standing.

Andre looks over with interest, and I rub my beard. I don't usually have issues with women like this. I'm a gentleman. I take care of them, treat them right, but something about her words and her tone when speaking about Daisy got to me, and I won't stand for it.

"Door is that way." I nod in the direction of the back of the room, and she huffs before grabbing her handbag and walking out. I lean back in my seat and push out a deep breath and let the last hour or so wash away from me. This is why I generally don't date. Women expect more from me, more of my money, more of my contacts, more, more, more.

While the game in front of me continues, I sit fuming,

wondering what Daisy's doing. I feel on edge the entire time. Wanting to look back to see her but forcing my head to remain facing forward. I told her I'd give her the weekend, but I'm itching to talk with her. Talk business, talk spa, talk about her, listen to her thoughts on things. She's captivating. I see movement out of the corner of my eye and look up, expecting her, but it's the male waitstaff, serving me snacks and another whiskey. Frowning, I spot her standing at the bar, polishing glasses, not looking in my direction. Completely ignoring me. Then she goes through a door out the back, and I internally curse.

I turn back around, my leg bouncing with pent-up energy. I leave my food to go cold as the game starts up again, and I watch the teams tussle it out. The game is tight, scores are even, and I stay right where I am, even though I'm itching to get out of this seat. I look back a few times, and each time I don't see her, I get even more worked up. There's a timeout called, and I look at the screen, seeing only minutes left to the game. The teams are tied, the tension in the stadium high, yet I've barely registered the play. I jump up, not able to stop myself a minute longer as I stride to the bar, my steps quick as I see her there, and she looks up.

"Can I get another whiskey, please, Daisy?" I ask her, feeling like a piece of shit.

"Certainly, sir," she says professionally, and I shake my head.

"Connor," I correct her as I watch her grab my favorite whiskey, one that's over ten grand a bottle, and she pulls the lid off like it's done her dirty.

"I need to address all clients here as sir." She's not

making eye contact, and I look quickly at the male staff member, who's farther back, pretending not to listen. I clear my throat.

"I would like to apologize—" I start to say, but she cuts me off.

"No need, sir." Giving me a fake-ass smile, she slides the whiskey over the bar in my direction.

There's no way she didn't hear what Bethany said earlier. I should've come straight to apologize then.

"No, I do—"

"No, you really don't." She stands firm. She's strong, has a solid backbone, seemingly not caring what others think of her.

"Will there be anything else, sir?" Not giving me an inch, she slides the glass again, closer to me, like I hadn't already seen it the first time she offered it.

"What are you doing here? I mean, I thought you worked at the wellness center?" I ask again, my head a scramble, not sure why I feel so out of sorts. I blame her. Since the minute I met her, I haven't been myself.

"I'm just filling in for a friend," she states, and I breathe out, my shoulders lowering. That makes sense, and I'm relieved to have an answer that isn't full of bite.

"Have you thought about my offer?" I ask, not wanting to push her, but I'm not used to waiting.

"A little," she says honestly, her lips tilting up at the sides, and I don't know why, but that subtle movement has my full attention.

"And?" I ask, the two of us playing a bit coy, and I equal parts love it and hate it. I hate it because I've never worked this hard for a woman to seem interested in anything I have to offer, and love it, because I feel like she's making me work for her.

"And you told me to call you Monday so... I have another day." Wiping down the counter, she gives me a smirk that tells me this woman isn't going to be a pushover. I pause with appreciation as we look at each other, my stare burning into hers, neither of us relenting. I swear I feel my dick jolt in my jeans, because she's a fucking firecracker, and I want to burn under her flames.

I hear it then. The crowd screams, the game starts up again, and both our eyes avert from each other as I turn around to see what I missed and she turns and looks at the clock. I stride back down to my seat at the balcony to look out and see that the Jets scored a touchdown, and with only a few seconds remaining, they win the game. My smile spreads, and I look back at the bar to celebrate with her, but she's gone.

Only the male server remains. Daisy is nowhere in sight, and I deflate immediately.

I throw back the whiskey and place the glass on the bar, feeling bereft. For the first time in what feels like forever, I'm intrigued by a woman, and she has completely disappeared on me. But she has my number and another twenty-four hours left to call me.

And if she doesn't, I know exactly where to find her.

7

DAISY

I stand leaning against the kitchen counter, strong aromas filling my senses.

"Pass me the turmeric, please, Daisy?" my mom asks, and I lean over, grabbing the freshly ground spice as my mouth waters. She's in the zone; she loves cooking, and her dahl is amazing.

"What's Dad doing?" I ask, peeking out the window at my father, who looks to be attempting some handyman work outside, and handy is one thing my father is not.

"Fixing the lock on the gate. It broke last week." Not looking at me, she stirs the curry.

"Does he need some help?" I ask as I see him give up on it already and walk back inside.

"You know your father. He'll get it, eventually." She sighs, and I smile before I look at the side table he made for Mom's crystals. It's on a little lean and is a bit wobbly, but she wouldn't change it for the world. He's great with numbers, not so great with tools.

"Will there be enough for me to take home?" I ask, remembering Trisha wanted some.

"I'll have a container for Trisha, don't worry," she says with a smile.

"Smells good in here," my dad says, announcing his entrance.

"Hey, Dad." I push off the counter to go to him.

"Hey, Sparkie." He says my nickname, something he's called me since I was a kid, because with red hair and a fiery personality, he always thought of me as a bit of a firecracker. I'm calmer now as I'm older, or so I thought. My interactions with Connor these past few days have uncovered my old traits and tested my limits of civility.

Dad wraps me up in a hug so big and so warm there's no safer place in the world. In his weekend uniform of slacks with trainers, he's the average suburban father, who works with numbers, is a little overweight, a little balding, and I'm pretty sure he's a member of the neighborhood watch committee. I think he was a nerd in school. He and Mom really shouldn't be together. They are complete opposites, as she is crazy and carefree and makes decisions based on the moon cycle, whereas Dad is straitlaced and focused on data. Yet when he was out driving one day, coming home from a conference, he picked up a beautiful hitchhiker, and they've been together ever since.

"No luck with the gate?" my mom asks him as I move around them and set the table. Sunday lunch is our weekly get-together.

"No. I need a different tool, I think," he says, and I grin before a small yawn filters through my lips.

"You seem a bit tired today, honey. Did you meditate this morning?" Mom asks me as we all take a seat and start to dig in.

"No. I had a late night," I tell her, my body soothing as the first bite hits my taste buds and the spices clear my nostrils immediately.

"Oh, anything exciting?" she asks.

"I covered Trisha's shift at the stadium. She had a date," I tell them, my dad quietly observing.

"Oh, with Graham?" she asks innocently.

"No." I shake my head.

"Oh, Christian."

"Nope." I shake my head, and she frowns, trying to recall.

"That girl…" My dad sighs, shaking his head, but otherwise remains quiet.

"His name is Tom," I say, and they both nod with knowing smiles. This is just how Trisha is. I can't wait to meet the guy she actually marries one day, since she thinks each person she goes on a date with is it for her.

"What about you, Daisy? Any man on the horizon?" Dad asks, and I give him a small smile. Because my parents met and married young, I think they expect the same of me.

"No. Still footloose and fancy-free," I tell him, pulling at my sweater, the mere thought of dating making my skin itch. My mind flicks to Connor last night and the buxom blond date he had. She was rude, completely horrible, but when I heard Connor admonish her for her horrible comments about me, and then tell her to leave, a part of my frustration and anger with him fell away. I haven't really had many people stick up for me before, and certainly not a man I barely know. It made me think that there's more to him than I first thought, and if he was willing to have my back in a situation like last night, then in business, I know he would be supportive too.

"Stop pulling at your sweater. Here, let me get the clear quartz," Mom says quickly, jumping up and going to the table of crystals she has nearby and passing one to me while holding one herself.

"I am strong. I am capable. I am enough," Mom chants, and I look at my dad, who gives me a soft, encouraging smile. He isn't into all this woo-woo, but he never dampens her shine. I hope I find a man just like him.

I close my eyes and grip on to the crystal, then take a few deep breaths.

"I am strong. I am capable. I am enough." I repeat her words of affirmation and keep my eyes closed a little longer, taking another few deep breaths.

"Thanks, Mom," I say, opening my eyes, feeling a little more relaxed, but hanging on to the crystal in my lap as she sits again.

"So how was it? The Jets had a hell of a game," my father says, grinning. He's a Jets fan. Has been all my life. I sometimes think if he had a son, he would be more involved in the sport, because he has only been to a few games. He says he doesn't like all the people and prefers to have some space. Hence why he and Mom live here in the outer suburbs, with more grass, more room. But he does love watching them on TV.

"I wouldn't even know. I just served drinks all night," I say, clenching the crystal in my lap tighter.

"Whose suite did you manage last night?" Dad asks, apparently more aware of the work that Trisha does than I am.

"Connor Whiteman," I say, my eyes flicking to Mom. Her eyebrows rise.

"The sound healing Adonis who came in on Friday?" she asks, putting two and two together.

"That's the one. His girlfriend was not overly friendly," I murmur, putting another forkful of curry into my mouth. I really need to stop talking. But he's all I've been thinking about. Six figures is a lot of money. Whispers looks like a nice town. At first, I was offended by his arrogance and the way he pointed out all the faults at Sunshine, but now, I'm feeling different. Like this opportunity is one that I would be silly to pass up.

"Bad words create ugly people, I've always told you that," Dad says, and I smile. He has always told me. In primary school, when the girls would be mean because I was bigger than them all, I would cry in my room and my dad would always be the one to console me.

Then in high school, when the boys started calling me Daisy Cow because of my weight, my dad marched down to school to see the principal, threw around a few professional words, such as *harassment* and *verbal assault*, and those boys got suspended. But it didn't stop. I've been teased about my weight all my life.

"I know, Dad," I say, sighing, thinking back to the woman. She was stunning. Model perfect. Exactly the kind of woman you would expect to be on Connor Whiteman's arm. Although certainly ugly on the inside, if her words about me are anything to go by.

"Did he remember you?" Mom asks, looking at me innocently, and my guilt starts to fester. *Am I really considering leaving her and Sunshine to work in a small town?*

"Well... about that." I put down my fork and look at both of them. "Connor actually offered me a job," I tell her, and she sits up straighter. My nerves dance, not sure what they'll say or think.

"A job?" my dad asks, frowning.

"He owns a whiskey distillery in a small town a few states over. They're opening a spa, and he needs a consultant to help him get it up and running." My palms sweat a little, and I grab on to the clear quartz harder.

"And he wants that to be you?" my dad asks, brows still pinched, clearly not liking the idea, which is in complete contrast to my mom, who's beaming.

"Mm-hmm. He fell asleep during my treatment and then stayed back for a bit afterward, asking me a lot of questions. I think he saw my passion and knowledge and wants to bring that to his business," I say, swallowing. I searched for him online last night when I got home from the game. Trisha was right. He's a gazillionaire. There were lots of images online of him in suits, at high-end bars, at different functions with the president. It was all a little overwhelming, to be honest. But he's clearly well regarded, his business brain in high demand, and he's also very well connected. I feel from a business perspective, I would learn a lot from him, and though our banter has been mostly snide comments, we do riff off each other well, both full of energy.

"Well, I did say the universe would decide..." my mom says, but my father isn't so easily convinced.

"So, he just expects you to, what? Pack up your life and move halfway across the country?" He's worried, I can tell. As an only child, I've been here with them all my life, so he's probably freaking out a little.

"Oh please, I was hitchhiking across the country when I was her age," Mom quips.

"Exactly!" Dad says, looking at her pointedly, like they share a piece of information I'm not privy to. I ignore them and continue explaining.

"He would fly me and provide accommodations, as well as a consulting fee."

"Whatever amount you're thinking of charging, I want you to double it," Dad grumbles. "It's basically a relocation. Whether you're there for a few days or a few weeks, it's the same. You have commitments here that you need to uphold. Your mother needs..." he trails off.

I look at Mom as my stomach dips. I feel bad about leaving her, but I know in my gut, despite how infuriating Connor is, that this job opportunity will be a good move for me. To my surprise, Mom interjects.

"Nothing. Actually, I'll cut down my hours and start to only open a few days a week when you're gone. My hands are giving me too much pain these days anyway, so this is perfect. It allows me to slow down, and it allows you to try something new. When you finish, you can come back and consult with some of the amazing places here in the city. It's a great skill set and experience to have," Mom says, giving me a smile, and I can't believe that I worried so much about what she would say. She may not like my ideas or growth plans for Sunshine, but she isn't going to hold me back. I shouldn't have underestimated her.

"I'm not totally sold on it," Dad murmurs, although I see him softening.

"I don't really have a lot of other options for career growth at the moment, Dad. I didn't go to college. I work all day at Sunshine. I feel like this might be a really good opportunity, and it isn't forever. It's a few weeks, a month or two, tops, maybe? You won't even know I'm gone," I tell him, and he sighs. The more I think about it, the more it feels like the right decision. I can't work for my mom forever, and this will give me the experience of not only learning more about business but having new colleagues and new bosses to report to.

"That's at least four Sundays..."

I give him a small smile, because that's as good of an approval as I'm going to get.

"Sounds like you've already made up your mind?" Mom asks, looking at me expectantly, and I huff a laugh.

"Not at all. The job would be great, the small town looks quaint. But Connor is frustrating. Pretty arrogant at times. I'm not sure working with him would be worth it." I scoop up more dahl as I think about it some more.

"Things don't always go to plan in business, Daisy. You and your mother work well together, but when you work for others, compromise is a key attribute to utilize, as are negotiation and communication," Dad says, as only a professional can.

"I know. But I enjoy what I do. I love working at Sunshine. I enjoy the treatments, yoga, the teas and elixirs, crystals."

My mom smiles proudly, and my heart sinks a little as I realize I want more. I want to be more.

"Sunshine is your mother's business. It doesn't have to be yours," my dad says, and Mom and I look at him.

"He's right, honey. Sunshine is my passion; it was what I always wanted to do. But it may not be the way forward for you. Not in the way it is now. You're always coming up with new ideas, but I'm happy with how things are. You need to find your passion."

"I enjoy instructing, teaching, and building the business... I feel like all these years working with you, Mom, and helping out running Sunshine has really given me all the skills I need to take on this new role." My creativity and positivity are now flowing as we talk more about it. Maybe it's because I'm still holding on to the clear quartz.

"Well, when you do yoga flow classes, they are always well attended. You have many skills, darling, and you would be perfect for this opportunity," Mom confirms, and I nod.

"Think about it some more. Just promise me you won't rush into anything." Dad gives me a serious look, and I can see the initial shock of it has worn off and he's slowly coming around to the idea.

"Meditate on it, honey. The right answer will come to you, and we'll be supportive of whatever you decide."

I tried meditating. I closed my eyes and tried to find the clarity I was searching for to help me with my decision. But all I saw was his bare torso and his hard-as-rock abs and that little V that delved into his shorts that makes my mouth water just thinking about it.

I clear my throat and grab my fork again, digging into my food. Nope. I won't meditate on it anymore.

But I can push my feelings for him aside in order to

create a better future for myself. I would be a fool for doing otherwise.

Connor Whiteman and his abs can stay deep in the recesses of my mind. I can be professional, and I'm sure he can too.

8

CONNOR

"So the expansion is on track," Dad says, looking at us all from where he sits at the head of the boardroom table. I tap a few buttons on my laptop, bringing up the numbers.

"We're on budget. A little under, actually." I review the figures carefully.

"I have most things secured for the interior. Once the build is complete this week, I can start," Victoria, my dad's fiancée and my soon-to-be new stepmom, says. My eyes flick to Dad quickly, and I see him looking at her with hearts in his eyes. He was alone for so long, I'm glad he finally found someone. The fact that she's younger than me threw me for a little while, but seeing them so happy now makes me happy for them.

"How did it go at the Sunshine Space Wellness Clinic?" Lacy asks me, taking notes. She has a lot on her plate at the moment, probably shouldn't even be here, given her mom is about to go in for a minor operation soon. But she had a great weekend in the city with Hudson, and I'm pretty sure the two of them are headed for the wedding chapel themselves one day. A perfect pair.

"Oh yes. Fiona goes to get her chakras cleansed there monthly. She swears by them. Mother-daughter duo who have been treating her for years apparently," Victoria says, and I did wonder how they found the place, Victoria's best friend from New York now the obvious connection.

"What the hell is a chakra?" Dad asks.

"Like, your aura..." Victoria says, and I frown, looking at Dad.

"What the hell is an aura?" I ask, getting confused with all this terminology. Daisy made it all make sense to me, giving me the information in business terms and not getting too woo-woo. Now all these words are flying around, and I feel like I need to read up on it all, be well versed. I look at my phone. It's Monday morning, and I still haven't heard from her. I'm not used to people not jumping at the chance to work with us. And while I did say I would give her the weekend, I thought she would've called before now. I run my hand over my beard, this unsettled feeling something new. I will give her until five before I call her.

"Kinda like your playboy, hot lumberjack vibes. It's the energy of a person," Lacy says.

"You think I'm hot?" I tease her. We have a sibling-like relationship, more so than boss and employee, so she gets my humor.

"Shut up," she says, throwing a pencil at me as Dad rubs his eyes, obviously frustrated.

"How was the sound massage and yoga flow?"

Victoria teases, trying to hold in her laugh, and even Dad has a sly grin on his face now. Should've known he would know all about it.

"It was actually pretty good," I say with a smile. The thought of the red-haired woman hasn't been far from my mind for days. Lacy spits out her coffee.

"Shit, sorry, I think I burned my tongue," she says quickly, mopping up the mess with a tissue as I throw the pencil back at her.

"It was relaxing. I don't know... healing?" I ask myself, not sure that's the answer I'm trying to convey. It certainly made an impact, and while I've learned a lot from college and years in the business, I lean on my gut instinct too, and my gut is telling me that Daisy is the perfect person to build our spa. "It got me thinking..."

"Go on," Dad says, interested, knowing that I have some thoughts and everyone looks at me. I lean back in my chair, feeling relaxed. Offering her the job was one of the best things I've done. If only she would accept it already.

"Well, what if we made our spa here more than just a fancy spa? Maybe more like a wellness retreat?" I say. I've thought about it more and more since the weekend. It's the perfect business move.

"It's not really what we're going for..." Dad says, frowning, thinking about it.

"I know, but a fancy spa isn't really Whispers either. I think something more for well-being. Like sound healing and yoga could be good for our visitors and the locals." As I look at everyone, they stare back at me like I've grown a second head.

"I could do with a bit of yoga and stress relief in my life," Lacy mumbles, tapping her pen on the table.

"Exactly!" I say, and Dad rubs his chin in thought.

"Daisy, from Sunshine, told me that the vibrations of the sound massage promote stress relief and healing. I thought it might be good to also incorporate some tonics and teas. We might be able to find something complementary to Whiskey, which could be a good marketing tactic. I mean, I fell asleep during my treatment," I say, shrugging.

"You fell asleep?" Victoria says, looking at me quickly.

"Yeah." I nod, still not believing it myself. I'm always on. At the ready for anything. While Whispers is a small town and a little sleepy at times, that doesn't mean the distillery sleeps. It never has and never will. Dad and I have big growth plans, and I'm going to make them happen.

"Wow... Connor Whiteman has a kryptonite, and it comes in the shape of a Daisy..." Lacy murmurs, and I ignore her, even though now all I can visualize is Daisy and her kissable lips.

"At Sunshine, they offer shiatsu, acupuncture, sound healing, and yoga. We could also have relaxation massages and body wraps, like we originally thought, and no doubt, they'll be popular... but we should think about incorporating the two. Beauty and wellness together, so to speak. Daisy also said that there are less issues around stock and products, so it seems fiscally sound to go in that direction."

"Daisy sounds like she knows what she's talking about," Dad says, and I almost hum in agreement. I thought he might appreciate it. He hates waste, likes to reclaim old timber and make furniture and things. He likes ensuring that everything old is new again. So the fact that some wellness treatments can produce less waste and consume less water makes it all sound really appealing from a business perspective.

"If they can make you fall asleep, I think it would work. You're one of the busiest, least likely people to even go for a massage, let alone fall asleep during one," Lacy says with a shrug.

"So do you think this Daisy might be interested in coming to Whispers? Maybe she can consult. Start the spa, hire the people?" Dad asks.

"I offered her a job already," I tell the table, and they all look up at me, shocked.

"A job?" Dad asks, expression turning serious. His eyes burn into mine. He knows that I never make a business decision without running it past him. This is new ground for us.

"To come to Whispers to consult; my thoughts mirror your own. Help us bring the spa to life."

My dad eyes me intensely, giving me a small nod, almost like he's proud of me for taking the reins on it. He's been doing that more and more lately. I've been ready to step up in the business, and he's ready to step back a little more. The switch is happening organically, and we can both feel it.

"It isn't a bad idea. There's no one here in Whispers who has experience in this type of thing. We would've either needed to hire from the city or train local people, so it fits within our plans," Victoria says, looking at me curiously.

"What about Williamstown?" Dad quizzes again, asking about out neighboring town and I frown.

"I want Daisy. She's the best."

"We'll have to offer her a good fee. I mean, she's used to city living, and she's an expert," Lacy says, looking at me. I clear my throat and glance back at my laptop, getting my head back into the numbers.

"We can make it work. I can fly her here on the jet; she can stay in Dad's old place next door to mine. I can have Sawyer draw up the contract today." I nod as I move in my seat, my body feeling antsy as sparkling blue eyes and red hair fill my vision, and I tap out the email to Sawyer right now to get it done.

"Sounds like you have it all planned out, son. Are you feeling alright?" Dad asks, as both women start talking about the spa.

"Fine. Why?" I ask him.

"Just look a little flushed is all," he murmurs.

"No. I'm good," I say, smiling. My grin is feeling brighter than it has in a while.

"Hmmm. Must be all those vibrations to your chakra," Dad says with a smirk.

"So you're on board with this?" I ask him.

"I trust your judgment, and I think Daisy sounds like she could be a nice addition to the team, albeit for a month or two. Let me know if she agrees to your offer."

I look at my watch again. Still no word from her. I roll my head on my shoulders, the tension building all over again.

"I should go call Sawyer, organize the contract." Shutting my laptop, I gather my things.

"Anything else going on with you?" Dad asks as I stand, and I balk.

"No. Everything's fine," I tell him, wondering what he's thinking.

"Hmmm. Tell Sawyer I said hello." Leaning back in his chair, he watches me as I walk out of the room, grabbing my cell and hitting Sawyer's number.

"Connor. Miss me already?" he says, having just seen me in New York over the weekend.

"No, asshole, I need you to actually do some work today." I make my way down the hall to my office. Sawyer has become a firm friend these past few years. A top lawyer and one who we want here in Whispers with us. Yet another thing we'll need to start moving on. I push through the door, the morning sun filtering through my large windows.

From here, I get a view of the entire back of our distillery. Green grass, our rose garden off to the side that my grandparents made. I also see my place and Dad's old place sitting at the back. It's completely private and lush, like my own private oasis.

"What do you need?" he asks.

"A contract drawn up. I made an offer to someone in New York to come consult and build the spa business for us. I just emailed you about it," I tell him, rolling my head on my shoulders, wondering why I feel so edgy.

"Great move. A city professional is exactly who you need." I can hear him tapping on his keyboard.

"I will fly her in, accommodate her here, and pay for

everything. I'm thinking six figures," I tell him, and he's quiet for a beat.

"Six figures? Plus relocation costs?" he confirms.

"Yes. For a month, with an extension for another month, maybe two. Timing is yet to be solidified on the project."

"That's a pretty generous offer," Sawyer says, and I swallow.

"It's an important move for the spa, for the business. She's a professional, has a lot of experience."

"Well, fine. I'll get it done today."

I sigh, not realizing I was holding my breath.

"She hasn't actually verbally accepted yet."

"What? You offered her relocation and six figures, and she still hasn't accepted?" Sawyer sounds gobsmacked. Glad to know I'm not the only one.

"Maybe we need to send her something to sweeten the deal?" I murmur to him as I look out at the garden, spotting a small daisy bush among my grandmother's roses.

"Is she worth this much?" he asks, and I answer without hesitation.

"Yes."

"Maybe a ten grand sign-on bonus can be sent with the contract?" Sawyer suggests, and my brow crumples, knowing money isn't the answer. Not for a woman like Daisy.

"No, it needs to be something more... meaningful," I think out loud.

"Meaningful? Well, you seem to know her. What do

you think?" he asks as I grin, coming up with just the thing.

"Organize a donation to the wilderness society. One that covers us for any trees that were chopped down for our business stationery requirements and put the donation in her name. Send her the certificate." I'm smirking as I think about her quip about how many trees died making my business cards.

"You want to buy her trees?" Sawyer asks, confused.

"Yeah. I want to buy her a fucking field of them."

"You know, I'm too busy to go down this rabbit hole to even question what the fuck is going on here. Leave it with me. I'll get my team to organize it. We'll send it to her today," Sawyer says, no doubt shaking his head at my antics.

"Thanks, Sawyer. Speak soon."

As I end the call. I'm hoping those trees get her over the line.

9
____

DAISY

I look at my cell. I'm not sure why I'm hesitating. Actually, no, that's a lie. Trisha showed me the heating bill, and I almost vomited. So now I'm going to call the one person in the world who can give me instant cash, even though I only met him three days ago.

My eyes flick to the piece of paper that was couriered to Sunshine today. A donation made in my honor to the America Wilderness Society for the reforestation of trees. I had no idea what it was initially, before realization took over and I had to sit down. It was a large donation, totally unnecessary, yet somehow also very, very kind. I flick his thick designer business card in my hand, and the grin I try to hold back peeks through. At least he listens to me.

His number stares at me from the cell screen, my heart beating out of my chest, and it has been all afternoon. I'm nervous, because damn, I want this. *I need this.* Yet this decision is about to turn my safe little world completely upside down. But the opportunity to work with him, build this spa, it's a job that people can only dream about. I know I'm ready for it. I've worked for years in this space, I'm good at what I do, and I have a passion for business and a willingness to learn what I don't already know. It's almost like this role was made for me.

I take in another breath, mentally going through the pros and cons. Pros: money, experience, a break from the city, and a break from Sunshine. Cons: he's rude and arrogant, and I won't be able to just play nice. He riles me up, brings out the fire in me, and I can't for the life of me figure out why. I am Zen now. I meditate, I do yoga, yet the minute I see or think about him, it's like I'm back to that fiery young girl I was when I was a kid. I have missed her, though. She's been mellow for far too long.

"Have you called him yet?" Trisha yells from the other side of the door, and I let go of the breath I was holding.

"No!" I yell back.

"Get one of those crystals in your hand. That always seems to help you," she says sarcastically, and I look down to my lap, seeing the clear quartz already there.

I roll my eyes. "Go away!"

I hear her chuckle as her footsteps retreat.

I'm not sure why I'm hesitating. It's the ideal opportunity at the ideal time. I close my eyes and take a few deep breaths, trying to center myself. But again, the minute my eyes close, the vision of him half-naked returns.

"It's now or never Daisy," I murmur to myself and hit the call button, putting the phone to my ear. Rolling my shoulders back, I sit up straight, not that he can see me, but Confidence Building 101 states that you talk with a smile, you sound friendly, you sit up straight, you can tackle anything.

"Daisy," Connor's voice hums through the line instantly, like he was waiting by his phone for my call. My name rumbles from his throat, and at his tone, my body involuntarily shivers.

"Connor," I say in greeting, following his lead. *Professional.*

"Do you usually leave all your business decisions to the eleventh hour?" he asks, and I still. I look at the clock on my bedside, seeing it's almost five p.m. I guess I did leave it a little longer than I thought. But I take a deep breath and center myself once more. I need to show him that I'm capable and business-minded.

"Well, I like to look at decisions from every angle. People are too quick these days and sometimes that isn't always beneficial. I want to make sure I'm getting as much out of this as you are," I tell him, feeling a little more confident, despite the nerves dancing in my body.

It's just a job, Daisy. Albeit a job of a lifetime, with a very ruggedly handsome boss, but still just a job.

"You know... sometimes, quick decisions are necessary. So you don't miss out on opportunities," he banters back, and I wonder if he's usually annoying like this to everyone or just me. I need to be mindful; he's offered me an opportunity, but there's no contract, no firm discussion on money or timelines.

"I'm a firm believer that good things are worth waiting for. Besides, I'm sure you don't want to invest in someone who's flippant or doesn't take large decisions seriously. You have this amazing spa to open, and you offered me a job to help you bring it to life. You need me, remember?"

"So what *is* your decision?" he asks, cutting straight to it, and I gulp.

"I would like to take you up on the opportunity. We'll need to discuss timing and remuneration, and—"

"I'll have my jet bring you here later in the week. I have a place ready for your stay. We're estimating a month, maybe two, to bring it all together. Remuneration will be on the contract that I have just sent to your phone."

I stall, pulling the phone from my ear and looking at the screen, and sure enough, it lights up with an incoming message.

"I'm sure you'll find the offer more than reasonable. Send me your address, sign the contract, and I will see you this week, Daisy. I'll have a car pick you up and take you to my jet," he says before he ends the call without even saying goodbye.

I'm left breathless, my heart hammering in my ears. I'm in awe of his business manner. Confident, not ruthless but demanding. I think I just experienced what everyone else must when they're in front of him. For someone who consults crystals and meditates, it's in complete contrast, yet there's something about it, about him, that has me feeling jittery, my body thrumming, my nerves on overdrive, and I quickly pull up the contract he sent through.

It's for a month, with the possible extension to a second month, depending if timelines require it. Start date is Thursday. He'll be paying me even on travel days. The Whiteman's Whiskey jet will transport me to Whispers and can bring me back to the city as required.

Accommodations will be provided in the form of a four-bedroom house on the grounds of the distillery. There will be full food services from the nearby diner or the distillery restaurant if required. My eyes widen as I look through the details about the job itself.

Chief Wellness Center Consultant. In charge of product selection for both treatments and retail opportunities. The hiring and training of staff, rostering systems, treatment menu development, retail and booking system... I pause on that one, because at Sunshine, we don't have a computer system for our clients. But there's a new software program that I've been researching that I tried to talk to Mom about implementing at Sunshine, so maybe that's something I can incorporate at Whiteman's.

I look back at the screen and scroll through the rest of the details. It outlines the project budget I have to work with, which is well into the millions, and my mouth goes dry. We've never made a million dollars at Sunshine, so I know for sure that I'll be able to deliver what he needs within that budget.

Scrolling further, I read through the remuneration package. He's offering me one hundred thousand dollars, and now as I look at it in black-and-white, in a formal contract, I think my heart stops.

"Please tell me you're off your call!" Trisha yells from the other side of my bedroom door.

"Umm!" I basically shout. This kind of money is more than I've ever had access to. It will set me up to not only pay off our heating bill and my other debts, but maybe start my own clinic when I come back to New York after the project. It's perfect. A month in Whispers, building confidence, experience, and expertise, and then I can open my own center. Maybe a yoga studio with a side office to do mini treatments?

"Soooooo?" Trisha asks as she opens my bedroom door and comes to sit at the end of my bed with me.

"So, I start this week," I tell her, trying to sort my thoughts.

"This week? Wow. What else?" she asks, and I stare at the contract in front of me.

"It's managing the entire process, essentially. They've done the build, so now it's up to me to help with the fit-out requirements and then turn it into a wellness center."

"Wow, that's a lot. In what time frame?" Her brows pinch.

"A month, but it can stretch to two." My mind whirls with ideas already forming. I need to speak to Mom to get her making and packaging our teas. I need to place a crystal order with Soren to get that ball rolling. Not to mention, choosing sound healing bowls and other equipment.

"That's a lot to do in a month. Staffing will probably be your biggest issue," Trisha says, thinking.

"Mm-hmm," I agree, thinking that's something I need to get straight onto as well. By the time you find people, interview them, and then train them, that could take the full four weeks as it is.

"He better be paying you well," she quips.

"Ahhhh, he, um... he is... Six figures."

"For a month!" she screeches.

"I know," I say, swallowing, reality not setting in just yet. "It's kinda crazy."

"The best kind of crazy! We should pack." Jumping up, she pulls my suitcase out from under the bed.

"Pack?" I question, head rearing back. "I don't leave for another few days."

"Well, it's either we get busy with packing, or I pour us both a shot or two of tequila. You look like you need it. But given that I already know you're a lightweight and don't need a hangover tomorrow, I think we can start packing. One less thing to worry about," Trisha says, her mind made up, and I nod, my body needing something to do.

"Wow. This is just... wow." Standing, I'm feeling a little unsteady on my feet, and she looks at me sharply.

"Daisy. You've got this. You're the expert. You know what you're doing. Hell, you could do this in your sleep backward, remember that. None of them have the skill, and that's why they want you. They might have money, but they don't have your knowledge and expertise. This is a great opportunity, and it also doesn't hurt to have a beautiful man to look at each day while you show him exactly what kind of girl boss you are."

I smile and try to ignore that statement about Connor. "Thanks. You're right, I can do this." This is my chance of a lifetime.

"Good, now sign that thing and let's get you sorted," she says, and I nod. I reread the contract for a second time as Trisha pulls out my clothes for me. I sign it, then I call and put Mom on speakerphone while I start packing my bags at the same time.

"Hi, sweetie."

"I accepted the job," I tell her, holding my breath, waiting for her response.

"Excellent, honey! I'm sure you'll be amazing. When do you start?"

"This week. They want me to start straightaway, so I need your help."

"This week! Wow, okay, what do you need?" she asks, sounding excited. I start talking with her about our tea line, crystals, our suppliers, all of whom she'll call for me tomorrow to get them on the front foot with things.

"I'll make sure I get the tea sorted tomorrow and ship it all to you express."

I smile, thankful to have Mom ready to go as well. Tea making is something she can do from home that doesn't hurt her hands as much, so she's probably happy that she can keep busy doing what she loves.

"Do you think Soren will be able to source some crystals?" I ask her as I open my underwear drawer and grab the essentials. As I do, Trisha leans over me and grabs a few of my nice lacy sets that I rarely wear and puts them in the bag. I look at her like she's lost her mind.

"You'll thank me later," she whispers to me so Mom can't hear before I see her dive back in and grab my special little bag of my battery friends. "You'll thank me for these too." Giving me a wink, she shoves them into the back of my suitcase. I don't fight her on it, but I shake my head at her antics.

"I'll get him to order not only the crystals, but also the singing bowls, and I have a contact at Yoga Express, so I'll send you their details for the yoga mats and other equipment," Mom continues.

So far, so good. Now I just need to figure out the staffing situation. I know Whispers is small, but surely, the town has some people I can train, because if not, I have no idea where to hire from.

"Okay, gotta go. Talk later," Trisha says, seemingly happy that I'm now back in control and half-packed. She's heading out for a date with Tom, and I give her a wave as she slips out the door.

"Write everything down," Mom says, and I almost forgot she was still on the phone.

"What?" I ask her, confused.

"I can tell your head is swimming with things. I'm going to start making some calls for you. You need to start planning what treatments you might want to incorporate, research the location and staffing. Write a list and start pulling things together so when you get there, you're already five steps ahead," Mom says, and I sit on my bed, releasing a heavy breath.

Nodding, I smile. "Thanks, Mom."

"You've got this, honey. I'll see you tomorrow," she says, and I hang up the phone.

With Trisha now gone on a date with Tom, and my phone call with Mom finished, I leave my suitcase half packed and sit at the small desk in my room. I do a brain dump of all my ideas, and when I'm done, I click through to the Whiteman's Whiskey website again to take a look.

It's impressive, and I read through their About Us section for what feels like the hundredth time. It talks all about how the distillery started, and I look through both Connor and his dad Tanner's bios. I can see where

Connor's looks come from; he's a younger version of his dad.

Then I click on Connor's profile picture and read his bio again. He went to one of the top colleges in the country and is now the CFO of the distillery, so he's obviously good with numbers and has lived in Whispers his entire life. I look at his features, and strong, dependable, honorable are all feelings I get when I look at him. Like I conjured him, my cell chimes, and I grab it, seeing a text from him in response to me sending the signed contract back earlier.

> Good decision-making, Daisy. I look forward to seeing you later in the week. Victoria from our team will pick you up when you land.

I shouldn't get butterflies at seeing his message. I clear my throat, wishing this new schoolgirl infatuation that's starting to build would go away.

> Thank you, Connor. See you then.

After replying professionally, I put my phone down and lean back in my chair. Trisha's right. I'm going to girl boss the shit out of this opportunity and set myself up for success.

There's no other option. I just need to ignore my attraction to Connor Whiteman. I close my eyes and rub them, the images I see reminding me just how impossible that's going to be.

10

CONNOR

I walk over to my window and look out at the sky. It's empty of clouds, stunningly blue, almost the same color as her eyes.

"She here yet?" Dad asks, walking into my office. Daisy's here. I sent her the jet, had confirmation that she's on it, and I've been location tracking it on my cell for the last few hours, so I know it landed ten minutes ago.

"Should be here any minute," I tell him, running my hand down my beard, walking back to my desk and picking up my cell, not looking at anything really because my mind is on high alert.

"Why are you nervous?" Dad asks, looking at me through narrowed eyes.

"I'm not nervous," I say with a huff, then throw my cell back on my desk and walk over to the mini whiskey bar in my office. It's before noon; otherwise, I would take a shot.

"You're rubbing your beard. It's your tell."

I look at him like he has gone mad.

"Pfft. It's not my tell. Is your old age making you think crazy thoughts, old man?" I ask him, before I walk back over to the window and look out again. He's right, though. I feel fidgety, nerves cycling through my body, and I have no idea why. Actually, I do, and it has everything to do with the curvaceous redhead who's about to walk into my distillery.

"I might be old, but I know my son, and at the moment, you're almost jumping out of your skin."

"I'm just vibrating at a high frequency, that's all." I shrug, like it's no big deal. It's something I've learned over the past few days of my research. I downloaded some books on wellness and chakras and things I still don't understand entirely, but I wanted to have some knowledge for when Daisy arrives, so she doesn't think I'm totally inept.

"What the hell does that mean?" he grumbles, frowning at me.

"Nothing." I wave off his question. "I just have a lot on my plate." Even though that's true, I thrive on the demands the distillery brings. I've been working here my entire life. It's the baby my father started, and now the child I'll develop and grow. Dad's starting to step back, preferring to spend more time with Victoria and her goats, and that works well for me, because I always wanted to be at the helm.

"Maybe you need another massage. She'll be here soon. Victoria is dying to try it out," he says, and my jaw tics.

Another massage? I imagine Daisy's hands on my body and swallow roughly. Or should I say, near my body? I huff a laugh, just thinking about it all. She was almost too scared to come near me during my treatment. Not to mention, last time we saw each other, we were nearly at each other's throats. My dad looks at me like I have grown a second head. My inner thoughts are probably playing out in my features. Maybe I've gone completely mad.

"We're here!" I hear Victoria yell out from the front doors, and I jump and pace to my desk.

"Well, shit," I hear him mumble. "You better get yourself under control before she takes one look at how eager you are and walks straight back out." He shakes his head at me, and I take a breath. I have no idea what the hell is wrong with me. I'm acting like some kid eager to get his rocks off. Not Connor fucking Whiteman.

"Boys?" Victoria yells again.

"In here," Dad calls out as he takes a seat in an armchair in my office, with an eye on both me and the door.

"Oh, here you are. Boys, this is Daisy. Daisy, you have already met Connor, and this is his father, Tanner. As outlined in the brief we sent, Tanner and Connor own the distillery and are both looking forward to the expansion," Victoria explains, and I stand, feet rooted to the floor, eyes on her as she walks through my office door.

She almost sparkles as the sun from my window coats her in amber. Her smile is wide, looking totally comfortable, in control, and so fucking beautiful. I swallow down my admiration, straightening my stance, pulling my shoulders back, standing tall, and I take a breath in to try to appear like my professional self. Not the ogling asshole I actually am when it comes to her.

"Nice to meet you," she says, looking at Dad with a big smile and shaking his hand. I can't breathe again. She looks better than the last couple of times I saw her. To be fair, both times, she was in some type of uniform, both at Sunshine and then also at the stadium.

This time, her hair is loose, long and shiny, her face glowing. She's wearing tailored black pants and a black top, which looks both corporate and sexy as hell. Her belt cinches her in at the waist, highlighting her hourglass shape, and I need to swallow my groan that threatens to escape because deep curves and a body to grab on to have always been my weakness.

"Daisy." I say her name in greeting, and I watch as her gaze falls to me and those bright blues that I've been dreaming about meet mine. I physically feel my chest expanding. I could barely sleep last night in anticipation of seeing her again. I'm not ashamed to admit that I thought about fisting her vibrant red hair when I gripped my cock in the shower this morning, coming harder than I have in a long while.

"Connor," she says simply, our words not laced with malice, but far from friendly. It seems we might still be at odds with each other. I notice Dad and Victoria looking between us, no doubt wondering what's going on, so I continue.

"How was the flight?" I ask, my body suddenly wanting to get closer. I step toward her, trying to remain professional and taming the small grin that pulls at the sides of my mouth. Flying private isn't something everyone experiences in life, and while we do it often, because it's more efficient and easier, I expect this is Daisy's first time.

"Well, it was my first time on a private jet, and it was pretty fabulous," she says, and her genuine honesty is refreshing. Anyone else would be acting like it's a simple thing and no big deal, that they themselves travel private all the time, or some have the opposite response; they have their guard up, almost acting like we're showing off by having our plane transport them. To her, it just is, and I hear my dad's chest rumble in what I think is a small laugh. When I look at him, his eyes are dancing as he glances between me and Daisy and back again. Shit, she even has my old man under her spell.

"Well, Tanner and I need to get to another appointment, so Connor will show you to your accommodations, where you can freshen up and unpack. Your bags are already there, and then we have dinner with the four of us at our bar in town tonight before we hit the ground running tomorrow," Victoria explains, and I watch Daisy nod, her tense swallow the only hint I get of her slight nervousness. I raise my eyebrows at Victoria's sudden change of plans. She was meant to show Daisy around and get her settled. I have meetings and appointments, but Victoria gives me a sly grin as she steps toward the door.

"Nice to meet you, Daisy," Dad says, giving her nod before looking at me with narrowed eyes, then he follows Victoria out the door to go who knows where.

"Nice to meet you both. See you later at dinner,"

Daisy says, her manners appreciated as we watch them go, and then it's just the two of us.

"So you're friendly to them and not me?" I ask her, and her head whips around to look at me.

"Well, so far, they haven't been jerks and insulted me or my mother's business, so I'm taking them at face value," she fires back, and I can't help the smirk that comes to my face.

"First day on the job, and you're calling your boss a jerk? Very professional." I lift an eyebrow.

"Not boss. I'm an independent contractor hired by the distillery to do a job, for a set fee, for a set time period," she states, full of confidence.

"My distillery, my rules, Daisy." As I step closer to her, she squares her shoulders. She grins then, like I humor her, and I've never wanted to kiss a woman more than I do right now.

"I'm more than happy to turn around and walk straight back out that door, Connor. You need me, remember?" Stepping toward me slowly, her hands find her hips, and my jaw clenches at her closeness.

"And go where? Back to Sunshine, that's falling apart around you?" It's a low blow, and she shakes her head, unamused.

"Sometimes, you find diamonds in the rough," she says, and no truer words have ever been spoken. "Besides, I'm sure your girlfriend would love to have you back in the city. She's such a super friendly woman." The sarcasm is clear as day.

"Not girlfriend. Not friend. Not even an acquaintance," I tell her, my eyes not leaving hers for a second. "Simply a favor for a friend."

She watches me carefully, no doubt to see if I'm being honest.

We stand in front of each other, both with fire in our eyes. I've never spoken to a staff member like this. I never explain myself to anyone. Hell, aside from Sawyer, I've never spoken to a contractor or supplier like this either. But this woman gets so far under my skin, I can barely concentrate.

"I have meetings, so let me show you around so I can get back to it," I say, acting like she's an inconvenience, when all I want to do is talk with her all day. Swiping my cell from my desk, I stride out of my office, with Daisy hot on my heels.

"This is our main corporate office. We have boardrooms, staff spaces, and all the administration for the distillery and our distribution here. Your office is down the hall."

She looks around, taking in the space. My steps are quick, as I have things to do, important people to speak with, so giving Little Miss Sassy Pants a tour is the last thing I should be doing. My strides are long, and I hear her almost running in her heels to keep up. I feel like an asshole, but this is how we work best, I'm starting to discover.

"Through here..." I say, opening a large timber door that leads to the main distillery. "This is where the magic happens." Pride fills me every time I enter this space. I like to think I'm smart and well rounded. I had good grades throughout college, and I've done well as the CFO of Whiteman's, but I've never been prouder of the business. Our growth plans, both locally and internationally, are ambitious, but I plan to meet every last one of them.

As we walk through, I can't help but notice her looking wide-eyed and taking it all in. She doesn't have her phone out taking selfies, doesn't look bored, and she eyes over everything with interest. As she looks around, I take the opportunity to drink her in. Her lips are painted soft pink, and that Cupid's bow teases me a little. With her short stature, I'm almost a giant next to her. Then there's her aroma. It smells vibrant, intoxicating, and I want to drown in it. When she looks back at me, I blink, having been caught staring at her, and I turn looking around the space myself, but not before I see her smile.

"So this is where you actually distill the whiskey?" she asks, looking back around at all our equipment.

"It is. Dad is our main distiller. We produce a few different varieties and products, then through here are our aging rooms." I take her down another hallway, and I see her mouth agape as she glances around at room after room of barrels.

Her brows pinch. "You have a lot of stock?"

"We do small batches, mostly, but a lot of them. It keeps things exclusive. We want to ensure that not everyone can get their hands on a bottle of Whiteman's."

"You can sell it for a higher price that way too, I assume?" she asks, and I raise my eyebrows, impressed.

"Yes, we can command higher prices. But it also helps us maintain quality."

"Do you store any barrels off-site?"

I almost hum in approval. I love the way her mind

works. Who would have thought that this curvaceous hippie would have the business mind of a shark.

"We have a variety of storage facilities, both here on-site and in other places around the country." I nod to her, not giving too much away.

"Minimizing risk? Shortening lead times and distribution channels?" she asks quickly, and I nod once again, appreciating her smart intellect and quick thoughts. Before I can get caught staring at her again, I push on.

"We have an on-site restaurant through here," I tell her, taking her through another door, where she can see the main space. "It's empty for the moment. Our chefs are busy preparing for the night of bookings we have... And then we have a large outdoor area. We do tastings, both inside and out, and run tours of the production rooms when we're not distilling." I open the large French doors and walk outside.

"It's beautiful." She looks around, taking it all in. "These gardens are amazing." Walking ahead of me, she moves into the distillery gardens that I can see from my office. The sun hits her hair, the red even more vibrant in the sunlight.

"My grandparents built this. The roses have been here for years. Generations, really."

She bends over and smells them, closing her eyes and taking in the scent.

"What do you do with all this space?" she asks as she looks over the vast amount of green lawn, the various pockets of gardens, and the small hidden-away floral oases we have.

"It's just gardens."

I can see her thinking, and I'm already wanting to know what's happening inside that head of hers.

"They smell amazing. Do you have any other gardens?" Daisy asks, looking around. Our land is vast, and there's a lot of room here.

"We have a large food garden that our chefs utilize. They have all sorts of vegetables, fruits, and herbs—"

"Herbs?" she asks, seemingly excited. "Can I take a look?"

"Sure. It's just over here." Stepping to the side, behind the kitchen, we walk through a little garden gate. I haven't been back here for a while, and it's grown in size from the last time I was here.

"Wow," Daisy says as she tentatively walks through the garden. "You have lemongrass, chamomile, ginger…"

I watch her inquisitively. She's in her element now, talking about herbs and plants, and I start to see her passion come through.

"We also have our own beehives for our own honey."

She looks up at me and smiles wide, like I hung the moon, and I feel my chest push out slightly.

"Your own honey?" Her eyes sparkle in delight.

"Well, whiskey and honey do go well together," I tell her, my voice sounding a little rough, and I swallow.

"That they do." Again, she's seemingly deep in thought as she walks back toward me.

"Are you into whiskey?" I ask her. I have no idea if she even drinks. Probably something I should have asked before I hired her, and now that I think about it, I'm dying to see my whiskey on her lips. Fuck, the vision is already making me ache for it.

"I don't really drink," she admits, and I stand still, my fingers twitching to touch her.

"Like ever?" I ask, frowning.

"Well, yes, I have before, on the odd occasion, but generally, no, I don't. I try to limit the amount of toxins in my environment, although..." With a pause, she looks at me. "It appears I have come to the wrong place for all that." Her subtle dig at me is almost humorous. I add funny to her list of attributes that's growing by the minute.

"Now you're calling me toxic. Name-calling your new boss, Daisy. *Tsk, tsk*," I tease.

"Not boss," she says, shaking her head, and I smirk.

"If not your boss, what am I?" I gloat, and she grins.

"Oh, so many things..."

I shake my head, the two of us clearly pushing each other, yet having fun with it now.

"How long does a good whiskey age?" she asks, coming to stop not far from me, but also too far away. I try to tame my satisfied smile. This is what I like about her. She asks good questions. She's smart as well as sexy.

"We have a variety of ages. My favorite is our seventeen-year-old batch," I tell her honestly.

"Why is it your favorite?"

"It was the first batch I made with Dad. Did it on my eighteenth birthday." The memory of that time makes me smile.

Her grin widens. "It sounds like it's special, then."

"Yeah, well, it also makes me feel old." I laugh, knowing that at thirty-five, I'm at least a decade older than her. "Let me show you the spa space."

"Great," she says as we walk in comfortable silence through the gardens to the other side of the distillery.

"So the fit-out is almost complete," I tell her as we walk inside. The mood here is different. It's all deep-brown woods from our recycled barrels, cream-colored stone, very earthy and raw, yet has curves that make it look soft and inviting. Our builder, Griffin, did a fantastic job, and now Victoria has added some final touches to it, but for the most part, it's a blank canvas, ready for Daisy and Victoria to add what they need to it.

"Wow, another amazing space." Looking around, she reaches out and touches the finishes.

"A little more aesthetically pleasing than the Sunshine Space Wellness Clinic, I think we can both agree," I murmur, not able to help myself. She throws me a look over her shoulder, her eyes narrowing, but remains quiet as her lips thin. I miss having her volley back an insult. But there's no denying it. The Whiteman Distillery Spa is top-of-the-line luxury.

"We have three rooms, plus restrooms and showers. An office and the front reception space. Then the back door..." I say, pacing ahead down the corridor to a door at the end. As I step outside, Daisy follows.

"This path takes you directly to our natural mineral springs," I tell her, pointing to the raw rock pavers that make a path through the back of the distillery and through a gate at the fence into Marie's Place next door, where the mineral springs are located.

"Mineral springs?" she confirms with a gasp, and I nod.

"Thermal springs, lots of minerals or whatnot. Very

good for the body." I don't really know the exact benefits, and I smile, seeing the surprise on her face.

"Okay, *that's* amazing..." she says, a little gobsmacked, and I can see her brain moving a million miles an hour, so I decide to give her a reprieve.

"Let me show you to your place. I have a few meetings to get to, and you probably want to unpack and have some time before dinner."

She follows me back inside, and we walk through the garden to where Dad's old house sits right next to mine.

"I think staff will be the biggest issue. I'm assuming that Whispers doesn't have a lot of options in regard to experienced and trained therapists?" she mentions as we walk.

"No, not really. We have Williamstown, though, a bigger town an hour or so away. I think we might find some good people there," I tell her, although I don't really know.

"Okay... do you have an option for staff quarters?"

I raise my eyebrows for a second time this afternoon.

"We have options..." I nod, thinking of both Dad's old place here, where she's staying and Marie's Place next door that we could utilize. "What are you thinking?" I ask her as we reach the front porch.

"It might be worth considering bringing in regular experts from the city for a week or two at a time," she says, and I barely have time to think about it before I'm nodding. Hudson is doing something similar at the hospital, with medical professionals, something that both Dad and I thought was a brilliant idea.

"Great idea," I say, liking that option. We'd not only

get the expertise, but potentially world-class people right here in Whispers, making it a spa destination of choice for many.

"It's just a thought." She shrugs. "I know you have enough patrons coming for the whiskey, but it certainly couldn't hurt to have world-class therapists on a fly-in fly-out basis."

"I like anything exclusive. I like having things that no one else has. Having a rotating visitation schedule of people not only from the city, but potentially worldwide would really set us apart. People come for the whiskey but stay for the wellness." My mind now races with possibilities, the marketing slogan sounding solid.

"I'll work on it. I have some contacts I can call." She nods, and I grin. I knew she would be amazing. She's thinking big, and I like it.

"Well, here's your place." Opening the door, the two of us step inside. Our cleaning people got it ready for her, and it looks sparkling and refreshed.

"Wow, this is stunning," she says, looking at the large open fire, the huge chandelier on the ceiling, and the vast amount of space.

"This is Dad's old place. I'm next door," I tell her, pointing to my place, which you can see through the window. "Your bags are here. Choose whatever bedroom you want. Bathrooms have towels and full amenities, and the fridge should be stocked. Victoria has left a welcome pack here for you, and all of our numbers are listed on the paperwork." Glancing around, I make sure everything is perfect for her.

"Great. Thank you," she says, smiling. And this smile,

it's sweeter than most of the others she's given me. It warms me up inside.

"I need to get back to work, but I'll come and get you around six to take us to the bar for dinner," I add, even though I would rather stay and talk with her than go to my next meeting, which is about issues with our barley supply, something we continually have so many issues with. It's immensely frustrating.

"Sure, um, what's the dress code?"

I can't help but let my eyes wander over her quickly before they snap back to meet hers, and I see a slight pink coloring her cheeks.

I clear my throat. "Anything you want to wear will be just fine." Then I quickly turn and walk out the door. I pace straight down the footpath, and my steps don't falter as I stride to my office. I have a million things to do before I leave for dinner, and after spending time showing her around, I have even less time to do them.

But she's here. In my distillery. And the distillery has never looked so good.

11

DAISY

I look at myself in the mirror. I couldn't wait to get those black pants off earlier; they were seriously starting to cut my diaphragm in half. Now, after unpacking, taking a quick shower, and redoing my hair, I've applied a light coat of makeup and am ready for dinner.

I will admit, I was nervous today. The car that picked me up from my apartment was new, polished, and the leather seats were so clean, I literally slid across them when we took a corner. Then I was driven straight onto the tarmac and stepped inside the private jet. That's an experience that I'll never forget.

As I swipe gloss onto my lips, I hear a knock at the front door. With one last glance at myself, I decide that jeans and a nice green top are what I'm going with, and I rush out.

When I first saw Connor, it left me breathless. He's even better-looking than I remember, yet also even more infuriating. The first two times I saw him, he was dressed casually. Today, however, he was in a business suit, and I had to clamp my jaw shut so it didn't fall to the floor. It didn't take long, though, before his arrogance came through, of course picking on Sunshine's lack of aesthetics, and he was definitely smug when he showed me the spa space. But I was almost too gobsmacked to fire back at him. It's amazing, and I have been pinching myself all afternoon that I got such a beautiful spa to develop into a thriving, profitable spa business.

Then to meet his dad, Tanner, and have the two of them in the same room was almost too much. Testosterone oozes from them. I'm not sure if it's because they're huge men, but they both have a commanding presence, yet kind eyes. It's an odd mix, but one I'm finding incredibly hard to ignore. I'm not sure what they put in the water here in Whispers, but it's working. Must be the mineral springs.

"Hey," I say, opening the door and then pulling up short. Connor has changed as well. Dark denim jeans, a navy button-down shirt open at the collar, and his cuffs are rolled up, showing arms that are thick and look like they could carry anything. I swallow before looking back at his eyes, just in time to see him do a quick canvass of me as well, his hand running down his beard. His expression's tight, making my nervousness even worse.

"Are you ready?" he asks me, frowning, like I've kept him waiting for hours. I bite my tongue so a sassy comment doesn't slip out.

The man is beautiful, but his personality sure leaves a lot to be desired, and while I try to live a life of peacefulness, with daily yoga and breathwork, I can't help my fiery nature every time I'm with him.

I look up at him and blink a few times. The sun is setting behind him, the soft orange glow giving him the kind of lighting that photographers dream of, and his natural good looks, his piercing eyes, and his broad shoulders sure give women something to swoon over.

"Yes, all set," I say, trying to be nice, grabbing my bag and walking out, proud that I can keep my smart-ass mouth in check for once as I follow him to his truck.

I peeked at his place earlier, hiding behind the thick, lush curtains of my quarters. The two homes are almost identical, log cabin style. Double story, featuring stone, and the one I'm in is like a luxury mansion, so I'm sure his is the same. The reality of exactly how wealthy this family is, is starting to show and it's eye-watering. I mean, all the media articles I read indicated that they were astronomically wealthy, but I didn't think too much about it all until now.

"Here," he almost barks at me, and I jolt to a stop as he leans over me and opens the passenger door to his truck. I haven't had anyone open a door for me before. I'm not sure how this is all meant to go or what the protocol is. It's something I envied whenever I saw it happen to other women, and when I see it on TV, I always swoon. Now, though, I'm so taken aback I'm not sure exactly what to say, standing here, wide-eyed.

"Ahhhh... Thank you," falls from my lips as his face remains hard-set. Clearly, he's had a bad afternoon or something, because he seems more agitated than earlier. I look back at the door that sits wide open. It's probably something he's done hundreds of times, for hundreds of women, and I take in a breath as I look up at the seat in the truck.

It seems almost too far away. His truck is huge, not unlike the man himself. Black, shiny, and I assume it's top of the line, if the luxurious look of it is anything to go by. It was something I noticed when I arrived and drove to the distillery with Victoria. Everyone in Whispers has a truck of some description. They were practically the only types of vehicles on the roads.

"Um, I..." I stutter as I step forward and grab on to the side of the door panel as my cheeks start to flame in embarrassment. I haven't been in a truck like this before, and I have no idea how to climb up into it while trying to remain well put together. Thank God, I didn't wear a dress tonight, because the chances of me falling on my butt are extremely high. Now I'm regretting the jeans I put on as well, because they're somewhat restrictive. Activewear would have been perfect for this. Although not suitable for a work dinner.

While I'm flexible, due to years of yoga, my legs are short and stocky, and my upper body strength isn't great, so I'm not entirely sure I can pull myself up into his truck.

"Problem?" he asks, like I'm deliberately causing an issue, and I look at him, frowning. His brow furrows in confusion.

"Yes, there's a problem," I start, disguising my embarrassment in slight anger and completely directing it at him. "How is any woman supposed to get up into this monstrosity of a truck?"

"It's not a monstrosity. It's the latest model," he grits out.

"Potato, potahto," I quip, because it doesn't matter, the issue is the same.

His frown deepens as he looks at me, then looks at the truck, and back again.

"The girls brought me a stepladder as a joke, but now it would probably be useful."

"Girls?" I ask and internally cringe because that came out too fast. It also isn't any of my business. Of course a man like Connor has girls. Multiple. God, I bet he satisfies every single one of them. *Probably simultaneously.*

"Lacy and Victoria."

I breathe out, trying to will my insides to stop having a disco in my stomach. When I searched Connor online, he had a myriad of women on his arms over the years, but I couldn't see any information on a permanent female in his life. I know he isn't married and doesn't have any children, the woman from the football game the other night clearly not anyone to him either, not that any of that should be of any concern to me.

"Here," he says, then grabs my waist and hoists me into the air and onto the seat. It happens so quickly that I don't have time to register what's going on before I'm seated in his truck and not sure I have the capacity to breathe. His soft leather seats are comfortable on my backside, and there's so much leg room, I feel like I can swing my legs. I'm so high up, I look down on everything. Except him. We're now eye to eye.

"You alright?" he asks, the frown gone and replaced with a small smirk that I want wiped off his face immediately. He's clearly taking too much enjoyment out of seeing my embarrassment as I sit, dumbfounded, a few feet up in the air.

"I... ahhhh, um, I mean... sure. Thank you." My mind swirls in disbelief, throat feeling dry, my cheeks flamed. No one has ever lifted me before. Never in my life has anyone even attempted. I can't remember my parents lifting me as a kid, with me being a bigger girl ever since I made it to double digits. Now, in a matter of a few seconds, Connor not only attempted, but succeeded in lifting me from the ground like I weighed nothing more than a matchstick. I look at him still standing on the ground at my open door, watching me. He isn't panting or sweating, doesn't look like it was hard work or exhausting. He isn't moaning about a sore back.

"Don't forget your seat belt." He slams the door closed, and I grab my seat belt and buckle in tight. Running around the truck to his side, he jumps in with complete ease, and I huff.

As we drive out, it's silent for a moment, before he asks, "So how do you feel about coming to Whispers?"

Is this a loaded question? Is he testing me? Are we making small talk right now? I look out the window and think carefully about my answer. The view is beautiful here. Rolling hills on one side, the large distillery on the other. Nothing but crisp, green pastures and clean air, and now that we're moving, I relax a little. There's something about Connor that makes me want to be completely honest with him, so I just go with that.

"So far, so good. I find it odd that someone like you calls this town home..."

He leans one arm on his door, the other gripping the wheel, the veins in his arms popping out every now and then as he turns this large truck with ease onto the road. I wasn't sure I had a thing for arms before now. But at this moment, I'm wondering what they would feel like around my naked body.

"Someone like me?" he asks, and I roll my lips to keep from smiling.

"Well, it's just that, you're so... tidy," I say and almost cringe.

"Tidy?"

"Tall, big... well... maintained." I slam my lips shut, wondering if I could be more awkward.

"Is that a compliment? Are you complimenting me, Daisy?" he teases, and I roll my eyes.

"Just... I figure you would be more of a city guy," I say, wishing I just started with that benign fact, as my cheeks heat. I turn my head to look out the window, but not before noticing his grin.

"Well, Whispers is pretty well maintained, so I like it here." He lets me off the hook. "So that there is called Marie's Place. Victoria owns it. Not sure if she told you about it?"

I shake my head while looking through the trees at what seems to be a beautiful white farmhouse with a large, new-looking red shed out back.

"No, she didn't mention it," I tell him, and he clears his throat.

"She's from New York, was left the place by her aunt when she passed, and moved here to remodel it."

I did see on the briefing paper they sent through that

Victoria was managing the fit-out of the spa, so it all makes sense.

"Sounds like she's very talented," I confirm.

"It takes around ten minutes to get to town. Most of this land here is farmland, and the mineral springs are on Victoria's land, just over that hill." He points out a few landmarks and things as he continues to give me a little info on the town. I remain quiet, taking it all in.

"So this is Main Street," he says as we make a turn, and I see the town come to life. It's magical. A quaint street, well maintained, colorful flowers, beautiful big trees. I fall in love with it immediately. It's everything that I imagined and the small amount of research I did hasn't done it justice, because it's absolutely stunning. I spot a small church on the corner that we pass, and I look over at Connor to see him watching me.

"Have you always lived here in Whispers?" I ask him, and his face softens.

"Except for college, and I spend a fair bit of time in New York at our office there, but I love being here."

I can see the love he has for this town written all over his face. It's refreshing. I'm sure he's ruthless when he wants to be, and to me, he's somewhat infuriating. He has this edge to him that makes me think that people don't cross him too much, but he seems almost soft and genuine too.

"We have a hardware store over there that's managed by Bob. Homewares over here, I'm pretty sure Victoria has a loyalty card to that place," he mumbles, and I laugh a little.

"What about that? What was that?" I ask, seeing a

nice shop all closed up, with newspapers lining the windows.

"Ahh, that was the old florist. They moved on, and we haven't found a new tenant for that space yet." His tone changes slightly, face falling, and I turn to look at the shop again. It's cute, double fronted, with large windows, and it's surrounded by gardens. From what I can see, a small lawn and garden out back. It looks almost picturesque.

"Whispers didn't need a florist? Did she go out of business?" I'm intrigued, because even though the town looks like it's thriving, I guess it would be hard as a small business to make money in a place like this unless you had something pretty special.

"She... ahhh. Well, truth time," he mumbles, and I look over to him with curiosity. "Jasmine was from the next town over. She was here for about a year, did a good trade, but unfortunately, had some mental health issues, one being that she was infatuated with my dad and didn't take too kindly to Victoria moving here. Burned down her shed at Marie's Place in a jealous rage."

I suck in a breath at that. While the small town is beautiful and quaint, I wonder if safety is an issue here. Should I triple lock my door at night?

"Does that kind of thing happen often?"

"Nope." He shakes his head before moving on, leaving me with a myriad of questions that he's obviously not prepared to answer. "We have the diner over there. Rochelle has been cooking for this town for years and will cook you anything you want. Farther down, we have the Toy Store, great for if you have any nieces or nephews," he adds, and I shake my head.

"Nope, I'm an only child," I tell him. Even though I do love kids, I'm not around them much.

"Me too."

"Wow, will you look at that? We actually have something in common," I say, my tone only half-sarcastic as I match his grin, which is fast becoming one of my favorite things about him.

"Hmmm, probably the only thing," he quips, and he's right. We're complete opposites, not just in the way we look, but everything about us. "We're here."

I whip my head around to the front, looking through the windshield, and take in the large building in front of me. The now familiar gold Whiteman's Whiskey badge is displayed front and center on the building, people wandering in, and the parking lot is full of trucks.

"Looks popular."

Connor jumps out of the truck and runs around to my side. My heart thuds a little. This is all so unusual. For the most part, I jump in and out of Ubers or taxis, the drivers rushing me out so they can get to their next job, but as he opens my door with a sweet chivalry that I'm now certain is only found in small towns, I take off my seat belt and swivel toward the door, looking down at the large drop that's before me. I could jump, but I would probably break an ankle.

"Come on, we haven't got all night," he grumbles and again grabs me around my waist, lowering me to the ground in front of him with complete ease. I grip on to the doorframe, scared I'm going to fall, but I shouldn't have been concerned. He lowers me right in front of him, and I pull in a breath as my body stills in shock. His scent wraps around me, a fresh, earthy aroma that smells almost natural, like a walk in the woods. I pick up scents of sandalwood and cedar, and I nearly hum at how delicious the combination is on him.

"Thank you," I say, feeling my blush creep from my chest up my neck. *God, how long has it been since a man had his hands on my body?*

"I can be nice sometimes." His voice is a rough rumble near my ear, reminding me exactly how close our bodies are. Like we notice it at the same time, he takes a quick step backward, holding the door open, and I move forward, needing the cool air against my heated skin.

This stupid crush I seem to have developed cannot be happening. He's just showing manners and would do it for any female with short legs, I'm sure of it. I have this job that could literally set me up for life; I can't forget that.

And while we're not technically boss and employee, with me on a consulting contract to his business, he might as well be, as much as that thought is something I've been pushing against this whole time. All this helping me into his truck and panty-melting grins are just part of small-town hospitality. Something an educated city girl like me should be more aware of.

I follow him up the stairs and into the bar, Connor holding the heavy timber door open for me to enter, and as I walk inside, I look around, smiling. It's exactly like you would see in the movies. Almost postcard perfect. Timber is showcased everywhere, and the ceiling has big antler chandeliers that I love. There's a large, roaring stone fireplace and tables and chairs spread around, with booths lining both sides.

The place is busy, full of people sitting at tables, standing up at the sparkling bright bar. and walking around chatting with each other like they're one happy family. There's a rustic timber dance floor off to the side, and when I see some people line dancing, my smile is immediate. Dancing is one of the things I love to do but rarely get the chance. My mom would love this place too. Having grown up in a commune, this kind of living would be second nature to her. Maybe that's why I've taken to the small town so quickly. It's in my blood. As I look at all the faces, my grin falters as I realize that they're all looking in one direction. At me.

"Don't worry about all the eyes. They always look at who the new people are. Small town, everyone likes to know everyone's business." I hear his voice in my ear again before I feel his hand at the small of my back. I know it's just manners, but it feels nice. It's simple yet appreciative gestures, not overstepping, but certainly taking control, assisting me yet keeping me close.

"Let's go, our table is at the back," he says, guiding me through. Everyone seems to know him, and they're all looking at the two of us with interest. A few men shake his hand and say hello, but he doesn't leave my side once, and his hand remains on my back the entire way, until I see Victoria and Tanner waiting for us at a booth. Victoria has a large smile that immediately puts me at ease, and Tanner looks between Connor and me, at where his hand is, like he's seeing something for the first time.

"You made it. Welcome to Whiteman's Bar," Victoria says, grinning as I slip into the booth on the opposite side of her, and Connor follows me in.

"Thank you, it's beautiful here," I tell them, relieved to be hiding in the booth, away from all the people, and Tanner gives me a small nod in what I think is appreciation for my words. The look on his face is similar to Connor's earlier when he drove me here, full of pride, and I'm starting to understand that these two men may run this town, if the size of this bar is anything to go by.

"Great burgers here too," Victoria says, winking as I grab a menu to look over. I'm not sure of the etiquette with work dinners, but I'm smart enough to know not to order the most expensive thing on the menu, so as the waitress takes our order, they all choose burgers, and I follow their lead.

"So, how did you find the house?" Victoria asks, and I smile.

"It's lovely, stunning." It's the truth. Total luxury and in complete contrast to the two-bedroom apartment I share with Trisha. I make a mental note to text her tonight to let her know I arrived, because I know she'll want all the details.

"And is your neighbor treating you well?" she teases as she looks at Connor, while Tanner sits back and surveys the atmosphere.

"Hey, I'm a perfect neighbor," Connor banters, and I grin. It's good to see him friendly with his staff members, although Victoria and Tanner do look rather cozy for a boss and employee.

"His choice of music can be questionable," Victoria says playfully.

"Better than yours. Thanks, *Mom*," Connor says sarcastically, and I still. *Did he just call her mom?* I look between the two of them, who continue with their conversation, and then to Tanner. He watches me as I feel confusion and slight panic at trying yet failing to understand this dynamic.

Connor and Victoria look to be the same age. I think back to the woman who owned the florist and who had issues, and I wonder what kind of place have I come to? I look around the bar again. Everything feels luxurious and normal, but am I in a commune or something? Mom hasn't really told me much about commune life, but I'm sure it looks nothing like this. *Shit, is this some small-town cult?*

"I can see your head about to explode. Victoria and I are partners. Connor is being a smart-ass," Tanner grumbles before Victoria and Connor stop talking and look at me.

It's then I feel my cheeks heat in slight embarrassment at jumping to stupid conclusions.

"Yeah, and my taste in music isn't that bad," Connor says before he lifts his glass of whiskey to his lips and looks at me over the rim of the glass.

"I will reserve my judgment." I want to make a good impression on everyone, yet I'm still trying to figure out the dynamics. I look over to the dance floor again, country music coming from a jukebox nearby and people, young and old, all move in time, doing the same routine. It's cute. Tanner runs his hand around the back of the booth and around Victoria's shoulders, and she leans into him a little. They actually really suit each other, despite what must be a massive age gap.

"Hmmm... I didn't pick you for a judgy person," Connor comments, and I look up at him.

"Not usually. But musical taste might be where I draw the line." My love for eighties music runs deep. It was the best era, in my opinion.

"Really?" Connor asks with a grin as he moves in his seat and faces me, Victoria and Tanner now talking among themselves.

I shrug. "Well, music says a lot about a person."

"So you like more than windpipes and waves crashing?" His eyes narrow on me, teasing.

"Eighties all the way," I tell him, and his eyebrows shoot to his hairline.

"Seriously?"

"Yes, seriously." I nod, wondering why I'm telling him one of my cringiest hobbies.

"I mean, Bon Jovi, Michael Jackson, Whitney Houston, there's a lot to love about that era." His eyes sparkle in delight as he watches me, and I'm enjoying this conversation just as much.

"Well, what's your favorite?" I ask inquisitively.

"Country, of course." He tilts his head in the direction of the dance floor. "Dolly and Kenny killed it in the eighties."

I look back at him as his smile widens. He seems

more relaxed now, sitting back in this booth, jeans on, whiskey in his hand.

"'Islands in the Stream.' It's a good one," I agree, nodding, actually loving that song. I smile at him as we watch each other with what feels like new admiration. Almost like we have crossed an invisible barrier, and I'm starting to think I perhaps misjudged him.

"Looks like we might have another thing in common now, doesn't it, Daisy?" he murmurs, his thick drawl as he says my name low and almost a rumble. My mouth dries at the sexy sound.

"Don't get ahead of yourself, cowboy," I quip, our eyes still only on each other as I feel my heart thumping a little more rapidly than it has in some time. "I see it now," I say, not at all covertly. I couldn't move my eyes from him if I tried.

"See what?" he asks as he moves his arm and places it at the back of the seat, turning his body to face me completely, not dissimilar to the way Tanner's is at the back of Victoria. The move cocoons us. We're close, yet I don't feel contained. I feel safe. Warm. Although that could be the fact that my temperature is rising the closer we get.

"See how this is your home," I tell him, thinking back to the conversation we had on the drive in.

"You can take the boy out of the country..."

"But you can't take the country out of the boy," I finish for him.

"Now you get it, Daisy. I love it here, and I think you're going to fall in love with Whispers the longer you're here too," he says with full confidence, his eyes searching mine. I swallow hard and wonder if they turned up the thermostat in here.

"I've never been in love..." I say, almost absentmindedly, the two of us so close now, I feel his breath on my cheeks.

"Sail away with me... to another world..."

I grin, the lyrics of the song so ingrained in my head.

"Cheesy... but I'll pass it," I say, both of us laughing together.

How am I supposed to get through this crush? It was fine when he was being arrogant and insulting at Sunshine. But now, I know he's a nice guy. I'm not going to survive.

As Victoria draws me into a new conversation, chatting about the spa again, I pretend my racing heart has more to do with the nerves of starting a new job than from sitting next to a man who can make my pussy clench just from the sound of his voice.

Yeah. This is going to be a long month.

12

CONNOR

My heart thuds heavily as sweat drips down my back. I discarded my t-shirt about a mile back, tucking it into the waistband of my shorts as my lungs gulp in the fresh air. I love running in the mornings in Whispers, and the sunrise here is hard to beat. I have flown all around the world, and not even Greece is better than this.

As I get closer to home, I slow to a saunter and cool down. I'm stressed. Our barley farms aren't producing what I need when I need it. The weather is wreaking havoc, my mind full of so many things I can't think straight, the five miles a day I do not even taming the thoughts, and it doesn't help that I have fucking "Islands in the Stream" playing on repeat in my mind. As I walk to cool down, I look over my own private running track. There's nothing but me and the clean air and the rising sun. It's quiet, no one else awake or at the distillery, especially since Dad and Victoria moved up to their new place on Billionaires Boulevard.

Running is my stress relief and one I desperately needed today. I hardly slept last night with visions of Daisy flicking through my mind like a movie reel. Her laughing at something I said. Her smiling next to me in the bar, listening to me intently, like she's interested in every word I say. The way I picked her up and put her in my truck. I shouldn't have touched her. It's not professional, and I didn't need to feel her in my hands, but damn, she looks good in my truck. I was permanently hard all night, my fist doing very little to tame the beast in my pants that seems to now have a mind of its own.

I walk around the corner of the tree line to get back to my place, knowing I need to shower and head to my office for an early morning conference call. But then I look up and stall. She's like a beacon, calling to me, and I watch her in awe as she does yoga in the front garden, my feet not moving, feeling like they are encased in cement, as I'm completely mesmerized.

She's wearing tight matching yoga pants and a crop top. I see her shape, her curves, and damn, has she got curves. So many curves. She has such a womanly figure, and I like that. I swallow, my mouth watering as I stand like a fucking stalker, watching her, peering over the high hedge. My eyes feast on her large, round peach of an ass, and I bite the inside of my cheek so I don't groan and completely startle her. She changes poses, and I get a front view of her perfect breasts that are almost spilling from her tight top as she lowers her hands to the ground.

"Good morning, Connor!" our gardener yells cheerily, and I jump, looking over at him on the far side of the garden, waving to me with a wide grin and a pitchfork in his hand. I grind my teeth together, waving back with a fake wide smile, pissed off that he interrupted my morning viewing. I forgot that fucker started early on Fridays. I look back at Daisy, who's now standing, hands on hips, looking straight at me. Shit.

"Good morning," I say, walking toward her slowly, confidence in my gait.

"You forgot your shirt?" she says, her flushed cheeks becoming a little more vibrant, still embarrassed by my half-nakedness, it seems. Yet I don't miss the way her eyes flick to my naked torso, which makes me smirk. Last week at Sunshine, she couldn't look at me, and now, her eyes are glued. I push my shoulders back, enjoying her attention.

"I just finished a run." I let my eyes roam a little. From a distance, she's stunning, and up close, she's delectable.

"Without a shirt?" she asks, and I shrug, feeling cocky. I work out. I look after myself, more for my mental health than anything else. But present me thanks past me for all those runs and weight sessions because Daisy seems flustered.

"I'm not used to having anyone here. Dad moved up to his ranch a while ago now, so his place here is rarely used." I brush my hand down my naked torso and watch her swallow. Good to know I affect her just as much as she affects me.

"I didn't realize anyone was up yet," she says, her hands still on her wide hips, and I tame the smirk pulling at my lips. I'm her boss, goddammit. I'm never thrown off my game. But for some reason, Daisy is now ingrained in my vision, and I can't get her out. I don't even want to.

"I usually go for a run to watch the sun come up. It's the best part of the day," I tell her honestly, coming to a stop about a foot in front of her. Her skin radiates in the morning light, a slight sheen to it, telling me she's been out here for a while herself. Her long red hair is piled onto her head in this messy yet sexy-as-hell bun, tendrils falling around her face. My fingers twitch to step forward and push them behind her ears so I can see her face more clearly. But I refrain.

"The sunrise showcases the start of something new. No matter what happened last night, yesterday, or even the days before, the sunrise allows us to reset, restart, and rejuvenate, ready for a brand-new day," she says in a tone that has me immediately relaxing and taking a deep breath. My shoulders lower instantly, and it feels like she's wrapping me up in a warm hug. I almost groan at feeling the stress melt away, simply from her voice and the morning sun showering me in warmth.

"I like sunrises too," she admits when I remain quietly staring at her.

"So... yoga?" I say, scrubbing my eyes, willing my brain to function. We haven't bitten each other's heads off yet, so the conversation feels more adult than the past week or so since I met her. Although it's early, so I'm sure her sass or sarcasm will come to the forefront at some point. I almost look forward to it.

"I try to have a daily practice each morning. That and meditation. It helps me to clear my mind and create some good energy for the day."

"Makes sense. Your office is all set up for you. I

assume you'll want to hit the ground running today?" I ask her, wondering what her plan of attack is.

"I have deliveries arriving, then some phone interviews to do, and I want to pull together a treatment menu by the end of the day for your approval."

I look at her, wide-eyed, and grin. She's organized and committed. I like that. Her work ethic is pretty strong, and I can see the determination in her gaze. My sight drops a little to her chest for a second too long, before meeting her eyes again. It's almost like her breasts are teasing me. The cute daisy chain necklace I notice she wears is dipping into her cleavage, playing a game of peek-a-boo as her chest rises and then quickly falls. A rush of heat travels through my body, and I move my t-shirt and tuck it into the front of my waistband to hide my growing infatuation with this woman.

"Sounds like a full day. I better get going so I can make a start myself. I've got a conference call with my lawyer, Sawyer, first up." I take a few steps in the direction of my place, needing to get my head out of my ass and get to work. I have a full day of meetings and conference calls. The work never stops.

"You have a lawyer named Sawyer?" she asks, laughing, and I grin as I walk backward, my eyes not ready to leave the sight of her just yet.

"Yeah. He's from New York," I tell her, by way of explanation.

"Sounds about right." She shakes her head. "See you at work."

"See you later," I say before turning and jogging up to my place, opening my front door, and pushing myself inside. I pace straight to the kitchen and tell myself it's to organize my morning coffee, and not because it has the window that looks over the back of the property, where I can torture myself with her downward dog one more time before I take a long, cold shower.

I need to stay away from this woman, because if I don't, there's no way I'll be able to keep my hands to myself.

I END the call with Sawyer, a little more frazzled than I'd like. It's been a big week, our expansion plans are going well, Daisy is now in place, and if I can just get a few other things sorted, then that would be a relief.

Walking out of my office, in search of caffeine, I spot Victoria in the restaurant doing the same.

As I get closer, I can tell she's disheveled, and I wonder if she's feeling alright.

"What's up? You okay?" I ask, meeting her at the coffee machine and pressing a few buttons as she takes a sip of her cup and sighs.

"I had a sound healing treatment this morning with Daisy, and I fell asleep," she says, and I grin.

"See, I'm not the only one," I quip, happy that Victoria now clearly approves of Daisy just as much as I do.

"Now I need coffee, lots of coffee." She takes another healthy sip, making me chuckle.

"So you enjoyed it?" I ask, stirring in a bit of sugar and cream, interested to hear her take on it all.

"It was amazing. Like she picked up on my trauma, my nightmares. Hell, if this gets me to sleep better every night, I think I might marry her instead of your father." She giggles, and I grin like a fool. I look at the large rock on her finger that my dad put there not too long ago. I never thought my dad would find his person. He was single for so long, for a variety of reasons. A trait I seemed to have picked up from him.

I think about that for a beat as I stir my coffee and take a sip. I've never really felt lonely before, always busy with work, jetting to the city and back often, and not lacking female attention. But I see what Dad has and how happy he is and have started thinking that it wouldn't be that bad to have a partner in my life.

"I'm getting your dad to have a treatment with her tomorrow," Victoria says, and I spit out coffee.

"Yeah, that's what he did when I told him just now."

I grab a napkin and clean up my spill, head shaking.

"I need photos or it didn't happen," I tell her, laughing, because my father on a spa bed with sound healing bowls on him is a sight I need to see. Although I already know Daisy won't agree to any photos. I can tell she has strong ethics and morals. There's no way she'll want any client photographed, especially during a treatment. I think back to her wanting me to put my clothes back on the first time I met her and the way she thoroughly studied my form for medications and injuries before we began. She's thorough and doesn't want to misdiagnose or incorrectly treat.

"She made me a sleepy tea, something herbal to take

before bed. Did you know she was an herbalist as well?" Victoria asks, clearly impressed.

"Had no idea…" I murmur, but I think back to the tea her mom made me, and even though it was bitter on the tongue, I felt on cloud nine all day after that.

"Anyway. I'm taking her into town tomorrow to get her some more supplies and introduce her to some people."

I roll my eyes good-naturedly. "Who, your best friend Bob?" I tease. Since remodeling Marie's place, Victoria is always in the hardware store, talking to Bob, and he loves it. It's the most attention that old guy has had in all his decades here in Whispers.

"What? Jealous? Scared Daisy might meet someone else who has better taste in music?" She eyes me accusingly, and I run my hand down my beard.

"Daisy is our consultant," I tell her like she doesn't know.

"Hmmmm… a consultant you couldn't stop looking at and talking to all last night at dinner. Tanner and I could have left the booth and you two wouldn't have even realized." She hums, watching me like a hawk. I sip my coffee and try to act nonchalant.

"She's here for a month. Of course I need to get to know her. She's managing one of our biggest investments. I'm many things, but stupid isn't one of them." Getting involved with a staff member or colleague is probably the riskiest thing I could do.

"Why are you stroking your beard like that?" Victoria asks, attention narrowing in on the movement, and I pause my hand immediately.

"Because he's nervous. It's his tell," Dad says, walking up behind me, and I drop my hand instantly.

"His tell?" she questions him, and the two of them start talking about me like I'm not standing a few feet away.

"He does it when he's nervous or uncomfortable. What are you talking about? Hang on, let me guess... Daisy?" Dad asks, and I suppress a groan of annoyance, not answering.

"Don't you two have some goats to milk or something?" I grumble. Victoria has a few goats as a hobby and now makes goat milk soap with Annabelle, a woman in town, who's a single mom and teacher at the local school.

"Kevin's doing it today..."

"Does he have a thing for Daisy?" she murmurs to Dad, the two of them looking at me, yet talking to each other.

"I'm right here, guys," I tell them with a huff, but they ignore me.

"I think it's more than a thing. Come on, let's go. I want to check in on Lacy and Hudson," Dad says, and Victoria grins as the two of them walk off together. I swallow down the bitter coffee and turn to head back to my office, my to-do list a mile long and now nothing but Daisy on my mind.

13

DAISY

I follow Victoria as we walk along the main street of Whispers, everyone looking at me, but this time, they have lots of smiles, coupled with their curious glances, so that helps. Whispers is so pretty. Exactly how you'd imagine a quaint town to be. Flower beds are brimming with color, people out and about, everyone seeming to know everyone, the small street bustling in a way only a small town can.

We've already visited Bob at the hardware store. Then I met the lovely Evelyn, who runs the homewares store. We stopped in the bar again for Victoria to pick something up, and I grabbed a few things from the local supermarket.

"Okay, here we are," she says, pushing open the door to the diner, and we walk in. The place is packed, the barstools all taken, a few tables also full. It has a nice hum of conversation to the place, everyone seems happy, talking, laughing, and of course, looking at me.

"Clearly, this is the place to be," I say, feeling like I'm

under the microscope the way everyone's gazes move to me. I see a few familiar faces from the bar the other night, but mostly new ones.

"Ladies, welcome. Hi, Daisy, I'm Rochelle, so nice to finally meet you," an older woman, whom I guess must be in her sixties, says. I remember Connor mentioning she's one of the best cooks in town.

"Nice to meet you too." I smile, enjoying the niceties that a small town brings. While Victoria drives a truck, I found it easier to get in and out of hers. It's a little lower, further cementing that Connor's is obviously made especially for his larger stature.

"We'll grab a seat at the back. What's on today?" Victoria asks as we walk through. I spot a group of women around my age sitting together at the front of the diner, watching us carefully. They don't look as approachable as everyone else, so that underbelly feeling creeps back into me for a moment.

"Chicken soup today. Shall I get two bowls?" Rochelle asks.

Victoria looks at me in question, and I smile.

"Sounds delicious."

Rochelle practically beams, and Victoria and I continue walking farther down, grabbing a booth toward the back.

"So that tea you made me yesterday that I drank before bed last night, it knocked me right out. I slept for eight hours straight!" she says, almost in disbelief.

"It was my sleepy time tea. All natural, a mix of herbs, such as chamomile, a little bit of rosehip, lavender, and other things," I tell her, glad that it helped her. It's one of my best sellers.

"Connor mentioned that you have a tea range? Is that something you might like to stock at the spa?"

At the mere mention of his name, the vision of Connor running shirtless is back in my mind. When I first saw him shirtless at Sunshine, I hid my eyes. It seemed unprofessional to ogle the man who was clearly confused about what the treatment entailed. But he knew exactly what he was doing on his morning run yesterday, and so I was going to look this time. And I can confirm that, yes, he is a real-life Adonis.

"Mom and I have been making tea for years and using it at our clinic. I would like to implement them at the spa as well. We have a small retail range that we can stock. But also, offering a different tea each day of the week in the reception area to get clients relaxed for both pre and post treatment would be good too." I think that it's not only beneficial to the spa, but also, long term, it's great for Mom and me. Having a spa stock our tea gets our name out there a bit more.

"I think it'd be perfect. I would like to see how we can incorporate whiskey a little more, though," she says, and I nod.

"I've been thinking about that. What if I developed something where we can blend both? In Scotland, they have hot tea toddys, which is essentially tea with a splash of whiskey. I can use the lemon and honey from the distillery gardens and add in some other herbs, like Whisper's chamomile, which I know grows here well.

That would make it very regional specific, could even be an exclusive tea of the region. We can sell that tea with a bottle of whiskey as a pair. It will be ideal for soothing a cough or cold and also great as a holiday gift idea," I suggest. Although I don't want any alcohol in my teas, it doesn't mean I can't use some of the more natural ingredients to make their whiskey a little more wellness friendly.

"I can see why Connor offered you a job. You think a lot like him, and that tea duo would be amazing. I know Lacy would love that idea," Victoria says, and I smile brightly, relieved we're on the same page.

"Here we are, two soups," a younger woman, who looks to be around my age, says as she places the two bowls on the table.

"Thanks, Nikki. Nikki, this is Daisy. She'll be working at the spa for a month or so. Daisy, this is Nikki, newish to town as well," Victoria says, introducing us.

"Oh great, I'm not the only newbie, then. Where are you from?" I ask, and when Nikki's smile falters a little, I feel like I've asked the wrong question.

"Uh, West Coast," she says vaguely, giving off a weird type of nervous energy. I can already tell she has secrets. I don't pry and just give her my kindest smile.

"Well, Whispers seems like a lovely place to settle," I tell her, and as her eyes meet mine, I give her a small nod. She swallows, smiling back.

"Enjoy your soup," she says to both of us before scurrying away, back behind the bar to top off the coffees.

"She's so hard to get to know. I wish she would open up more, but we only ever see her here at the diner. She never comes to the bar. She's a single mom, but boy, she must have had her child young, because she barely looks old enough to have a driver's license herself. I think she actually cycles to work most days."

I look over at Nikki, seeing her keeping busy, her head down. She's polite but not drawing attention to herself.

"So, you obviously love Whispers since you haven't moved back to the city, right?" I ask the question that's been on my mind since I arrived. The small-town vibe is great, one that I instantly took to, but it's a change of pace from New York, that's for sure.

"I think it all happened at the right time for me. I wasn't really succeeding in my career. I was let go from my job, actually. My fiancé at the time wasn't who I thought he was, so we broke up. Then I got a letter explaining my long-lost aunt left me a property here in Whispers, so I made the move. I met Tanner, and that was it. My life is now here, and I don't want to be anywhere else." She pauses for a moment, then adds, "Although I do miss the shopping, the bars, and the food selection sometimes..."

I giggle at that last bit, totally understanding.

"Did you go to Benny's? That's one of my favorite places," I ask, and she lights up.

"Oh my God, I love Benny's. It's my go-to place," she whines, and I laugh. The two of us have more in common than I first thought.

"So you're friends with Fiona?" That's how this connection came about. Fiona being one of our clients at Sunshine.

"Yes, she's one of my best friends and told me all about Sunshine. I knew I had to try it, but unfortunately, I had to send Connor to the city to do it instead. I can't believe he fell asleep on you!" She grins as she starts to spoon her soup.

My mind goes right back to the man's half-naked body, but also his smug smirk, his kind eyes, the way I catch him watching me sometimes, the way his hands felt on my body. I clear my throat, shaking away the thoughts.

"Yeah. It isn't uncommon..." I say, thinking about it. "But he was certainly a different type of client. He had no idea what he was in for, really."

She laughs, then her expression softens. "Yeah, well, we didn't tell him on purpose. Connor's probably the most typical male, bossy billionaire I know. Still a little more laid-back than the city types, but he's a go-getter, thinks about things from all angles, and has a good eye for the numbers. Between him and Tanner, they've built the distillery into this amazing business and put so much into this town that they love so much."

"I've found him to be a little arrogant and certainly frustrating..." I murmur, thinking about how the two of us interact. We seem to always be slightly pushing each other. It's new, and I don't totally hate it. Victoria grins like she knows what I'm thinking.

"He usually isn't. You must just push his buttons," she adds with a wink, and I remain quiet, spooning the soup into my mouth to stop me from dissecting my new boss too much to his soon-to-be stepmom. That thought is still hard to grasp because of their ages.

"So, what about you? Any boyfriend back in the city waiting for you?"

My cheeks heat. It's almost like I'm with Trisha and

talking to a close friend. It's nice. I don't have lots of friends; in fact, making friends as an adult is harder than I ever thought it would be. But Victoria is lovely, and this lunch catch-up is almost like we have been friends for years.

"No. No one," I tell her, shaking my head. "Just the clinic, my parents, friends... the usual. The city is so busy, full of... I don't know... people." I can't find the word I'm looking for.

Now that I've been out of the city for a few days, I feel like I can breathe. It wasn't that I was stressed in the city, but nothing really felt like mine. I share a home with Trisha; Sunshine is my mom's business; I don't have dates unless Trisha sets them up, and really, I kinda felt like I've just been floating along, not pushing myself into any direction in life. Now, even after a few days, my initial nerves have dissipated, and I feel a new fire starting to build inside of me, and the excitement of opportunity swirls.

"Assholes?" she offers, and I laugh.

"Yeah... I seem to meet a lot of those."

"Urghhh, I hated dating in the city. The apps, the meet-ups. It was all just... horrible." Scrunching her face, her shoulders shake like she gets a cold chill from thinking about it.

"Exactly. And they all end up being total boys. Not men. But boys." Now I understand the difference. It's not just their physical appearance, but maturity and decency.

"Well, you've come to the right place, because believe me, there's something in the water here in Whispers, because the men are amazing."

Yet again, my mind flicks to Connor's very fine physique, his abs of steel something that can't be removed from my memory, no matter how hard I try. If I can't get this damn image out of my mind, I have no idea what I'm going to do.

"Oh, speaking of water, Connor mentioned you have mineral springs at your place next door to the distillery?" I ask her, and she nods.

"They're amazing. You should definitely get there soon and check them out."

"I would like to offer that as an upsell on treatments..." I put it out there.

"I think that would be great, and the whole reason we built the spa on that side of the distillery was so that we could have access."

That's great news. "Maybe, like, a thirty- or sixty-minute soak before your treatment to get into a state of relaxation... No stock required, no therapist needed, it would be pure profit. We'll just need to ensure the safety of the path to the springs and provide footwear and robes."

"It's exactly what we were thinking."

I feel good that we're on the same page.

"So, I finalized the treatment plan," I tell her, moving the conversation on to specific business topics.

She smiles. "I read through it last night. I need to speak to Tanner and Connor, but from what I can tell, I think it'll be perfect. Everything you have outlined will be amazing, and I personally can't wait to try it all. Connor is better to look at the numbers and staffing, but I can help you start on planning out the retail space for shelving and cupboards and also the treatment rooms."

"Awesome. I've ordered the treatment beds and some supplies already, so they should arrive next week," I tell her, my tone filled with excitement, and she looks impressed.

"This spa is going to be amazing. I'm so glad you're here to build it with us. Speaking of which, we need to eat. Tanner will be almost ready for his treatment back at the distillery, and I can't wait for him to give it a go."

I took my sleepy time tea last night as well, and after my morning meditation earlier, I feel ready to do Tanner's treatment. He's a big man, like his son, so I know there will be a lot of energy to manage, but me and my singing bowls are ready for the challenge.

14

CONNOR

The numbers blur as I stare at the screen in front of me.

I throw my pen on the desk and rub my eyes. They're dry, itchy, and as I look at my watch, I know why. I've had my head buried in my screen for hours. I had a late night last night, talking with my distributors, and then an early morning on conference calls. Even then, I can't sleep unless I'm imagining red hair and deep-blue eyes, and it's driving me insane.

Even my morning runs are not helping. Usually, my motto of *exhaust the body to tame the mind* is my go-to and helps me every day, but lately, even though I try to take a different running track, I still see her. In her yoga gear, head down, beautiful ass up and...

I stand up at my desk, my chair pushing behind me with force.

"Stop. Just stop." I talk to myself because, apparently, this is what I've become. A rich, powerful business leader who's losing his mind over the new woman who sits a few doors down in her office. A woman I can't touch. A woman who doesn't even like me. Who thought I was an axe murderer, who covered her eyes at the sight of my bare chest, and who I insulted the first time I met her. A woman who every time I speak to her, I end up saying the wrong thing.

I really need to get my shit together.

I've kept my distance from her as much as I can these past few days. I know she spent the weekend with Victoria and gave Dad a treatment. I didn't get photos, but I heard he fell asleep as well and has only spoken highly of it all since then. He's now firmly in the Daisy Fan Club. Everyone is. I knew hiring her would be an excellent move for the business, and so far, I've been proven right. But I had no idea I would turn into a fucking daydreaming asshole in the process.

I walk out my door and look down the hall in the distillery office, seeing only two lights left on. Hers and mine, and before I even think about it, my feet are moving in her direction. I don't even hesitate. It's almost like my mind is telling me I'm a fool and I need to get back to work and stop thinking about her, but my body, clearly led by my dick, is saying *No way, buddy, let me just go insult her some more so that she might actually notice me.*

Everything's quiet as I stand at her door, looking in, watching her work. She's deep in concentration, biting her bottom lip, writing furiously on a page in front of her, brow furrowed. She's a hard worker. I feel a sense of pride for finding her and almost smile, before she must sense me, and with a gasp, looks up.

"Oh. Spying again, I see?" she sasses, and my jaw

tenses. There she is. The woman I've missed. She's been here for hours, just like me. Yet she doesn't look stressed or disheveled. She looks just like she did this morning. Bright eyes, fresh face, and although I know she's been working hard, you wouldn't know it.

"Not spying if it's in my own building," I tell her, sounding more arrogant than ever as I step slowly into her office. I shouldn't. I should just keep walking down the hall, grab some water or a coffee, as there are hours left ahead of me. I should stop looking, stop loitering, and for the love of God, probably stop talking in this asshole tone I've developed around her. She's now part of my team. But as my mind heats up in debate, my body moves automatically again, my feet leading me to take a seat in the armchair in her office.

"Potato, potahto," she mumbles, and I bite the inside of my cheek so I don't grin too hard at the cute saying she has.

"What are you working on? Or are you just online shopping or something?" I ask cheekily, leaning back in the chair. Her scowl tells me I hit a nerve.

"Just thinking about rosters and treatments, what skills I need for staffing," she says, eyes narrowed.

"Ahhh, the people. Usually, the hardest part of running a business is managing the people," I tell her as I look around her space. It's just how we prepared it for her. Apart from the addition of a crystal on her desk, which is sitting next to a steamy pot of tea and cups on a tray that she obviously just put together. There are a few boxes at the side of the room, full of more crystals, and I also see some tea and herbs nearby.

"Hmm, well, I could just insult them like you do, but that seems counterproductive." Eyes gleaming, a smirk is back on her face. I look at her, realizing that, regardless of what facial expression she has for me, I'm getting an appetite for all of them.

"I got you here, didn't I?" I say, smirking right back, and she relaxes into her seat, watching me. Our power play excites me. I pull, she pushes, then she pulls, and I push. It's almost like a dance.

"I've called a few people. Some experts I floated the visitation schedule to. Some were interested."

"Good. Sounds positive."

"I've also found a few people in Williamstown who could be suitable for more permanent positions, but it just doesn't all work together. The therapists I spoke to would all love to work here at the new spa, excited by the opportunity, actually, but if we were to have a rotating visitation schedule of experts, then this would eat into their hours, due to the number of rooms we have, meaning that we couldn't employ them full-time, and those full-time, permanent hours are really what they're looking for." As she bites her bottom lip in thought, my gaze latches on it.

"It's common around here. Local people want that security. There aren't a lot of new job opportunities in small towns, so they would be hesitant to leave a secure job for something new if they couldn't be guaranteed the same assurance of long-term employment," I tell her. It's probably one of the downsides to small-town living.

"I mean, can you see any way around this?" she asks.

"What if we supplemented their hours elsewhere?" I

offer, thinking on the fly. Her body language changes a little as she sits forward, more interested.

"How so?" she asks, clearly intrigued.

"Well, we would have to brainstorm with Dad, but we're expanding into accommodation, so maybe they can supplement their hours by working in that division? Whether it's cleaning, concierge..." I suggest, liking this idea.

"In-room treatments..." she says, and our eyes connect. The excitement of coming up with new plans is clearly something we both experience.

"In-room treatments... I like that," I murmur, brushing my beard. As I do, I notice her eyes flick to the movement before she quickly looks back at me.

"It's probably a good strategy for the distillery overall."

"What are you thinking?" I ask her. Watching her brain work is one of the sexiest things I've ever witnessed.

"That Whitemans could have a team of staff that are trained to be cross functional. Therapists can learn reception; they can learn cleaning and the restaurant. Also, your waiters can learn accommodation bookings, can be trained about wellness for the retail and reception of the spa..." she trails off, and I can't help the large grin pulling at my lips. This kind of thinking is well outside her responsibility of the wellness spa as it encompasses a whole business approach, but I love it.

"By cross-training staff, when times are slower, then we move them into the areas of the business that have demand. If people are sick, need time off or go on vacation, they're then covered almost immediately." Sitting forward in my seat, my body's now almost humming. I have more energy in this moment than I've had all day.

"It's a great risk management tool. The only consideration will be costs of training and remuneration, because they could demand a higher salary and hourly rate due to increased skill set, but—"

"But... then you can really offer your staff opportunities for not just a job, but a solid career, give them the chance to discover and learn new skills. Who knows, maybe your receptionist would be an amazing therapist, or maybe your head waiter has always dreamed of being a gardener?" she says, smiling, and I like the fact that, not only can she talk business, but she also connects the human element. Doing good for my people, not just my bottom line. That kind of thinking is what makes a business a great place to work. I sit back in the armchair, the two of us watching each other carefully, the room now charged with clear admiration.

"Here," she says as she grabs the pot of tea on her desk and pours me a cup. I don't even hesitate, leaning in and grabbing it from her and bringing the steamy cup to my nose. It's yellow and looks more like what goes into the toilet bowl than what should be going into my body. But it smells like dried flowers.

"What is it?" I ask, wondering if, like her mother, the tea that she's given me is going to taste like shit. Regardless, I bring it to my lips and sip. It tastes just as it smells. Not totally repugnant, but not tasty either.

"It's chrysanthemum tea," she says, sitting back, sipping her own cup of the steaming brew.

"What's it going to do to me?" I ask her as I look at her

from over the rim of the cup, knowing this is some kind of elixir of hers.

"It's my special truth elixir. After you drink this, I can ask you anything, and you won't lie."

Just as I swallow, I almost choke, and she laughs, a sound I wasn't ready for. Her giggle penetrates my body in a way I can't even begin to describe. I'm coughing up a lung, yet laughing at the same time, my heart pulsing at a rate it hasn't before.

"Kidding. *Obviously*," she says, wiping tears of joy from her eyes that she experiences from my pain and suffering. I take a deep breath, glad she's joking, because she doesn't want to know the truth about what I'm thinking about. The dirty thoughts I've been having about her are hard enough to contain as it is.

"It'll actually help relieve stress, cools the body down, helps with high blood pressure, and will keep you focused so the words or numbers won't be as blurry," she says, and I take another sip.

"Thank you. It's not great, but it isn't completely terrible," I tell her with a smirk.

"This doesn't mean you're forgiven for being an ass when we first met, or that we are, in any way, considered friends," she says cheekily, those blue eyes locked on mine.

"Potato, potahto," I quip, and her smile is instant and wide.

We sit sipping our tea, and I help her work around some staff planning, forgetting all about my own deadlines. While I love our banter, I've just caught a glimpse of how we are when we work on a common goal, and it's undeniably electric, the thought making my body hot.

So much so, I think I'll need to drink a gallon of this fucking tea.

15

DAISY

I've been here for a week, and I feel like I'm part of the furniture at the distillery already, and with the hours I'm working, I might as well be. I'm usually here early and leave late, but I love it. I knew that I would enjoy the change, and I was excited about the challenge, but I've never loved something as much as building this spa business, being here in a small town, and creating something from scratch. It's like I arrived and suddenly everything in my life just clicked. The feelings I get from doing the work and being in this small pocket of the world just feel right.

"So, is it everything you wanted it to be?" Trisha asks as we chat on the phone, our first real conversation since I left the city, even though it's noon on a Wednesday.

"It is. More so, really. I mean, the job is great, but Whispers is..." I say to her, pausing to think of the right word. Not wanting to understate my feelings, yet not wanting to totally fangirl over this new town that has captured my heart in an instant.

"Cold? Barren? Full of old, sleazy farmers who can't get it up?" she asks, and I laugh.

"No. It's beautiful. The fresh air is amazing, and my sleep in the quiet of the night is the best I've ever had." I don't miss the sirens and noise of the city that filtered through my small bedroom window every night.

"How's the good-looking, arrogant boss with the big balls?" she asks, and at the mention of Connor, my body hums. Warmth spreads through my joints like I'm lying out in the sunshine for the first time all year, and I look up at my office door to ensure he isn't spying again.

"He's the trifecta," I huff out, defeated. I tried hating him, and at first, he made it easy. But now I feel like the goalposts have moved a little, and I have to admit, I've never met a man like him before.

"Holy shit," she says in shock. Trisha and I often score her dating potentials based on a few things. Usually, most men have one or two things, but never all three, and while Connor and I still have some resistance to each other, I think we crossed the threshold the other night in my office, moving from insulting each other to admiring each other. He spent time going through staffing solutions with me, crunching numbers, working potential rosters. He didn't need to do any of it, and no doubt had a million other things to do, but he did, and we worked well together. Too well.

Which isn't great, because now not only is he devastatingly handsome, but his arrogance has decreased, the suave-o-meter has increased, and I've seen his passion for the work he does on full display, not to mention his business smarts. So he's the trifecta. Good-looking, smart, and somewhat charming.

"Yeah, well, first impressions obviously weren't great, and he still carries an air of arrogance, but he's so smart and this distillery of his is amazing," I tell her, looking around my office and appreciating how indulgent it is. I'm not even sure the five-star spas in New York could rival this.

"Soooo, been on a date yet?" She fishes for information.

"Oh no. That's not happening," I state clearly, needing to instill that fact not only into this conversation, but also into my brain. "I said he was a trifecta, not that I'm going to do anything about it. He'll remain a trifecta from a distance. It was simply an observation on my behalf." Scrubbing my eyes, I will the thoughts about Connor to go away, far, far away. "We work together. I'm here for a month, and he's the owner of this place. There's *no way* we can cross that line."

"Come on, Daisy. Rules are there so we can break them," she says, full of cheeky confidence, confidence that I just don't have when it comes to the opposite sex.

I release a sigh. "Not that one. Don't fall in love with your boss is the almighty rule that's never to be broken."

"Who said anything above love, Daisy? Why not just go for hot, sweaty sex? You know that kind that makes you want to rip each other's clothes off. The kind where he pushes you against the desk, throwing all the paperwork across the room in his urgency to get your clothes off," Trisha says, and I take a breath. I've never had that. Wouldn't even know how that would feel, other than my traitorous body is becoming hot all over, just thinking about it.

My limited sexual encounters have all been slightly awkward. A tangle of limbs in the wrong places, my jiggly body seemingly too much for some men who just don't know what to do with me. Other than missionary, where they don't even look at me, and usually, the ending isn't satisfactory for me at all.

A man has never made me come. *I bet Connor Whiteman could.* I swallow, looking at my desk, the images filtering through my mind rapidly, making my cheeks burn hotter. I take a sip of tea and shake my head. Because there's no way that will be happening. I'm a realist. Those kinds of movie star things never happen to a girl like me.

"Not happening. Anyway, how's Tom?" I ask her, not wanting to talk about my boss any longer. Especially not at his distillery, where anyone could hear me.

"Who?"

I huff a laugh and roll my eyes, because it's a new week, and of course, Trisha has a new man already.

"You know Tom? The guy you were in love with and were going to name your firstborn after me with?" I quiz her, smiling. She's crazy, but I love her.

"Oh yeah, no, he turned out to be a bit of a dud. But I met Jeff, and *he* is amazing!" she gushes, my workplace romance now forgotten as she tells me all about her new love interest.

After hearing all about Jeff, a guy she met when he came in to order pizza the other night and left her a huge tip, I end the call with Trisha and get my head back into my workload.

I have a few interviews lined up later in the week and a few more applications to look over. After working with Connor the other night, I'm close to making some offers with flexible staff members who are looking for full-time hours and are happy to have those hours not only in the spa but all around other functions in the distillery.

I'm expecting another delivery of goods today, some yoga mats and equipment, so I'll be finding a spot for all that later. Victoria's currently in the space, measuring the shelving for the retail space and cupboards for the treatment rooms, cross-checking the colors for the linen and towels I chose before we place that order next. It's slowly falling into place, and while I'm not sure if we're moving fast on this or not, compared to how spas usually open, it feels like things are coming together quickly and without issue.

"Daisy?" a voice from my door says, and I look up and smile at the receptionist, Stephanie.

"There's a gentleman here to see you. Says his name is Soren?" she asks, frowning, and I sit up, slightly shocked he's here personally.

"Oh, sure, I'll be right out." I was expecting Soren to ship the crystals I needed, not come all the way to Whispers to hand-deliver them.

I walk out and spot him standing in reception with a few boxes at his feet. The receptionist is keeping a close eye on him, clearly wary of him since he's new and not someone she's familiar with. He does look totally out of place, yet doesn't seem to care one bit. Skinny, too tanned to the point his skin is almost rubbery. Wispy long blond hair that's thinning at the top. He practices what he preaches, which is daily yoga, a strict vegetarian diet, and a very hippie lifestyle. Which is completely at odds with the building he's standing in.

"Soren," I say, smiling in greeting, and he turns to me with a grin.

"Ahhh, good to see you, my dear," he says in that borderline condescending tone he has. One which doesn't seem to worry Mom at all, but it gives me the creeps.

"What are you doing here? I thought you would courier these ones, just like the last ones?" I ask him, looking at the boxes at his feet. This is my second crystal delivery from him already.

"I was in the area," he says a little cryptically.

"You have other clients out this way?" I ask, confused. I don't know him well. His relationship with my mother goes back decades, from her commune days, I think. But I know Dad doesn't like him much, even though they have only met a few times.

"I visit the commune not far from here for deep medi-tation work. Your mother's old commune, actually. Since I was coming this way, I thought I would drop them off."

I nod, his words making sense. I have no idea about communes or how they work. But I do know the more traditional ones are usually out of cities and in places that are hard to find, unless you're looking for them. But one thing about what he said bothers me.

"Mom's commune? Where's that?" I'm surprised, intrigued, and a little miffed that Mom didn't tell me herself. She knew where I was coming and made no mention of knowing this area at all.

"Ohhh, it's buried deep. They're isolated and don't take kindly to strangers. But I call past once or twice a year to deliver goods they require and sit in silence for a week."

I feel like he isn't telling me something, but I leave it. That's Mom's history, not mine, and if she wanted me to know anything about it, then she would tell me. She never really talks about that time at all, actually.

"Can I offer you a tea? Take you on a tour of the new spa?" I offer, because it's a long way to come, and I'm sure he would like to walk around.

"I wouldn't say no to one of your energizing teas," he says, hopeful, and I smile, having received a big batch from Mom only a few days ago.

I help him move the boxes into my office, putting them with the others, and get busy with my teapot, my own little tea station already set up in my office, not dissimilar to the whiskey bars in all the others.

"How long was your drive?" I ask, making small talk. This is the most I've spoken to him ever, and it feels a little weird, if I'm honest.

"A few hours. Here, I got you this. A gift from your mother."

I turn, passing him the tea, and see a large rose quartz now sitting on my desk.

"Oh, wow. That's beautiful," I say, in awe. It's raw, which I love. Large, the pink color really strong and vibrant. I reach out to touch it immediately.

"It is. She knew the minute she saw it that she wanted you to have it."

I melt at the generosity of my mother. It must've cost a fortune. I need to lift it with both hands, it's that heavy.

"She wanted you to be surrounded by love, even though you're away from her and your father," he says, and I run my hand over the rough stone. I'm drawn to it, so I know that it's a stone I'm very much in alignment with already.

"She's too kind." I need to call her to thank her for it all.

"Daisy, I—" Connor starts as he walks into my office with his head down, looking at some paperwork before he stops short. "Sorry, I didn't realize you were with someone."

"Ohhh, the energy is strong with this one," Soren says under his breath, just loud enough for me to catch.

"Connor, this is Soren. He's the supplier for all our crystals, some herbs, and a few other things that we use at Sunshine and now at the distillery." I introduce the two men, who couldn't be more opposite.

"Connor Whiteman," Connor says formally, stepping forward with his hand outstretched. Dressed impeccably in his suit, full business mode activated, it feels like he takes up all the oxygen in the room, his large physique almost domineering in a way.

Soren looks at him, then his hand, before shaking it somewhat lukewarmly. "Soren." I notice he doesn't offer a last name, and to be honest, I don't know what it is either.

"I didn't mean to interrupt. Clearly, you're in the middle of something," he says to me quickly before looking back at Soren. The two of them are definitely on edge, the temperature in the room changing as Connor looks at Soren suspiciously. I assume it's because Soren is a man in his distillery whom he's never met before.

"I was just offering Soren a tea before he heads on his way," I tell Connor, who then looks at me, the tea on my desk, and then the large rose quartz.

"We can't go sitting around and drinking tea all day. We have a spa to open," Connor grits out.

"I'm merely being hospitable to our suppliers." I try to remain calm and friendly as Soren watches us both closely.

"Who needs a calming tea at this time of the day?" Connor pushes, and I have no idea why he's being so rude at the moment.

"You, apparently. Shall I make you a cup?" I ask with full sarcasm, because I'm not making him a damn thing, although the way he looks at me, like he's ready to throw me over his shoulder and walk me out of here, has my body tingling.

"I'm not in the mood for tea parties," he grumbles before he turns and walks out just as quickly as he came in. My mouth is agape as I watch him leave. It seems he's back to his asshole ways.

"Sorry, Soren, he's just really busy and stressed. He has a lot on his plate."

"Interesting..." he says in his assessing tone before turning and looking at me.

"What is?" I ask, grabbing my own tea and taking a seat as Soren does the same.

"His aura, it was a muddy green all over," Soren says,

and I almost burn my tongue as I try to swallow quickly. I don't respond. I can't. Muddy green indicates jealousy and insecurities. And I have no idea why Connor would have those feelings. He's a billionaire, owns this entire operation, and from what I've seen, most of the town too. There's no way a man like him would be jealous or insecure about anything.

"I'm sure it wasn't," I tell him, and he frowns.

"Auras don't lie, Daisy."

"What color am I?" I ask, knowing he's seeing it, feeling a little unsettled and vulnerable as he makes his assessment.

"A good mix. Mainly red. Clearly, you are passionate about something here," he murmurs, before sipping his tea and looking at me pointedly. I divert my eyes and look back at the beautiful rose quartz before I quietly chant to myself.

I am not falling for Connor Whiteman.
I am not falling for Connor Whiteman.
I am not falling for Connor Whiteman.

16

———

CONNOR

The tea Daisy made me last night worked like a treat.

I had the best sleep I've had in weeks, which meant I was up early, feeling refreshed and energized. All morning, I moved through my work rapidly, everything going my way. I've been on fire, approving, assessing. Our quarterly reports are almost done, and our figures are well above my estimates, which makes me even happier.

Although my mind is focused, Daisy's still front and center. She's been here just over a week, and the progress she's made is amazing. Her work ethic is strong, her intelligence apparent with every passing day, and my morning runs keep getting better and better.

I saw her this week in a matching green ensemble, which was my favorite on Sunday. On Monday, it was purple. Yesterday, it was orange, and this morning, she was classic in black, which almost had me tripping on a tree root and stumbling. Thank God for the large hedges that surround that part of my run; otherwise, she would have noticed me. I now delight in my morning runs, just to see what color she wears next. She has a whole wardrobe of yoga outfits, and watching her bend and stretch is now part of my routine too.

As is the relief I get imagining her while in my shower afterward, when my dick is so hard I can barely make it two minutes before my release leaves me, and I hang my head in shame. She's a consultant here, and for all intents and purposes, that means a worker. There's a power imbalance, whether she wants to see that or not. I can't go looking at her and fantasizing about her and fucking coming every morning to the visual I have of her in her yoga gear.

Now as I pace back to my office, my shoulders are tense again, my jaw clenching. I think I need to order one of those fancy ice baths everyone is doing these days.

I have no idea who that guy was having a fucking tea party with her, but I didn't like him one bit. The look of him, the critical gaze he had on me, his assessing eyes and the arrogant tone. Not to mention, he stood to greet me and completely blocked my vision of Daisy, which I despised, not liking anyone coming between her and me.

I have a good bullshit radar, and it was pinging off the charts when it came to him. I tried to be civil, but as I do whenever I'm around her, I turned into an asshole, and her visitor got most of it.

Throwing my paperwork on my desk, I walk over to my window, looking out at the distillery gardens Daisy likes so much. I draw in a deep breath, noticing a few bumblebees flying around, the clouds moving overhead.

Then my eyes rest on a small white and yellow flower. *A daisy.* Is there nothing I can look at now that doesn't make me think of the buxom redhead down the hallway?

I rub my eyes with the heels of my hands, squeezing them, trying to erase all thoughts of her from my brain, but it's futile. My cell rings, and I pull it out. It's Dad.

"Hey," I say, taking a seat and leaning back in my large brown leather chair. I look around my office, same as it's always been. Timber, deep browns, a sofa and armchairs, a meeting table, my whiskey bar. The only thing difference is the small pink teacup that now adorns my desk. And I wonder for a beat if Daisy can make me some more of the tea she had yesterday, wishing I had the energy now that I had this morning.

"What's up with you?" he asks, and I sigh.

"Some guy is here at the distillery. I don't know him, and I don't like it," I tell him honestly. We run a tight ship here, now more so than ever. We don't like having a lot of outsiders in our space, especially people we haven't met before. It's hard to manage, though, as we're a business that's open to the public, which means we have strangers come and go every day.

"What guy?" Dad quizzes immediately, and I cringe. I should've been more sensitive. Ever since the incident next door at Marie's Place with Victoria and Lacy, he's been super protective of Victoria, our business, and this town. I need to be more mindful.

"A spa supplier. He's in with Daisy," I explain.

"A friend of hers?" he asks, clearly wanting more information. He was a weird-looking guy. An old hippie, if I can call him that. Tall, thin, not much to him, but very centered in an unsettling type of way.

"I guess. Not sure. Looked like a hippie who rose from the Garden of Eden," I mumble, thinking of a suitable insult but coming up short.

"Are you jealous?" Dad asks, and I pull back.

"Pfft. No, why would you think that?" I jump up and walk back to the window. The feeling in my gut tells me that he could be right, but I push it away, not wanting to even start thinking like that about a person on my team. My hand automatically runs down my beard.

"You're touching your beard, aren't you?" he says, and I drop my hand immediately.

"No." My body feels antsy, and I move again, back to my desk, shuffling some papers.

"You like her, just admit it," he presses, and my jaw tics.

"We don't get along," I tell him, shaking my head at the thought, even though those words are no longer one hundred percent accurate. A week ago, we could fling insults at each other like we were professionals at it, but now, after working together all night on the staffing issues for the spa and bouncing different ideas off each other, that could not just benefit the spa but also my business overall, it's clear we do actually get along and my admiration for her has grown.

"God, it feels like I've been waiting forever for this day," Dad says, and although I can't see him, I can tell he's smirking.

"What day? What are you talking about?" I ask, wondering what in the world he's thinking.

"The day where you would meet someone you felt was worthy of your time."

"I didn't say that," I spit out at him, refuting all his nonsense. It can't happen. This is a professional workplace. I'm the fucking CFO.

"Oh, Connor, remember how much teasing you had for me when I met Victoria," he says slyly, and my eyes narrow.

"What are you talking about?" I ask him, sensing something's up.

"My boy. Payback's a bitch." As he laughs, I drop my head, shaking it, a small smile threatening to dance on my lips.

"No need for payback. She's just a staff member. That's all," I tell him with finality.

"Great! Well, then you won't mind taking our new staff member to the mineral springs tomorrow. Victoria is meant to do it, but she has to go away for the day with Griffin for another project," Dad says, and I don't need to hear his laugh to know he's grinning.

"I can't, I'm busy," I rush out, though not with any real determination. Taking Daisy to the mineral springs would be like putting chocolate in front of a dog. The deep desire to have it will overrun the sense not to touch it.

"Too bad. Make room in your busy calendar. She needs to see it, and we need to look at the best ways to walk clients down there so they don't trip and break their legs and sue us for damages in the process," he grumbles, and I know he's right. One of us needs to go and assess things and then talk to Griffin about a pathway plan.

"Fine. I'll take her, then I'll speak to Griffin and get the path sorted once we know the best and shortest way to get there from the back door of the spa."

Putting the entire trip into the work box of my brain and not the box that sends any type of signals to my growing infatuation with the woman down the hall, I try to shake it off.

I also know that Griffin is waiting for me to start talking to him about my empty plot of land up near Dad and Victoria's on Billionaire Boulevard. I should start building soon. While my place here on the distillery grounds is nice, I've been thinking about it a bit lately, especially since we also need to finalize the plans for our accommodation over on the other side of the distillery. Six luxury villas, all with mod cons, and I already know they're going to book out as soon as we open, and my once peaceful country home will become less private and have less security for me.

I have my penthouse in New York and my place here at the distillery, but I'm not getting any younger, and while I thought I might've found somebody to build my new luxury ranch with, single life is looking more and more like my future.

Except for the woman currently residing in Dad's old house next door. She's someone I see every night. Someone I can barely get through the day without thinking about.

And I'm not sure how to reconcile that in my mind. Because it can't happen.

17

———

DAISY

I don't know what made me pack a bathing suit, given that I can't swim and didn't think I would need it here in Whispers, but I did, and now it's riding up my ass. My body's clearly bigger now than it was when I bought my swimwear years ago.

But I'm still smiling, because I've been waiting for this all week.

"We need to work out the best path to the springs, the one that will be easiest for our clients," Connor says. He seems off today. The trek from the distillery was quiet, the scowl on his face looking permanent. We're back to insulting each other, the small peace treaty I thought we made no longer a viable option, apparently. Ever since Soren came to the office yesterday, he's been either ignoring me or short and to the point. But surely, I'm allowed to have suppliers visit; that's all part of networking and building a brand, and until he tells me I can't, then I'll continue doing the work my way. Although

Soren dropping by was a surprise, and one I could've done without.

"I've been thinking about that. I suspect we may also have some older clients who come to the mineral springs. I did some research on the springs. They're renowned for their healing properties. Mineral-rich waters can help boost circulation, improve hypertension, alleviate stress, help with pain, and reduce inflammation, not to mention a slew of other health benefits." I assume he already knows this, since he's a local.

"We'll need to install a proper path…" he says, seemingly ignoring my comment as I follow him down a well-worn dirt path through the fields. As we descend, the world quiets even more, until all I can hear is the peaceful hum of nature surrounding us.

I stop for a moment to soak it all in, because this isn't something that's found anywhere in New York. Looking around, I close my eyes and take a deep breath. People pay a lot of money to try to capture this sound and the feeling it evokes. The slight rustle of the long grass, the little creaks of bugs and insects nearby, the careful movement of the trees swaying in the small breeze, the singing of birds up above, and the feeling of protectiveness from being at one with nature.

"What are you doing?" Connor barks, interrupting my impromptu meditation, and my eyes fling open. He's standing in front of me, his eyes narrowing, brow furrowed. I have no idea why he's extra grumpy today. But even with a slight scowl, he's still handsome. Suppressing a groan of frustration, I push that thought to the side.

"Taking a moment. Soaking in nature. It's very relaxing. You should try it. It might stop you being such an ass today," I say sweetly with a shrug, totally stepping over the line of workplace courtesy, but we've toed that line since we met.

"I'm not being an ass. You're too slow. Come on, let's go." His snappy tone has me tensing, before he turns and starts walking again. I'm not sure if he went for his run earlier, but he clearly woke up on the wrong side of the bed.

"I'm not slow, you're too fast. Your giant-sized strides are at least three of mine," I gripe back, my feet racing to keep up and struggling with that task. Despite his assholery ways, I admire him from behind. He's wearing jeans and a button-down shirt, one of my favorite looks of his. Walking in front of me means that he's front and center in my vision. Not that he hasn't been since I met him a few weeks ago. Connor Whiteman seems to be permanently branded into my brain these days.

"We're in a beautiful place, and you still have something to complain about," he murmurs, and now it's my turn to frown, because I'm the least likely person to complain about anything.

"I'm not complaining. This place is beautiful, it's *you* I have a problem with."

"So *I'm* the problem?" he asks, exaggerating his tone, slight sarcasm sneaking in as he continues to walk down the sloping hill toward the springs.

"You're so infuriating today, really. What is your... Ohhhh!" I gasp as my foot slides on an open tree root that I didn't see sticking from the ground. I slip slightly and feel my heart leaping from my mouth as I fall. Trying to brace myself for the impact, I squeeze my eyes shut, holding my breath and waiting for my heavy frame to thud on the hard ground. But Connor is quick. In an instant, his hands are on me, his large palms wrapping around my waist as he pulls me close so I don't fall over completely.

My eyes ping open, and I look straight at him. We're almost chest to chest, barely an inch between us. His hands hold on to me tight, firmly around my waist, his body leaning over me, as he grabbed me mid-fall. My hands automatically latched on to his arms, and now my fingers grip his shirt, my breathing labored as we continue to stare at each other. I lick my dry lips and swallow, trying to bring myself back to reality. His eyes lower to my mouth, his face hardening.

"I'm infuriating? You can't even walk straight." He huffs, like I'm the one annoying him, rather than the other way around.

"I can so." It sounds immature, but I'm almost lost for words. My body tingles, my breathing rapid, and my heart is racing as he looms over me. I feel completely at his mercy right now. Pulling away slightly, his eyes inspect me for injury while I try to calm my breathing. I notice his nostrils flare as his attention roams my body, his beard covering a world of emotions flicking across his face that are impossible to decipher.

"You need to watch where you're walkin'," he says, his accent thick, and I almost stumble again as my knees go weak. Sure, he talks all the time, and yes, I've heard small slithers of his Southern country accent slip in and out of his dialect, but out here in the field, the sounds of nature surrounding us and no one else here but the two of us, it's thicker and slides down my body like warm honey, making my pussy throb in a way it hasn't for some time.

"I was watching," I push back, and he looks like he doesn't believe me. Which would be right, since I was too busy looking at his fine ass, rather than where I was planting my feet.

"I don't need an insurance claim on you if you hurt yourself already."

"Well, like I said, stop walking so fast. I can't keep up with your giant steps." It's obvious I'm still a little breathless. My heart thuds, the pull I feel for him increasing, and the way he's looking at me could melt my clothes right off. It's warm today, and I'm wearing a long shirt over some shorts, the shirt open at my collar, my swimwear underneath that. Although riding up my butt, it does cinch me in at the waist and pulls my breasts together, giving my already excellent cleavage a little more oomph. It's a great confidence builder.

"Come on," he snaps, startling me from my thoughts and dropping his hands from my waist. My body feels bereft for a beat before something strange happens. His hand grabs mine, holding tightly, and he starts walking again, this time a little slower. I think my soul has left my body, but my feet move along with him. He looks straight ahead, which is good, because if he looked at me, I'm not sure I could hide the feelings from my face. Shock, mixed with excitement, mixed with appreciation. His hand is huge, mine small in his firm hold, until he moves his hand a little so our fingers intertwine. I'm not sure if he's just being helpful or trying to ensure I don't fall or actually wants to touch me and hold my hand. But I let my fingers grip his just as tight.

"We'll need to put in a handrail," I say, my voice sounding a little nervous. I have no idea what's happening, but my body is responding like she's been waiting for this moment forever, gripping on to his hand tight, even now that the walkway has leveled off a little and there are no rocks or roots sticking up to trip me.

"I can get Griffin going on building a better path, with rails and maybe some small seating along the way. So people can sit and let nature soak over them," he grumbles, and my eyes widen. Did he just agree with me?

"Griffin?" I ask.

"My builder."

I huff. Of course he has his own builder.

"Careful here, the rocks can be slippery." His hold on my hand tightens again as I step over some rocks that are glistening, then finally stop and look up and around. My mouth drops open in awe at the sight before me.

"Wow," I say, stunned into silence. I'm not sure what I was expecting, but it wasn't this. "This is beautiful." The water is calm, the spring larger than I was anticipating. Big boulders run around the perimeter, making it look like a natural pool. The water's amazing, so clear, you can almost see the bottom. I've never wanted to jump into a pool this much before in my life. I swallow, pulling at my shirt a little, because even though I want to get in, I feel apprehensive about Connor seeing me in my bathing suit.

"Local kids come and hang out sometimes, but they generally stick to that side. Here, closest to our property, is quieter." I can see out of the corner of my eye him watching me take it all in.

I see a small area off to the side that's a little flatter and stare at it for a beat.

"What?" he asks, and it isn't lost on me that we're still standing side by side and he hasn't let go of my hand.

"I'm just thinking..." I say as my mind starts to whirl.

"Care to share?"

I take in a deep breath, trying not to let his impatience bother me.

"Can we utilize this space?" I point out where I'm looking.

He frowns, looking over it before nodding.

"It's on Victoria's land. It's near our private pathway."

"We could put a cold plunge pool here. Utilize this entire area for cold and hot plunges. It's called contrast therapy, and it's great for pain relief, improved blood flow. It reduces inflammation, stress..." I say, thinking out loud.

"We have enough room." He doesn't deny the idea, so I take that as a win.

"It also improves mood, so it might be good for you to use daily," I say, not able to help myself, and his eyes whip to me, slight amusement in his gaze, though he remains silent.

I look back to the springs, noticing a small amount of steam rising from the water, and before I can think too hard about it, my body moves on autopilot as I let go of his hand and pull my clothes from my frame.

"What are you doing?" he asks as I kick off my shoes.

"What does it look like I'm doing?" I sass as I unbutton my shorts. While I'm aware of my size, it isn't ever something I have hidden. Not until that disaster of a date I had a few months ago. But I'm here in this amazing place, and I can't let this opportunity pass me by, just because some city douchebag decided he had a problem with my weight. While being in a bathing suit isn't something I do often, I'm just going for a swim, and I have a one-piece on. Everything is covered.

"You're going in?" He looks a little shocked, like a deer caught in headlights.

"Yeah, are you?" I ask him, because he certainly isn't dressed like he is.

"No. I'm just showing you the place, not swimming," he rushes out, looking at me, before looking away, and then looking back at me. I notice his hands running down his beard, his eyes aflame with what looks like panic.

"I need to try every treatment before we can assume others will want to pay for them. So yeah. Call it research, you're good at that. Sure you aren't coming?" I shimmy off my shorts and start undoing the buttons to my shirt before my fear takes over and I lose my confidence.

"No," is all he says, eyes darting all around the springs as I open my shirt and pull it from my frame. The sun is nice on my bare skin, and I take a deep breath in, quickly tiptoeing into the water before he turns around to look at me again. I'm not ashamed of my body, but being in a swimsuit right in front of him isn't something that my confidence levels are ready for just yet.

"Suit yourself," I say on a sigh as the warm water pulls me in deeper, and I fully submerge myself. This is the best warm bath ever, and I'm so glad I got in. I open my eyes and look at Connor. He's rigid, standing on the edge of the water like he's been bitten by a million bees. Shaking off my concerns with him, I close my eyes and lean my head back, my body floating on the top of the water.

This is bliss.

18

CONNOR

Fuck me.

I have no idea what I did to piss God off, but he's sure making me pay today.

Spending the day with the woman I can't get out of my mind is one thing. Seeing her half-naked right in front of me and being unable to touch her is a completely different level of control I wasn't sure I had. I grit my teeth and swallow hard as she lies back in the water like she's sleeping. Completely afloat, totally at ease, her beautiful curves on full display. Meanwhile, my dick is rock-hard and straining against my zipper and has been ever since I glimpsed her glorious round ass poking out from her swimwear as she stripped off her clothes.

My eyes canvass the area for the millionth time. If anyone else was here, I would have thrown that towel around her so quickly she wouldn't have known what hit her. No one else can see her like this, and as it is, I shouldn't be looking.

But I am. Fuck, seeing her every day in her yoga gear is one thing, but seeing her ass out, her pale peaches and cream skin, and her full tits almost falling out of her swimsuit has my mouth watering. She's confident in her body, and I like that. Yet another thing to add to my *Things I love about Daisy* list that's growing daily.

"You sure you don't want to come in?" she asks again, and my eyes meet hers. *Oh, I want to come, alright. Right down her pretty little throat.*

"I'm fine," I grit out, forcing my feet to stay on the ground. There's no way I'm getting in that water, because I know if I do, my resolve will snap. I've been an asshole to her all morning because all I can think about is that guy in her office yesterday. The one who gave me the creeps, and now, my resolve is stretching, because I'm spending time with her and wanting to touch her but can't. I'm being pushed to my limits.

"Just don't drown," I warn, my eyes are now glued to her, and she grins.

"Well, I can't swim, so that's probably likely," she quips back, and I still.

"What the hell did you just say?" I ask her, angry now as I take a step forward, ready to kick off my shoes and jeans and dive in after her.

"Don't worry, I can float." Still lying on her back, she looks like she should be sunbathing in Ibiza, rather than floating around a mineral spring in Whispers. I wonder if I could take her to Ibiza, rub sun lotion on her, and watch her suntan topless. I shake my head of the thoughts.

"Daisy. Get out of the water." The spring isn't deep for

someone like me, but for her, she won't be able to touch the bottom in some places.

"No, I'm not getting out."

I swear this woman always does the opposite of what I ask of her.

"Daisy, it's deep," I warn her, fear and frustration wrapping around my heart.

"Connor, I'm fine," she grits out, her hands moving slowly around in the water, almost steering her body.

"I swear to God, Daisy. If you drown in this mineral spring, I will kill you." I'm ready to jump in and haul her beautiful big ass out of that water. I might throw her over my shoulder while I'm at it, stalk back up to my place, and lock her in my bedroom.

"Hey, Connor!" I hear shouted from behind me, and I look up, seeing a bunch of local kids running down the hill on the opposite side.

"Daisy, time to get out," I tell her once again, grabbing her towel, trying not to sound like an asshole, but they're not seeing her like this, practically naked, wet body, her long red hair dripping.

"Why?" she asks, exasperated, looking up at me.

"Because you can't swim and because all the kids are coming." I barely finish speaking, just as they start running and jumping in the water, creating ripples and waves.

"Oh." Her brows pinch, feeling the water change from still and peaceful to waves created by a full-on frat party.

"Float over here. I'll grab you." I tell her, angry that she'd get in the water when she knows she can't swim.

"I'm fine, Connor." She gets closer and moves around,

now standing on the bottom and starting to walk toward me.

I clench my jaw, my teeth almost at breaking point as she steps out of the water like a goddamn James Bond girl. Water drips from her body, her swimsuit plastered to her like latex. I hear the boys start to whistle, and I jump into action. Striding over to her, I wrap her towel around her so they can no longer see her juicy plump ass that I know is on display.

"Mighty chivalrous of you." She raises her eyebrow in question as she grabs the ends of the towel and pulls it to her chest. She's pushing me. I know it, and if she isn't careful, I'll pounce. I'm about five seconds away from doing just that.

"What the hell were you thinking getting in the water when you can't swim?" I growl, stepping between her and the boys to shield her from their eyes, even though she's now covered in a large towel.

"I was thinking that I'd be fine. I'm an adult; I know my limits. Besides, you were there. You would've saved me if I got into trouble." She throws on her shirt and shorts, and I bite the inside of my cheeks, because she's right. I would've saved her, obviously. Given her mouth-to-mouth, and then once she was okay, turned her over and made her ass red.

"Daisy, you don't know the water. The spring is uneven, so you shouldn't have done that. What if I wasn't here?" I demand, my frustration now peaking.

Swiping her things, she starts walking up the path, past me, saying over her shoulder, "I'm not stupid, Connor."

"Could've fooled me." I stride up behind her, the two of us full of steam, our pace back to the distillery now much quicker than the trip here.

She looks at me, shaking her head. "Seriously, what's up with you today?"

"Who in their right mind jumps into a spring when they know they can't swim!" My voice rises, along with my temperature. I move ahead of her, needing to calm myself.

I push through the distillery door and stalk right to my office. It's the weekend. No one's here. The restaurant is busy, but our offices are all locked. I hear the door being pushed open just as violently behind me, and I know she's hot on my heels.

Slamming the door shut behind her, she raises her voice right back. "In case you forgot, I'm capable of making my own decisions, and as I said, I know my limits!"

"Yeah, well, I have just about hit my limit," I tell her as I turn and look at her. I'm not sure if she can see it in my face, but I'm about to lose my composure, and my nostrils flare as I try to suck in the air I need.

She looks at me curiously with her sparkling blues, hair long and damp, face flushed but clear like porcelain. Her shirt is open, her bathing suit still wet underneath. The air around us shifts as her stubbornness softens, and my anger gives way to relief that she's here, she's safe, not drowned, lying face down in the springs. I'm sick of denying it. Daisy is beautiful, smart, and so goddamn sexy, and I need to taste her. I need her... just once.

"Come here," I say in a low growl as I stand by my

desk. I need her to come to me. I need to know she's feeling the same way I do. My stare remains intense as I watch her, and her hand lets go of her towel, it hitting the floor at her feet. Her eyes don't move from mine as she steps forward, toward me, and my breathing quickens. Shit, this is happening.

She doesn't stop until our toes meet. I look down at her and watch her hair fall down her back as she looks up at me, hearing a shaky breath leave her lips that calls to my own desperation. My head moves before my brain catches up, and I'm putting my lips to hers.

Her mouth opens on a gasp, and she's still for a beat, before her hands grip on to my shirt at my chest and she pulls me down to her, sealing her lips to mine fully. A rough growl rumbles from my core in appreciation, now knowing that her feelings for me mirror my own for her as my hands sweep around her damp waist and I pull her body flush to mine. We're connected, our tongues tangling, lips meshing, and I swear I feel my soul leave my body because this woman will be my undoing, I just know it.

Relaxing her hold on my shirt, her hands move up around my neck and land on the back of my head, and she pulls me closer. I lower my hands past her waist, my palms cupping her round ass, and I groan at the feeling. My large hands are full of her, appreciating her body as I pull her hips to meet mine, letting her feel exactly what she does to me. I revel in the moan she releases into my mouth.

As our kiss becomes more frantic, I trail a hand to her

front, sliding it up her body, until I can cup her breast, squeezing once. I think I'm in heaven.

"Connor…" she whispers as I mold her large breast, really wanting to put my mouth on her. She pulls my hair and I can barely get a hold of myself. But as I open my eyes for a second to look at her, I see my pile of reports on my desk, and reality sets in that I'm groping my fucking employee. My brain kicks back into gear like it's yanked the emergency brake, and I drop my hands and step back.

Swallowing, we look at each other. Both panting, both a little shocked, and both obviously feeling a certain way about the other.

"I shouldn't have done that," I say, my hands threading through my hair, waiting to see what she says. I'm praying to God I got this right and she wants me as much as I want her. That I didn't just take advantage in any way.

"Me neither," she says breathily as her hands run down her front and she fixes herself up a little.

"We work together. We… We need to build the spa," I say, shaking my head, feeling like I'm telling myself rather than her, needing to keep this professional.

"I'm here for just a few more weeks. I need to focus." She nods, and I hate the words of truth she speaks.

"We can't do that again." Even though I really, really want to.

"Definitely not. Absolutely can't happen," she agrees, and I step farther away from her. If I don't, then this will escalate. Quickly.

"I need a shower." Gathering her towel, she moves toward my door, opening it but hesitating before looking back at me. She remains quiet before quickly opening the door wider and walking through, closing it behind her. I release a big breath, watching where she left. All I can think about now is lathering her naked body in soap and fucking her in my shower.

But that definitely cannot happen. No, absolutely not.

19

CONNOR

"Good, you're here. I need to talk to you," I say to Sawyer the minute he steps inside my office. I'm up, out of my chair, and striding to the door, closing it behind him. I flew him in today to go over a few things with the spa, and then we're heading to Hudson's place for the day. Lacy's mom is going in for an operation, and we need to keep Hudson busy so he doesn't go mad waiting for news. Lacy has delegated him to stay at home, not allowing him to go to the hospital with them. Too independent for her own good, that girl.

"Okaaaay. You have my attention." He's watching me like a hawk, knowing something's up. I've been feeling a mix of emotions all day. I haven't seen Daisy since the mineral springs yesterday, and we're deliberately ignoring each other, yet I feel like I'm sitting on the edge of a cliff, ready to jump, because all I can think about is her. My eyes move to the small parcel on my desk. The one that houses arm floaties I bought for her, given swimming isn't her strong suit and drowning isn't something I want her to experience.

"I've done something..." I start, now pacing my office. I've thought of nothing else other than that bruising kiss yesterday, and now I want more.

"What?" he asks sharply, and I run my hand through my hair, then stand with my hands on my hips.

"I kissed her," I admit. "I couldn't fucking stay away. She was there in her swimsuit, her body on full display, and I couldn't take it. I've been itching to kiss her since she arrived." I start to pace again. As a boss, it was a stupid thing to do. I mean, we're both consenting adults, but still, there's a line, and I crossed it. After she left my office yesterday, I went straight home and sat under a cold shower for an hour. Since then, the two of us have been busy, but we both wanted it, and we both agreed we couldn't. But now I really, really want to do it again.

"Kissed who?" he asks, his eyes narrowing.

"Daisy," I breathe out. He looks confused for a moment before his eyes widen once the pieces click together.

"Your new consultant?" he clarifies, and I nod.

"Well, shit." He slumps in the armchair, my news obviously not what he was expecting to hear. "And so...?" he asks, wanting more information.

"And it was fucking amazing, but we both agreed it can't happen again."

"You're in agreement? So she was happily involved in this incident?"

I pause my strides and look at him sharply.

"I didn't fucking assault her, if that's what you're implying." His accusation makes me feel ill.

"Just asking the questions to see if it will open us up for a lawsuit."

"No, but…" I start, having thought of this all last night.

"But what?" he pushes.

"I've been thinking… can we get a contract drawn up?" I ask.

"What kind of contract?"

"One that states we're entering into a mutually beneficial private arrangement and that it has no impact on her work or the distillery. I can't fire her or end her contract. Etc., etc.," I say, and he looks at me like he's seeing me for the first time.

"Are you feeling alright?" he questions, his brow furrowed.

"Fine," I lie, because I need sleep, I need a cup of fucking tea, and I need to see Daisy.

"Fuck, you really like her," he says in awe, his eyebrows rising almost comically.

"Pfft…" I wave him off, not contradicting his words. Clearly, I'm not very good at hiding how I feel because his shock turns into a shit-eating grin.

"Holy shit. Connor Whiteman has fucking feelings. I never thought I would see the day," he teases.

"Shut up. Can you do it or not?" I push, and he nods.

"It's actually pretty common, and given she's a consultant and not an employee, then it's even easier. I'll get the team to draw it up now." Sawyer gets busy on his phone and laptop for the next few minutes as I breathe out, feeling relieved. We agreed it was a one-time thing. Just a kiss, just a blip in time. But I haven't felt like this before, and I know I can't stop at just one taste.

"I just emailed you something," he murmurs and I raise my eyebrows. "Told you it was common. We have a template on file," he says, giving me a smart-ass grin.

I move to my laptop and scan the contract quickly. It's standard terminology and says everything I need it to say so I print it out and sign it, handing the paperwork back to him.

"You'll give it to her," I tell him.

"Me?" he questions.

"That way she won't feel like I'm pouncing on her. It gives her some breathing space to make her own decision," I tell him and he takes the file, adding it to his pile.

"Fine. I'm charging you a delivery fee, though," he says as he stands, a smirk on his face. He's joking, of course. Sawyer's legal expertise is unrivaled. He has negotiated our biggest deals and has worked with us for a long time. He's well and truly part of the family.

"Asshole," I grit out, my shoulders tense as I think about all that is needed is her signature.

"What does Tanner think?" he asks, and I can only stare at him.

"Ohhh, shit. He doesn't know." Sawyer grins, and I roll my eyes.

"And I would like to keep it that way," I mention, not exactly sure what Dad will think.

"Fine. Your dirty little secret is safe with me," he says, grinning from ear to ear.

"We need to get going. They're all waiting in the meeting room for us. We need to go over the spa legalities in relation to the treatments and the insurances." Grabbing my laptop, I'm itching to get down the hall to the rest of the team, but really, I just want to see Daisy.

We walk briskly, already late, my shoulders tense, which isn't helped by the fact that Sawyer hasn't stopped grinning since I spoke with him.

"Sawyer," Dad says, nodding to Sawyer in greeting as the conversation Victoria and Daisy are having ceases.

"What's going on?" I ask, seeing one of our support staff here changing cables over, the computer in here apparently not working.

"Technical difficulties," Victoria says, smiling, and I take a seat, my eyes flicking to Daisy, who has a nice little flush coloring her cheeks. She raises her eyes to meet mine, and I watch her swallow.

"Daisy," I say by way of greeting, not wanting to treat her any differently than I have been, although the corners of my mouth are quirking.

"Connor," she says, and Sawyer clears his throat next to me.

"Daisy, nice to finally meet you. I'm Sawyer." He holds out his hand, and Daisy leans over to shake it.

"Nice to meet you too, Sawyer."

My shoulders lower, her voice hitting my spine, instant relaxation of just being around her evident.

"The bottling machine is down again," Dad says, looking at me, and I stroke my beard and open my laptop to get my head into the meeting.

"Again?" I ask, frowning. "I heard from the team in California this morning. The storm last night hit our crops." None of this news is good, since both issues will put a stop to our production in some way or another.

"Oh my God. Sorry!" Victoria says, spilling her coffee, and she and Daisy jump up, fetching tissues to mop up the mess.

Dad looks at me and frowns.

"What the hell is going on today?" he asks everyone.

"Mercury is in retrograde," both Daisy and Victoria say simultaneously, like it's a normal thing. They both continue cleaning and talking, as if what they said makes any sense, and the three of us men just look at each other in confusion before I feel Sawyer lean over to me.

"Holy shit, they are so alike... they could be twins," he whispers, and my hand flies out to hit him in the arm. Not my finest moment, and certainly not professional, but our team is close, more like family, and everyone's used to these antics.

The girls don't pay any attention. But Dad does, and his eyes on me are burning as his lips quirk.

"Payback's going to be a bitch," he murmurs, and I smile, not able to hide a thing.

20

DAISY

I kissed him. I kissed him, and I loved it, and I want to do it again. Over and over again.

It wasn't a drunken night out or a pity kiss at the end of a date. No, it was a scorching hot, bruising kiss that lifted me from my feet. We both wanted it, and God,, it felt good. I've never experienced anything like it. Sure, my history with men isn't excessive; in fact, it's almost embarrassingly nonexistent, but Connor and that kiss, there was no faking that. That was too good.

Even now, I touch my lips, remembering it in detail as I look at him across the boardroom table as he, his father, and the lawyer named Sawyer all discuss insurances and liabilities in regard to the spa and the mineral springs. His attention flicks to me, dropping to my lips, watching me brush my finger across my bottom one, and his eyes fill with heat and longing. I swallow, the tension between us so thick you could light a flame with it. Then he returns his attention back to Sawyer, to the conversation at hand.

Obviously, we can't even go there. That's why we stopped it yesterday. We can't entertain anything. But as I sit in this meeting, trying to understand insurances and legal costs, I feel my already hot cheeks get hotter, because the man across the table from me continues to look at me like he wants to eat me whole, and I want to let him.

I couldn't sleep last night. The kiss just played over and over in my mind on repeat. It left me wanting, my body in a new state of heightened tension that needed a release. So I retrieved the little bag that Trisha threw into my suitcase, the one that contains my battery-operated friends, and sent a thanks to the universe for having Trisha in my life.

I came so hard that I had to bite the pillow, for fear my sexy neighbor would hear my screams. But I shouldn't be worried; I'm sure the walls in my place are soundproof because I hear nothing. A person could walk right into the house, and I wouldn't even know.

"Okay, I'll file these copies, and then Griffin can start the path. I think everything you've said makes sense and should cover us completely if there were to be any incidents," Sawyer says as he shuffles some paperwork that Tanner and Connor just signed.

He looks at me and smiles. He's done that a few times in this meeting, and I'm starting to get a complex as I look down at myself, wondering if I have spilled something on my top.

"I would just like to raise something else?" I ask the room, and all eyes are on me.

"Go for it." Connor nods, looking at me intently.

"When we were at the springs yesterday..." I start and can't help but look right at him. I see him swallow, and I continue. "The local kids came, and while they obviously love the springs, kids running and jumping is not something that encourages relaxation," I tell them, and Victoria nods.

"You're right, and in the height of summer, it's even busier." She nods.

"Well, it's private property. We can just close the access down," Sawyer says with a shrug, but Tanner and Connor growl.

"Not happening," Connor says quickly.

"The springs are for the community." Tanner follows up, and I grin, thinking it's cute these two burly businessmen actually want to do good by the people in this town.

"So what options do we have?" Victoria asks.

I think about it for a moment.

"We could only offer a mineral soak on particular days or at certain times? During school hours, for example. Make it known to the kids and the community those are the days that it'll be locked down for private soaks for the distillery, but all other times it can remain open for the community," I suggest, and Connor looks at me and nods.

"I mean, it's on Victoria's private land. She doesn't need to let any of them on it at all," Sawyer pushes.

"But it's nice for the people of Whispers to enjoy it," Victoria says, and I can feel the love the boys and she have for this town move through me. Sure, they're part of this big business, leaders in the whiskey industry world-wide, but they don't tread on the little guy to get where they want to go. It's admirable.

"I like Daisy's idea. Keeps it doable for everyone. Dad?" Connor asks, and I turn to look at Tanner and see his eyes on me.

"I think what Daisy offers makes the most sense. Get me the days and hours, and I will talk with the community. Get their buy-in." Tanner nods to me, like he appreciates my thoughts, and I smile, relishing this feeling of acceptance.

"Oh, before I forget, the local mayor mentioned that there's a submission currently being reviewed for a new business in town," Tanner says as we all start to gather our laptops and paperwork.

"Really?" Sawyer looks surprised.

"What's it for?" Victoria asks, and I just wait and listen, not sure what they're talking about.

"A bakery. Someone from out of town, apparently. But I told them I think a bakery would be a great addition and one we would support," Tanner explains.

"Yum, fresh pastries every morning sounds delicious," Victoria says, grinning.

"Great, well, let me grab my things, Sawyer, and I will meet you out front," Connor says, and as we all stand from the table, his gaze moves to me again quickly before he walks out the door, the rest of us following suit. I swallow my newfound feelings. All that fighting and tension when we first met has melted into an interest and arousal I've never experienced before, and I have no idea what to do about it.

We shuffle out of the meeting room, and I walk with Sawyer toward reception.

"So, how are you enjoying the job so far?" he asks, making small talk, and I smile.

"I'm really enjoying the opportunity. The spa is going to be amazing once it's complete."

"A few more weeks, right? What are you going to do then?"

It's something I haven't really thought about too much yet.

"At this stage, I'll be here for probably another month. While things are on track, I need to ensure that the staff are trained and the opening week or two goes well. After that, I'll head back to the city. I enjoy pulling this kind of thing together, but my real passion is yoga. I did a lot of it back in the city at my mom's wellness center, so it's almost second nature. I'll be looking for the next opportunity where I can broaden my skills even further."

The more time I spend here in Whispers, the less I feel like going back to the noise and grind of New York, though. And the less I feel like going back to Sunshine and having my business ideas restricted again.

"Before I forget, I have some new paperwork here for you to read over and sign," he says, handing over a folder.

"Oh, is it time sensitive? I have a few other things I need to go through in regard to product contracts and things at the moment," I tell him, putting the folder under my other work that I'm holding, knowing the pile on my desk is growing by the minute.

He gives me a weird grin. "No. Not at all. Take your time with it. It's not urgent."

Before I can ask more, we get interrupted.

"Oh, Daisy?" Stephanie, the receptionist, says, and Sawyer and I both look at her from where we stand at the front area. Him waiting for Connor, me heading to my office.

"Yes?" I ask her. She's a young girl, very friendly, always has a smile.

"The team at the restaurant said there was a man who came to the distillery for lunch and asked about treatments."

"Oh wow, really?" I feel proud that we have some inquiries already. We haven't even started advertising.

"Hmm, it seems like your reputation is already out," she says with a bright smile, clearly happy too, but I frown in confusion.

"What do you mean by my reputation?" I ask.

"Well, he was asking for you, specifically."

"For me?" I ask again, because that's weird. I'm a consultant. I'm not listed on the website and haven't been on any social media for the spa or distillery. I'm not part of the permanent team in any way.

"Who's asking after Daisy?" Connor's voice barks from behind me, so firm that I jolt. Unease fills me slightly as I think about who would even know I'm here. It's just the team here, and then, of course, my family, Trisha, and a few suppliers. Maybe it was a supplier?

I turn to him, his face tense as he looks at Stephanie.

"Ahh, he didn't leave a name or number..." she says hesitantly. "Maybe the restaurant team knows more?" she offers, now feeling unsure herself, and I dare say, a little taken aback by Connor's intensity. I know he's been stressed lately. Something happened with Lacy and his friend Hudson. I didn't ask questions—it's none of my business—but whatever it is, it seems major. Lacy won't be back at work for a while, and both Sawyer and Connor are about to go over to Hudson's place now.

He now stands by my side, so close I can smell him and feel the heat from his body. Sawyer stands opposite us, watching everyone and everything as Connor looks down at me, his gaze burning into mine.

"We haven't put anything out to the media yet. No one knows you're here. Who would be asking for you personally?" His brows pinch in thought, and I don't know why we all feel uneasy about this. I take a deep breath, trying to think about it logically.

"It might have been a supplier? Maybe Soren again?" I'm trying to ease everyone's confusion and concern, yet as I say the words, I doubt them. I know Soren is having his quiet week at the commune, so I don't think it would be him. I also don't have any more deliveries coming. In fact, I have more than enough stock from him to last me months.

"Maybe it was just a tourist. He probably heard about it in town. You know how Rochelle loves to talk." Stephanie shrugs, and I nod.

"Yeah. That must be it," I say, smiling at her and nodding as she moves back to her desk to take a call. Meanwhile, Connor is still tense beside me. I hear a cell ring and look at Sawyer, who holds up his phone.

"Sorry, I've got to take this," he says, stepping out to the front of the distillery, leaving Connor and me alone.

"Can you think of anyone else it might be?" he asks me, frowning. I'm not sure why he's suddenly so concerned about this.

"I'm sure it's nothing. Maybe a contact of my mom's or something. She's been telling everyone where I am." I try to put him at ease. His stance softens a bit.

"Sorry, we just don't like strangers around here much, and I want to ensure you're safe." His hand touches the small of my back, and his thumb rubs up and down in a soft motion that sends butterflies into flight in my stomach. I pause, the feelings building between us almost too big for me to handle. Any words I had get stuck in my throat as his eyes search mine.

We both agreed after the kiss yesterday that we needed to remain professional, but this side of him, this caring, protective nature of his that has started to come through, his passionate kiss, the way he rests his hand on the small of my back when we walk places, or the way he lifted me into his truck. All these little moments are chipping away at my initial assessment of him, and I can now see that I was way off the mark in how I judged him.

"I need to go. You alright?" he asks me quietly, startling me from my thoughts, his tone low, like we're having our own private conversation, and I'm not sure if he's referring to this situation or the situation we had in his office yesterday, but I smile up at him. I heard him and Tanner talking about the machine breaking down and the crops that were affected by the storm, so I know he has a lot on his mind. Stress is such an impacting factor on our health these days, and I prefer Connor doesn't suffer because of it. That thought makes my healing nature come to the forefront.

"I'm fine. But you seem to have a lot going on. Why don't you join me for yoga on the weekend? It might help your stress levels," I offer genuinely, and while it probably isn't the best idea for us to start doing more activities together, given our need to remain professional, as a healer and understanding the power of yoga and meditation like I do, I know that it'll benefit him. His eyes widen a little before his lips curve up at the sides just slightly.

"I might give it a try." He nods before he drops his hand and walks out the door, and I stand, watching as he and Sawyer jump into his truck and drive away.

"I called the restaurant to ask for more details." Stephanie's voice startles me, and I turn to look at her.

"Oh, what did they say?" I ask, walking over to her desk.

"They said it was an older gentleman who was there with a few younger men. A group of four of them. They asked to see you, wanted to walk into the office, but the waiter stopped them."

"Did they give a name?" I ask.

"No. But he saw them leave in an old van."

It was obviously Soren, here with some friends or hitchhikers, no doubt.

"Oh, that's fine. I know him. He's a supplier," I tell her, feeling somewhat relieved to put the puzzle together, and she smiles, happy the mystery is solved.

As I walk down to my office, ready to tackle the afternoon workload, I think about Mom and Dad. I should go home to see them soon. I'm here for a month, maybe two, but I can leave on weekends, and maybe flying back to see them would be nice. I put the new paperwork from Sawyer underneath all the rest, knowing it isn't urgent, before I get back to tackling my to-do list.

I will meditate on it. While I'm in no rush to get back to the city, I'm really craving Mom's dahl.

DAISY

As the morning sun coats me in its rays, I close my eyes, my body nimble, feeling the movements automatically as I breathe in through my nose and out through my mouth. It's been a long week, and I'm so glad to have the weekend in front of me now.

A goat bleats in the distance, and I hear the slow movements of a cow walking in a nearby field and the rustle of a tiny breeze through the trees. This is surreal and beautiful.

I continue to bend, stretching my body, feeling my muscles lengthen and awaken. My bare feet press firmly on the grass, grounding my body with nature as I move into the downward dog. Feeling tight in my calves, I hold the pose for a moment before I roll up again. Every joint in my spine stacks on top of each other as I stand, and I take in a big breath, slowly opening my eyes.

"Ahhhhhh!" I scream, jumping back and clenching

my hands at my chest as Connor stands right in front of me, half-naked. And he's laughing.

"You said to join you for yoga?" His eyes trail up and down my body, not so subtly, as I try to calm my frightened heart. Yeah, staying away from each other is proving difficult, but we're adults. We can behave ourselves.

"Deciding to scare people is a new tactic of yours, is it?" I ask, the slight sass I get around him back in action.

"Well, that, and attempting to do whatever it is you were just doing." A small smile dances on his lips.

"I'm surprised you came." My smile spreads wider now that the adrenaline rush from fright disappears, because I was sure he wouldn't join me for this. It's been a few days since I mentioned it, the two of us busy with work and barely having time to chat.

"I did. Not sure if I'm going to regret this or not..." he says, sounding unsure. Throwing his damp t-shirt that's tucked into the waistband of his shorts onto the ground, his amazing physique is showcased to me in nothing but a pair of black gym shorts. He's confident, clearly happy with his body, and he should be. My mouth salivates at the sight.

"Hmmmm, you might," I say with a grin. I can't wait for this. It's clear he's not a yogi. In fact, most things that we discuss about the spa, he has no idea about. He's very much a man's man, although open to new ideas and trying new things, which I appreciate.

"Okay, where do you want me?" he asks, obviously eager to give it a go. Either that, or he has a meeting he needs to dash to. But he seems a little jumpy, almost nervous, which isn't like him.

"Have you done yoga before?"

"I've never done any yoga or Pilates or slow, stretchy movements before, and if my father could see me now, I know he'd be rolling around on the grass, laughing his ass off. But I'm interested in trying out everything you suggest, because work is handing me my ass at the moment." As he kicks off his shoes to go barefoot like me, my smile widens.

"Okay, well, let's start with a mountain pose," I tell him, my voice immediately calming. After years of practice, I can barely notice when it changes, the melodic tone second nature now. We stand opposite each other, facing one another.

"Put your feet hip width apart and flat on the ground." Showing him, he follows my lead. "Spread your toes, create awareness at all four corners of your feet and draw the energy up through your legs, bringing your palms together at the heart." I continue and close my eyes as my hands move up into a prayer motion, showing him and assuming he follows suit. I pause for a moment and take a few deep breaths, and as I open my eyes, I see him struggling. His feet are moving; he's clearly getting frustrated, and I can tell he isn't as grounded as he should be.

"Take your time. Get comfortable with just standing firm, connecting to the ground."

"I'm still trying to work out how my feet have four corners and how I can recover my barley crops after the storm damaged them the other day," he says honestly, his shoulders tight around his ears and his body tense. I can tell his mind's still racing, and I think for a moment.

"You know, it might be best to do some meditation

today. Try to relax your mind before we relax your body. Let's sit." I lower myself to the grass and sit cross-legged, waiting for him to do the same.

"Ahh, meditation?" he asks hesitantly.

"Trust me," I tell him, and he nods, sitting down, crossing his legs awkwardly as he sits in front of me, our knees now touching.

"Give me your hands," I tell him, and he puts out his hands. Taking them in mine, I shake them a little, trying to loosen up his upper body, moving them around and up and down, literally shaking the stress right out of his shoulders. I feel them relax before I gently place them palm down on his knees.

"Close your eyes." I watch him as he does, then I do too.

"Now, take a deep breath in through your nose for four counts..." I say, my voice calm as I count the beats and breathe in and hear him do the same. "Now breathe out through the mouth for four."

"And again," I say, this time not counting, but I can hear his breath as we both inhale, then exhale.

My eyes open to take a look at him. "Feel the breeze in your hair and as it brushes over your skin." This massive man is sitting cross-legged in front of me with his eyes closed, deep breathing, and I can physically see his shoulders have lowered. It makes me smile.

"Take a deep breath in through your nose... and then out through your mouth."

His diaphragm expands and then contracts with each direction I give him, going on for another five minutes until his breaths are perfectly steady and his face has smoothed into one of serenity.

"Now, open your eyes," I say quietly, and he opens his eyes, his gaze right on mine. Our knees still touching, we both sit quietly for a moment, comfortable in each other's presence. Basking in the morning light, the sounds of nature on a quiet sunny morning fill our ears. I don't want to move, and he doesn't seem to want to either.

"You're very good at all this," he says, his voice sounding calmer and more deliberate.

The compliment means a lot to me. "I've been practicing my whole life."

"Any tips for when I get stressed?" he asks.

"Deep breathing like we've done is super simple and very effective. Sometimes, a hand on heart can help to really ground you too," I suggest, thinking about what would be quick and easy for him to implement into his stressful days.

"Hand on heart?"

"Put your hand on your heart like this." I lift my hand and place it palm down on my chest, and he copies my movement.

"Feel your heartbeat under your palm and close your eyes. Continue to breathe slowly, and eventually, your deep breathing will align with your beating heart. The heart is the most central and significant part of our body. It's rhythmic, a steady warrior in stressful times. Placing your hand on your heart and that of your loved ones can represent great connectedness to yourself and others." This move is more aligned with partners, but the theory is the same.

He opens his eyes but doesn't move his hand, and we stare at each other, just breathing in the peaceful morning for a moment. Lifting his other hand, he places it over mine, which is covering my own heart, and my breathing changes.

"Like this?" he asks, his gaze burning into mine, and I swallow roughly.

"Yes, like this," I say, mirroring his movement, placing my own palm onto the back of his hand where it lays on his chest. Our soul gazing turns into a hands-on heart circuit. These movements have gravitated from general meditation to the beginnings of Tantric sex methods, something I haven't studied at length, but I know the basics, even if I've never tried.

"The heart chakra is one of the most vulnerable chakras and can be easily wounded by emotional pain or loss. Sometimes, we hold on to things for a long period of time and deep breathing and heart connection helps alleviate those feelings. The heart chakra is also the center of our ability to love and be loved," I murmur, feeling connected, as one, the emotions I'm feeling growing in intensity.

As we sit here in the quiet, looking into each other's eyes, I can feel the pure life force emanating from him. Tantric sex is often shared in a sacred place, something partners do to connect on deeper levels. It's intimate, bringing the fire of sexual energy, passion, and desires into alignment with your heart and your spirit. This connection makes sex healing, empowering, transcendent, and profoundly beautiful. The kind of lovemaking that feels *truly* connected, aligned, massively powerful, and filled with the utmost respect and devotion.

Connor and I haven't had sex, but the connection I feel to him right now is overwhelming and almost too much. My body tingles, my heart races, and my need for him becomes undeniable.

"Let the love that's in your heart shine out through your eyes." My meditative state is still talking as our gaze on each other doesn't waver. It's raw, emotional, and like nothing else I've experienced. I feel like I'm baring my soul to him, showing him everything inside of me, not hiding a thing. Trusting him to keep it safe. In return, I feel his strong, masculine energy emitting from him, his protectiveness, his emotions, all of it. I watch his Adam's apple bob as he swallows, seeming just as affected by this as me.

"This feels special, Daise," he whispers, the cute nickname making me feel even more connected.

"It is special, Connor," I whisper back as we take a few more deep breaths. If this was a Tantric sex moment, the movement would begin to change. I would probably sit on his lap. Our hands would start exploring, maybe our lips would start trailing each other's skin. Just thinking about it sets my skin on fire, has my heart racing and my pussy pulsing. I clear my throat, bringing myself back into the moment and allowing us time to refocus on the here and now. Lowering my hand from his chest, he trails his down my arm slowly, electrical current pinging from my skin before he grabs my hand and gives it a squeeze.

"That was..." he starts to say, mouth parting, then closing. It's confirmation this has affected him. My mind is clear, my body humming, centered around my one true north, which, right now, is Connor.

"Meditation can take many different forms. Mostly, it's about quieting the mind and deep breathing techniques, but sometimes it can feel spiritual, intense, different." I'm still trying to understand it all myself. In all my years of meditation and yoga, both in class environments or with my previous one-on-one coaching, I've never experienced anything like that. My mind's a little frazzled.

"I liked it. I liked doing it with you," he admits, grinning as he entwines our fingers together, resting our joined hands on my knee. My stomach flutters at his openness, the way his simple touch feels.

He starts to stand, pulling me up with him as we both begin to feel our own bodies again. It isn't lost on me that neither of us has let go of the other's hand. I don't want to, and he doesn't look like he's in a hurry either.

He smiles as he looks down at me. "So... um... Connor gave you some paperwork earlier in the week... Do you have any questions about it?" he asks, and my brow furrows in confusion at the sharp pivot of the conversation back to work topics.

"Paperwork?" I think of all those contracts and forms sitting on my desk before I remember Sawyer passing that folder to me.

"Sawyer said he gave it to you..."

"Oh yes! Sorry, it's at the bottom of my pile of contracts. He said it wasn't urgent, so I haven't even looked at it," I tell him, now wondering if it *was* more urgent and I've messed up somehow.

"Damn Sawyer," he grumbles as he grabs his beard, something I notice he does at times.

"I can look at it today. Is that okay?" I offer, planning to get through some work on the weekend anyway.

"It's fine. Take a look on Monday," he says with a slight shake of his head, looking almost deflated. "I need to go. Thanks for the yoga session, Daisy." A sweet smirk curls his lips as he squeezes my hand before walking back to his place, swiping his shoes and shirt from the ground mid-step.

"You're very welcome..." I whisper, in a daze as I watch him go, my body still buzzing from what we just experienced together. I think it's time to do more research on Tantric sex.

22

CONNOR

I'm buzzing. I have no idea how she does it, but every time I'm with Daisy, my stress lowers, my need for her grows, and I ache for her like no other. Yoga with her on the weekend has emphasized that feeling, and even though Mondays are usually frantic, I'm killing it today. I own the day. Like, *own the fucking day*. I have been on fire at work for hours, finalizing overseas orders, getting our new product into branding, and even with Lacy not here at the moment and my workload doubled, I'm getting things done quicker than we would if she were here.

"Why do you have a spring in your step?" my dad asks as he walks into my office, taking a seat in the armchair and leaning back, relaxing, watching me.

"I'm having a good day is all," I tell him simply, barely able to keep the smile off my face. I have no idea what Daisy and I did on the weekend. Maybe it was some of her voodoo magic, but sitting on the fucking grass, holding her heart in my palm, like I was a fourteen-year-old boy again, was a moment I want more of. I've never done anything like that before. Sure, it was somewhat calming, got my mind off work, and I was able to relax. But it also gave me a raging hard-on, a new understanding for connectedness, and an appreciation for the work she does in this wellness space she seems to love so much.

It threw me at first, because I wasn't really sure what I was doing. I didn't want to be awkward or have her look at me like I wasn't capable, but then when I got hold of my racing thoughts and felt her heartbeat under my skin, all I could feel was charged. Charged for her. It was a good test of my self-control, one which I think I mastered well. Although I had to leave her almost immediately after; otherwise, I would have kissed her again. That and the fact that she hadn't even seen the contract yet had me tangled in a bundle of nerves like never before. I'm not ashamed to say I called Sawyer straightaway to confront him over telling her it wasn't urgent. All he did was laugh at me, like a schoolboy who couldn't control his giggling, leaving me even more frustrated and him with too much ammunition on me. But I will pay him back. I didn't want to push her on it, so I left her thinking it wasn't too urgent, preferring that she reads it through in her own time. Now, as I run my hand down my beard, I feel jumpy, nervous, wondering when she'll sign it, or if she'll sign it at all.

"Our crops are dead, our bottling machine needs a major overhaul, and I just spoke to Lacy. She's going to be away for a little longer than we first thought. What the hell is good about any of that?" he grumbles like the grumpy old man he is, and I grin.

"Yeah, but I've got a plan for new crops, bottling will only be down another day because I'm flying in a new engineer from Germany to take a look at it, and don't worry about Lacy's workload. I've got it." I'm feeling cocky and pumped. Pumped for more yoga with the woman down the hall. One who may end up in a downward dog of my own creation.

Dad's eyes narrow on me. "You organized that all this morning?"

"Yeah, I was up early, went for a run, did some yoga on the weekend that had me feeling good, too, so I started work early." Now that he lives on his new ranch, he isn't in as early as he used to be.

"Yoga?" My dad's eyebrows shoot to his hairline.

Fuck, probably should have skipped that detail.

"Yeah, just some meditation... mindfulness..." I say, fobbing it off like it's nothing, but like a shark that smells blood in the water, my dad smiles.

"Oh, meditation, huh?" he asks, a shit-eating grin on his face, and I shake my head.

"It's good for stress." I try to tame his humorous thoughts.

"Well, hell, I'm feeling pretty stressed. Maybe I should get up early tomorrow and come join you—"

"No," I cut him off, sounding like an overprotective asshole, but I don't care. Dad starts laughing at me. I know he's deliberately trying to get under my skin, but there's no way that Daisy is doing anything like we did on the weekend with another man. It was raw, it was vulnerable. It was one big foreplay session that I couldn't finish and that has now made me so worked up that my energy is firing into work because there's no other way to let it go. Not until she signs that contract, then we might have a different outcome.

"No? I'm sure Daisy would like to teach others her ways. I heard it's something that requires a lot of flexibility?" Dad continues, and I grind my teeth. Maybe I'm already too possessive. But hell, I want time with Daisy all to myself for as long as I can get it.

"You'll just have to wait for the classes to start then," I tell him with a shrug.

"Classes?" he quizzes.

"Yeah, I thought Daisy could stay on a bit longer, run some regular classes, you know, for the staff as a free benefit, and maybe even for the townspeople and community." I only thought of it this morning, but I'm trying hard to think of anything that might get her to stay a little longer. As it is, she's now staying on for the full two-month term. The spa, although going well, isn't going to be ready for her to leave at the end of a month's time. Something I'm secretly happy about, even if it pushes our plans back a little.

"So only you get the one-on-one attention, then? Teacher's pet?"

I shake my head. He's letting me off easy. The times I made fun of him when he was courting Victoria, he has so much payback to deliver, but deep down, I don't care.

I'm doing all I can to stop grinning like a fool about the thought of it all myself.

"What's going on between the two of you?" he asks seriously, watching me.

"Nothing." It's as honest as I can be right now.

"But you want there to be something, right?" he asks, and I look him in the eye. I can't lie to him. He's my dad but also my best friend. We've been through a lot together, so I nod, remaining tight-lipped.

"Are you concerned about the business? The working arrangement?"

I lean back in my chair, not expecting this conversation, yet here we are.

"Yeah. It's something to consider. But I had Sawyer draw up a contract that protects her and the business." I'm a smart businessman. I've seen too many companies go through negative press or legal consequences because their leaders couldn't keep it in their pants. I don't want to be like that, and I don't want to make her feel uncomfortable. Hell, kissing her was already a step too far. But if she signs this contract, then I'll know where to take things. And I'm hoping I can take her—in the shower, in my bed, on the desk here in my office. I look down at the desk, already imagining her perfect voluptuous body and wondering how she'll jiggle as I thrust into her.

"Did she sign it?" he asks. My gaze flicks to his, and he nods in understanding. My expression must be as pained as I feel.

"So that's what's eating you alive, then? She hasn't signed it. How does she feel about it all?" His eyes narrow.

I want to tell him that she feels fucking fantastic in my arms. That her body when I pull her close fits just right. That I'm insanely attracted to her brain as well as her beauty. That her sassy personality that comes through lights a fire in me that I haven't felt before.

"I think we're aligned," I tell him the safest thing I can without spewing my true thoughts.

"I've never seen you this worked up about a woman before."

I swallow roughly. "Maybe she's drugged my tea," I say cheekily, and he huffs a laugh.

"Maybe you've just been waiting for the right one," he comments, and my smile softens at his serious tone.

"No other woman has made this impression on me, that's for sure."

I'm no saint. I've dated and bedded a lot of women. But that's all it's ever been. For years, I've played the field. Lived a life that most men envy. But never having that connection, that feeling of being linked to someone for more than just a physical release. Daisy provides that, but more. I can already envision talking to her about business decisions, helping each other through difficult times, and leaning on each other. The feeling of dependability I get with her is something I haven't felt with a woman before, ever. I can trust her. Explicitly.

"Just make smart decisions," Dad says, all jokes now gone. We think similarly, so I know he's now thinking about the business ramifications of the situation.

I nod, a small smirk coming to my face just thinking about her.

"Oh, my boy, I live to see the day!" he yells before

slapping the doorframe and walking out, and I look at my watch. It's now well into the afternoon, and I still haven't seen or heard from my sexy yoga instructor.

What will I do about these feelings if she doesn't sign those papers?

23

DAISY

I look at the folder on my desk, the one housing the contract that I've read three times over. I haven't seen Connor since our yoga session on the weekend. He's clearly giving me space after our heated exchange, and now this contract is now all I can think about. But my body is fully in her feminine energy, and if I could be any animal right now, it would be a sex kitten. Maybe even a crazed sex kitten, because I'm on edge.

"So you loved the rose quartz?" my mom asks, and I shake my head and focus back on our conversation. I haven't spoken to her and Dad for almost a week, and I miss them terribly.

"Mom, it's so beautiful. I have no idea where Soren got it, but it's huge," I tell her, smiling as my eyes flick to the large pink rock on my desk. It sits firm, solid, a thing of pure beauty.

"They have a few around my old commune, which is up that way," she says, and I frown.

"Soren mentioned he was going there. How come you never told me about it?" I ask her.

"There isn't much to say about it, really. I grew up there as a child, then left when I was in my late teens. Met your father on the road, and the rest is history." She says the same words she's told me throughout the years, but unlike the other times, a question pops into my mind about it.

"Why did you leave the commune?" I ask her, intrigued. I wonder if I could find it if I looked. Maybe Soren would take me. For no other reason than to see where Mom grew up and what it's like.

"It was just my time, honey. My journey there was over, and I was led onto a different path." The way she says it almost sounds cryptic, so I drop it, resigned to never knowing further details.

"So, I have all our teas here. They look great on the shelf in the new spa," I tell her, smiling, because seeing our brand of tea on a retail shelf that we don't own was one of my earlier goals. I'm so proud to have them stocked here at Whitemans I could almost burst.

"Oh, you mentioned that the chamomile grows well up there. You should try making a few new ones."

"Already thinking about it. They have a great herb garden, plus they have their own hives for honey," I tell her, getting excited about the new possibilities. Although I'm bereft when I think about my time here coming to an end soon.

"I would say you should stay on, play around with mixing some new elixirs, but your father says just take the cash and come home. He misses you."

It's true, the consultation rates I'm being paid by Whiteman's are well over and above anything we made at the shop. I've already received half of my monthly fee in my account. It's the most money I've ever had in my life, and I had to refresh my screen three times before I could believe it was real.

"Can you tell Dad I will email him tomorrow? I want to start putting some into my 401k," I tell her.

"Pfft, don't give anything to the government," Mom says, dismissing me with one of her old hangups from commune days.

"That's smart, honey," Dad yells out from the background, and I laugh, wondering how in the world they actually make their relationship work when they're so opposite.

"So how is that big hunk of spunk?" Mom teases, and I cough out a laugh.

"Mom!"

"Rainbow! I heard that!" My dad usually calls her Rain or Rainy, but whenever she's in trouble, he uses her full name.

"Well, that's what Trisha called him," Mom justifies with a chuckle.

"Have you been speaking to Trisha?" I ask her.

"Yes, she came over last night to grab some dahl."

My mouth waters just thinking about it. "I'm craving your dahl..." I tell her, and she laughs.

"You'll get some soon enough."

We talk for a few more moments before we end the call, with me slightly homesick and craving dahl and she and Dad in a deep conversation about Mom's lack of a 401k.

I look out the window, seeing it's dark out, not realizing that I've been so busy all day that I barely noticed the time. I pack up my office and look at the folder with the contract again. I signed it this morning. I signed it after the first read. I barely had to think twice. I know he's notorious for his dating life, if the search online that Trisha and I did back in New York is anything to go by. But the Connor I'm getting to know here in Whispers is nothing like his paparazzi presence makes him out to be. Other than being devastatingly handsome and a whiskey tycoon, since those things remain true.

It was my disbelief about it all that made me read it two more times, just to ensure I was reading it right. It took me by surprise. When he mentioned a contract, I was thinking it was something to do with the spa, but when I opened it and started to read, a whirl of emotions ran through me. Is it even real? What does it all mean? Does Connor Whiteman like me? Shock and disbelief turned into certainty and a signature pretty quickly. I'm not sure what's going to happen, or if anything will, but I do know that for the first time in a long time, he's a man who I'm acutely aware of and he's starting to infiltrate most of my thoughts. The way he moves around the office with this arrogant yet charming allure. The way he talks, committed to his thoughts, steadfast in his approach to business. Obviously, after we kissed, things became a little clearer to both of us. Tempted is too loose of a word for what we're feeling toward each other. It feels deeper than that.

Is it hormones? Just sexual expression? Will we have each other once, and then the fire will go out? Is it the fact that I'm away, here in Whispers, and living essentially a new life that has me feeling more carefree than I ordinarily would? Like when you go on holiday and throw all caution to the wind. I don't know exactly, but I do know it feels different. I want him to touch me all over, including the parts of my body that I usually wouldn't be confident with, like my soft tummy and thicker thighs. I want to kiss him, feel his hands grab me again, let his tongue explore some more, and if we need a legal document signed in order for us to discover whatever burning feelings we're currently dabbling in, then sign me up.

Everything Connor has outlined in the contract is all beneficial to me. My job and full salary and benefits were protected. If something happens, and I choose to leave immediately, I'll be paid out and given a full reference and letters of support. There was a confidentiality clause and clear lines of communication outlined. But I don't need any of that. I know Connor is a good man, and just like I told him at the mineral springs, I'm an adult, and I know what I want.

So with that thought in mind, I grab the folder and walk out of my office, knowing that everyone has left for the day, yet I'm acutely aware that the only person besides me who works this late and is remaining in the office is the man himself. The two of us are more alike than we probably care to admit.

I stride down the hall, seeing darkness around me, except for the glow of his office light, and I pause in his doorway, as I can hear other voices. He's on a call, the other people on speaker as he sits back, looking at his screen intently. His eyes are focused, his fingers running back and forth across his lip as he takes in whatever they're talking about. He hasn't noticed me, so deep in concentration, so I walk into his office quietly, not sure if I'm overstepping, but his door was wide open.

As I do, he looks up and a small grin dances on his face at seeing me, then he leans back in his large leather chair. He looks like a king ruling over his kingdom as his eyes flick to the folder, and then back to me, before they travel down my front and back up again, like he's surveying something he desires. My hips sway a little more than usual, the flowing, corporate appropriate dress I wore today, skimming my curves, and by the look on his face, he appreciates it.

Remaining tight-lipped, I move straight to the side of his desk, standing close to him but just out of reach. His eyes burn into me the entire way. I place the folder down in front of him, and his eyebrows rise as I stand and wait. My heart is thudding. I've never done anything like this before. I don't know the rules; workplace romances are things I've only read about or seen on TV. He leans forward, opening the folder and flicking through the pages until he gets to the last one and sees both our signatures on it. Before I can even digest what's happening, he stands abruptly and grabs my waist, pulling me to him like I'm his lifeline, and smashes his lips into mine.

It's unexpected, but my gasp is swallowed by his mouth as his hand wraps around the nape of my neck. My brain finally fires into action as I grip on to his shirt and hold him to me, my body now aching for his touch.

His beard is a little scratchy. I've never kissed a man with so much facial hair before. It's not harsh, but rather soft and thick, and I lift my hands to cup his face, wanting to touch it.

He pulls back slightly before lowering his lips to my ear. His warm breath dances across my skin as he whispers, "Can you be quiet, baby girl?"

My heart races as I nod, having lost the ability to speak. *Baby girl.* God, I think my underwear melted right off my body just with his words.

The men on the other end of the conference call start talking about crops and harvests as Connor grabs my waist and lifts me onto his desk with ease. I hold my breath. This is the second time he's lifted me, and as he places my butt on the edge of his very nice, very sturdy timber desk, he stands tall in front of me, shoulders back, like he's proud to have me right where he wants me. I think back to the conversation I had with Trisha, where she talked about hot sex on his desk, and I swallow. *Um... yes, please.*

"I'm happy with that. Very happy," he says, his voice loud, and it takes me a minute to understand he's still taking part in the conference call, yet his eyes are firmly on me. I barely notice the conversation happening around us as the call moves on to the weather cycles, rain forecasted, and wild winds while he lowers, his face meeting mine, our lips a hair's breadth apart.

"No noise. Not a sound..." he whispers, and I smile as he leans forward an inch and takes my lips with his again. I should've been prepared. I mean, the few kisses we've shared have been all-encompassing. But as we lean against each other, our lips move like they know exactly what the other likes. It's sultry, all lips and tongue, tasting each other, his hands gripping into my hair and moving my head, positioning me exactly where he wants me to deepen our connection. Our hands start to roam then, discovering each other, and I run my palms up and down his torso, the feel of his hard chest underneath the soft silkiness of his business shirt a contradiction like nothing I've felt before. His large, warm hands smooth down my sides and back up, feeling like they cover most of my body, his thumb brushing across my nipple teasingly, and with every pass, I moan a little.

"Do you agree, Connor?" a man asks, and we both freeze. Connor pulls back, grinning at me.

"One hundred percent. Let's go with that option," he says, then he hits the mute button on his laptop and dives back in, his kiss getting more demanding. The woman in me purrs, my chest pushing out against his, my full feminine energy coming through as he moves his body so he's standing between my legs. I spread them wider for him, glad I wore a flowing dress to work today. His hands drop to the back of my knees, where he pulls me and slides me toward the edge of the desk, toward him, and I feel my core brush his. The heat we share, his hard length against me, makes my hips move, wanting more.

As his hands continue up my legs, he gathers the fabric of my dress, the material skirting up my bare legs, my skin feeling cool without coverage as he pushes it to my waist. He moves slowly, like he's waiting for me to stop him, but I'm too far gone.

"Don't stop..." I whisper against his mouth, telling

him I want it. I want more, I want him. My mind is mush, but my body is aching, desperate to feel more of him. I've lost all consideration for the workplace. The professional in me would tut at my behavior, seeing as I'm almost spread-eagle on my boss's desk, yet this feels like the most natural, safest interaction I've ever had with a man.

I'm almost shivering with need, and he acts like he has all the time in the world. Like there's no desire to get it over with and get back to his call. He caresses my skin, like he wants to memorize it, taking his time, all the while his lips continue to move demandingly over mine, brandishing me, and I know that I will feel this kiss for hours after it ends.

"Connor," I moan as I lean back on his desk on one hand while my other digs into the nape of his neck, pulling him closer. He leans over me, not separating our mouths, his hands gripping on to my waist.

"You feel good, baby girl... so fucking good in my arms," he growls low, and my pussy pulses at his words. I need to mine whatever is in the soil here in Whispers because the men around here are surely the eighth wonder of the world.

His lips move from my mouth down my neck and warmth spreads across my body as his beard tickles my skin, the friction a perfect tease as his palms mold my breasts. I've always been big-chested, and finding bras that fit plus look good and are comfortable is a constant challenge, so I've always hated my breasts. Until now.

"Fucking phenomenal..." I hear him murmur as his lips lower across my shoulders, his fingers getting busy undoing the buttons at the front of my dress and pulling the fabric to the side, baring my chest to him, my white bra now on full display. His movements quicken, like he suddenly can't hold back any longer, and my breaths turn to pants as my hips start to grind against his.

I lean farther back, my body arching like I'm doing a yoga pose as he pulls down the cups of my bra. My breasts tumble out, and I almost shudder as he moves quickly, taking a nipple into his mouth, swiping his tongue across before sucking.

"Ohhhh..." I moan, my head falling backwards, eyes closed, feeling his hard length pushing against my throbbing pussy. I hear him growl, the rumble from his chest turning me on even more as he sucks my skin, pushing my breasts together, his fingers digging in, his tongue and mouth giving both nipples attention.

"A breast man?" I pant, not recognizing the sound of my own voice, enjoying the sensation of having a man devouring me like this.

"A breast man, an ass man..." he says as his hands move down my body, and he palms my butt cheeks, pulling them to him and grinding me into him. The feeling of him controlling the friction over his hard length takes my breath away before he latches on to one nipple and sucks hard, grabbing both my breast and my ass. I gasp and look at him, seeing a wicked gleam in his eye.

With our eyes hooked on each other's, I feel his hand move across my body and slowly slide across my hip, under the fabric of my dress.

"A pussy man..." he adds, tone like gravel, and I

swallow as his fingers gently swipe across the outside of my underwear, and I nod.

"Yes... please," I tell him, sounding embarrassingly needy, not knowing if he's asking, but telling him I want more.

"Fuck, Daisy, you're so wet." With a groan, his lips crash into mine, and I grab on to his shoulders as he rubs me.

"More, Connor, more," I pant against his lips, wondering what's happening to my voice and how I've become a porn star all of a sudden. I guess this is what happens when a man showers you in lust like you've never experienced before. I'm usually quiet with men. Letting them lead. Most experiences I've had were missionary, never feeling comfortable to explore anything else and them not really wanting me on top or to do anything remotely exciting. But with Connor, my true self seems to come out, and I can't help it.

I want him, and I want him to do everything with me.

When I feel his hand swipe beneath the material of my underwear, his fingers hitting my center, I almost explode just from the simple touch.

"Such a good girl for signing the contract, Daisy. We're going to have so much fun together," he murmurs, and if this is the kind of fun he's thinking, then sign me up a million times over.

"Yes... oh God, yes," I moan as his finger plays with me, teasingly slow, achingly tantalizing.

"Hmmmm, are you a greedy girl? Tell me what you want, baby girl." His accent is thick in this moment, purring against my lips, and I'm about ten seconds from losing myself to this man.

"You... I want... you," I pant. The men on the phone are still talking, their conversation a very distant distraction as my breaths quicken, my orgasm building.

"God, I want to fuck you every way I know how... Your pussy is so wet for me. I'm never going to be able to look at this desk without wanting you spread out naked for me to enjoy like this," he says as he slides a finger inside of me, and I gasp. His mouth is on mine in an instant, swallowing my moans, capturing my whimpers as he slides a second finger in, then pulls them out, rubbing them against my clit and then doing the same move over and over again.

"That feels so good," I groan as my fingers dig into his hair, pulling his head to me harder, not wanting any space between us. If anyone was to walk in right now, they would certainly get a sight. My breasts are still out, pushed against his chest, my dress half-open, legs spread for him. He's still fully dressed, although his hair is disheveled and his hand is in my underwear, but I care very little at this point as I run my other hand down his torso until I hit his belt buckle.

"I want to feel you," I tell him as I rub my hand on the outside of his trousers. He's big and rock-hard, all for me.

"Mm, I want that too, but not now. Now, it's just about you." His movements speed up, and he rubs my clit harder.

"Oh shit..." I gasp, never experiencing anything like this. "Connor..." My release is so close. I don't think I've ever come so fast or so easily under someone else's touch.

"That's it, baby girl. Come for me... on my fingers... right here on my desk. Let go for me."

Moaning, I slap my hands on the desk behind me, leaning back on both hands, letting him play me like he wants to. His fingers continue rubbing my clit, and his head lowers, taking my nipple in his mouth again and biting. That's all I need to let go.

"Connor!" I gasp, holding back the scream tearing through me. My legs shake, the orgasm so intense my mind goes blank. I do as he asks and come on his fingers, right here on his desk, during his business call. The emotions are thick, my body humming, and I wonder if this is all a dream. I swallow as I slowly come back to earth, Connor continuing to kiss up my throat to my mouth before he pulls back slightly to look into my eyes.

I grin, in a total daze, and he smiles.

"Best damn conference call I've had in a while," he says as he moves his hand from my center and brings his fingers to his lips, sucking me from his skin. I watch, enraptured. It's at this moment I know that the contract I signed earlier was the best decision I've ever made.

24

CONNOR

I can barely get her out of my mind.

After hearing her moans on my desk last night, I kissed her for what felt like all night until I had another conference call with our international supply chain that I couldn't miss and had to actually participate in. So I buttoned her up and watched her walk away from me, out of my office and down the hall to the garden path, then from my window until she walked inside her accommodations.

Now as I pound the ground, I nearly race to get to the hedge that surrounds our homes so I can see her doing her yoga this morning. I wonder if she's wearing the black or red matching set, then thinking about how good she looks in green and wondering if she'll let me peel it from her body and suck on her perfect breasts like last night. God, I could die happy just kissing her body.

But as I turn around the hedge, the little grassy patch that she's made her own these past few weeks is empty. I slow my steps, walking toward her area, panting as I cool down from my run. Looking around, I can't see her. I wipe the sweat from my brow with my t-shirt, before peeling it from my body and tucking it into my shorts, then walk to the house, wondering if she's in a different space today.

The garden on the other side is empty, as is the kitchen garden she seems to like so much. Frowning, I walk through the offices, seeing no one here yet. All the lights are still off and her office sits empty. My panic grows as I notice the spa is still locked up without lights on, and I pull out my cell, checking our shared work diary to see if she had to go to some kind of early meeting I didn't know about. But there's nothing scheduled. She should be doing yoga, should be out enjoying the sunrise.

Pacing back to our homes, I see her curtains still drawn, and for anyone else, that wouldn't cause concern because it's still early, but for Daisy, it's odd. She loves to see the sunrise. She could've slept in, but the sun has been up for a while now, and it's very out of character. For the entire time she's been here, she's always up early. Even on Sundays. I can't help the feeling inside that starts to fester. Did something happen? Is she okay? I've never cared enough about a woman before to know how to handle the ache in my chest at the thought. My eyes scan everywhere I can think of, but I can't find her.

I step up to her porch and knock on the door, softly at first, but as I wait, my skin tingles, something not feeling right. I don't know why I feel overprotective of her. Hell, she's dynamite, beautiful, funny, smart, but we've only just met, and I don't know where this will all lead. But as the quietness stretches, my unease increases.

"Daisy?" I yell, knocking on the door again before I try the handle, and it opens almost instantly.

"Shit," I murmur, my heart now racing, wondering why her door isn't locked, and I open it a fraction to peek inside. Fear consumes me, as does anger that someone may have gotten to her. My thoughts are not rational, I know this, but I'm too far gone now to even start to rein them back in. I have morning meetings, so I should be hitting the shower and getting to work, but all that's on my mind now is finding Daisy and making sure she's alright.

"Daisy?" I yell a little louder, but again, nothing. I take a quick look around. Nothing is out of place, and there are no signs of a struggle, but I have no idea where she is. We're pretty secure here at the distillery, but nothing is a hundred percent. I think about where she could be, and my chest hurts as I wonder if she's fallen and hurt herself, hit her head, or is in pain. Those thoughts spur me on, and I stalk down the hall, checking every room.

"Daisy?" I stop short as I hear a noise, something akin to a muffle, although it's soft, barely audible. The walls are thick in this house, with soundproofing something we invested in, due to being so close to the distillery.

"Shit. Daisy?" Slight panic takes over my tone as my pace quickens. I look down the hallway, spotting all bedroom doors open except one. All logical thinking now out the window, my brain expects to find her tied up or murdered on the bed, and I throw the door open and lunge inside.

Nothing could have prepared me for what I'm seeing.

"Connor!" she pants, her beautiful naked body

splayed out on the large bed, legs spread wide, cheeks flushed, and a fucking pink vibrator in her hand. Desire thrums through my veins as I look her over, her large breasts rising and falling quickly as she starts to close her legs and grab the blanket.

"Don't you stop," I grit out, swallowing hard as my eyes remain glued to her. I fist my hands. The effort it's taking me not to take another step toward her is intense. Instant relief that she's safe now mixes with a ferocious need to have her right here and right now. I swallow hard, my heart thudding and my temperature heating. Lifting the t-shirt from my waistband, I throw it on the floor.

"What?" she pants, her body frozen in shock, no doubt, her hands still between her legs, bare pussy on full fucking display.

"Don't you fucking stop," I repeat, letting myself step forward. The only other sound in the room is the slight buzz of her pleasure toy.

"Oh God..." she says breathily, clearly in the moment. Her cheeks blush as she holds the blanket tight in one hand, the vibrator in the other, and she starts to cover herself.

"Don't cover your beautiful body. Let go of the blanket, spread those legs wider, and fucking show me how you touch yourself, baby girl..." My nostrils flare as I try to take in the oxygen I need. I approach her slowly, like I'm approaching a wild or injured animal. Ready to pounce, but not wanting to scare her.

Her eyes latch on mine, and whatever she sees has her releasing the blanket. Then her knees part again, legs falling open wider. Now I'm really able to appreciate all her yoga work; her flexibility is visually delicious. My eyes drop to her glistening bare center as her hand moves, placing her battery friend back into place at her clit, and her immediate gasp has me falling to the floor, my knees buckling.

"That's it..." I groan, my running shorts tented as I walk on my knees to the edge of the bed, closer to her parted legs.

"Connor," she hiccups, still in shock and almost overcome by her orgasm. I can tell she's close, her breaths rapid, her toes starting to curl, the skin of her chest flushing deeper.

"Mmmmm. Fuck, Daise," I say, palming myself. I'm so fucking hard I can barely stand it. I have no idea what voodoo this woman has over me. But she's fast becoming my obsession, and I barely have any control over myself when it comes to her.

"Baby girl, look at how fucking pretty you are," I tell her, in awe of the beauty surrounded by ruffled bedsheets, her vibrant red hair flowing over the pillow.

"I need more," she pants the invitation, and I pause. I want to watch. I want to watch her come. I don't want my eyes to leave this sight that I've stumbled upon, but my mouth waters. I had a small taste of her last night, but not enough to savor, and I almost growl thinking about how good it was. Now her flavor is all I fucking think about.

"More?" I ask as I move closer, swallowing roughly, barely keeping it together as I drop my shorts, peeling them off, my raging dick so hard I think I'm going to come just from the visual. I palm my length, hot and heavy in my hand, my balls so fucking full, I need to clench my jaw.

She doesn't realize it, but the room she's chosen to sleep in was once mine. My teenage self never predicted this scenario, though, but I'm sure I imagined it in my dreams many times all those years ago.

"Oh God, Connor..." Biting her bottom lip, her back arches slightly, equal parts frustrated by my slow movements to get to her and still so turned on that she can't stop herself. I watch her move her toy over her clit, and every time she does, her breath catches, offering me a whimper that does something to my insides.

"You want my mouth, Daise?" I ask her, the words barely audible, my chest heaving.

"Yes, God, yesssss. Please, please, please..." she begs, just as I meet the end of the bed. I kiss her ankle, my hands running up her bare legs. Her skin is so soft, I can't stop touching her, and I lean forward, my mouth leaving lazy kisses to the inside of her thigh. Working my way up, I put my hand on hers, pushing her toy around with her as I lower my mouth and slowly lick along her folds.

She moans, sounding relieved, as I do it again, savoring the taste of her while our fingers connect on her toy. The vibrations on her clit continue as I lick her, and her other hand digs into my hair, pushing my head down. I grin against her wetness. My girl likes my head in her pussy, which is good, because I fucking love being here just as much.

"Yes, Connor... Yes. You're gonna make me come," she pants, and I suck and lick as her hips start to grind over my mouth. Her pussy quivering, her hand gripping in my hair, she comes with my fucking name on her lips.

As she removes the vibrator, panting, her hands scramble to find me, and I move up, sucking her swollen, sensitive clit. She gasps as both her hands dig into my hair and scratch my scalp. My dick's weeping for her.

"What are you doing here?" she whispers as I kiss up her body, her fucking fantastic hips, the small hill of her soft tummy, to her amazing breasts. Her hands caress my back, the feeling of her bare skin against mine almost too much for me to handle.

"I didn't see you at yoga. I looked everywhere, and I got worried." I tell her the truth, in between nipping at her skin, my lips unable to leave her body. As her hands move up and down my back, her nails leave a slight scratch that makes my chest rumble. We're now both naked, my clothes long forgotten on the floor somewhere.

"So you just walk into my house? Ever heard of knocking?" she asks, and I hear the slight teasing sass that I'm grateful for. That was crazy for me to do. When I look up at her, she's smiling.

"You need to lock your door," I murmur, kissing up her chest, across her beautiful breasts to her neck, and she sighs. Her legs relax and part even more for me, my body right on top of hers, yet not resting on her. Not yet. I hold my weight on my hands and knees, still looking over this vision underneath me.

"Maybe I like you coming inside," she says coyly as her fingers travel to my chest, her nails leaving their mark as a sexy-as-sin look takes over her face.

I nudge her nose with mine, just as her fingers scrape

down my hips, and I feel her hand grab my dick. With a growl, my lips meet hers. I suck on her tongue as she palms my cock, stroking me, feeling all of me as I try very fucking hard not to come in her hands.

"What are you doing, baby girl?" I ask, my voice rumbling over her parted lips.

"My turn to taste you," she says as her leg hooks around my back, and I let her push me to the side and onto my back as she straddles me.

I wasn't ready for this sight. Her naked body sitting on top of mine. Not wanting to miss seeing any part of her, I run my hands down her bare thighs as hers move down my torso again before palming me, rubbing her thumb over the tip of my cock, where pre-cum has started to build.

Understanding washes over me that I'm going to miss my conference call this morning, and probably the meeting after that as well. But I don't care, because all I can think about is her.

25

DAISY

I don't know who this Daisy is or where she came from, but I'm liking her. I've never straddled a man before. Hell, I've never sat on anyone's knee either. But Connor looking up at me is giving me the confidence I need. As is his hard-on. I can't stop touching him.

"You keep playing with me like that, baby girl, and I have no idea what's going to happen..." He groans, thrusting his hips up a little, lifting me from the bed an inch. *Baby girl.* There's that nickname again, and I almost melted into a puddle on the floor at hearing it. I thought it was just in movies. Cute nicknames that also sound hot as hell, given to you from a man who looks like he wants to own your body just like he owns this town.

"I like touching you," I whisper, wondering if it feels like this for everyone, and all these years, I've been missing out. We haven't even had sex yet, but we're so comfortable with each other.

"I like it too. But why don't you turn around, baby girl,

and bring your fine ass to my face. Let me taste you again. That way, we can both play."

I almost choke. He just had his head buried between my legs not five minutes ago. I still tingle where his beard teased my thighs, already wanting more.

His hands don't stop as they run up and down my bare thighs and he watches me carefully, no doubt wondering what I will do. My heart pounds. I've never done a 69 before, but my body is on autopilot as I start to move.

"Good girl," he murmurs, a satisfied smirk on his face, as I turn and his hands find my waist. He holds me tight, pulling me toward his mouth, and I shuffle down the bed, excited, nervous, and turned on all at the same time.

"Bring your pussy to my mouth. Let me eat."

I think I almost die as his hands grip around my thick thighs, palming my ass, and he pulls my hips, doing exactly that. I rest down on my hands and knees, not wanting to put my full weight on him, but not able to stop him when he seals my front to his, and I feel his tongue lick me again.

"Ohhh..." I moan as his beard touches my clit. Looking at him hard and thick in my face, I grab on to his length, putting my lips around his tip and sucking, which enlists a deep rumble from him that vibrates onto my pussy. It feels good, so I do it again.

I take him in a little more and get lost in the moment. The two of us tasting, sucking, discovering each other. This is by far the hottest experience I've ever had. My body is now fully relaxed, and I take him deeper down my throat. If our yoga session yesterday was the start of

Tantric sex, then this is well within the depths of it. The way we're discovering each other, needy, but refraining almost like we know as soon as we let go, it will be explosive. Cupping his balls, I suck on the way up, hungry for him.

"Fuck, like that, Daise. Baby girl, just like that."

I keep up the movement and rhythm as his tongue swipes across my already sensitive clit, my orgasm not far away at all. His beard scratches my inner thighs a little, almost teasingly so. Then his hands are moving, traveling across my back and up to my hair. He gathers it up, the length easy for him to hold, then pulls it a little. As he does, my head tilts back a mere inch, and his hips thrust up into my mouth, just as he licks me from my clit to my opening and flicks his tongue inside me. He does it again and again, the two of us now completely gone for each other as I feel my skin start to tingle and he thickens even more in my mouth.

"Connor!" I gasp as he latches on to my clit tight, and stars explode in my eyes as I come hard and fast. My throat relaxes as I moan, and he slides into my mouth one last time before he's coming too. I swallow it down, my head almost dizzy with satisfaction.

I can barely move, and he's in no hurry to move me as his hands run up and down my back again, and he peppers kisses to my inner thighs.

"Hmmmm, I should've had that contract drawn up weeks ago," he murmurs, and I grin as I roll over and turn to look at him.

"Weeks ago, huh?" I ask teasingly, feeling happy, both physically and mentally.

"We could've been enjoying each other a hell of a lot sooner."

He's wanted me for a while, our push-and-pull from when we met now making sense.

"Well, we'll just have to enjoy each other for the time we have left," I tell him. Because whether I like it or not, I'm on a deadline here. Sure, the spa delivery project has blown out a few more weeks, so I'll be here longer than we first thought, but after that, no more job, no more Whispers, and no more Connor.

That thought gives me pause. It isn't like I knew this would happen and hell, we've only just fallen into bed with each other. It isn't like something like this can last. We're clearly totally different people. He probably pours whiskey on his cereal for breakfast, and mine consists of almond milk and organic quinoa. I mean, what are we now? Fuck buddies? It feels intimate, the most intimate I've ever been with anyone. But I can't let my thoughts get too big. I need to remember what Trisha said. *It isn't love, Daisy, just hot, sweaty sex on his desk...*

With that, I grab the blanket, wanting to shield my body, the high from my orgasm now diminishing.

"Don't shy away from me," he says, leaning over, his large hand skimming across my soft tummy and pulling me toward him. "I fucking love your body." With a rumbling groan, his warm palm continues to roam over my skin, keeping me close as his words coat my insides, building back up the confidence I once lost. I look at him, his delicious grin, his eyes sparkling, and there's no regret showing anywhere on his face. He isn't in a hurry to jump out of this bed, even though he's probably missing a meeting or a phone call or something. He isn't in a hurry to get away from me, even though he's sexually satisfied. Again, so different from any other man I've been with.

"Bossy in bed as well," I murmur playfully, a lazy smile spreading across my face as I give in to this and let myself enjoy it. After all, I was touching myself to thoughts of him before he bulldozed his way in here. I may as well enjoy this fantasy fully playing out.

"Yes. Now come here and give me that mouth," he says, and I don't know how, but even after two orgasms, my pussy pulses. And I listen without any hesitation, kissing him thoroughly.

My sexual awakening is starting, and Connor Whiteman is one hell of a teacher.

26

CONNOR

I need to research. I need to find some books, an academia article, a fucking podcast, because I have no idea how I'm meant to work with her all day and not touch her. After this morning, feeling the sexual chemistry between us, something that I never thought I would find with any woman, I now realize I'm completely smitten. Even more so than before. Yesterday in the office, she wore a long, flowing dress, and today, it's a tighter one. Black, the fabric following her curves, finishing at that sexy length just below the knees that shows off her hourglass figure like she's teasing me on purpose.

"So it's model day today," Daisy says as Dad, Victoria, and I sit around the boardroom, going over the project plan with her. If I had my way, we'd both still be in bed, naked. But with the spa project needing to be kept on track, meetings and issues to resolve, we had to peel ourselves off each other, the walk to my place the hardest one I've ever done.

The spa opening has been pushed out a bit, but I'm

thankful. Daisy would only have another week here if we had stuck to our original schedule, and that thought leaves a very bitter taste in my mouth.

"Model day?" I ask, looking around at them, wondering what I've missed.

"Ooooh, who's coming in?" Victoria asks, grinning.

"Again, what's model day?" I ask again, then look at Daisy.

"I have a few locals coming in to get the staff ready and trained, as well as to trial some of the treatments to get feedback. The team put it out on social media last week, so we might get a few new people to the distillery. But we need all kinds of people to see how it all works," she says, smiling, and I feel my brow furrow. I don't want her touching anyone but me. I know it's her job, but I still don't like it.

She grins at me with that saucy smirk, the one where she looks like she knows what I'm thinking. I know she doesn't, because if she did, she'd be flushed cherry red. I have to fist my hand under the table to prevent me from asking her to crawl on her knees to me in that fucking dress so I can peel it off her.

"Who's coming in?" I ask her, and I see my father frown, clearly not sure why I'm so invested in the information.

"So, there's Rochelle from the diner, and Tina, who I think is married to Tim from the toy store?" she says, unsure, but we all nod. We know Tina; she and Tim have lived in Whispers forever as well.

"Oh, and we have a small group that is going to try

out the springs, some yoga, and maybe a group meditation. Which I'll run," Daisy says.

"Griffin's team is working on the path, but it should be fine to use. Do you need me to go to the springs with you?" I ask, because now that I know she's heading back to the water, I'm uneasy.

"No, I'll be fine." There's a different kind of heat in her gaze now, not liking me raising the issue of her lack of swimming skills again. "Griffin is quick?" Daisy asks, surprised, moving the conversation on, while I wonder what time she's going to be down by the water and if I can move my meetings around to go with her. Knowing she can't swim makes panic prickle beneath my skin.

"Griffin is the best builder in the country. He has teams located everywhere and pretty much an office or supply factory in almost every state. He works quickly, does quality work, and he's in high demand," Dad explains.

"Wow, sounds like a busy guy," she quips and I smile, seeing her processing the information.

"You'll meet him soon. At the spa opening," I tell her, looking forward to introducing her to a few people she hasn't met yet. I make a mental note to see if Harrison might swing past, although I'm sure he'll be too busy, considering he's president of the country now and everything.

"Spa opening?" Daisy asks, looking blankly at all of us.

"Yeah, a party to celebrate the opening. I'm organizing it with the team. We didn't want you thinking about organizing a party when you're head down into getting the spa ready," Victoria says.

"Oh, fun!" Her giddy expression makes my chest clench in a way I'm not used to feeling.

"Okay, well, that's it for this morning. I think we have covered everything, and I see some people already arriving," Victoria says, and we all stand, looking out at the reception area, and sure enough, both Rochelle and Tina are there already.

"Let us know what the feedback is and if there are any major adjustments we need to make," Dad asks of Daisy.

She nods. "Of course. I'll make note of everything."

We watch him and Victoria walk out, going who knows where.

When they're out of sight, she turns and looks at me. "You need to stop that," she says, trying to act in control, when I know she's barely hanging on herself.

"Stop what?" I ask, playing dumb, walking over to her on the other side of the table.

She rolls her eyes. "Looking at me like that."

"Like what?" I ask with a taunting smirk as I stand tall and look down at her. There's pure lust in my gaze as she looks back at me, and I watch her swallow, clearly affected.

"Connor," she warns, her tone serious, yet I'm sure I could have her moaning in mere seconds.

"Daisy..." I say back to her, my hand reaching around her waist.

A sigh of exasperation leaves her lips, but she doesn't push me away. "We can't be like this at work. We need to be professional. What will people say?"

"I don't care what people say. In fact, I want to take you out tonight," I tell her, just thinking about it now.

"Out?" she asks, head tilting.

"Yeah, to the bar. We have a live band playing, so maybe I can get you to try my whiskey?" I tease, my thoughts already filthy all over again.

"If I say yes, will you stop looking at me like you've seen me naked?" she sasses, and I raise my eyebrows.

"Mmmmm, no. That's a visual I'm referring to every damn minute of every day, baby girl," I tell her, and she groans. Even though her lips curl just a tiny bit.

"Okay, I'm out of here; otherwise, I won't be able to concentrate."

"Before you go... here," I say, passing her the small parcel that I've had on my desk.

"What is it?" She looks it over before opening the wrapping paper.

"I bought you some inflatable armbands," I tell her quickly. My anxiety about her being at the springs today without me is already building. "I've only just met you. I don't want you drowning already."

"Water wings?" she asks, a small smile on her face, her eyes wide as she opens the parcel. "I promise you, Connor, I won't drown." Her tone is adamant, even as she waves one of the inflatable armbands around.

"Well, at least now I know you'll float," I tell her, and she rolls her eyes before grinning and walking out the door.

My eyes trail her until she's out of sight.

I walk out of my office on my way to the spa. My meetings have finished, and I've been on edge all day, wondering if Daisy made it to the springs and back in one piece. I know she did. I saw them all leave, Victoria with them, so I relaxed a little, knowing that she had a lot of people with her. Plus, she had her new armbands, which I hope she wore. But I still didn't like it.

"Oh, Connor," our young receptionist, Stephanie, says, and I pause mid-stride as I walk past her desk. "The man was back," she says, and I frown, trying to remember what she's talking about. But I have so many meetings and calls that it really could be anyone.

"Man?" I question, wondering if she's purposefully being elusive or if she's not handling her job very well. One of the key parts of being a receptionist is taking the calls and messages, and if she can't do that, then we may have an issue.

"The man looking for Daisy. The one who was here the other day," she explains, and I feel my body stiffen.

"Someone was looking for me?" Daisy breezes in from the side door, smiling, clearly having a good day, while my jaw is clenched tight. She looks at me, then to Stephanie, and back again, sensing something is off.

"The man who was here the other day looking for you. He came back today."

Daisy blinks a few times before realization comes to her face. "Oh," is all she says, but I need more.

"What did he want?" I ask, now very invested in what she has to say.

"He wanted a treatment. He saw the social media call-out and just turned up. I explained that he needed to make an appointment," Stephanie says, and I don't like it.

"You call me immediately if you see him again. Interrupt me, even if I'm in a meeting," I tell Stephanie, who looks at me, unsure.

"Connor. It's just Soren," Daisy says, staring at me like I'm the weird one. But in my soul, I don't like it. If it was him, then he's been here three times in as many weeks. Sure, they might be familiar, but I'm still not happy, because I don't like him either.

"Call me," I reiterate to Stephanie, and she nods. Daisy rolls her eyes at me for another time today, then starts walking down the hall to her office. When I turn on my heel and follow her, she pauses and spins around, sighing like she's frustrated with me.

"You don't need to worry. Soren is a friend of my mom's. She's known him for years," she explains, then continues walking. I follow her down the hall, and we walk into her office. Once she puts her stuff down, one hand finds her hip, giving me her sass. I think back to her mom, Rainbow, the alternative middle-aged woman who reminded me of a witch the first time I met her. I'm not sure that she's the best judge of character, but I try to let it go.

"At least you didn't drown today," I murmur, my relief about that fact relaxing me more than the words she says. And when she smiles, I'm glad my attempt to lighten the mood worked.

"Well, I didn't wear your armbands. I would've looked ridiculous, but I was careful."

My eyes thin in question, but I don't say anything.

"Would you have come to give me mouth to mouth if I had gone under?" she teases, walking toward me, her hips swaying, and my eyes dance down her frame. I stand tall and proud, waiting, feeling fucking lucky to have her eyes firmly on me.

"You know I would've." My body temperature rises just from having her near. I reach out to her, my hand sliding around her middle, like her curves were made just for me, and I pull her close, pinning her body to mine.

"Then once you came to, I would pull your swimsuit to the side and make you come so hard on my dick you wouldn't want to go anywhere near the water without me again," I murmur my filthy thoughts onto her lips, and her eyes widen slightly as she looks at me.

"Hmmmm, promises, promises... I need to get back to work so I can finish up on time. I have a hot date tonight."

I almost groan as she steps away from me and circles back to her desk, leaving me hard and horny.

"Make sure you wear your dancing shoes, baby girl," I tell her, walking backward, a few things to finish myself.

"Dancing?" she asks, looking at me quickly, surprise on her face.

"I'll come to your place after work," is all I tell her before I leave her office with a raging hard-on and a head full of questions. I pace back to my office, still thinking about the male visitor we had, so when I arrive at my desk, I pull up the security camera feed from the distillery. This Soren guy has me on edge. I didn't like him when I met him, and I don't like him now.

The footage doesn't give me a very good angle, although I see a van, and the frame of the man who enters reception is similar to that of Soren. I lean back in my chair, wondering what the deal is between them. It could be nothing. It could be something. I will get my security team to run a background check.

At least then I'll see if he's hiding anything.

27

———

DAISY

We walk into the bar, and it's the sound that hits me straightaway this time. Connor mentioned there was a band tonight, but what he failed to mention is that it looks like the entire town is here and the bar is packed.

"Ready?" he asks me as his hand slips around my waist, guiding me inside.

"Sure," I say, not feeling sure at all. I mean, I've met some of these people, but not many of them, and I'm relieved that most of them are too busy chatting and dancing to even be looking my way. But just like last time, it's almost as if Connor's parting the seas when he walks in. People turn and look, smile, talk, some older ladies pulling him down and kissing his cheek, who get a wicked grin and a wink from him that has them swooning. It's adorable, really.

But one thing I don't miss is the fact that his hand remains on my back. Just like last time, he keeps me close, and we get a few looks, but everyone's smiling.

Connor introduces me to a few people as we walk through, and by the time we get to the bar, I'm thankful to perch up on the barstool, while Connor stands close to me, surveying the room.

"What'll it be, boss?" a young guy from behind the bar asks Connor.

"My usual." He nods, and then they both look at me.

"Oh, ummmm..." I'm not sure what I feel like.

"You came!" Victoria yells over the music. "Come on, let's dance!" She pulls me from the barstool, and I laugh. Connor's grinning as I stumble to the dance floor after her.

"Just follow everyone else," Victoria yells, and I glance around me, seeing people move in time to the music. They're lined up, boots on, hips swaying. They look awesome, and a smile takes over my face immediately. My love for live music and dancing is high, and I'm now in my element. I may be a big girl, but the Lord did grace me with a few key attributes. I happen to be a quick learner and have excellent rhythm. I watch for a beat, and my feet start to move. I make a few missteps, but after a while, I get the hang of it pretty well, and soon, Victoria and I are laughing and having a great time.

When I look back at the bar, Tanner's with Connor, the two of them in conversation, but Connor's eyes are firmly on me. It lights me up, knowing I have his full attention, and I move my hips with a little more sway just for him.

The songs change, as do the steps with each one, line dancing apparently very popular around here, but again, I pick it up quickly, following Victoria's lead. I look around the dance floor, full of both men and women of all ages, and it's nice to see.

As the song ends, I'm grateful to have a song next that's made for couples so I can cool down a bit. I start to walk back to Connor, my smile wide, where he stands tall, waiting for me, but an older man steps toward me.

"May I have this dance?" a gentleman I haven't met yet, who I think is Jeff, the local taxi man, asks. He's an older man, more my father's age.

There's only one man I want to dance with here. "Oh, actually, I—" I start to say.

"Sorry, Jeff, she's all mine," Connor says from behind me, and I turn on my heel in surprise to see him on the dance floor. He stands protectively next to me, and I hear Jeff chuckle.

"Thanks, your dad now owes me a fifty," I hear him murmur as he shakes his head and walks over to Tanner, and sure enough, the two of them laugh. I spot Tanner hand over a fifty-dollar bill to Jeff, the two of them grinning at us.

"Ahhh, what's that all about?" I ask, my cheeks feeling even more flushed, and I see Connor's eyes throwing flames at his dad.

"That's my dad being a pain in my ass. Let's go." Grabbing my hand, he spins me into him before we start to dance.

"You dance?" I blurt out, shocked. In my experience, men don't dance that much, and a man like Connor I thought for sure would never step foot on a dance floor.

"Apparently," he grits out, and I laugh as we start to move. I can't remember the last time I danced with a man. Maybe at school, but I can't really remember. While I love to dance, it's usually a solo endeavor, with friends or just in my room with the music blaring.

I raise my eyebrows as he moves, clearly very rhythmic himself and knowing all the steps. Before long, I get the hang of it, letting him lead as he spins me away from him and then pulls me close, and we sway for a little longer before he spins me out again.

I lose myself in the music. The song has a sultry swing to it, making my hips move, and Connor knows exactly what to do with me. I trust him completely as he starts to spin me out faster, pulling me back to him and catching me against his chest and our hips grind together.

"Who taught you to dance?" I ask, trying to ignore the tension brewing between us. Otherwise, I won't be able to keep my hands to myself in a less-than-audience-friendly way.

"My grandma. And the ladies from the sewing club," he says with a boyish smile, one that warms my heart and makes me giggle.

"Well, they did a good job."

"They taught me the steps. It isn't until you get the right partner that you feel the beats through your boots and your hips know exactly where they need to go," he tells me, eyes on mine, and I suck in a breath.

"Well, I'm just following your lead," I admit, although I'm not missing any steps. Instead, I'm giving up all control to the man whose hands haven't left my body.

"I'll never lead you wrong. I've got you."

I look up at his eyes, and he gives me a sly wink before he spins me quickly, then back in, and I go with it. That is, until I feel myself falling backward, my heart stuttering before his hand catches me at the back of my neck and flips me to standing just as quickly. As he does, his hands remain, gripping in my hair as he pulls my face to meet his in a chaste kiss that has me feeling all kinds of things. My heart feels like it moves out of my chest, both with the speed of the move and the feeling of his lips quickly taking mine.

"Told you I've got you," he murmurs against my mouth, his own pulled up into a sexy-as-sin smirk, which has my body now entirely under his control as my mind turns to mush.

We just kissed in public. I'm not sure if anyone saw. I mean, we moved fast, and we're surrounded by other couples doing similar dance moves. No one else looks at me, other than Tanner, who eyes his son like he's grown a second head. I get the feeling that Connor doesn't dance very often. I'm not sure why, though, as he clearly has the talent. But that thought sparks a small flame of jealousy in my stomach, because if this is the way Connor dances, then I don't want any other woman experiencing it.

I've seen this kind of dancing on the internet. Country Swing, I think it's called. I always loved watching it, but never in a million years did I think I would try it. Not only because you would be hard-pressed to find a place in New York that would have this kind of thing authentically, but also because being a bigger girl, all the spinning and lifting and quick steps, I assumed it would be a little more difficult.

But I was wrong, because while I don't know all the steps, my body is just going with whatever Connor delivers. I spin out again, and he pulls me back to him, lifting me slightly, and grabbing my ass, wrapping my leg over his hip. Again, the move is not unusual to what the others around us are doing, but he squeezes my ass, holds me tight, and I swear this is starting to feel more like foreplay than actual dancing. Especially with how my core clenches and stomach flutters.

Connor, in his jeans and button-down shirt, looks like every woman's wet dream. But I'm the woman he's with right now, and he never once lets go of my hand.

We're in perfect sync, and I shouldn't be surprised; it's almost like our bodies know exactly what to do each time we're together. Whether it's yoga on the lawn or oral pleasure in my bed this morning. As I think about him naked, I swallow, watching him watch me just as intently and the feeling between the two of us continues to build, his hands cupping my waist, before spinning me again, the beat faster, then he pulls me back in and we do some more hip grinding. This time, his thigh is between my legs, and I almost groan at the contact my pussy makes with his jeans, the friction needed yet also building more yearning inside me. He grins like he knows exactly what he's doing.

"You're doing that on purpose," I whisper, eyes narrowed as I look up at him, feeling worked up.

"Hmmmm, if there is any time I can touch you, I'm going to take it." he grits out, and I know he feels it too. My pussy is already pulsing.

"Even in a packed bar?" I sway my hips, deliberately sliding them across his and feeling how hard he is.

A hiss slips through his teeth. "Fuck me, Daise... you're the one doing the teasing."

"Just giving you some of your own medicine."

"You could give me any damn medicine, and I would take it." He spins me around, making me gasp at the sudden movement, then places his hands firmly on my hips, bringing us back to swaying together.

"Really? Maybe I should buy you some water wings?" I tease, loving this caring side of him. The gift itself was small, but the feelings behind it were clear, and that's what makes me giddy about this man.

"They're called arm inflatables, and they're for your safety," he says with a serious look on his face.

"Potato, potahto," I say, grinning, and he pulls me closer.

"Maybe I just need to lock you up so you don't go near the water without me ever again."

Quirking my eyebrow, I ask, "Are you worried for my safety, cowboy?"

"What can I say, you do something to me that I can't explain..."

I hold my breath, the words he says starting to feel too real.

"When I hold you close, I feel no pain..." he says before he smiles wide, and I roll my eyes at him.

"Every beat of my heart, we got something going on..." I say, completing the lyrics to "Islands in the Stream," even though other music blares around us.

"Do you always refer to Dolly and Kenny when you're on a date?" I ask, given the last time we were here, the lyrics to the song were featured in our conversation.

"Weirdly, it only seems to happen when I'm with you."

That has me smiling wider. "I'm glad I bring out the music in you."

"You sure bring out something, baby girl." His low and rumbly voice skims over my skin, making goosebumps break out on my arms.

I take a quick look around, wondering if everyone's eyes are on us, because right now, it feels like we're so into each other that it may not be safe for public consumption, but everyone's smiling and having their own great times, not paying us any mind.

"What are you thinking about, baby girl?" he asks as the song slows, and he pulls me in tight to him.

"I'm just thinking about Whispers and how much I love it," I tell him honestly, barely able to talk, and his smile is instant.

"Hmmm, I think Whispers looks good on you." His hand grabs mine, and I don't answer as I take in some breaths.

"You know what else would look good?" he asks, his gaze alight with a look filled with desire. It makes me shiver in the best way.

"What's that?" I sound breathy, my heart racing.

"You naked, in my sheets, in about ten minutes. You want to go?" he asks against my ear, and I swallow as I nod.

I had a great night. Danced for over an hour, I think, and now as Connor leads me out of the bar, I realize I didn't even have one drink. But as if he knows exactly what I'm thinking, Connor swipes two bottles of water from the bartop on our way out.

"You're leaving so soon?" Tanner asks him as we walk past, a smug grin on his face as he eyeballs his son.

"Got better things to do," I hear Connor say to him.

"Oh, payback is too good." Tanner laughs, and I frown, not really understanding what they're talking about, but with anticipation between Connor and me building, and the heat flowing through my body, I really don't care.

Because Connor is dragging me out of here like the place is on fire, and I know exactly what's going to happen next.

We both want it. And tonight, there's no stopping us.

28

CONNOR

I'm acting like a goddamn fool, but I can't stop. After practically dragging her out of the bar and putting her in my truck, we're now home, at my place, and I'm pulling her inside.

"In a hurry?" she teases, a grin on her face, which has been there all night. With her hand firmly in mine, her steps are quick, keeping pace with my own.

"Not even sure how I managed to last this long," I tell her, before my lips hit hers, and suddenly the world feels right again. I'm not sure how that happens. That just by touching her, my stress levels dissipate, my hunger grows, and my feelings for her build.

I can't move my mouth from hers. I want her so fucking badly, I can barely think straight. Gripping her waist, I walk her through the house backward. We half stumble, the two of us so consumed with each other, we aren't really watching where we're going. Her hands get busy opening my shirt buttons. Clearly, I'm not the only one in a hurry.

"You sure know how to dance," she comments, pulling away from me briefly, before we stumble again, and I move her back against the wall. Caging her in, I open her jeans, with her now trying to push my shirt from my shoulders. I relent and pull off her, yanking the shirt from my frame at the same time her hands dive for my belt buckle.

"I haven't danced in years," I murmur as I pull up her top, and she raises her arms into the air for me to peel it clean off her body. I stare at her for a moment, her racing breaths and her perfect breasts so beautifully wrapped in a sexy lace bra I wasn't expecting. But I come back to the present quick enough as she opens my jeans button and lowers my zipper, hand diving into my underwear.

"I don't believe you." Her hand grabs my cock, and I slap my palm against the wall near her head so I don't topple. My legs feel weak at her touch.

"I speak the truth, baby girl. Haven't danced in years." I groan through my words, her hand pumping me and pulling my underwear off, leaving me now naked. My words are truthful. I can't really remember the last time I danced like that. At school, maybe. People were definitely looking at me because me on the dance floor is a novelty. But growing up here, you learn the moves, and on the odd occasion, I might get Rochelle up or even one of the older ladies from the knitting club when they have their Christmas get-togethers, for no other reason than I know it makes them laugh and brings a smile to their face.

But dancing with Daisy was something new. It was the hottest dancing I've ever done. Feeling her body move in time with mine. Her letting go and trusting me to lead her. Taking her any way I wanted, spinning her, lifting her, fucking grinding my hips into hers.

"So why tonight?" she asks as I start to kiss down her neck, her back still sealed to the hallway wall as she pants breaths. My hands run around her waist and down to her ass, where I squeeze, teeth grinding at how good she feels. With her hand still wrapped around my dick, she keeps pumping, doing magical things that make my body tingle and my balls tighten.

"Because when Jeff asked you to dance, all I saw was green." I tell her the truth. It was a setup. My dad clearly instigated it, paying Jeff fifty dollars to ask Daisy to dance, knowing that I don't want any man, no matter how innocent, to be throwing her around a dance floor. Especially not in my own bar. If anyone is doing that, it'll be me. Hence why I stepped straight onto the dance floor, to claim what's mine.

Much to my father's amusement.

"Connor..." She moans my name, all breathy and achy, making my balls tighten even more.

"Shit, what are you doing to me, baby girl?" I groan, feeling mere moments from coming in her hand and not wanting to. So I pull away, grab her hand, and drag her down the hall to my room.

I don't bother closing the door as I tug her inside my room and walk her backward to the bed. My hands smooth up her back as we walk, my mouth on hers. I can't let her go. I can't stop touching her, kissing her, feeling her soft skin or swallowing her moans. I unclip her bra, feeling her breasts fall free as the lace slips from her arms. My head immediately drops to one of my favorite places, right near her heart, and to her full breasts I can't get enough of.

"This is going to be hard and fast, baby," I tell her, dragging my lips back up to hers, and she nods quickly.

"Yes, please. Just get inside me," she breathes out against my lips, her neediness matching mine. I grab the lace at her hips, just as the back of her knees hit the bed, and she falls back. Pulling the lace down her body, I throw her underwear to the side, then grab a condom from my nightstand. As I sheath myself, she moves up the bed, watching me, her skin flushed, and I growl at the sight. She looks good lying in the middle of my bed. Any other time, I would like to kiss her from head to toe and fuck her with my tongue, but tonight, I'm too far gone. The attention she's already given my cock has pushed me too far.

"Get on all fours," I tell her as I step toward the bed. She moves instantly, and I grin. I love this side of her. By day, she's business-minded, focused, and will push me and sass me all day long. But at night, naked before me, she does exactly what I tell her. It's such a turn-on. She's my little devil in disguise. I stand on the floor at the end of the bed, and she shuffles down, giving me a great view of her fantastic ass. I groan as I reach out, palming her cheek and squeezing, seeing her ass jiggle a little, and I bite my lower lip.

"Oh God..." she says, and I notice her hand between her legs, playing with her clit.

"Keep touching yourself, baby girl. Such a good girl, so worked up for me." Not able to wait another second, I grab my cock and slide it up and down her entrance, her wetness coating me before I press inside and fill her up.

"Connor!" Her gasp turns into a whimper as she pushes back into me, and I grit my teeth.

"That's it, baby girl. Take me in your sweet, sweet pussy," I growl, the sensation already too much.

"Yes... More..." she pants, her voice higher pitched, like she's barely hanging on herself.

"You feel good... so fucking good," I moan as I pull out and glide back in again, her wet warmth surrounding me. My rhythm builds, thrusting into her, her panting increasing, and I grip her hip with one hand as I run the other one up her back. I hold her tight, no doubt leaving bruises, but I can't help it. I want to bury myself deep, feel every inch of her.

"Yes... Oh my God, Connor, yes..."

I push her head down, lifting her ass farther up to me and watch, fascinated, as her body wiggles with every thrust. I'm salivating at the sight.

"Fuck, your ass is fantastic," I grit out as my orgasm lingers just on the horizon, our skin slapping with the ferocity of not ever getting enough of each other. I grab her hair, looping it up in my hand and pull her head back a little. She bends so her back is arched, her body a thing of magic, flexible as fuck, and I can now see her perfect tits bouncing with every slap of our skin. When she moans this time, I can feel she's close, her core fluttering around me as her fingers work over her clit faster. "That's it, baby girl."

"Oh God, I'm going to come," she moans, and so am I, so I move my hands, placing them both solidly on her hips and drive into her. My need to take her savagely is almost overwhelming.

"Yes, you are, baby girl. You're going to be a good girl and come all over my cock," I grit out, never so turned on in my life.

"Yes! Yes... yes... yes. Please don't stop, Connor, please," she pants, her words tumbling over each other before she's crying out and tensing. As she clenches around me, the pulsing of her release is enough to have my balls tightening.

"Daisy," I roar, thrusting into her deep, coming with her. The feeling of her losing herself sets me off, and I almost see stars as I let go. We're both left panting, our bodies spent as I run my hand up and down her back, and we pull in the air we need. I step back and get rid of the condom quickly as she lies in my sheets, a sweet look of contentment on her face.

"You alright?" I ask, realizing that was one of the most intense experiences I've ever had and hoping she enjoyed it too.

Her eyes meet mine and she grins. "Mm-hmm. I'm better than alright. That was amazing," she murmurs, and I get into bed, pull her close, and cover us in blankets. My hand still roams as I pepper kisses to her shoulder, her back now to my front. I pull at her hips, ensuring her ass is flush with my pelvis, not wanting any space between us.

Her breathing slows, becomes rhythmic, and I shouldn't be surprised. After a busy week, a night of dancing, and what we just experienced, we're both exhausted.

But as she sleeps, my hand caresses up and down her side. With her naked body against mine, a new feeling builds. One that's more intense than I have ever felt with anyone, and I swallow roughly. I want her now more than ever. And I have no idea how to keep her.

29

DAISY

I wake to my body feeling deliciously sore. I'm not sure of the time, but as I move around on these soft sheets, I know I don't need my morning yoga. Not only did we have enough exercise last night on the dance floor, but Connor woke me up two more times during the night, each one more pleasurable than the last.

"Mmmm. Good morning, baby girl," he murmurs as his lips touch my bare shoulder, the heat of his body at my back. His beard is rough against my skin, but I like it.

"Morning. No run for you today?" I ask, turning my head back to look at him. I'm met with eyes that sparkle and a grin that promises too many things. It makes my belly swoop.

"I think my cardio over the last twenty-four hours warrants a rest day," he says, making me chuckle.

"My muscles feel the same way," I tell him, and he peppers a few more kisses to my skin.

"Let me help with that a bit..."

I wonder what he means before I feel his large hands

on my back, and he starts to massage me.

"Ohhhhhh," I moan. It feels fantastic. As someone who gives a lot of treatments, I'm usually too busy to get them for myself, and right now, Connor's hands are warm and strong, moving around my back, exactly where I need them. "Wow. You're good at this." My eyes close as I enjoy his touch.

"I like touching you. Besides, I made your muscles sore, so it's the least I can do to make you feel better," he teases, and I smile.

"If you didn't have plans today, I would like to do something with you."

My breath catches. Am I surprised? Not entirely. Am I excited? Beyond belief. But I'm almost a little taken aback. I mean, I wasn't sure we were anything. Last night was amazing, but he could just ask me to leave and we go on our merry way. Instead, he wants to spend time with me, and I know that shouldn't be unusual, and maybe to anyone else, it isn't. But my history tells me that in the morning, men make excuses and leave. Connor wants to spend the daylight hours with me too. On a weekend, with no rushing out this morning. My heart blooms at the prospect.

"I'm free," I tell him, watching him carefully.

"Good. I want us to go to the springs," he says, and I raise my eyebrows, smile widening.

"The springs?" I confirm as I roll around, my chest now against his. His hand moves instantly, skimming up my side, grabbing my ass cheek before running down my leg and hooking around the back of my knee. As he pulls my leg over his hips, I feel him hard at my core.

My pulse thuds in my ears as arousal builds in my center, my hips moving automatically against his.

"Mm-hmm... I'm going to teach you to swim."

I blink a few times, wondering if I heard him right.

"Teach me to swim?"

"Well, after knowing you were there yesterday with the models for the spa, I couldn't work at all thinking that you had drowned. So yeah, I'm going to teach you to swim."

The fact that he was worried about me like that warms me from the inside out. I've always wanted to learn how to swim; it just wasn't something I did growing up. My parents weren't really into the beach or water, so it hasn't ever been something I gravitated to.

"I guess a drowned staff member isn't good for business," I quip, biting my bottom lip as his finger hits my clit, and I gasp in a breath. "Now it makes sense why you barged in here yesterday like a man on a mission. Here I thought you were just being a Peeping Tom." I can't hold back my giggle at how his eyes narrow with my teasing.

"I thought I may have fucked the sass right out of you last night, but it appears I was wrong," he murmurs deep and low.

"I guess so..." My eyes close as he continues to circle my clit. "What time do you want to go?" I ask, though there's no way I'm leaving this bed with his hands working me over like this.

"After I make you come again one more time," he says, moving his hips against mine, and in a matter of moments, his name is the only thing on my lips, the sass completely fucked right out of me.

"At least you can float without your inflatables," Connor says as I step into the water quicker than he has time to disrobe. But he throws off his t-shirt and steps in just after me, grabbing my hand and keeping me close. I bite down a grin at his protectiveness, his moves swift, almost panicked.

"That I can," I say, smiling.

"You have no fear of the water, do you?" he asks, almost gobsmacked, and I shake my head.

"No. Not at all. I probably should, but…" I shrug, not really sure where my lack of fear comes from. I guess, having not been around it, it's not like I have a fear of the water or anything; I just don't have the ability to swim. Like someone may not have the ability to do some yoga poses. But I'm hopeful with practice that I can do it.

"So how is it that you never learned how to swim?" he asks as the water gets deeper. My heart races a little because I haven't been this deep before when walking in. Usually, I'm floating about now.

"I've got you." Still able to touch the bottom, he pulls me to him, my body gliding through the water to him effortlessly, and I hook my arms around his neck.

"We were never a water family, really. It wasn't our thing. No one has ever offered to teach me to swim before," I tell him as his large hands grip on to my waist. Our bodies are used to each other now, yet the sensation still makes me gasp when my breasts push up against his bare chest.

"If you're coming down here, then I want you to at

least be able to get yourself out of trouble if needed. To be able to get to the edge quickly and safely," he says, and I can tell he's in serious mode.

"Okay, so what do I do?" I ask, keen to learn.

"Well, you can float on your back, so let's practice you floating upright. I'm going to let go of you. I want you to move your arms around a little to keep you buoyant in the water. Do you think you can try that?"

"Sure," I say, not really knowing exactly what he wants me to do, but I'll try.

"I'll be right here to grab you if you go under. Okay. One, two, three." Suddenly, his hands are gone, and my body starts to sink. I move my hands, slight panic crawling up my skin as my mouth gets covered with water. I can see a look of complete fear in Connor's eyes before I glide my hands in a strong motion around the water and bob back up again.

"Oh my God, I'm doing it!" I shout and laugh. It's a major workout for my arms, but I'm too excited to care.

"Good girl," he praises me, watching my every move, like he's ready to pounce.

"I can bob in the water! I can bob in the water!"

"Okay, I want you to see if you can do the same motion, but move toward me a little."

I nod before I move my hands like he shows me. It's harder than I thought, and I start to go under again. Pushing my lips together tight, my legs and arms keep moving, but I'm not making any ground, and I go under. My head completely submerges.

My panic is short-lived as large hands wrap around

me and hoist me up like I weigh nothing, and I blow out the breath I was holding.

"I've got you. You're alright," he murmurs, his hands firmly on me, not letting me go as I brush the wet hair from my face and squint the water from my eyes.

"I couldn't get the right motion. I tried to circle them, but I couldn't move." I frown, not liking not being able to get something right the first time.

"Try again. Take a few deep breaths and calm yourself." I listen to him and do as I'm told to slow my breathing again.

"Alright, this time, instead of circles with your hands, I want you to pretend you're reaching out in front of you and grabbing something, and then cupping it and pulling it back toward you."

My mind immediately goes to a place that's not G-rated.

"I have no idea what you're thinking, but if you want a reward at the end, I'm more than happy to oblige," he says with a chuckle, a wicked grin on his face.

"I always liked being the teacher's pet," I tease, smiling, with him still holding me tightly.

"One... two... three..." he says before letting me go slowly and stepping out of reach, and I do as he says, imagining I'm grabbing an apple, cupping it and pulling it to my chest. I keep repeating the motion, my head bobbing on the surface of the water, my mouth closed and my eyes squinting due to all the splashes.

"That's it. Keep going..." He continually steps back, and I continue to swim toward him, Connor staying just out of reach, yet close enough to grab me, should I need it. Before long, I see the water is up to his waist, which means I can probably touch the bottom. I tentatively put my feet down, feeling the solid rocks underneath as I stand.

"Oh my God, I did it!" I say with a giddy squeal, not sure I could actually do it.

"You did. That was amazing. You, my girl, are amazing," Connor says, and I look up at him, seeing the pure pride in his eyes. I swallow, my feelings building. *My girl.* Was it just a turn of phrase, or does he mean the words he says? While sex together is great, I shouldn't think I'm special. Just the right woman at the right time, maybe?

But I do wonder what it would be like to be Connor's girl more permanently, and my feelings for him are growing every minute of every day. Surely, he wouldn't be here on the weekend, teaching me to swim, if what we had was nothing. But then I look at the half-finished path and remember I'm here to build the spa business, and I roll my shoulders. I said it earlier as a joke, but maybe Connor is just trying to mitigate the risk of me drowning, obviously not needing that to happen for his business. I look back at him, knowing that my feelings for him are growing, and they have been ever since I met him. But I have no way of knowing if he feels the same.

"Let's do it again," I tell him, already stepping back into the deep, wanting to perfect it.

"Let's go." Grinning, he follows me back to the deep, and I try again. This time, I'm not as successful, so we try a third, then a fourth time, each time with different levels of success.

"Let's take a break. You're getting tired," he says,

before grabbing my hand and pulling me to him. "Wrap your legs around me." He walks out deeper, still able to touch the bottom, but I have no chance. So I do as he said and wrap my legs around him, his hands immediately cupping my ass and pulling me against him tight.

"It's really nice down here," I say, feeling relaxed in his hold, enjoying the serenity.

"It is." His eyes meet mine, and he smiles, then his gaze drops to my neck. "Tell me about this necklace. I see that you wear it every day."

I immediately look down and grab the small daisy chain that lies around my neck.

"It was my mother's. She made it when she was younger and passed it on to me when I turned twenty-one. I never take it off." Twisting the daisy between my fingers, I smile, thinking of my mom.

"Like a family heirloom of sorts?"

"Of sorts. How often do you come swimming here?" I ask him, changing the subject back to our location, the peacefulness of the springs now something I fully take in. I'm not sure where the local kids are. Maybe it's still too early for them.

"Hardly ever. I'm usually too busy. I can't remember the last time I was down here for a swim," he says, and I frown.

"So, what, you don't usually dance and you don't usually swim? Why the change of heart?" I ask curiously.

"It's all you. You make me do things I haven't done in forever, reminding me how good they are, and how much better they are with someone you enjoy spending time with." As he looks at me intently, I can hardly breathe.

"Oh…" is all I can get out, not expecting his honesty.

"You're making me do all kinds of things that I wouldn't ordinarily do, Daise. I'm starting to think maybe you've been drugging me with your tea?" he says, grinning, and I bark out a laugh.

"No, not yet," I tease, making him chuckle. I lean into him and take a deep breath as I look around.

"What are you thinking about, baby girl? Tell me what's going on in that head of yours," he asks as we bob around in the peace and quiet, my legs wrapped around him, his hand running up and down my back.

"I'm thinking of my mom's dahl. Tomorrow is Sunday. I usually visit them every Sunday and she makes me dahl," I say on a sigh.

"You miss your family?" he asks, frowning like it never occurred to him.

"Yeah. I know it sounds silly. I mean, it's only been a few weeks, but we're close, and I haven't really been away from them for a long time before."

"Well, do you want to go? We could fly out this afternoon. I need to go to New York for a few things this week anyway, and I'm sure whatever you need to do with the spa can be done remotely for a few days," he says, like it's a trip into town to do some groceries, not hopping on a private jet at a moment's notice and spending time in the city together.

I pause, thinking about it. Mentally going through my project plan, trying to remember what I have on this week.

"I could probably make it work for a few days. I just want to be back midweek so I can do the next training with the new staff," I tell him, not quite believing what we're talking about, but excitement bubbles in my tummy. I really want to check on my parents, and I want to talk to Mom about a few new tea recipes that I'm putting together for the spa menu with the chef from the distillery.

"Great, we can leave later this afternoon. Stay at my penthouse on Madison Avenue."

"Penthouse?" I question, eyes wide, and a smirk quirks his lips.

"Well, I can't make you scream every night when you have a roommate down the hall, but if you prefer to have me at your place, then I will do my best to swallow your moans, baby girl."

I feel like I'm having an out-of-body experience.

Is this happening? Is one of the wealthiest bachelors in the country flying me home to see my parents and wanting me to spend time with him in the city?

"What do you say?" he asks, always wanting my approval before he moves forward with anything. It means a lot to me every time.

"I think that sounds like a great idea," I tell him, grinning, still not believing any of this is real, but going with it. I want to spend more time with him, even though I only have a few more weeks left here in Whispers. Here's to hoping I can keep my heart from getting too carried away...

"Good." Leaning forward, he seals the trip with a kiss.

30

DAISY

Connor had the jet fueled and ready, our teams briefed, and we landed in New York before the day's end. It was a whirlwind, yet nothing felt rushed or stressed. Traveling privately is definitely a luxury. One I'm not used to, and even though I flew in his jet to arrive in Whispers weeks ago, flying back to the city just because I missed my parents seems indulgent.

The way the air hostess greeted him, offering him obviously curated food and drinks, the pilot having a private conversation with him about the flight path and landing routes, the drivers who take care of all the luggage upon arriving at the penthouse, a fridge full of high-end food, not a speck of dust to be seen; a glittering view of the New York skyline that only multimillionaires could buy, it's all overwhelming and completely different from my life. It's going to be hard to go back to using the subway to get to work when I'm back at Sunshine with Mom.

We arrived in darkness and went straight to the

bedroom, eager to make love on almost every surface we could. The high achievers we both are, we succeeded in that quest.

Now in the light of a new day, I stand up from my morning salutation and look around. My bare feet sink into the thick, luxurious carpet, the white tones of the room I'm in a relaxing color palette. I do my morning yoga with the sunlight seeping in from the large floor-to-ceiling windows, the view unobstructed and the green of Central Park nearby. Taking a deep breath, I try to center myself.

Connor's penthouse is amazing. Over two levels, it's modern yet still cozy. It has everything you could imagine: a large kitchen, a living room with a massive TV, bathrooms, bedrooms, a gym, an office, a private elevator... I mean, the list is endless. And it's in complete contrast to my small two-bedroom abode I share with Trisha.

I can't even do yoga in our apartment. There's no room. We're squashed together like sardines, and he's right; had Connor stayed with me, our walls are paper thin and Trisha would've been given a show last night, for sure. The kitchen is literally a cupboard and a small fridge. The oven hasn't worked since I moved in and is currently where I store my winter sweaters. And the one bathroom we share is barely big enough for me to shower in.

I look over at his bar, fully stocked with whiskey, like something from a deluxe cocktail lounge, with backlights and glass shelving and mirrors. I still haven't tried his whiskey. I'm not even sure I could stomach it. I swallow as the startling differences between our two lives make my tongue stick to the roof of my mouth. The opulence of this place is like nothing I could ever imagine, and I feel like a fraud for even being here.

"Hey, baby girl." His voice is a mere murmur that rumbles over my skin as his hands move around my waist from behind. I didn't even hear him walk into the second living room, where I've perched myself this morning. I want to fall back into his embrace, sigh in contentment, and imagine that this is all normal. That this life I've stepped into could be real. That we might become something. But it isn't. This is just two people having a good time that will end as soon as the spa opens and he flies me back here permanently. I'm not stupid. Connor is a ladies' man, a billionaire bachelor whom many women crave, but with every touch, and every *baby girl* that rolls from his lips, I fall a little more for the man I crave like no other. The pain at the end of it all will be worth it, just to feel like this with him right now.

"Finished your run?" I ask, knowing he has if the sweat I feel on him is anything to go by. Even though we're in a new place, our morning routine has remained. He went to the gym to run a few miles on the treadmill, and I found this little sun-soaked spot for my yoga. His head ducks into the crook of my neck, his kisses making my heart race and my knees weak. God, I don't know how he does it, but I melt like putty in his hands, putting my head back on his shoulder as his grip around me tightens.

"I have. What are you thinking about, looking out at the city skyline here?" His hot breath skims my throat as he pulls me back against him firmly so I have no option but to sink into his protective embrace.

"Just life," I say, not wanting to get into it.

"Hmmmmm, I can hear your brain ticking over," he comments, and I can't help but grin.

"This is just so... beautiful," I tell him honestly. Opulence aside, the view, the stillness, it's something I never thought you could find in the city, the open space with lots of blue sky above me, seeing the sun, the beauty of the world around us... It's stunning.

"I'm glad you like it. I don't really like the hustle and bustle of the city, so I wanted a place where I could spend time that wasn't too loud, too congested. It's the country in me, I suppose." He speaks against my skin, where he continues to pepper kisses.

"What do you prefer, New York or Whispers?" I ask. Looking at him, you would think the city. Tall, handsome, a ladies' man, wearing business suits and making corporate deals.

"Whispers," he answers with conviction.

"Really?" I ask, somewhat surprised.

"I grew up there. My dad's there. The distillery is there. I enjoy the city, and I'm here often. I went to college close by here, and most of my friends are from here too, but I prefer the genuine people from Whispers. The fresh air, no traffic. I feel more relaxed there."

I think about it. There's a lot to love about Whispers, that's for sure.

"What time do you want to leave for your parents' place?"

"I was just going to walk to the subway and catch the

train at around eleven," I tell him, and I feel his body stiffen behind me.

"Subway?" he questions, pulling his mouth from my neck and looking down at me with a pinched brow. I turn to look at him fully, puzzled.

"Yeah, I called Mom, told her I was coming, and she was beside herself with excitement. She's going to make an extra big batch of dahl so I can bring some back to Whispers with me."

"Why don't we take the car?" he asks, and my head tilts.

"Car?" Clearly, the two of us aren't on the same page.

"Yeah, I have some cars downstairs. I can drive us," he says, and the realization dawns on me.

"Some cars?" I ask, because how many cars does one man need?

"Well, you can choose which one we take, since I'm not familiar with the area your parents live in," he says with a shrug, like this is a normal conversation, when nothing about this is normal.

"Familiar with the area?" My brain's not connecting. It must be the way his hands run up and down my sides, keeping me close, the fireworks sprinkling across my skin at every pass.

"The area where your parents live? We can take something sporty, or if it's a longer drive, we can take the SUV."

I raise my eyebrows as it dawns on me.

"You want to come meet my parents?" I almost squeak out, gobsmacked.

"Well, technically, I've already met your mom..." he

says tentatively, watching me as a million different things race through my mind. I've never taken a man home to meet my parents. To be honest, I really like the idea of taking Connor. I'm hesitant, though, because in a few weeks, this love affair we're having will be over. But as I start to smile, happiness wins out. I've spent weeks in his hometown, and I like the idea of introducing him to my dad.

"Unless you don't want me to..." He pulls away from me slightly, looking conflicted.

"Do you even like dahl?" I ask him, quirking an eyebrow to tease him.

"I don't even know what the fuck darrrrlllll is. But you love it, so I will too."

I laugh at his exaggeration of the word.

"I just thought since the Jets were playing that you might have had plans to go to the game. To your suite." I say, knowing that Trisha is working today and his love for football runs deep.

"Do your parents have a TV?" he asks, and my smile widens.

"Yes," I tell him, nodding, the giddiness I feel almost overtaking any sense of preservation I've been holding on to. Meeting my parents isn't casual, and I've given him an out that he hasn't taken.

"Well, I'll be fine. As long as your mom's darrrrlllll doesn't kill me."

I'm giggling as he pulls me close, this all feeling too good and too perfect.

"Well, it's spicy...." I say, leaving him hanging, and he grins.

"It can't be any worse than that tea she made me at Sunshine."

That interaction was just over a month ago, yet it feels like a lifetime.

"That was our aphrodisiac tea." I roll my lips together so I don't laugh as his eyebrows shoot up.

"Well, that explains it then..." he trails off, and I frown, waiting for him to continue.

"Explains what?"

"Why I'm totally bewitched by you and have been since the moment I first met you."

Humming, I say, "Well, good to know that our tea actually works."

"Oh, it isn't the tea..." he says, suddenly looking serious. My body stills as I feel our conversation morphing into something less playful.

"No?" I ask, almost breathless.

"It's all you, baby girl. Every inch of you, from your fantastic round ass, your perfect curves, your killer smile, your intelligence, and your humor. I could keep that list going if you need more convincing."

My gasp is caught by his lips as he kisses me wholly, and I mesh into his hold, wondering how I'm ever going to recover from this man before he pulls back just a little to whisper.

"Your downward dog is pretty fantastic too."

31

CONNOR

I'm smiling as we pull up to Daisy's family home.

"He still hasn't fixed the gate," she mumbles next to me, looking at who I assume is her father. He stands at the front gate with a small scattering of tools at his feet.

"Are you ready?" I ask, quickly checking my mirrors. We had paparazzi at the front of my building earlier. They followed us for a while, but they obviously got their shot, as I saw them peel off a while ago. I'm somewhat used to them. But I don't like them always making up stories about people and issues they know nothing about. Clickbait these days is out of control. I also don't want to subject Daisy or her family to that. Especially before I've even formally met them. I need to make a good impression. And with that thought, I jump out and run around to her side door.

"Oh," she says, surprised.

"You think I left my manners back in Whispers?" I ask her, seeing her father look up at us.

"Well, I guess not." She laughs lightly, and I help her from the car, grabbing her hand and walking by her side toward her father.

"Hey, Dad." As she steps up to him, I let go of her briefly, the two of them hugging.

"Hey, Sparkie," I hear her dad say, and my lips twitch.

"Sparkie?" I ask, smiling, and Daisy rolls her eyes at me.

"She has always been a bit of a firecracker, a bright spark. It's the red hair. I think it brings out a little fire in her personality. It's stuck since she was a child," he says, and I stretch out my hand.

"Connor Whiteman," I say, introducing myself. I feel my heart thud. I've never done this before. Met the parents. While I meet new people all the time, I've never felt this nervous before.

"Good to meet you," he says, his handshake firm. As Daisy starts asking him about the gate, I look at him and the house, taking it all in. It's a standard suburban street, the house a white single-story, well kept but old. Their garden is neat. Nothing like Whispers, but pretty enough.

Her father looks exactly how you imagine an accountant to look. Thinning hair, glasses, white collar on with slacks, even though it's a Sunday. He's taller than Daisy, but not by much. I tower over both of them, my frame bigger than most. There are no signs of meditation, herbal remedies, or fucking crystals in sight.

"You've been fixing this for weeks," Daisy says as I look back at the gate.

"I need something to stop the neighbors' kids' balls coming in and ruining my daisy bushes. That one I planted with you was thriving until the soccer ball from next door hit it."

"Daisies?" I ask.

"I have my garden full of them. After our Daisy here," he says, and Daisy smiles adoringly. I look around the small garden, and sure enough, there are daisy bushes everywhere, most in bloom, looking full and lush.

"We make tea with them. They have just as much vitamin C as a lemon. Good for coughs and colds," Daisy tells me. I swear this woman could live off-grid for years if she needed to.

"You're here!"

I look up, seeing Rainbow, Daisy's mother, step out the front door, and the smile on Daisy's face is instant as she hurries over to her. It's heartwarming to see.

"Oh, you brought the hunk of s—"

Daisy's quick to interrupt. "Mom! You remember Connor?"

I step forward to greet her. I've met Rainbow already at Sunshine. Hell, she saw me checking Daisy out the minute we met. I rub my eyes at the thought, embarrassed. Yet not at all remorseful. Daisy has a great ass, and I still look at it every chance I get.

"Good to see you again." I offer my hand, and she tuts.

"None of that formal stuff. We believe in the healing nature of touch in our home... Come here." Grabbing me by the upper arms, she pulls me down and gives me a small hug. She's just how I remember. Thin, long black hair with streaks of purple and gray. Her natural appearance has a little more warmth than what I remember. The visions of her as a witch are less so today, even though she's still dressed similarly, her dress flowing.

"Shall I brew you some tea?" she asks me, and I glance at Daisy.

"Some of that tea you made me at Sunshine would be amazing, if you have it?" I ask innocently. Daisy's eyes widen, and I try hard to tame my smirk. It tasted like shit, but I will throw it back. Not that I need an aphrodisiac, as just looking at Daisy gets me going.

Daisy's mom's eyes alight, oblivious to my filthy thoughts about her daughter, and her grin is instant.

"Oh, I knew you liked it. I will get a pot going."

I'm happy that I have her mother's approval already. Now I just need to work on her dad.

"Are you still going with that gate?" she asks her husband, and I look at it again and take in the tools he has out. It's clear that he doesn't work with his hands very often.

"I can help you out, if you'd like?" I offer, because from the quick glance, I'm pretty sure it just needs a small tweak and a re-screw.

"Oh, that would be lovely," Rainbow says as she loops her arm around Daisy's. "We'll be inside if you need us. Dahl and tea will be ready soon."

Daisy takes a quick look at me, and I give her a nod, telling her that I'm fine, and I watch them both walk inside, talking about herbs and tea and a myriad of other things.

"Rainbow's dahl is some of the best you will ever try," he says to me.

"So I've heard. I'm looking forward to it," I tell him,

smiling, before I look at the gate. "Do you want me to have a look?"

"Sure." He sighs like he's given up. "I've been trying to fix this for weeks, but working with the tools isn't really my forte." He steps back as I roll up my shirtsleeves and get to work. I'm a businessman. I work on computers and with numbers every day, probably not unlike Daisy's father. But my dad made me learn every tool and every home and outdoor task since I was a kid. By age five, I could pick a lock. At eight, I was mowing lawns and cutting trees at the distillery. By ten, I could change a car tire. By fifteen, I could service a vehicle, sleep in the forest without a tent, and chop a load of wood for a fire. I have learned many things, some of which I still do today, and as I pick apart the lock and reattach it, using different screws to adhere it to the gate, I feel confident in my abilities.

"A real-life MacGyver," he murmurs, making me chuckle.

"Not really, just lucky with a few tools is all," I tell him before I stand up and test the lock, the gate now fixed.

"I have read up about you."

I'm not surprised. One simple online search yields thousands of results about me, some of them true, while others, not so much.

"I would expect any father to do some research on where their daughter is working," I tell him, nodding.

"You're extremely successful. You and your father."

I nod. "We are. We worked hard for it, though." I want him to know I'm not just some rich kid living off Daddy's money. I met a few of those in college, and most of them are assholes.

"You have an office here in New York as well?" he asks.

"I have a full office and staff team in the city, so I divide my time between here and Whispers, usually."

"How is Daisy doing in Whispers?" With that question, I notice he's looking at me more carefully.

"She's doing great at the distillery. The spa is amazing; she's done a really incredible job. Whispers and she seem to go well together." I wonder where he's going with this.

"I'm a little familiar with the area. My wife was born into a commune from up that way."

I raise my eyebrows. I've heard that there are communes around, but we never see anyone in Whispers who is from that lifestyle.

"Really? I didn't know," I tell him honestly, because Daisy never mentioned it.

"Daisy doesn't know where it is, and I would like to keep it that way, if you understand my meaning," he says, his gaze on me now hardened. I don't know much about communes, but I know they're an alternative way of living, some more restrictive than others. Cults being the more extreme end of that spectrum. I think about Soren. His visits still feel a little weird to me. My security team didn't find much about him, though, so I assume he also lives off-grid. He certainly looked like he does.

"Do you know a man named Soren?" I ask him, my interest now piqued.

"A crystal supplier of Rainbow's. I don't know him well and tend to leave Rainbow to manage her own business contacts. But I think they know each other from the commune days, so again, he's probably not someone worth having around much, if you can help it. They all get a bit territorial. Rainbow got out and never went back, something I don't think was well received. So we keep away. Not wanting to bring up old issues."

I nod, still not really understanding it all, but pocketing the information away.

"Well, I don't know the location of any communes, so I certainly won't be taking her near any. Daisy is safe with me," I assure him, and his eyes narrow.

"From the way you're speaking, it seems you have feelings for my daughter. Is that right?" he asks, watching me like a hawk. Waiting for me to trip up. But I rarely trip up. Daisy is the only person with the talent to do that.

"I do," I say confidently, taking in a breath, not prepared for this conversation so early on in meeting him. But he's obviously worried about his daughter. I look back up to the house, not seeing her, yet my heart chakra feels like it's pulsating. A month ago, I didn't even know what a fucking chakra was, and now I feel it in my body. She's under my skin. My feelings for this girl are building to a level that almost scares me, and I hope I get his approval.

"You will look after her? While she's in Whispers?"

"I will look after her for as long as she lets me," I tell him, letting it be known that I'm in it for more than just the timeline of her working arrangement. We haven't talked about it. Daisy and I are just getting to know each other and enjoying each other, but the weeks are going by fast, and I already know I don't want it to end. But given how much she misses her parents, maybe Whispers isn't the place she wants to be, and I would never make her choose. My answer must appease him because he gives me a small smile.

"Well, she tells me you are a Jets fan, so you get my approval," he says quickly with a clap on my shoulder, grinning before picking up the tools. I smile. I now see where Daisy gets her sassy and sarcastic sense of humor. It's all him. An accountant. Who would've thought.

"What a year they've had," I say to him as we walk inside, discussing my second favorite topic—football. As we open the door, the smell hits me. Instead of the drying incense from the clinic, it's now an eye-watering amount of spice. The aromas are already sinking into my skin.

"Dahl is ready!" I hear Daisy's mother call out as we walk down the hall, and I swallow, having no idea what I'm in for. But as I spot Daisy setting the table, seeing her move around the house, looking beautifully carefree, I realize that there's nowhere else I want to be.

Even if I burn my insides with some very spicy darrrlllll.

32

DAISY

"I think they liked me," Connor says from the driver's seat. The light sweat from the spicy dahl is now gone from his brow, as is about a half gallon of milk he had to drink to tame the burn in his mouth. But he ate it all, never once complained, and I may have fallen for him a little harder with every bite he took.

My mom adores him, probably because he's the first guy I've brought home. My dad was surprisingly welcoming as well. That makes this all so much harder. He has three people's hearts and feelings now. If this ends, the heartbreak is going to be gut-wrenching. But, thinking positively, I'm now fully stocked with dahl and tea and herbs and all sorts of things that I hope we can fit on the jet for our trip back. At least that'll bring me comfort.

"You bribed my dad with tickets to see the Jets," I say, rolling my eyes as he grins.

"I didn't bribe him." Connor scoffs before he laughs. My grin is instant.

"You offered, very generously, for him to come to your suite. I call that a bribe." I love how we both had such a great day, and it was just a simple meal in a simple house with my parents.

"Potato, potahto," he mumbles, making me giggle, my usual quip rubbing off on him.

We hit traffic as we get back into the city and turn to drive down toward his penthouse, and I notice he begins shuffling in his seat.

"What's wrong?" I ask, sensing a change in the air. Before he can answer, a motorbike speeds past us. A guy on the back has a camera, his lens pointed at us. I frown, looking around and seeing a few others behind us as well. *Paparazzi.* They're like bees, swarming the car, and Connor's need for concentration increases.

"What's going on?" I ask curiously, wondering if there is a celebrity nearby.

"They're trying to get photos," he grits out, his hands white-knuckled on the steering wheel as we're now almost back to his building.

"Of who?" I wonder if Tom Cruise or George Clooney are in a car beside us or something.

"Of us," he says as we turn the corner, and I see the parking garage up ahead. When his words sink in, I nearly balk.

"What?" I look at him like he's being ridiculous.

He glances at me, looking remorseful. "Sorry, I should've warned you."

"Why do they want photos of us?" It's the most ridiculous thing I've ever heard.

"They try to get me when they can, knowing I'm not here all the time. I don't keep a consistent schedule of when I'm in the city, which helps alleviate the invasion slightly. But they saw us leave earlier, and seeing that I'm with a woman, they've come circling for blood."

Suddenly, I'm just as uneasy as he is.

As we slow down to enter the parking garage, flashes start to go off, as there are media standing on the sidewalk, watching us, cameras up and aimed. This whole thing is new and completely bizarre, and my heart races as nervousness takes over.

After we drive through the gate, it closes securely behind us, and we make our way down to his private basement, the people and flashes now long gone.

"What will they publish?" I ask, trying to figure it all out.

"Well, did you search me up online before you came to Whispers?" he asks as he parks the car and shuts off the engine, turning in his seat to look at me fully. I bite my bottom lip, the answer clearly written all over my face.

"Most people do, it isn't a big deal. But I would say most of the images and gossip you found online came from situations like this. People taking photos when I'm unaware, and then making up the story to suit their narrative to sell magazines or have as clickbait."

"So there will be photos of me and you? In the car?" My privacy now feels violated.

"Yes. They'll probably accompany a speculative head-line about the new woman in my life." He releases a heavy sigh. "I'm sorry. I should've better prepared you for it all." Reaching over, he grabs my hand and gives it a squeeze.

"It isn't your fault," I tell him, because it isn't, and now, I'm wondering about all the things Trisha and I saw when we looked him up online and how much of it is probably fake news.

"Just don't read anything they write. Social media can be toxic, and it's best not to look at any of it," he says, and I nod.

"I'm now starting to understand why you prefer to be in Whispers," I murmur.

With another sigh, he nods. "Let's go. I think your mom's tea is working." He jumps out and runs around to my door, and as he opens it, I cackle a laugh. Under-standing washes over me about what he said before my laughter is whipped from my body as his hands grab me from the car, his lips take mine, and we walk to the elevator and head into the apartment, the media now a mere speed bump in our glorious day together.

"You got a delivery?" I ask as we walk inside, the amazing penthouse looking just as beautiful as when we left this morning—apart from some boxes that sit on his kitchen counter.

"I got a few things." He walks over and opens one of the boxes. I watch as he pulls out a few things, unwrap-ping them, and I gasp when he pulls out one of the items.

"Is that a teapot?"

"Yeah. I wasn't sure what you liked, but there's nothing good here in the apartment for you to brew your teas, so I got the team at Bergdorf to send something over. Do you like it?" he asks, stepping back and looking at me.

I can barely breathe. I mean, it's only a teapot, but it's white and green, made from what I think is porcelain, and I step forward to touch it.

"It's beautiful," I say, looking it over, my eyes almost bugging from my head when I see the familiar Gucci brand mark. I swallow, not wanting to know what he spent on it. "You didn't have to get this. It's too much…"

"I wanted to. I want you to feel at home here, with me. And nothing is too much for you, baby girl."

I swear this man has my knees wobbling every day. Again, his caring nature peeks through, and I wonder if I'm the only one who gets to see this side of him. I feel honored that I might be.

"What else did you get?" Seeing more boxes, I take a moment to gather my thoughts and calm my breathing.

"Delivery of some whiskey that I had sent over from the office," he tells me, opening the box and pulling out a few bottles from his range. None of which I recognize, but they all have slightly different labels, so I assume they're all different. I look at his already full bar, not knowing where he's going to put them.

I see one called Next Door, and one says something about a single malt, another one is double aged, and then my hands rest on a bottle, the label intriguing me.

"Father Son?" I question, reading the name on the

label and looking further at the details. "Aged in Whis-pers for seventeen years?"

"That's my favorite," he says, placing all the bottles on the counter, the box out of the way.

"The one you made with your dad when you were younger?" I remember him telling me about it when I first landed in Whispers.

"You remember?" he asks, smiling.

"Of course," I tell him, biting my lip as his grin widens.

"So, how 'bout it?" he asks, gesturing to the bottle, and I look at him, confused.

"About what?" I ask, then place the bottle down as he steps toward me, his hands circling my waist, my temper-ature rising at his touch, already breathless from the way he looks at me.

"Want to try some of my whiskey, baby girl? Because I sure as hell want to see it on your lips," he growls.

I barely nod, before he's taking my lips in a searing kiss, our night of whiskey tasting starting now.

33

CONNOR

I blame the tea her mother gave me. The minute Daisy nodded at my request to put whiskey on her lips, I devoured her. I stripped her bare, exactly where we stood, and kissed her pussy until she screamed. Now my cock is hard, my taste buds are eager for more, and her body is stress free as she sits on the sofa, completely naked except for my shirt draped over her shoulders, looking like every man's wet dream.

I gather the things I need on a tray and take it over, placing it all on the large coffee table and taking a seat beside her.

"Mmmmm, I always wanted to be served by a topless waiter," she teases, her eyes sparkling, and it's one of my favorite things to see.

"Well, glad I can be of service," I say with a chuckle as I open the bottles.

"Wow, so we're really doing this." Sitting up, she looks at what I have, taking it all in.

"Are you ready?" I ask, my dick so hard at the visual of

her naked in just my open shirt. There's no doubt my orgasm will be building from the moment I see the amber liquid spill from her mouth.

"I'm not sure I'll like it, and I don't want to offend you," she says more softly, looking a little unsure. I grin as I sit next to her, the two of us close, facing each other.

"We'll start easy," I murmur as I grab one of my single malts. I take a sip, loving the taste, and she waits patiently for me to pass her the bottle, but instead, I lean forward, grab her at the nape of her neck, and bring her lips to mine. She moans as I kiss her, gripping her jaw and tilting her head up a little before I roll my tongue into her mouth, finding her own, the whiskey now coating both our mouths, passing her a little liquid with my tongue. She swallows it down, and I do the same, our kisses not wavering. When I pull back, a drop trails from her mouth, so I lean forward to lick it from her skin.

"Wow," she says quietly, and I grab the small jar of Whiteman's honey, dipping my finger in it and scooping up a small amount.

"Open your mouth, baby girl."

Smiling, she does, and I slide my honey-dipped finger into her mouth. Her lips close around me, and I growl as she sucks, pulling my finger into her mouth and cleaning it with her tongue.

Fuck me, this woman is digging herself further and further into my chest with every moment we share. As I slide my finger out of her greedy mouth, her eyes are a little glassy with lust, her lips tinted pink.

"Well?" I ask her, barely hanging on to my self-control, seemingly a common occurrence with her.

"It wasn't bad," she teases with a slight shrug, acting nonchalant. When she does, my shirt opens where it hangs from her shoulders, her beautiful bare body underneath. My eyes drop to her naked form, and I take in some air, before looking back at her.

"Try this one." I take a swig of one of our newest releases, Next Door. A small boutique batch we made. Again, I roll the whiskey around in my mouth and pull her face to mine. My movements are strong, the ache I have for her overtaking my mind. This foreplay with my whiskey is something that's going to stick with me for a very long time.

I devour her lips, sucking on them, the whiskey coating us both. It's messy, the liquor running down her chin and into my beard, but I crave her taste too much to care. I pull back again, seeing more drops running down her bare chest, and again, I dip my finger in the honey. I'm aware that she isn't a whiskey drinker and know alcohol isn't her thing, but the burn of the whiskey, the kiss, and then the honey chaser make it all so seductively sweet, so I know she enjoys it.

Honey drips from my finger and lands on her nipple before I put it in her mouth. She sucks it down again, her tongue curving around me, licking it from my skin, and then she moves back slightly, her shoulders hitting the sofa. Arching, the open shirt falls to her sides, exposing her naked body to me completely.

She's a little minx. Her hands travel across my still jean-clothed knee, and she smooths it up my thigh, palming my hard cock where it strains under my zipper. Suppressing a groan, I lean over, taking her nipple in my mouth, sucking the sweet honey from her skin. I lick up her chest, sweeping up the drops of whiskey that make trails down her body, her skin soft and warm and made for this.

"That one was a little better," she teases, rubbing her hand up and down my crotch as I remove my finger from her mouth. She pants, taking in some breaths, and I lean forward more, pecking her on the lips. They're hot from our kissing, from the whiskey, probably both.

"This one is my favorite," I murmur, grabbing the last bottle.

"Is this the seventeen-year-old one?" she asks, already knowing the answer as she opens my jeans button and lowers the zipper. Her small hand reaches inside and grips me, and I clench my jaw, loving her hands on me so much, I already feel like I could combust.

"It is. I don't have many bottles of it left. I don't share this with anyone. Until now. It's smoother than the others. A buttery taste that's softer on the tongue. It's almost as delicious as your pussy," I tell her, nearly losing my breath as her hand continues to toy with me. I speak the truth. I loved the taste of this whiskey until I tasted her. Now her flavor is by far my favorite. I wish I could bottle her and drink her whenever I wanted.

I take a heavy swig of my favorite whiskey, the one that really kick-started my whole business and put Dad and me on the map. The one that we now keep hidden, only available for our own consumption or very rarely for special friends or for a charitable cause.

As I move closer, she takes the opportunity to push my jeans over my ass, and I grab her jaw tight and bring her mouth to mine. She opens her mouth for me, and I slowly release the liquor, my tongue pushing it into her mouth, the softness of butter, the hint of spice, all combining with her sweetness, and I groan. I don't offer her honey. I can't. I can't remove my lips from hers, and instead, I lower my hands, grab hold of her ass, and pull her up off the sofa to straddle me.

Her thick thighs fall to either side of mine, and the whiskey spills from our mouths all over our bare torsos. The liquid coats us both, my beard wet. I run my hands up her body, pushing my shirt from her shoulders, and she throws it across the floor so that she's now completely bare, sitting on top of me as I get to drink her in.

Our eyes meet as she loops her hands around the back of my neck, and I run my hands up and down her sides. I love the feel of her. I relax back as her fingers dig into the base of my neck, a mini massage of sorts that has me groaning in pleasure. She's on top. She's controlling it all, but I feel like an arrogant son of bitch with my head leaning back on the sofa, just watching her.

I draw patterns on her bare skin with my fingers, tracing down her chest, circling her nipple and feeling the whiskey and honey still on her skin. Her hands move behind her to rest on my knees, leaving her even more open and beautifully on display.

"Is this all for me, baby girl?" I groan. Her gorgeous body right in front of me, no longer hidden, shows me exactly who she is and what she's got.

"All yours," she murmurs, a sultry grin on her face, and I sit forward with a growl at how that sounds. Taking her nipple into my mouth, my hands smooth up her thighs to her center, and I dip a finger inside.

She moans my name, her body rolling as her hips grind into my hand. Her panting my name like a prayer is something I notice she does when she's desperately turned on, like I almost leave her breathless. Which is good, because she leaves me almost incapacitated. My will is always tested, my disbelief that I found her all-encompassing. I pull her nipple into my mouth, sucking hard as my finger circles her clit, and her hips start moving more.

"I want you to come and slide up and down my cock for me," I say against her skin as I slide my mouth across her chest to her other nipple. "I want your body to move on me like it's moving on my hand." I continue, hardly able to pull my mouth away from her. "And while you ride me, baby girl, I'm going to pour my whiskey all over your fucking beautiful naked body." Nibbling and dragging my lips across her body, I hear her pant, her hips moving faster. "And I'm gonna lick you clean." My mumbled desires have her chest rising and falling rapidly, her skin flushed.

She starts to move then, sitting up a little, getting into position as I pull down my underwear, my cock springing up hard. Grabbing on to me, she strokes me a little, and I growl. I lean over and get a condom from my jeans, ripping it open. She takes it from my hand eagerly and rolls it onto my length, until I'm perfectly sheathed and ready to feel her around me.

"Sit, baby girl," I grit out, because I'm trying very hard not to come in her hand. She moves instantly as the words leave my mouth, and as I feel her warm, wet pussy take me in, I almost come undone. "Fuuuuuccckkkkkk."

"Oh... my..." she pants out as she starts to move up and down on my cock, finding a rhythm that's comfortable for her. I don't care either way. I have prime viewing. I have the most amazing, beautiful woman riding my cock and a bottle of my favorite whiskey in my hand.

"That's it," I tell her, her hands now back behind her, resting on my knees as her body rolls onto me. I lift the bottle and pour a little down her chest, making her gasp. The liquor cascading down her breast and dripping from her nipple is photo worthy, and it's only a second before I'm sucking and licking my way up her chest.

"Yes... Oh, Connor," she moans, sounding nearly feral as her bouncing quickens.

"Fucking delicious," I groan. The way she's moving and the taste of her has my cock throbbing. I pour again, this time over the second breast, giving it the same attention.

"You're making a mess," she pants, a light laugh leaving her, but she doesn't stop riding me like it's her job. Her body jiggles, her breasts bouncing in my face, and I grab on to her hip with one hand, pulling her down onto me harder.

"Hmmmmmm, now it's your turn, baby girl. Make a mess on my cock for me," I tell her, putting the bottle down and grabbing her other hip as I start to lift her up and down on my cock, helping her reach that spot inside her that I know will have her exploding. Every time we connect, our skin slaps together, but my view is still unmatched. Her naked body is for my eyes only.

"I'm going to... come..." she whimpers, and I can tell she's close, which is good, because so am I.

"Look at you, so perfect for me, your pretty pussy taking me so well."

"Yes... yes..." She's almost there, her cheeks flushed, her body still bouncing, but her movements begin tensing, her eyes rolling to the back of her head.

"Made for me, baby girl. You were made just for me," I pant out, also breathless, and then I feel her coming undone.

"Connor, Connor, Connor! Yesssssssss!" Her orgasm rips through her, and she screams and cries out, her entire body shaking, with me right behind her.

"Fuuuuccccckkkkk," I grit out as I take over fully, thrusting up and chasing my release. I feel like my mind blanks for a second. My release is so big it takes the wind right out of me, and I lean back on the sofa as Daisy falls forward, hugging her tight to my chest.

We quietly stay like that for a moment because it feels like we just achieved something really special. I'm so fucking happy right now; I didn't even realize something like this was possible. Finding a girl who fits in with my lifestyle, someone who's smart and challenges me. Someone who can teach me new things and completely take me by surprise while also being absolute perfection in bed. I meant what I said earlier; I feel like she was made just for me.

I swallow roughly. My feelings for Daisy are so strong, and I'm not sure what it means.

"You okay, baby girl?" I ask, because she's still silent, and I feel her grin against my bare chest. Then, in the worst small-town country accent I've ever heard, she answers me.

"That's the best damn whiskey I've ever tasted."

We laugh together, and for the first time ever, I start thinking about shopping for a diamond. One so big that they can see it from space, because I want every fucker that comes within a ten-mile radius of where Daisy is to know she's mine.

I just hope she feels the same.

34

DAISY

We're showered and lying in Connor's bed, the two of us in that post-sex haze of contentment. Still naked and cuddling, he hasn't removed his hands from my body all night. Whether it's a caress of my bare shoulder, a kiss peppered to my lips, or an ass grab to move me closer to him, Connor can't stop touching me. And I don't want him to ever stop.

I'm not sure what was different about our time together today, but something shifted. The sex was intense, as it usually is. But our connectedness is like something I've never known. It's like our entire beings are aligned.

"How is that heart chakra of yours going now, baby girl?" he asks, and I smile. It's like he read my mind.

"It's going just fine." My head rests on his chest, hearing his big, strong heart thud in constant rhythm under my ear. I think about him and the media chasing us today. I wonder how the other women in his life have dealt with it. My mind then wanders, thinking about if this is what he always does when he comes to the city. Have amazing sex with a woman and fall asleep cuddling.

"I can tell you're thinking about something. Spit it out, baby girl." His hand trails up and down my back, tickling in the most comforting way.

"Is this how all your work trips go when you come to New York?" I ask, swallowing quickly, and his hand stops mid-caress on my shoulder.

"Never," he says adamantly.

"Never?" I ask because, apparently, I like to torture myself. I'm not sure what's happening between us, but it feels strong, and I need to know if it feels different for him too.

"Daisy, this is new for me. I've never had a girlfriend. Not like this." His fingers start up again, drawing lazy patterns on my shoulder as my body freezes.

"Girlfriend?" I ask, my breath catching. We haven't labeled us until now, and it's almost like I'm too shocked to believe it.

"Yeah, that's what you are, my girlfriend. I met my girlfriend's parents today. I fixed my girlfriend's father's gate. I'm spending time in the city with *my girlfriend* this week."

I can't help the grin that comes to my face as my heart expands and a feeling of complete joy wraps around me.

"Are you sure? I mean, we haven't known each other long. I know people keep things casual for a while before..." I start, because even though I've never been someone's girlfriend, I do know through most men I meet that they like to keep things casual for a long time. They never like to discuss commitment of any kind. Not with me, anyway.

"If it's alright with you, when we go back to Whispers, I'm telling everyone who will listen that you're mine."

We're doing this. He feels the same. I had no idea something this good was waiting for me. It's so true what they say, that you need to kiss a few frogs before you find your prince. And I think I may have finally found mine.

"Are you sure?" I offer, giving him an out. My brain is fighting with itself. One half of me wants to jump up and down, tell him that I'm falling for him, that I want to be his. The other is trying to preserve my heart, knowing how much pain I'm going to be in if this doesn't work out.

"Yes, very sure, Daisy. I want us to be exclusive."

I lift my head up and look at him. I'm wide-eyed, and as the silence becomes deafening, I will my mouth to talk and say *yes!* But it doesn't, and he looks at me seriously, seemingly becoming a bit nervous himself at my reaction.

"If you have someone else here in the city or someone who you were seeing before you moved to Whispers who you're not over, you need to let me know, because I need to tell them that you're no longer theirs." He says it so seriously I think I might faint. The butterflies he elicits are rampaging my insides.

"Yours?" I ask tentatively, looking into his eyes.

He nods, his gaze searing into mine. "Mine, baby girl. All mine."

"I'm not anybody else's but yours, Connor White-man," I confirm, and he smiles, releasing a breath.

"Good. Seems like our frequencies are in alignment, then," he adds simply, and I burst out a laugh.

"Seems like it." As I giggle against him, he lifts up, kissing me tenderly, like he's ensuring I know exactly how he feels. And I do. I can feel it. It isn't my imagination. It isn't a casual thing. What we have, what we're feeling, is strong. For both of us.

As we pull away, I lie back down, and his hand goes back to caressing my arm.

"Did you know your mom's old commune is somewhere near Whispers?" he asks me. I lift my head, resting my chin on his chest to look at him.

"Yeah. I have no idea where. I'd like to go and find it actually, so I can get some insight into her upbringing. Learn a bit about my family history," I tell him honestly, grinning as I ponder that possibility, but he's frowning.

"I don't think that's a good idea." His tone is careful, like he doesn't want to upset me.

"Why not?" I can feel my lips pulling into a pout. "It'll just be a day trip. You know, to look around, maybe say hi to some of her old friends," I tell him as I warm up to the idea even more.

"People who live in those kinds of places generally like to keep to themselves. Your dad mentioned it to me this afternoon. He said it probably wasn't smart to go looking for them. They don't often welcome strangers."

I think over his words for a moment, taking into consideration that my dad had something to say about it. "Well, I'm technically not a stranger..." I murmur, but his creased brows don't smooth out just yet.

"From what I understand, your mom left a long time ago. They probably don't even know that she had a child.

Best to leave the past where it is, I think," he offers, and I take a deep breath.

I sigh. "Yeah, maybe."

He's right, of course. I would never go and just turn up, unannounced. But I do like the idea of learning more about that way of life and more about my mom's childhood.

"Can't you just give your mom a truth tea or something?" he asks, and I lift my head, looking at him with confusion.

"Truth tea?" I question, my smile growing as I try not to laugh.

"Yeah. You have tea for everything else. Can't you make something that has people telling the truth from the first sip they take?" He's grinning now, clearly teasing me.

"I think that's called whiskey... If I gave you such a tea, what would the first true thing be that comes from your lips, Mr. Whiteman?" I ask playfully.

"Hmm, maybe you need to make it for me and find out."

I laugh as his hands grab my waist and roll me onto my back, and he lowers on top of me, settling between my legs to remind me yet again how good we are together.

35

———

CONNOR

Waking up alone, I go in search of the woman I can't stop thinking about. I feel groggy. The few days I've had here at the office in New York have been some of my most productive. I've had back-to-back meetings, negotiated some new deals, and signed off on some new crops for our barley production. But that, coupled with late nights making love to Daisy numerous times, has me feeling exhausted. She's been working hard too. She had a few meetings as well, has been reviewing staff protocols, making new tea elixirs with her mom, and deciding on a few new ones that I think she'll want to bring to the spa. Her tea business is a big passion of hers, as is the yoga—more so than the spa side of things—but her business mind is really where she thrives, and I've been trying to think of things she can explore for her future. Ones that she can do from Whispers, because I really want her to stay with me. Not that she has to work. I would take care of her, but I know if I suggested such a thing, she would probably concoct a death elixir. One sip, and I'd be gone.

"Good morning," she says as I spot her in my kitchen, showered and changed, a cup of tea in one hand and a glass of green juice in the other. I walk toward her, the stupid grin on my face at seeing her in my space not able to be wiped away, as she stretches out her hands to me.

"What's this?" I groan, looking at what she's offering me, feeling my body aching from all the exercise we did last night, the night before, and the night before that. I can't get enough of her. Not that I'm complaining. I love how Daisy is so into it; her confidence with me is building every day, startlingly different to that woman I first met at Sunshine who couldn't look at me naked. Now, she can't keep her hands off me.

"It's a hot mixture of ginseng and echinacea that will help with both energy and immunity. The green juice is mainly celery and packed full of antioxidants. We've had a big few days, and I thought you might need it." She puts them on the kitchen counter next to me.

"Let me jump into the shower, and then I'll be ready to go," I tell her, because I obviously slept in, something I never do.

"You don't have to come. I can just meet you at the airport later," she offers, but I'm already shaking my head and throwing back the juice, which makes me almost gag, enlisting a giggle from her.

"You don't want me to go with you?" I ask. As I stand totally naked, she looks amazing in some jeans and a shirt.

"No, I mean, Trisha's and my apartment isn't..."

Glancing around my penthouse, she waves her hand a little as I watch her and take a sip of the tea. It isn't terrible and a bit easier to consume than the green shit. Maybe I'm getting used to all these hot tonics she gives me.

"Daisy, I don't care what your apartment is like. But we only have this morning before we need to be on the jet, so we can call on Trisha, and then head straight to the airport together."

"Sure, just... you know, keep an open mind."

I grin. "I have a very open mind. In fact, I'm open to anything..." I say, grabbing her by the hips and pulling her to me.

"Connor! Go, or we will be late." She laughs and swats at my shoulder playfully, my clear attempt at seduction falling on deaf ears. But I'm still smiling as I take my tea and head to the shower, making it a quick and very cold one.

MY DRIVER PULLS UP to a laundromat on a side of town I've never been to. It isn't bad... but it isn't great either. My lips thin as I look around. My security team got back to me overnight, finding nothing amiss with Soren other than he hasn't filed taxes in forever and he doesn't seem to have a permanent place of residence. But I know how people in that lifestyle live off-grid, and his taxes are not my problem. So for the moment, he is clean.

"We're here!" she says, opening the door and stepping out, and I follow her quickly, the sidewalk busy. I look up and down the street, seeing a mix of retail and food shops, many of which have seen better days. "Come on. Let's go."

Grabbing my hand, I look at my driver, who gives me a nod. He'll wait here, just in case. I look around once more, seeing a few motorbikes pull up opposite us on the other side of the road, and clench my jaw. The paparazzi are following us. I shouldn't be surprised. I haven't seen any articles yet. But I know they have images. I have briefed my PR team, and they're aware that something is coming.

Daisy drags me across the sidewalk, and we walk into a twenty-four seven dry cleaners.

"Hey, Daisy! Where have you been?" an older woman, who appears to be too old to even be working, says in a heavy French accent. I watch her carefully. Her eyes seem deceptive as she moves her gaze to me, clearly interested in who I am. I wonder if this dry cleaners is a front for a mafia mob or something. I make a mental note to ask Daisy about it later.

"Hey, Anna, just out of town for a few. Back again soon, though," Daisy says as she continues pulling me down a side hallway.

We hit a back door and open it, and I notice the lock is broken before I close it behind me. As we walk up a few flights of stairs, I'm grateful for the cardio I do; otherwise, it would be a challenge.

"We're here." She sounds a little puffed, and I see her swallow down some nerves before she opens the door and we step inside.

As we walk in, the first thing I do is duck. The ceilings

seem lower than usual. Although, I do have high ceilings everywhere I am, the office fit-out was done purposefully for that. My penthouse and everything we have in Whispers is the same.

"Hey, Trisha," she says, and I spot a woman sitting on the sofa, eating a tub of ice cream, even though it's the morning, and she sits up quickly. She smiles at Daisy, then looks at me, her mouth dropping open.

"Holy hell, it's big dick guy!"

My eyebrows hit my hairline, and Daisy splutters a cough before going a cute shade of pink.

"Sorry, she didn't mean that." Daisy covers for her, and I smirk.

"It's good to know I please you, baby girl," I whisper to her, grinning like a fool, thinking about Daisy talking about me to her friends.

She blushes some more, her hand slapping my chest, and I grab it, holding it in mine. "Come, let's sit. Trisha, this is Connor. Connor, this is Trisha." Daisy makes the introductions, and Trisha waves her spoon at me. I give her a nod as I follow Daisy into her apartment.

We can barely fit on the extremely small sofa, and as the girls catch up, I take in her space. The building is old. Maybe pre-war, but it has had some renovations done at some point, because the ceiling is really low and the rooms are small. Almost like they took one large apartment and cut it into two. The window frames are chipped, a big crack running up the corner of the wall beside me, and I wonder if it's structurally sound. I turn to look at the other side, noticing the kitchen is almost nonexistent and doesn't look like it gets a lot of use.

"What's with the ice cream?" Daisy asks her.

"I'm eating my feelings," Trisha says. "I found Josh kissing another woman last night." She scoops out another big bite of ice cream.

"Really? What happened?" Daisy asks. I still have hold of her hand, keeping her close.

"We went to this restaurant. It was new, pretty fancy. Had a great meal, and then he excused himself to use the restroom. When he didn't come back for a while, I went looking for him and found him sucking face with some girl behind the wine racks."

I feel bad for her. Clearly, he isn't the kind of guy you want around.

"Oh no!" Daisy says, her expression pinched.

"Can you believe I thought he was marriage material!"

"I'm sorry, Trisha. Not all men are like that. How long were you together?" I ask. She's Daisy's friend, so I want to make an effort and get to know her. She's heartbroken and almost married this guy, so they must have been together for a long time.

"Two weeks. Two weeks, and he just got up and sucked face with someone else." She huffs, and I look at Daisy like she's crazy. She gives me a close-lipped smile and a small nod, and I know she'll fill me in on the smaller details later.

"When are you coming home?" Trisha asks her, and my body stills. *Never.*

"Well, I still have another week or two in Whispers, but then I'll be back and can help you find your next Mr. Right." She smiles at Trisha, and my stomach twists. I want her to stay in Whispers, and while we haven't talked about it, I didn't realize she was so committed to coming back to the city.

"I've missed you," Trisha says, and I frown, because "missed you" is too light a saying for the feelings I'll have if Daisy moves back here. I start thinking about how I can work from my New York office more so I can still see her, the pain in my gut intensifying, because I know I'm also needed in Whispers a lot, at the distillery, the home of my business. My entire life.

"I've missed you too. Here, I've put next month's rent in here, plus extra for bills," Daisy says, handing Trisha a yellow envelope that I'm now assuming contains cash, and I try to swallow, this whole thing leaving a very bitter taste in my mouth.

"But you aren't even here!" Trisha says, even though she takes Daisy's money.

"I know, but a bit extra to help."

I take in some air to try to tame my feelings. I'm not sure what their annual rental fees are, but I would happily pay them. I look at Trisha, and she looks at me.

"You're my waitress in my suite, aren't you?" I ask her.

"Yes. I'm working this weekend. Will you be there?" she asks innocently.

"No, I've given it to my friend, Huxley, but he's great and won't give you any trouble," I tell her, knowing that some suites and corporate spaces can contain some real arrogant assholes.

"Good. Is he single?" she asks quickly, her face full of hope, and I realize that she's one of those girls who's in love with the thought of being in love. I give her a grin.

"No, very happily married," I confirm.

"All the good ones are," she mumbles, and Daisy looks at me in a way that makes me think she feels the same about me as I do her. I squeeze her hand in mine, and she does it back.

All the while, my stomach rolls, and my head is busy, trying to think of how to keep her in Whispers.

How to keep her with me.

36

———

CONNOR

I'm glad to be home. It's been a week since New York, and things are moving quickly. With the spa, and with Daisy and me.

I love the city, but the older I get, the more I just want to be in Whispers. With her. Seeing Daisy do her morning yoga on the lawn brings me peace. I like falling asleep with her in my arms. We work all day, and sometimes see each other around the office, sometimes not, but my days are starting and ending with her now, and I can't remember them being any different.

Now I survey my new building plans that are stretched out across my desk, looking over them with a critical eye with my builder, Griffin.

"So is this what you're thinking?" Griffin asks me, the two of us working on these plans on and off for months now. Dad and I purchased separate plots of land farther out of town years ago. He built on his, a large ranch-style home, and now he and Victoria and their myriad of animals all live there happily. My land is next to his, the borders thick with pines for privacy, but we have a gate between us, so he and I can walk over to each other's place anytime we want. It isn't far from Hudson and Huxley's family ranch, and there are a few other large allotments still vacant around us. One I know Griffin has already purchased, the others still waiting for the right buyer. Prices are so high for the land, it's out of reach for most locals.

But even though I own the land, I don't have a house yet. It was always something I thought I would build when I was older, ready to settle down. But now, as I stare at the plans we've designed over the last few weeks, it's feeling like it's the right time to make it happen.

"Yeah, I think we're nearly there. Can we extend this a little?" I ask, looking at the landscaping. There's a space to the east that I was going to make into a pool, but I have since changed it to be a large, expansive lawn.

"Sure. The other option is to have the pool over here on the north side, which is probably better," Griffin suggests, watching me. "Why do you want so much lawn over there?" he asks, and I look up from the plans at him. He's grinning at me, like he knows exactly why I want such a big lawn, and I roll my eyes.

"Just say it," I tell him, throwing my pen on the desk and pocketing my hands, waiting for his teasing to start.

"Your dad told me that you're into yoga now..." He's not able to help the laughter that spills from his mouth. I grin then, because I don't care.

"You've been talking to Dad?" I ask him, scratching the back of my head, and it makes sense. They've probably been having a good old gossip about me, especially since Daisy and I haven't really been hiding anything since we got back.

"What's happening?" my dad asks, walking into my office.

"Speak of the devil," I murmur as he shakes hands with Griffin.

"We're just tweaking a few things. Your son here wants more grass for his morning yoga," Griffin says, his smile wide.

Dad looks at me, his grin one that makes me grin right back, and now all three of us grown men stand around my office, smiling like fools.

"Yeah, well, love will make you do crazy things, Griffin. You'll learn that soon enough," Dad says, and I scoff.

"I'm not in love." Only, the words taste bitter on my tongue. I can't be, though, right...? I mean, we work together every day and spend every night together too. I've met her parents, and she's met mine. We've traveled to the city and have practically been inseparable this entire time. The thought of being separated gives me hives.

"Oh, well, I'm no expert, but..." Griffin trails off, looking back at the house plans and then back to me accusingly, and I sigh before running my hand down my beard. "Keep these. Look over them, and then just email me any changes. I need to go chat with Victoria about a new project that's coming up."

"I'll catch up with you later," Dad tells him, and I give him a wave as he walks out of my office.

"You alright?" Dad asks seriously.

"Yeah, it's just Daisy."

"Daisy? I thought it was going well with her?" His brow creases with concern.

"That's the problem," I tell him, looking at him firmly.

He shakes his head. "I don't understand?"

"She's brilliant. Also, fucking smart, funny, quirky, she makes me tea every morning, and she's so fucking flexible..." I groan, and my dad grins.

"I just... How do I get her to stay? How do I get her to stay in Whispers? Here, with me?" I ask him, feeling my chest open up, vulnerability sneaking out.

"Well, shit." His grin widens as he chuckles.

"How did you get Victoria to stay?" I ask him, thinking he'll have the answer for me.

"I simply didn't let her go. There was no way she was leaving Whispers, and I told her as much," Dad says, and I shake my head. I'm not going to go about it that way with Daisy, that's for sure.

"Have you told Daisy how you feel, since you're clearly in love with her?"

My heart stutters at his call-out. "I'm not in love..." I can't even finish my denial, not believing the words for a second. The way I feel when I'm with her and the way I feel when I'm without her, it's too intense to be anything other than burning, deep love. My dad looks at me the same way he looked at me the time I hid bullfrogs in his whiskey cask when I was ten. He doesn't believe me.

"So you're okay that she packs up and leaves in another week or so? Because that's what she's going to do unless you get your head out of your ass and ask her to stay."

Exhaling a whoosh of breath, I run my hand down my beard again.

"I can't ask her to stay. She has a life, family, friends, work in New York." I don't want to take her away from everything she loves. That feels like a selfish move on my part.

"But how do you know she doesn't want to? She sure fits in well around here, seems to love the lifestyle Whispers offers. She can go back to the city with you every month, see her friends and family," Dad says, and it all makes sense to me, but I'm not sure Daisy will feel the same.

"She has a strong business brain..." I murmur, because she isn't going to be a kept woman. She will want to work, want to do something productive that challenges her and makes her happy.

"So do you, so why don't you put it to work and get something organized for her? Hell, she has a lot of skills we could use in our business."

I look at him sharply. He's okay with me offering her something permanent, and for that, I'm grateful.

"Maybe..." I murmur, already thinking about it.

"It feels good, doesn't it?"

"What does?" I ask, wondering where he's going with this serious tone.

"To find a woman who feels like the other half of yourself?"

"Hey!" Daisy steps into the office like a breath of fresh air, just as I'm about to respond. But my dad already knows how I feel. That my answer would be a resounding yes. "Oh sorry, I didn't realize you were in a meeting." She starts to step out.

"No. I'm just leaving." Dad steps toward the door and looks at me. "Think about it, son," he reiterates, and I nod.

"Thanks, Dad."

He gives Daisy a big shit-eating grin as he leaves us alone.

"Things have progressed quickly with the spa this week. I've finalized the long treatment food menu with the chef, and once I tweak a few things, that will be done. Staff are all confirmed and all trained. I have booked Marie's Place next door for the next few months, and then you can reassess. The booking system is all in, and the team is starting to take advanced bookings. Products have all been allocated and stock counted, ready to go," she tells me with a wide, proud smile on her face. I grin back at her, even though my stomach drops.

She's almost done. Her project is complete. The end of her tenure with us is coming too soon.

"What's this?" she asks, stepping closer and looking down at the plans for my new place that are spread all over my desk.

"Oh, house plans. I'm building a ranch out of town," I tell her, and she looks up at me, surprised.

"Really? A new house?"

"Yeah, I can't live at the distillery forever. We're going to break ground on the accommodation buildings soon, and then it will be too busy, too loud..."

"Wow, this looks amazing." Her fingers run across the drawings, taking it all in.

"Do you like it?" I ask, holding my breath, hoping she does.

"Look at all that lawn. That's going to be amazing." Awe softens her tone, wrapping around my heart, and I grin, feeling like I made the right decisions.

"Bedrooms all along here, a large living space, and a kitchen that overlooks Whispers." I point out a few details.

"Oh, what's this room?" she asks, and I swallow. I should've known she'd catch that.

Before I can answer, Stephanie, the receptionist, walks in.

"Connor. The PR team is on the phone. They said to check your emails right away."

I move quickly, opening up my laptop and seeing the email in question.

"Everything alright?" Daisy asks, frowning, and I look at the screen, my eyes moving through the email.

"The media have published photos..." I grit out, before I click on the attachment and draw in a sharp breath.

"Photos?" she asks tentatively.

"Of us," I tell her, and she steps forward to look at my computer over my shoulder.

"Oh..." As the article opens, we both stare at it in silence. It's a leading story in one of the online news and gossip websites, with photos of us walking around town, going to her apartment, driving into my penthouse. With my nerves rushing, I look at her, seeing her face has paled. The photos aren't great, and the headline is commenting on her size, clearly for clickbait, even though she's fucking beautiful just the way she is. My shoulders stiffen, realizing how hurtful this must be for her. They write shit about me all the time, but the frustration and anger I'm feeling now is focused solely on them commenting on Daisy. I make a mental note to have a meeting with my PR team. The media needs to know Daisy is off-limits.

"Ignore it. They're vultures. They don't know me, they don't know you. They don't know us," I tell her as I stand and grab her hand. She looks at me, searching my eyes for something, and I grab her other hand, standing toe-to-toe with her.

"Breathe with me, Daisy," I ask her quietly, and her eyes widen before she nods.

"In, two, three, four..." she says as her eyes close.

"Out, two, three, four..." I say as we stand together, holding hands and breathing in sync for a few more beats before we open our eyes and look back at each other.

"You're getting good at that." Her smile is small, but there.

"Deep breathing is a new hobby of mine. I was taught by the best," I quip, and her smile widens a bit, making me feel better.

"Are you ready for the party tonight?" I ask her, knowing the spa opening has been all that anyone has spoken about all week, as Victoria has been busy pulling it together.

"As ready as I'll ever be. Thank you for organizing a dress and hair, makeup, shoes, the works. A real-life glam squad is coming for me." She hums, still smiling up at me. This is her night to shine. Our night to shine. I was always going to ensure she had everything she needed. Because while I love Whispers, I know it doesn't have the shops or people to help her for a formal night like tonight. So I flew them in, especially for her.

"You don't need glam; you're always the most beautiful woman to me." Leaning down, I take her lips in a chaste kiss.

"Well, on that note, I should go. I have a few things to finish up before I head out." Stepping backward, away from me, she slides out of my grip.

"See you tonight," I tell her, watching her go.

"See you tonight," she says, sending me one more sweet smile over her shoulder before she's out of my office, and I'm slumping down in my seat.

My dad's right. I'm completely and utterly in love with her.

37

DAISY

With quick steps, I strut back to my office and go straight to my laptop, my heart pounding. I put on a brave face with Connor, but all my old insecurities came flooding back in an instant when I saw that article.

I find the article online and look it over properly, immediately feeling sick. The photos they captured are a total invasion of our privacy. There are some of us in the car, others of us walking into the dry cleaners at the bottom of my apartment. A few taken from a long-range lens, no doubt, of us stepping onto the jet together. There's a whole montage of our entire trip to the city. To make matters worse, the images of me are not flattering whatsoever. The article headline reads "Connor Whiteman is Trying on Someone Different for Size," clearly a jab at my weight while also pointing out that I'm not like his usual girlfriends.

I think back to the trip, to him telling me that he hasn't ever really had a girlfriend. Dates, yes. Casual hookups, yes, but nothing like this. I really look at the pictures then, of the two of us, and I still. Not from the angles or what we are doing, but the way Connor is looking at me when I hadn't realized. His eyes look at me with pure adoration. There's another photo of me gleaming up at him, and it's one of the happiest photos of me I've ever seen. But what's consistent in all of them is the clear, open body language we have that speaks volumes of how we feel about each other. We're always touching, smiling, laughing and you can't fake that.

I swallow and continue reading. The article goes into details about Connor, like his wealth and status, before the journalist questions what he's doing with someone like me. I'm not sure how, but they have found old photos of me and published those too. They mention Sunshine and call me a hippie.

"Got a minute?" Tanner's voice is rough as he startles me, and my gaze whips up to his.

"Sure," I rush to say as I click off the screen and clear my throat, trying to get my head into gear.

"I wanted to say congratulations on the spa. You've done a great job," he says as he walks toward my desk, leaning on the back of the armchair opposite me.

"Well, it isn't over yet, but thank you. I appreciate that," I tell him, grateful.

"Victoria has arranged one hell of a party tonight." He looks at me seriously for a moment, so I wait for him to continue. "Are you looking at the article?" he asks.

I can't hide anything from him. My emotions are clearly written all over my face, not just about the article, but also about my work, Whispers, and Connor. So, I just go with the truth. "Yeah..."

"It won't be the first hurdle that you and Connor face together," he says, and I remain silent. "I know my son. He's never brought a girl home to introduce me to."

My breathing stalls at that information.

"Sure, he dates, has been a bit of a ladies' man over the years, but he has never committed before now. I blamed myself for that. I was always a loner. I was thinking he might be more like me than I realized." He continues with a sigh. "But, hell, he hired you after meeting you the first day and brought you straight here, so clearly, he's had feelings for you from the start."

I swallow past the lump in my throat, knowing he still has more to say.

"And I can see in the way you two interact that those feelings are reciprocated." He watches me carefully, and I take a deep breath.

"They are. But... how can it work? I'm from the city." My voice cracks, my head a whirl, my heart a mess.

"Anything can work if you want it badly enough. So I guess the question is, do you?" he asks.

I don't even hesitate. "I do. I one hundred percent do." I'm not sure if I'm talking to my boss, my boyfriend's father, a mentor, or all three right now.

"You fit in well here, the distillery, the town, our family. I'd be proud to have you as part of my son's life."

It hits me right in the chest as I realize that this is true acceptance. I've never felt this before. I have my parents' love, of course, and the great friendship with Trisha, but with Connor, his family, this town, all of it makes me feel so welcomed, so accepted, just for being my true self. It's refreshing and energizing.

"Wow..." I say on an exhale, almost speechless.

"But I need to know... Are you any good with goats?" he asks with a grin, breaking the heaviness of the conversation. I laugh heartily, and he tells me more about Victoria's goat Gertie, and then he leaves me to it.

There's no more time for me to overthink. The glam squad is waiting, and I need to get ready for the party.

38

CONNOR

The party is amazing. It's been a big night, people everywhere. The distillery and spa look six-star quality, the room full of locals, suppliers, both new and old faces. And overwhelmingly, the response has been positive. All due to the amazing woman who I've been watching all night. In a black dress that makes her look like a goddess, with her hair long and shiny, the curls flowing down her back. Her bright-blue eyes sparkle, just how I like them. She takes my breath away every time I see her.

I step toward her, my voice almost gone from talking so much, and lean over her shoulder, whispering in her ear.

"Can I steal you for a moment?" I murmur as I grab her hand, and she politely ends the conversation with one of our new staff members. I've hardly spoken to her all night. I've been networking, and she's been meeting and greeting people, taking them on tours of the new space. It's been busy.

"Where are you taking me?" she asks with a smile as I guide her through the crowd and take her out a side door into the cool, crisp fresh air of Whispers. I remain quiet as we head down the side garden path, the night clear, the stars bright, and the silence golden. We walk down the length of the distillery, somewhere she hasn't really been since her first day here when I gave her a quick tour. Thinking about that time makes me want to chuckle. How much she pushed me, how arrogant I was with her. The path ends, and we step out into a large, vibrant green lawn that I have since had landscaped.

"Oh my God." Stopping abruptly, she looks up, her eyes nearly bugging out of her head, which has me even more excited about this reveal. "Connor?"

"I can't take all the credit. Your father gave me the idea from his garden," I tell her as she looks around the hundreds of Daisy bushes that surround us. All in full bloom, all planted together tightly, so all we can see is a mass of white and yellow with the backdrop of the manicured lawn. Looking from above, the bushes are positioned in the outline of a daisy, the middle circle a trimmed grassy area, where we are currently standing now.

"What's this?" she asks, still looking gobsmacked.

"This is our garden," I say simply.

"Our garden?"

"A place here at the distillery that's just for us. For yoga, for breathwork, for picnics, long nights with a bottle of whiskey..." I tell her, not able to help my grin, thinking about the image my memory pulls of her from that night in my penthouse.

"It's perfect." Her expression is one of awe. "I love this. So much." When she turns that pretty face to me, I can tell she's ready to say more. But I just want her in my arms.

"Come dance with me." This is only the second time in my life I've asked a woman to dance with me, her taking up the first time as well a few weeks ago at the bar.

"Here?" she asks with a tilt of her head, and I hit a button on my cell in response. The outdoor speakers come alive with the sweet sounds of Dolly and Kenny, as do some sparkly fairy lights that I had placed in the daisies. Our very own magical garden comes to life.

"Connor," she whispers, her eyes glassing over slightly. "You've really thought of everything."

"Dance with me, baby girl."

She steps forward, into my arms, and I hold her to me tight as we start to sway.

"I thought you hardly ever danced?" she comments, smiling up at me. "I guess I must be a lucky gal."

"Just with you. I'll always dance with you." The honesty tears through me almost violently. I feel vulnerable, my heart completely open. I feel a mix of nerves, yet so self-assured, like nothing else in my life has been the right decision but her. She stops swaying then and lifts onto her tiptoes, her lips touching mine in a way that seals us together.

Running my palm over her back, I wrap my arms around her tightly, the feeling of not wanting to let her go taking over. As Dolly's voice filters through the night air, singing about doing something to me that I can't explain, I feel those lyrics to my core.

"Come with me. I want to show you something else," I say, pulling away from her slightly and taking her hand, leading her farther away from the party and past the thick daisies to a smaller clearing cocooned by large bushes of lavender.

"What's this? Another surprise?" she asks as I lead her to the structure I had specially made for her, currently decorated in fairy lights. The sounds of the party hum in the distance, this area private, quiet, and just for us.

"It's a glass house that has counters and a sitting area and a place where you can grow your specific herbs that may not be suitable for the kitchen garden," I tell her as she takes everything in. I have a space with a large daybed where she can meditate if she wishes. All the tools and pots are already here, glossy and new, just waiting for her to use.

"Connor..." I watch as her eyes well with tears, and I swallow. "All of this, it's... I can't believe you did this for me." Shaking her head, she asks, "How did you get this built so quickly? How didn't I notice this was happening? This is so thoughtful and intricate and I... I just... Why?"

I cut off her questions with a kiss. If I start explaining the hows and whys now, it'll only lead back to three little words from me that I'm not sure she's ready to hear. "Have I told you how stunning you look tonight, baby girl?" My words fall onto her lips as her palms run up my chest. She smiles up at me, relaxing into my touch, her questions saved for later.

"This old thing..." she teases, and my hands move then, smoothing down her curvaceous body before trailing up her back. I revel in her little shiver and the flare of her gaze when I hit her zipper and I start to lower it, wanting to see and feel all of her.

"Connor, someone might come," she whispers but doesn't stop me, the look in her eyes full of desire. As the zip lowers, the straps fall from her shoulders, and she bites her plush lip in anticipation.

"We're in complete privacy. The only person coming will be you." I speak against her skin as I press a kiss to her now bare shoulder, dragging my lips up her neck. She moans softly, and my cock thickens as she lets the dress fall to the ground. She's a vision. Bathed in moonlight, in a lacy set of lingerie that has me salivating.

"God, you're beautiful…" I croak, wondering how I got so lucky.

"You have such a way with words…." she whispers, her grin seductively sexy as she unbuttons my shirt and I slide off my jacket.

"I speak the truth. Your body is fucking amazing," I growl as I run my hands up and down her sides, not able to stop touching her for even a moment. "And I'd do anything for you, you know that? You could ask me for anything, and the answer would always be yes, Daise…" I admit as I lose my shirt, and her hands and lips are on my chest and neck. I make quick work of my pants before I lower her down onto the daybed, the new plush cushions making for a luxurious spot under the night sky.

"I just want you," she says as I kiss her shoulders and down her neck, her body arching as I do, her large breasts begging for release. Unclipping her bra, I cup them, moaning as I kiss her all over.

She pushes down my underwear as I grip her hip,

grabbing the lace and pulling it from her body. Giggling at my eagerness, her feet quickly kick them off her as she lies underneath me.

Her red hair is spread out across the fabric of the cushions, her body now at my mercy. I run my finger across her perfect lips and look into her eyes before I lower my touch, right to her core.

"Yes..." she gasps as I touch her clit, jolting a little before I put my lips on hers and swallow her moans. She loops her hands around my neck, pulling me closer as her breasts seal against my chest.

"I love the feel of you against me," I murmur, and her legs spread wider. Running my hand back up, I mold her breast in my palm as my pelvis grinds into hers.

"Connor, please," she whimpers almost impatiently, and I grin as I maneuver myself, edging my way into her slowly, wanting to burn this moment into my brain. I watch as her mouth opens on a moan as she takes me in so well that I almost lose my composure.

"Yeahhh, baby girl," I say, pulling out slightly and then moving back in, my eyes not leaving her face. Seeing the pleasure as she bites her bottom lip, I start to move a little quicker. I can't get enough of the way her body moves with my thrusts, how her eyes roll back, her sounds becoming desperate as I work her closer to the edge. As close as we are, it'll never feel close enough.

"Soooo good," she moans, long and low. Knowing that she's enjoying this teasing pace, I take my time, our mouths and hands exploring and consuming one another.

"You respond so well to me, baby girl... You were

made for me, there's no doubt in my mind." I moan, voice choked as my balls tighten, and I clench my jaw, needing to get her to come first.

"Only you, Connor." And with that, I feel her body clenching and pulsing before she's panting, "Yes... Yes, I'm going to come..." Her breaths grow quicker, her moves urgent, and she lifts her hips to meet my harder thrusts.

"Connor!" she shouts my name, convulsing, her fingers digging into my shoulders, and I speed up until I'm seeing stars.

"Fuck, Daise. Perfect... Mine... All mine." With a groan, I join her in ecstasy, holding her tight and never wanting to let her go.

39

DAISY

y mind and body feel like mush. The way Connor touches me, the way he's honest with me, his sweetness and thoughtfulness, I've never experienced that with a man. As we slowly catch our breaths, I look around, hoping this is all real. That I haven't dreamed up this scenario with the perfect man for me.

"You okay, baby girl?" he asks, peppering kisses to my bare shoulder as we both lie side by side in the glass house on the cozy daybed.

"I couldn't be any better," I tell him honestly, not able to tame my grin.

"This is such a special spot, Connor. I really can't believe you did all this," I tell him as I look around. It's like my own private little fairy tale. The small lights reflect off the glass, making it seem like there are thousands of them. The care and attention he's taken with the gardening tools, this daybed, and the meditation space, never mind the garden outside that took my breath away.

And don't get me started on the huge amounts of lavender.

"Well, I feel like I really had to sell Whispers... and me," he says, and I look at him, seeing the sincerity in his eyes. I reach up and cup his cheek, scratching my fingers in his beard.

"Sell?" I question, my heart back to beating erratically as I wait for his explanation. Tonight, this moment, feels different between us, like we have just solidified our relationship even more.

"There's something you don't know about me, Daise..."

I swallow roughly, waiting, sensing the importance of the conversation in the air.

"What's that?" I ask, voice quiet.

"I'm selfish. And... And I don't want you to leave."

"What?" I ask tentatively, wondering if I heard him right, my heartbeat thundering in my ears.

"I want you to be with me, and I want you to stay here. In Whispers. With me." He punctuates each sentence, ensuring there's no confusion. Watching me carefully, he waits for my response, looking nervous. He clearly doesn't understand how deeply I feel about him.

I wet my lips and take a breath before I say the only word that I know, down to my soul, is the right one.

"Yes," I whisper. I don't dare move; this bubble we're in is so magical, I want to remember everything about this moment. The way he's looking at me is how every woman wants their man to look at them. He's *my* man, isn't he?

"You want to stay in Whispers, or you want to stay with me?" he asks for clarity, eyes searching mine.

"With you. I love Whispers, and I..." I pause, my nerves calming, only solidifying my decision. Leaning in, I press my lips to his, then pull back and say, "And I love you."

When his lips spread in a grin, my heart bursts wide open, and a big smile sweeps across my face.

"Oh, baby girl... I loved you the moment you told me to put my clothes back on. I've fallen completely and madly in love with you. Just being in your presence brings me so much peace and happiness. If I have you with me, then everything else just falls into place," Connor says quickly, like he's rushing to get all the words out, and I giggle at his excitement, the smile on my face one that can't be wiped anytime soon, my eyes watering in both disbelief and an overwhelming sensation of pure love.

"My mom was right," I tell him, thinking back to what my mother said to me months ago.

"How so?" Cupping my jaw, his thumb brushes against my cheek, wiping away a lone tear that's fallen.

"She said that the universe will decide my life, and it went and put me right here in Whispers so I could find you."

"Come here," he growls, pulling my face to meet his once more. I grab him tight, and he holds my face like he never wants to let me go, kissing me breathless. We slowly pull away to look at each other.

"I love it here, and I meant what I said. I love you, Connor.

You've changed my life. Glass house or no glass house, you're an incredible man and I want to be with you. But..." With a steady inhale, I ask the question that's been haunting me every time I think about staying. "But what would I do? I will need to work. Do something... I love what I do now, the work I did at my mom's spa, and I don't want to give up that part of me," I say, but I'm smiling as I finish speaking, because he's looking back at me with a shit-eating grin, clearly happy.

"I've been thinking about that too. How about you project manage the new accommodations? It entails managing all the same things as the spa. Suppliers, staff, booking systems... We're breaking ground in a few weeks. You seem pretty good at managing new business units. I think you could also create that online yoga class you always wanted to do. Mix your teas and we can run them through our distribution channels to get you into retailers right around the country. Whatever your dreams are, let's make them happen. You can do anything you want, Daisy. I just want you to do it here with me," he says, and my body warms, heart full. He's thought of everything.

"I've been daydreaming about that kind of thing for a long time," I tell him, and his hold on me becomes firmer. This night has been perfect and is going to be ingrained in my mind for eternity.

"Those plans you saw today... of my house..." He takes a deep breath, and I look at him curiously. "I want them to be of our house."

"What?" I ask, eyes wide as I still in his arms.

"That room you saw. You asked me what that room was on the plans. It's a meditation and crystal room.

Right in the middle of the house. In the heart chakra of what I hope to be our home. You told me the heart chakra is the center of our ability to love and be loved. So in our house, I want that room to be the heart of our home, one with all our crystals. A safe, quiet space for you to meditate, for me to meditate... maybe for us to meditate together... I know it's a lot all at once. With you deciding to stay and starting a new job, us officially being together. I don't want you to feel pressured, but I'm serious about us, and I need you to know that."

I can't believe what I'm hearing. Connor Whiteman would be the last person to ever have a meditation room in his home. A place for crystals or anything like that. Yet here he is, wanting to talk about building a life together. A life that I never in a million years thought I'd ever get. A man who is kind, funny, generous, and handsome. A man who makes me feel like nothing else matters but the two of us. A man who flies me to see my parents at a moment's notice because he knows that I miss them. I feel like a real-life Cinderella. I can't help the tear that trails down my cheek, and he kisses it away.

"What do you say, baby girl? Want to build a future together?" he asks me, and I realize I haven't responded yet. I want what he described more than anything. So, for the second time tonight, I say the words that feel right.

"Yes, Connor, let's build a future. Here in Whispers. Together," I tell him with a watery smile. And as he lowers his mouth to mine, we seal our fates, our chakras perfectly aligned.

40

———

DAISY

As I get out of the springs, my body feels good.

I wipe down quickly, having snuck out this morning while Connor was on his run. I probably should've told him, but all he does is worry when I come down here to the springs on my own. But I'm trying to practice my swimming, so I can surprise him with my skill when he offers to give me another lesson.

Throwing my clothes on over my wet swimwear, I walk up the path, taking in the silent surroundings and the beautiful landscape.

Excitement bubbles in my chest while I also feel a little sad. I need to speak to my parents, as my life moving forward will look a lot different. I won't be going back to Sunshine or to live with Trisha. But I get to do something new, something that's all mine, maybe do some yoga online and expand our tea business, which will be great to do with Mom's help.

My thoughts are whirling as I step through the gate

back onto the distillery land, and that's probably why I don't see the man before he's next to me.

"Daisy Beckett?" a man's voice announces from over my shoulder, and I swivel quickly.

"Yes?" I say, almost out of breath from being so startled. Unease fills me with the man right by my side, barely an inch between us, my space invaded. I swallow as my heart rate increases. I probably shouldn't have identified myself, but put it down to shock. My gaze darts around, seeing no one else here in the parking lot, other than the usual business vehicles that park here overnight and a run-down off-white Kombi van.

"We need to talk," he says, not appearing friendly, but not aggressive either.

"I'm sorry, you are?" I ask as I step away from him to try to create some distance and get me closer to the door. But he's quick and already stepping with me, apparently aware of my moves before I even make them. My body is still damp, my hair a rat's nest, and I feel vulnerable as the clothes I threw on barely cover my wet swimsuit.

"Not here. We need to go," he grits out, and I see him looking around.

"Go? I'm not going anywhere with you." Something about this isn't right. He isn't lost, not asking for directions. Seems to know exactly who I am, yet I have no idea who he is. There's something about him that reminds me of Soren. Similar height and build. His hair is past his shoulders, skin weathered and tanned, like he has spent his life outside in the elements. Not dissimilar to my mom, really. Although he's younger and fitter, more my age, I would guess. Before I can make a run for the door, his hand grips on to my arm tightly.

"Keep quiet and walk now."

Coolness of metal presses into my side, and I look down, seeing a gun in his hand pointed right at me. My panic flares.

"What do you want?" I ask, gritting my teeth so I don't vomit. I want to scream. I want to run. I want to get away from him and his sweaty stench. Deodorant is clearly not something he uses.

"Shut up and walk," he hisses low, pushing me along. I look up and around as he pushes me toward the van, praying someone comes. But I know Connor is on the other side of the distillery on his running track and the only other person out at this early hour is usually the gardener, who I know for fact isn't working this morning because he was at the party with us all last night, and Connor told everyone to come in later today.

"Are you going to kill me? Is that what you're planning to do? Why? Who are you? I don't even know who you are," I quiz him, my words stumbling out over the top of each other, and the gun pushes into my skin harder, causing me to grimace. I wonder if this is it. Is my life about to be over? Just when it's really getting started? I think of Connor and how much he opened up to me last night, how he's seeing me as part of his future, and I trip over the road toward the van as dizziness hits me. It doesn't help that when he straightens me with a curse, he just pushes me forward again. I try to slow my steps, clinging on to the hope that someone might spot me. Is this human trafficking? Is this what happens? Is this how it starts? When I try to ask him more questions, he cuts me off with a rough shove that has my knees buckling.

"You need to shut up," he warns, but I don't care, I need to make this as difficult for him as possible without getting myself killed.

"What's this about? Where are you taking me?" I ask again, but he pushes me harder, so I walk faster, my feet tripping on the ground with every step.

"We're going for a little drive, Daisy," he says in a mock sweet, yet dangerous voice that makes me shiver. We make it to the van, and reality dawns on me that I can't get in. If I get in, then it's over, I'm as good as gone.

"No," I state firmly as I try to wriggle out of his grip with all my might, but his hand clamps down on my arm harder, his strength something I can't fight against.

"Get in the van, Daisy." Opening the large side door, he gestures with a wave of his hand. I notice there's no back seat. It's completely empty, except for the two seats at the front for the driver and one passenger.

"No. Where are you taking me?" I plead as he pushes the metal into my side so hard I let out a sob.

"I'm sure Daddy Dearest will tell you all about it."

I frown, confused, my breaths quickening.

"Dad?" I ask, before he grabs my hair at the back of my head and shoves me forward. I wasn't prepared for it, and I lose my balance easily, my shins hitting the door with a painful thud.

"No, no, please. What do you want? Please, don't do this." I'm begging, but he doesn't care to hear it. His foot lifts to my butt, and he kicks me in, but not before my head and neck slam against the doorframe. I feel something pulling against my neck as it scrapes on some rough metal, and my hand immediately reaches up to soothe the pain. My necklace is gone. All I feel is wetness, and I don't even have to look to know that I'm bleeding. I'm panting, anxiety fully taking over, but my fight-or-flight has failed me. I'm half-in and half-out of this van, the man right at my back. There's nowhere for me to go. I have no escape.

"For fuck's sake," I hear him mutter before I turn to look at him, and he raises his hand, the one holding the gun. I move quickly, but not quick enough as the butt of the gun comes down onto my head, the pain excruciating, the darkness instant.

41

CONNOR

I pace the office, brow pinched and body coiled tight.

"Have you seen Daisy?" I ask Stephanie as she walks in later than usual. I told all staff to start later today because of the event last night, so even though I've been awake for a little while, no one else has been around. Except Daisy. Or she's meant to be. I left her in bed when I went for a run earlier. When I got back, she was gone, but I assumed she was doing yoga in our new garden, so I hit the shower and made us breakfast. Only, it still sits cold on my kitchen counter, because she never came back.

I looked around the lawns and went to our new garden, but she wasn't there. After that, I came to the office, looking for her here, thinking she may have started work early since it would be quiet. But I have walked around the offices three times and can't find her.

"Ahhh, no. Haven't seen her since last night," she says,

and I just give her a nod, an uncomfortable feeling seeping into my veins.

I think about where else she could be, and my mind immediately goes to the springs. She's gone there twice since we got back from New York without telling me. I caught her the first time sneaking off and followed her, watching her from a distance with pride as she worked hard at accomplishing a new skill of swimming. I know she's smart and competent, and getting into trouble when she's in the water is an almost unthinkable issue now. But it's still not impossible. What if she drowned? What if she slipped on a rock and hit her head? I would never forgive myself if that happened.

Feeling a fresh rush of panic, I run out the door and down the path toward the springs, looking around on my journey, and there's no sign of her. I speed up my steps, frazzled, having no idea where else she might be if she isn't by the water.

I reach the springs, and the water is calm. The gravel's a little messy in the area where I know she normally steps, so she may have been here, but there's no other sign of her. No towel, shoes. Nothing.

"Daisy!" I yell out her name, the feeling of something being off building. I hear nothing, I see nothing, and with nowhere else to search, I run back up the path, my mind spinning.

We had a great night. We laid out our cards. I told her how I feel about her, and she feels the same. It was so good to have her in my arms, dancing in our garden of daisies, and while I know we still have a few things to iron out, we're both committed to merging our futures.

There's a pit in my stomach, and I rub my chest as my heart pounds hard and fast. Something feels really wrong, like the connection we have is in jeopardy. I shake my head. I'm sounding woo-woo, but... I feel it in my gut.

"What's going on?" Dad asks, having just pulled up to the distillery and seeing me come through the gate. "What's wrong?" he asks again, striding over to me, my panic written all over my face, no doubt.

"I can't find her," I tell him, my breathing rapid.

"Who?"

"Daisy. I went for a run. I thought she was going to do yoga, but I can't find her on the lawn. Then I checked the office, and she hasn't been in yet. I just went down to the springs, and she isn't there either, although I think she might have been," I rush out, and a frown creases his face immediately.

"Do you think... Do you think she left?" I ask him, swallowing as self-doubt creeps in. I know it's not possible. We feel tethered together, Daisy and me. Our feelings are too real and too big to even consider that she would run from me, but I need to look at all angles.

"Left you?" he asks, already shaking his head.

"Maybe last night was too much for her?" I mention, and he inhales a sharp breath.

"Call her parents," he says, and I nod, grabbing my cell. Finding their details, I immediately call them.

"It's Connor Whiteman," I say as soon as someone answers.

"Connor. Good morning," her father says.

"Sorry for the early call, but I can't find Daisy. She normally does morning yoga while I run, but when I got back, she wasn't there, and I've looked everywhere. I can't find her. I'm calling to see if you have heard from her..." I ask, knowing that this is an odd phone call, and I have taken him by surprise. I hold my breath. On the one hand, I want him to tell me that he has heard from her and she's on her way home to them. I would be devastated, but at least I'd know she's okay. On the other hand, if he hasn't heard from her, then I know my gut feeling is right.

"We haven't heard from her. Are you sure you've looked everywhere? Called her cell?" he asks, and Dad looks at me. It's a silent question, asking if she's with her parents. I shake my head, and he's quick to pull out his phone.

"I've called her cell, but her phone, along with her purse, are still sitting on the table at my place. She doesn't have anything with her," I tell him, thinking about seeing her handbag, her crystals, yoga gear. Everything is still as it was last night. Safely in my house.

"Connor, you're starting to worry me," he says, his voice taking on an edge of panic. The kind I've felt all morning.

"I am worried, sir," I admit. My palms start to sweat, my shoulders tense as I wait for his response.

"Did the two of you have a fight or anything?" he asks, and I look up to the sky.

"No, the opposite. I told her last night that I loved her and I want her to build a life with me," I tell him honestly.

"Was she okay with that?" he asks hesitantly, and I swallow.

"She reciprocated her love for me. She smiled, laughed, we danced under the stars for a bit, before we had to come back inside for the remainder of the party, and then we went home. She was happy last night and still asleep in bed this morning when I left for my run."

"What time did you last see her?"

I look at my watch. "About three hours ago."

"She isn't a runner, Connor. She has never run away from anything in her life. Rainbow and I will pack a bag and come to Whispers right away. Something doesn't feel right," he says, and I nod, even though he can't see me.

"I'll arrange a car to be at your place in half an hour. I can fly you both here to Whispers this morning."

I hear my dad on his phone, calling the staff in. Starting a search party, the gardener, the restaurant team, he's asking everyone if they've seen her and to come in to start looking around the area.

"Okay. We'll see you soon, Connor," he says, ending the call, and I send a quick text to my team to arrange the flight before pocketing my cell.

"Would she be at Marie's Place?" I ask my dad as it pops into my head.

"Nope. Victoria's there already, and there's no sign of her."

My heart feels like it's about to blow up as I pace around the parking lot, pulling at my hair. Some staff are already arriving, and I walk from the gate of the springs toward the distillery door, feeling like I need to retrace her steps or something.

Not wasting any precious moments, I look around, seeing the garden unbothered, and as I'm about to turn, I see a small sparkle hit my eye and pause. Walking closer, I bend down and pick it up.

Dread chills me down to my bones, anxiety crawling through my body like black tar.

"Dad!" I yell.

"What is it?" he shouts back as he runs over, and I hold up the silver daisy chain necklace that I found on the ground.

"This is Daisy's. Her mom gave it to her for her birthday. She never takes it off. Never," I state, and we both look at it closely. "Is that..."

"Blood. I'll call the sheriff," Dad says quickly, and I think I lose the ability to breathe before I look up, spotting our security cameras on the side of the building.

"I need to see the cameras." Placing the necklace into a clean tissue, I run up the stairs to my office, my dad right behind me, already talking to the local sheriff.

I race to my computer, bringing up the security feed. I rewind it until I spot some movement.

"There!" Dad yells in my ear, and I pause it, playing it back slowly. We see a van in the parking lot, not sure what time it arrived. With the party yesterday, we had so many cars coming and going all night, it would have been easy for it to come on-site. Our security when we travel or when we are in the city is tight. We have our own team that we use when we need to. But out here, in such a small town, where everyone knows everyone, we haven't needed full guards or locked gates before.

"That's her." I spot her coming up through the gate from the springs, her hair wet, towel in her hand. So she did go to the springs for a swim this morning. Then she looks up sharply at a man I recognize stepping toward her.

"Who is that?" Dad asks.

"He's been here before. I think it's a supplier. Soren," I say, because it definitely looks like him. But then the man turns, shoving something into her waist, and I freeze.

"Was that a gun?" I ask my dad, who's looking over my shoulder. He leans closer because I can't move my hands from where they're gripping my desk, white-knuckled as fear takes over my body and we replay that part of the footage. The two of us watch intently, holding our breaths.

"Fuck," Dad spits, and my anger now rises to join my fear and anxiety. I can't see the man's face, but as he moves, I notice his hair is a little different from the man I met in her office all those weeks ago. He's also bigger and broader than I remember Soren being.

Pure terror takes over Daisy's body language, and I watch her stumble into the van before he hits her. My teeth grind, my jaw tight as he throws her limp body into the van, slamming the door shut and driving off.

"Download the footage and send it to the team," Dad says, and I move on autopilot.

"Who would want anything from Daisy?" he asks me, and I shake my head.

"I have no idea. She doesn't know anyone here." Downloading the footage, I send it out immediately to our team for facial recognition and any other trace elements we can find.

"What about her parents?" Dad asks. And I pause.

"The commune..." I say, thinking out loud. The

kidnapper was wearing flowing cream linen clothing, nothing like the denim and button-down shirts most people around here wear. Long hair, earthy, nature-loving type profile.

"The what?" Dad asks, looking at me like I'm crazy.

"Daisy's mom was raised in a commune not far away from here," I tell him.

"Where?" he barks.

"I have no idea, but her parents will know." Running my hand through my hair, I pull at the ends, wishing I knew more about it. But I know exactly who does, and they're on my plane and going to be here within a few hours. So I send them the footage, hoping they have the answers we all need, before I call them to work out a location. At the moment, we don't have much.

And I need my Daisy girl back.

42

DAISY

"Urgghhhhh," I moan, my headache feeling like it's splitting me in two. I squeeze my eyes shut, gritting my teeth, my jaw aching as I try to breathe through the pain.

"It will subside soon," I hear a deep voice say, and I startle, my eyes pinging open before I cringe, squeezing them shut again. A sharp bolt of pain shoots through the base of my neck and up through to my brain.

I try to get my bearings. Birds chirp outside, and the brief moment my eyes were open, I saw blue skies and sunlight streaming in through a small window. The thud in my head is constant, but I slowly open my eyes again and am looking straight at one man whom I've never seen before and another whom I have. My memories all flood back to me.

"Where am I?" I look around a little more, trying to gauge where I am, but nothing is familiar. We're not in the distillery, and from what I can see out the tiny window, I don't think we're in Whispers. The forest outside looks dense, like it cocoons us.

"You are where you belong," the man I don't recognize says cryptically, and I look back at him. He's older, very weathered. His hair is long, gray, and thinning on top. His eyes are bright blue, his teeth brown, and his clothes look too big for him. I smell incense burning— ylang ylang. It's a calming scent; I use it sometimes at night to help rest my body and mind before sleep.

"And where is that?" I ask, unable to hide the bite in my tone as I look between him and the man next to him, the one who grabbed me from the parking lot at the distillery. He's somewhat more familiar, but still a stranger.

"Here, I made you tea." He offers me a terracotta cup, the contents steaming. I swallow, my mouth dry, tongue feeling like sandpaper, but I don't take it. I just look at him.

"It's not poison, my child. It's chamomile. We grow it here on our land, so it's fresh, organic," he says, still extending the cup to me. But I continue to ignore him.

He huffs.

"Painful, just like your mother," he murmurs, and now he has my attention.

"How do you know my mother?" I ask, my eyes narrowing on him. I try to think if I've met him before at Sunshine.

"You're currently in her commune." Taking back the cup, he places it next to him, and I sit up. My body hurts as I straighten on the hard timber floor. It isn't polished, but it is sanded. This room is small and looks like some type of living space in a small, run-down cabin.

"Commune?" As I look between him and my kidnapper, my heart starts to race all over again. They look like they live in a commune. Both with long hair, very natural clothing. Not dissimilar to Soren or some of my mom's other contacts whom I've met over the years.

"Yes, my child, you're at Forest Falls. Your family home," he says, and I frown. I've never heard of Forest Falls. Never heard a thing about this place, but it's starting to make sense. I look out the window again, and the sun is still high. It couldn't have taken long to get here from Whispers. Mom did say her commune was close.

"Rainbow was one of us. She was born here. Her life is meant to be here. As is yours, my child."

"Stop calling me your child," I tell him, shoulders tense, not liking the wording, nor the familiarity that he uses it with.

"But that's what you are. You are a child of Forest Falls, yes. But you are also my child. My blood," he says, and I stop breathing.

"What?" I ask, my mind whirling, feeling the air around me go still.

"I procreated with your mother. Her breasts swelled, as did her belly, before she left in the dead of night, and we never saw her again. She stole you from me."

Everything he's saying has me feeling like I might be sick.

"I already have a father, so that must have been a different pregnancy," I state with a shake of my head, the feeling of terror mixed with shock and disbelief filtering through my body.

"You have my eyes."

I look right at his pupils and swallow down the bile rising up my throat. He's right. I do.

"Most of the population has blue eyes." My confidence in my heritage is waning. He's right. I look nothing like my father. I look like Mom, and I always thought I took after her in every way. But she doesn't have vibrant blue eyes, and neither does Dad.

The thump in my head starts to worsen, and the feeling of nausea because overwhelming.

"I was devastated when she left. I looked for days, sure that she was met with danger in the forest. The whole commune searched and searched. It wasn't until my friend, Soren, found her in the city almost a decade later that we knew where she was."

My blood chills.

"Soren?" I ask, because if he knows Soren, then his story just became a hell of a lot more believable.

"Yes. Soren is a crystal finder. He comes here annually and sits in peace before he mines for quartz in the rock faces nearby," he explains, and I feel my hands start to shake. He knows too much. The information is exactly what Soren told me in my office weeks ago. Everything he says is making perfect sense. My heart breaks as the feeling that my dad isn't my real dad sinks in.

"So if I'm your daughter, why didn't you come and get me then?" I ask, because, surely, a parent would at least want to see their child.

"I didn't need you then."

"But you need me now?" I ask, having no idea what he's talking about, my splitting headache not helping as I take all of this in.

"Here. Drink up so I can tell you more about your family and your history. I hate to see you parched. I've scolded Joseph here for hitting you. He was just trying to bring you home for me." When he stretches out his hand, offering the cup again, this time, I take it. My mouth is too dry and my head a mess. I take a sip, immediately glad I did, as I feel the tea soothe my dryness, and I try to think back to my life as a child. Trying to think of anything that I missed about my father that may have indicated that he's not my biological parent.

With my mind swirling, I continue to sip. This chamomile tea is really good.

"That's it, my child. Drink up. Then the two of you can consummate," he says simply, and I choke, coughing as the tea falls from my lips and dribbles down my chin.

"Consummate?" Spluttering, I look from him to the other guy, who appears younger, although just as weathered by the elements and natural living.

"Consummate your union." He stands, smiling down at me, where I remain on the floor, my hips sore from lying on the timber floorboards for so long.

"Our union?" I ask, then instantly pause. *Is my speech slurring?* My vision blurs at the edges, and I look down at the cup before I look back at him, knowing that he drugged me with something.

"Our numbers are not what they used to be."

The terror I felt earlier is back in full throttle as my hands start to shake.

"Probably because you're forcing people here against their will," I tell him, my fiery nature coming out as I try to stand. But my legs feel like Jell-O, and I fail miserably.

"So we need more children, born into this life." He ignores my comment, now looking at me like he cares very little.

"And what do I have to do with that?" I ask, my words tripping over each other as I try to stand again. Joseph waits patiently next to him, remaining silent, yet looking me over.

"As my daughter, your womb is what will bring new life. Mother Nature has blessed us with you, and now she'll help you birth our babies."

This can't be happening. Why did I drink this tea? Why is my dad not my dad? Why does this man have eyes that look like my own?

"There was no blessing, only kidnapping, which I'm pretty sure is a federal offense." I'm trying to keep the vomit down as the room starts to spin. I can't take a full breath.

"We don't live life by other man's law. We have our own law," he grits out, clearly not happy with all my questions.

"Kidnapping is kidnapping," I tell him, because even though my body doesn't seem to have strength, my mouth is still semi-functional, and she isn't going down without a fight.

"You are my daughter. You're my only blood. Your role is here. You are to breed babies with Joseph. Joseph has been here since birth. He's our favorite son here at Forest Falls."

"No..." I stutter out, shocked at what I'm hearing. The fear that I can't move my body starts to consume me. I think of Connor. Of what my life was about to become. How happy I was that we were going to bring our lives together.

"Hmmmm, good child. The tea is working. You will be blessed by the mother of fertility..." the man who says he is my father hums.

"No," I say, but it's weak, my voice barely audible now.

"It's okay, my child. You're home now. We take care of our own."

My eyes close, yet the last thing I see is his smile, and I know it will haunt me forever.

43

CONNOR

"Tell me you know who it is?" I ask the minute Daisy's parents step out of the jet. I need to ensure my pilot gets a raise, because he flew here faster than I knew was possible, knowing how urgent it was. Dad, our security team, the sheriff and his men, and I have all been here for half an hour, waiting for them to land. Our small airstrip has been overrun with cars, choppers nearby at the ready. I've even spoken to Harrison, the president, and he's waiting for my call, should he need to help get more feet on the ground.

It's early afternoon. The sheriff has called in support from nearby counties, and my father has called in our security firm. We're all ready to find her but have absolutely nothing to go on.

"It's a man from the commune I left over twenty-five years ago," Daisy's mother, Rainbow, says, almost breathless as they walk quickly to meet us. She looks remorseful, and her husband puts his arm around her. Their eyes are red and swollen, clearly shaken up.

"Does Daisy know them? Were they in contact?" Dad asks, and they both shake their heads.

"No. Never. I have never seen him or spoken to him since I left."

"Daisy doesn't know anything about them. It's a past life..." her father starts, and I interject.

"Not anymore. Now it's very fucking present." I'm angry, knowing that they were aware of the threat before Daisy made her way to Whispers and never once mentioned it. I move around a little, wanting to start doing something, anything, that will get me closer to finding her.

"We didn't know they were capable of this. We didn't know he would even find her," Rainbow implores.

"Why did you leave the commune?" the sheriff asks her, his pen and notepad out, taking notes, when all I want to do is get in a fucking truck and drive to where they are.

"I was born into it. From a young age, we are taught to obey the men. From the age of fourteen onward, I was repeatedly forced into bed with a young man whom I now understand to be the leader of the commune. It was there I fell pregnant with Daisy," she explains, and my head whips around to look at Daisy's father.

"Daisy isn't my biological daughter," he admits.

I'm shocked into stillness for a moment.

"Daisy didn't mention that," I say, frowning, wondering why she hasn't confided in me.

"Daisy doesn't know," he says, concern lining his features. I feel like I have been hit in the gut, knowing how much pain this is going to bring to Daisy.

"Once I was pregnant, I knew I couldn't raise a baby up there, especially if it was a girl. I didn't want her to go through the same horrible experiences I did. So in the middle of the night, I left. I had memorized the way to the highway from our few trips to town to get supplies. I ran and ran until I got to the road," Rainbow says, pausing for a moment as she wipes her teary eyes.

"I picked her up on my way home from an accounting conference. Thought a hitchhiker might make good company on the long drive back to the city," Daisy's father continues for her.

"It wasn't until I got out of the commune life and met Gerald that I learned I'd been brainwashed, and it was more likely a cult. Psychedelics will do that to you." She looks at the sheriff, but I don't care about her drug-fueled past.

"Where is it? This commune?" I ask, too harshly. I'm going to break out of my skin. Daisy could be there, subjected to what her mother had experienced.

"It's called Forest Falls. It's about three hours south of here," she tells us.

"Can you indicate the location on the map?" the sheriff asks, showing her a screen, a map of the area already up and synced to all our phones.

"Three hours south, in the forest next to the border," she says, pointing to a spot within a thick forest. There are no roads or dwellings on the map, nothing at all to indicate people live there.

"She's in the middle of fucking nowhere!" I yell, frustrated I can't just get her and bring her home to me right this second.

"Helicopters?" Dad asks, and I pull out my cell, ready to get a whole fucking fleet here if I need to.

"No, the forest is too dense. You can't land," the sheriff says, and I fist my hand so hard I almost crack my phone.

"We will need to drive all the way in," Dad says as we all look over the map and zoom in, seeing a small dirt road.

"The roads are barely drivable. We need to wait for backup. We don't know what they have by way of weapons. Cultists usually stockpile a range of things, and they don't like visitors. We'll get some drones into the air," the sheriff says.

"No. They will hear them, know we are coming, and scatter deeper into the forest," Rainbow says, panicked, and I nod in agreement.

"No drones," Dad agrees, and I grit my teeth. This is all taking too long.

"Fuck them. I'm going." I'm already walking to my truck, sick of waiting, sick of standing around, not wanting to think of what they may have already done to her.

"I'll go with you," Dad says, grabbing Victoria, who looks concerned, giving her a quick kiss before he runs after me to the truck.

"We're coming too," Daisy's parents say in unison, and the two of them run behind me, jumping into the back as the sheriff continues yelling at us to stop and wait.

But we don't.

I'm already out of the airport before he and his team are running to their cars as well, as does our security team. It's three hours away, and we need to get there *now*.

44

CONNOR

This is fucking déjà vu.

Dad grips on to the door handle as I drive like a madman down the gravel road. Not unlike we were a year or so ago, racing to Marie's Place to try to save Victoria and Lacy from the horrific ordeal they endured. Seems like us Whitemans have to suffer for our women before we surrender completely to them. And I promise to God that if Daisy is alive, that's what I will do. Fall onto my knees for her and do anything she damn well asks me to for the rest of our lives.

Dust, dirt, and stones fly up, hitting the truck. We have our security team behind us, and police cars behind them.

"Who the fuck could ever live out here?" I say, the sun starting to set, the glow of the afternoon hour making it look creepy rather than tranquil. I see nothing but shrubs, overgrowth, and forest. The large escalades we're surrounded by barely show through the trees as they overhang onto the road, scratching down the paintwork and making us cringe.

"This is what cults do. They segregate," Daisy's father says.

"If he has harmed her..." I growl, knowing that if she is hurt in any way, I will lose it.

"He's her father. A father won't harm his daughter," Dad says to try to placate me.

"He's no father. She has a father, and he's in the back of this truck," I spit out, knowing her biological father is going to regret this act, whether he's harmed her or not.

As I continue to drive, our GPS tells us we're close. I know why they call it Forest Falls, because there is nothing but forest as far as the eye can see. You would think that it would be beautiful, lush, green, and welcoming. But Whispers is far more beautiful. This is almost like overgrown swamplands.

I see a small clearing up ahead, but I don't slow down. A few people nearby look up at the approaching vehicle, shocked and startled as we barrel in. At the hum of the engine, a small flock of chickens scatters, and I slam on the brakes, putting it in park, ready to find my girl without any more waiting.

Jumping out of the car, I start looking around. The people are almost frozen solid. They are quiet, wide-eyed, like they've never seen anything like us before. I turn and look at my other side, and I notice a cow, the bell around its neck heavier than it should be.

"Get off my land!" a voice barks. I hear the cock of a shotgun and turn to see a man who looks to be about seventy, with long gray hair, weathered skin, and vibrant blue eyes I would know from anywhere.

"I will as soon as you give me my goddamn wife," I grit out as I step toward him, not afraid of the gun. I didn't mean to say wife. But that's exactly what she'll be the minute I get her away from this shithole. I'm going to put a ring on her finger, and I'm never letting her out of my sight again.

"Wife?" he questions, pulling his head back from the gauge of the shotgun to look at me. I'm still in my suit, having dressed for the day before I realized she was missing, and too preoccupied to bother changing.

"You have exactly five minutes before the federal police surround this place and exactly two minutes until my team shoots you in the head," I tell him, not afraid. This wiry old man will probably have a heart attack just from pulling the trigger.

I spot my father out of the corner of my eye, looking apprehensive, like he's about to push me out of the way and take the bullet himself.

"Raymond!" Daisy's mom comes forward, and his attention goes to her. He looks shocked briefly before his face morphs with pure anger.

"Knew you would be back eventually," he mocks her, still not lowering his gun.

"Take me instead of Daisy." She starts walking forward, toward him, offering herself up to this idiot.

"He's not taking anyone," I mumble to Dad, who has stepped up next to me, and he nods.

"Where is Daisy?!" I shout, grabbing his attention again as I step forward in front of Rainbow. I'm not a small man, and even from a distance, I know I tower over him. He looks at me and Dad, the two of us coming for him, and dare I say he only has the ability to pull the trigger once, meaning he knows he's fucked. The rest of the people who were here are now gone, stepping back into the shadows and disappearing completely. But another man comes forward to stand beside Raymond, also with a shotgun, aimed right at us.

"Daisy!" I shout once more, needing to see her, hear her, anything that tells me she's still alive and okay. "Daisy!"

"She can't hear you. She's indisposed…" the man next to Raymond says, and my jaw clenches to the point of cramping.

"You fucking asshole," I grit out, knowing he's done something. Rainbow screams behind me, looking unhinged herself when he only smiles instead of explaining.

"You are under arrest," a voice over an amplifier booms as I hear cars coming in by the dozen behind us, enough to distract them, and I make a run for it.

"Connor!" my dad yells. As I tackle the old guy to the ground, a gunshot goes off. Bedlam ensues as I see Dad pounce on the other man, the rest of our security grabbing any men and women who come forward with an array of shovels and pitchforks like we're from the fucking nineteen twenties. I wrestle the gun from his hand, the burn to my side intensifying, and grip his collar tight, cutting off his air supply.

"I'm going to fucking kill you right here, right now. Tell me where Daisy is," I scream in his face. He doesn't respond. He can't, but he smiles, and it's pure evil, like the devil himself is inside of him.

"Never."

I lift his head and slam it back into the ground, and he groans.

"Connor! Connor! This way!" Rainbow yells as Dad hauls me off him, which is a good thing, because I would have killed him. Police run onto the scene, and one of them grabs the man underneath me as I jump up and follow her mom through the small clearing. We're running, in between chickens and goats and small run-down timber houses all the way, but my vision is zeroed in on the path we're headed in.

"In this one. This is my old one. He held me here for months once," she says, panting, as the three of us race to an old run-down cabin that looks like it isn't fit for animals, let alone humans.

I don't hesitate as I slam my shoulder into the door. It cracks open immediately and the timber flies into the room. I stand there, letting my eyes adjust to the darkness, before I see her. Crumpled in the corner. Covered in a rug. My heart drops to my feet.

"Daisy!" I scream as I run to her, falling to my knees and gently rolling her over.

"Medics! We need medics!" her dad yells out the door as I feel for her pulse along her cut and bloodied neck, hands shaking as I touch her seemingly lifeless body. When I feel her pulse, nice and strong, I can breathe for the first time all day.

"She's breathing," her mom says beside me.

"Pulse is strong," I say as I look her over. There's a

large lump on her head and blood down her neck onto her top, but otherwise, she looks okay.

"She's sedated," Rainbow says, looking over her daughter carefully before she lifts the blanket that covers her. I hold my breath and don't release it until I see Daisy is still fully clothed, wearing the same clothes she had on this morning, none of it torn or misplaced. No one has touched her. We got here in time.

"Oh, thank God," her mom cries out, releasing a breath with me.

"How do you know they drugged her?" I ask, looking over Daisy's face, seeing her eyes closed, her breathing shallow.

"Their favorite way to consummate and create life is a game of cat and mouse. They drug you, then wait until you wake up slightly, and then let you attempt to run while still under the influence, so you stagger and stumble around the forest before they hunt you down. They say it's the closest way to Mother Earth. Like an animal preying on its mate," she explains, and I grit my teeth. This commune is so fucked up. I'm going to burn this place to the ground.

"I'm getting her out of here." I put an arm under her legs and one under her shoulders and lift her into my embrace.

"Are you sure you're okay to lift her?" her dad asks worriedly.

"I've got her," I tell him, walking out of this shithole with her cuddled close to my chest, straight to the car, where the medics check over her quickly before we lay her in the back seat, her parents on either side of her.

Dad and I let the police look after the rest as we jump in the truck, and I drive like a madman out of this poor excuse for a commune to the main road, where a medic chopper waits to take us to the nearest hospital. Which just so happens to be in Whispers, where Hudson is prepared for our arrival.

Which is a good thing, considering that bullet that went off is lodged in my side.

With a bloody shirt and burning pain, my worry stays on the love of my life.

45

DAISY

I wake slowly, the thud in my head only slight. Holding my breath, I open my eyes slowly, carefully, waiting to see Joseph and fisting my hands, ready to throw a punch.

"Baby girl?" The voice doesn't match who I expect to see. "Hey... there she is," he murmurs, his voice sounding sweeter than I've ever heard him sound.

"Connor?" I ask, opening my eyes wider and seeing him at my bedside. I panic a little, looking around quickly before realizing I'm in a hospital bed, and the faint memory of flying here enters my mind.

"You're in the Whispers hospital. You're safe. We all are," he says, and my panic subsides as I take a breath.

"Hospital?" I ask, my brain still foggy and trying to keep up with everything.

"We found you at the commune. Your mom and dad and I..." he says, and in his words, I get a flash of a vision with vibrant blue eyes.

"My dad?" I ask him, frowning.

"The man at the commune has been arrested. Most of the people there were taken in for questioning. Your mom has already given a full statement and provided a myriad of information on them. There will be historical charges as well."

"You came?" I ask shakily as a tear falls down my face. The reality of the situation now makes sense. I was kidnapped, taken against my will, and drugged. "How did you even know?"

"There was never any doubt. I saw on the distillery cameras that you were taken. Your parents filled in the rest for me. I got to you as soon as I could." He grabs my hand, and as he moves, I see him wince. My nerves come back with a flurry.

"What happened to you?" I ask as I quickly look over him.

"Just a little gunshot graze to my side, baby girl. Nothing for you to worry about," he murmurs and squeezes my hand reassuringly.

"A gunshot! Oh my God, you were shot!" I nearly scream as I frantically try to sit up, my head still feeling heavy but not able to stop myself.

"Easy, baby. Relax. I'm fine, I promise." He soothes me as I settle back in the bed, brushing hair away from my face and pressing a kiss to my head. I see a thick bandage under his shirt, and my heart gallops.

"You took a bullet saving me?" I ask as a tear falls down my cheek.

"Pretty heroic, really, isn't it," he says, giving me a smirk, throwing in a little humor, which I know is his way of trying to calm me down.

"Very heroic. But are you okay? Really?" I ask again, more worried about him than myself.

"Just a graze, baby girl. I will be fully healed in no time."

Nodding, I take a deep breath, and he wipes my tears. But I have more questions than answers at this point.

"He said he was my father? Said he knew Soren?" I ask, my brow furrowing, confused.

"Yeah. Well, I will let your parents talk to you about that one, but in my mind, a father is a man who raises you. They are a different species than a sperm donor."

I agree with him, but it doesn't take away the pain in my chest.

"In terms of Soren, he knew nothing about this. Your mom got hold of him. He was a few states over, digging up some rose quartz, but is on his way, happy to answer any questions police might have about what he knows of the commune. Your mom mentioned that he wouldn't know anything. Being a visitor, he would have been kept segregated from the daily happenings of the commune, and probably only tolerated anything because he usually brought news or information on the outside world for them. Including where he mentioned your mom and you, and how you were in Whispers."

"My mom?"

"They're right outside. Waiting. I even flew Trisha in, because she was blowing up my phone. Apparently, your mom filled her in on the day, and she called me and demanded that I, and I quote, 'get my big balls together and get her here for you.'"

I huff a small laugh at my crazy friend, even as my mind whirls, trying to sort through everything.

"I don't even know who I am anymore... Who my dad is... What my surname is..." I tell him. My family history is all unknown now.

"Sure, you do. You're the beautiful, sassy yoga queen, kick-ass businesswoman, who's about to take the world by storm with me by her side," he says, looking at me with so much love and adoration, another tear falls.

"Here, your mom made you a cup of tea," he murmurs to me as he helps me sit up, then passes me the cup, the tea still nice and warm. I smell lemon and honey and close my eyes, taking a sip, feeling it soothe me from the inside out. I don't think I'll be drinking chamomile for a while.

"Thank you, Connor. For everything. I don't know what would have happened if you hadn't found me. I was so, so scared," I tell him, knowing there's still a lot about today that I don't know, yet knowing that he found me and stopped at nothing until he did blankets me with a whole new sense of safety and comfort.

"Today was the scariest day of my entire life. I knew before this that I loved you. I knew before this that you were the other half of my soul. But after today, there's no way I want to be apart from you in any way. I was willing to put my life down for you, and I would do it again in a heartbeat."

More tears form, and I shake my head, not wanting him to do that. Yet I'm sure there's nothing I can say that will change his mind, because I feel the exact same way.

"Let's hope our days of kidnapping and assault are

behind us..." I tell him, smiling as playfully as I can muster, trying to find a little light in what's our darkest day.

"No, no more. Only sunshine from here on out, baby." Like he just remembered something, he pats his pocket, then pulls something out. "I almost forgot. This is yours. It's how I knew something happened. I found this near the distillery."

"Oh, my necklace!" I gasp in awe, more tears at the ready.

"It led me to you. And I know how important it is to you. Daisies have a whole new meaning now. I think we're gonna need to plant some more around our new home, don't you think?" he says, and I swallow roughly. This man is truly meant for me.

Nodding, I tug on his sleeve to pull him closer. "I love you, Connor."

"And I love you, Daise," he says, before placing his lips on mine.

DAISY - EPILOGUE

"Why are we here?" I ask Connor as my stomach growls. "You said we were going to the diner. I'm starving!" With a groan, I jump out of the truck that he has parked up the other end of the street of Rochelle's, her vegetable soup already calling my name. Not waiting for Connor to open my door, like he always does, his frown tells me he's not pleased about that fact.

"I have a surprise," he says, meeting me at the front of the truck.

"Surprise? Don't you think I've had enough surprises so far this year?" I ask him, my hand moving automatically to the small scar on my neck, the reminder of what I've endured.

It's been a few months, and we're doing well. I had to give a lot of police interviews, I'm going to therapy regularly, and I've been meditating and doing yoga daily. I still love it, and I now know that yoga is the thing I want to concentrate on, along with our herbal teas. My parents and I have spent a lot of time together, here in Whispers, thanks to Connor, who constantly flies them or me anywhere we want to go as we process and talk through everything. It took a while, but my dad is still my dad, whether or not we share the same blood type.

My bio dad is in jail. He had a slew of charges laid against him and not any interest in hiring any legal representation. He remained tight-lipped, not confirming or denying any of the allegations, so it was an open-and-shut case. The media hasn't been as simple. Due to Connor's name and our connection, we have had to increase both our security and our PR team. But I thank God for this town called Whispers. They say it's a town where the billionaires come to hide, but it's also the perfect hiding spot for me. The townsfolk keep our secrets. They're often the first to spot a paparazzi or an outsider, and the calls we get to inform us are sometimes hilarious, but I know they all care. It has all started to die down a little now. Life is feeling more and more normal.

"This is a good one. I promise." He grabs my hand and leads me down the sidewalk and we stop outside the old florist shop. Newspapers still cover the windows.

"Connor?" I ask him, confused.

"Daisy, welcome to Yoga by Daisy. Your own yoga studio. I know you love it, and I know the people in town will love it too. I want you to have something of your own, and working at the distillery full-time isn't it. So, this is all yours..." he says as he opens the door and pulls me inside, where I spot Sawyer standing there with paperwork and a box in his hand. Excitement swirls in my belly, but I feel frozen in place for a second.

"What?" Looking at him before I look around the space, I'm thoroughly shocked. It needs a total fit-out, but it's huge, with rooms out the back, and from memory, I'm pretty sure the garden is amazing too.

"I'm signing this place over to you. This is entirely yours. Not a penny of it goes to the distillery or to me. This is your baby. Make your teas, do your yoga, grow an herb garden. Whatever you want to do, baby girl." He grabs the keys and paperwork and the box from Sawyer, leaving me staring wide-eyed, making Sawyer grin.

"Enjoy, you two," he says with a chuckle as he starts to walk out.

"Thanks, Sawyer. Where are you off to?" Connor asks him.

"I've got to go see Victoria's goat milk soap partner," he says before looking at his cell to confirm her details. "Annabelle something or other."

"Sounds like you're becoming the town's lawyer?" Connor teases him, and I grin, knowing that Connor and his dad want Sawyer to take over the law firm here in Whispers when Jerry, the current local lawyer, retires.

"Not in your lifetime," Sawyer says quickly, but I look at Connor, who just smirks. He's told me that Annabelle and her sons are a handful, so they'll give Sawyer the runaround this afternoon.

"That city boy doesn't know what's about to hit him," Connor says to me as Sawyer exits the shop, leaving the two of us alone.

"So what do you think?" he asks me as he glances around, smiling.

"I think it's too much," I tell him, not sure how to feel other than overwhelmed and loved.

"You lost your sparkle for a while, baby girl, but with each day, I see it coming back. The distillery is my baby, and I get so much joy from it and I know you do too. But you're too brilliant to live in anyone's shadow. You need to sparkle bright like a diamond yourself. So I bought this property for you to enjoy, however you please. Your name is on the title. I want you to do whatever it is that'll bring you joy. I may still get you to consult for the distillery from time to time, though, because your brain is one of the many things I love about you."

My heart swells at the pride in his voice. "Thank you. For everything. You're amazing, you know that?" I tell him, grinning, the reality of all this not sinking in.

"Let's look around." He grabs my hand and we walk out the back, where there's plenty of room for my tea supplies and, as I remembered, a great garden where I can plant some herbs.

"Oh look, daisies!" I say with a little hop. My name-sake flowers are now almost everywhere we go in Whispers, always bringing a smile to my face. I walk over to the large bush, seeing it full of flowers that bring me so much happiness. When I turn to look at Connor, he isn't there.

"Connor?" I ask, turning around fully, and there he is. Down on a bended knee, holding a box the size of a football, one way too big to be what you need to be on bended knee for.

"Daisy..." he says, clearing his throat, acting nervous.

"What? What's going on?" I ask, glancing around as I step back toward him, and he takes my hand.

"Daisy, I knew the moment we met that you were special. The only woman to ever talk back to me, push me, challenge me. The only woman I've ever met who's the most beautiful, caring, genuine, funny, intelligent, sarcastic, and amazing person, one I'm so grateful to have in my life."

A lone tear falls as I try to breathe, the simple requirement harder and harder with every word he speaks.

"So Daisy, my baby girl. Will you do me the honor of being my wife?" he asks before he spins around the box, and I almost faint.

"What?" I gasp in total disbelief.

"I have looked for the biggest diamond I could find that I felt was representative of the love and commitment I have for you. The ones that go on your finger were not big enough, although I got you one of those too," he explains as my widened gaze falls from his face to the box and back again.

It is a black velvet box, with a clear glass front and inside is a crystal that looks similar to a clear quartz.

"Is that a..." I start to ask tentatively, because I think I'm having a heart attack.

"A raw diamond. A gemstone that represents steadfast love. This is the world's biggest that will sit in the heart chakra of our new home. I wanted to get you something that represented you, us, and the life we're going to build together." Then he pulls out another black velvet box, one that fits in his palm. "This one will go on your finger," he says quickly, showcasing a magnificent solitaire that sparkles brightly in the sun.

"What do you say, Daise? Will you marry me?" he asks, and it's then I realize I haven't answered him, too shocked at seeing a raw diamond in real life.

Through tear-filled eyes, I smile, nodding eagerly. "Yes, Connor, in a thousand lifetimes, my answer will always be yes," I tell him before he stands, holding me tight and kissing me just like the first time.

Only this time, our chakras are perfectly aligned.

To find out where Connor and Daisy are now, grab their bonus epilogue HERE

ALSO BY SAMANTHA SKYE

SAWYER

Working the land and raising my boys as a **single mom** is the only life I've ever known. Teaching during the day and parenting at night, my world begins and ends with them. But between managing a struggling farm in **small town** Whispers and nurturing a growing side hustle, I dream of a life beyond poverty—a chance to turn our hopes into reality.

I'm done living on handouts.

Then Sawyer shows up on my doorstep—the new local lawyer. A **billionaire** from the city, polished and privileged, he's clueless about **small-town** struggles, where food stamps and church donations mean survival. He says he wants to help, but I'm not some damsel in distress. His suits are pristine, my jeans are torn. His shoes gleam, my hair's a wild mess. He's polished perfection, and I'm pure chaos. **Total opposites.**

Yet, somehow, he breaks through my walls. And when he does, we're like a wildfire—intense, consuming, unstoppable. He's everything I never dared to want, offering me a fairytale I never thought I'd have.

But just as I begin to believe in a future beyond the struggle, danger comes knocking. The farm feels less like home and more like a target, my side business teeters on collapse, and my fears grow louder than ever. Life has knocked me down before, but this time, getting back up feels impossible. And the last thing I want is for Sawyer to fall down with me.

ALSO BY SAMANTHA SKYE

The Billionaires of Whispers

Tanner

Hudson

Connor

Sawyer

Sutton

Griffin

SCROOGE: A Billionaire Christmas Story

The Baltimore Boys

The Charming Billionaire

The Arrogant Billionaire

The Damaged Billionaire

The Secret Billionaire

The Bossy Billionaire

The Billionaire Babe

Men Of New York

My Legacy

My Destiny

My Fight

My Chance

Boston Billionaires

Coming Home

Finding Home

Leaving Home

Building Home

ABOUT THE AUTHOR

Samantha Skye is an international bestselling author. A country kid turned city slicker, she writes spicy and suspenseful contemporary romance novels that leave you hot under the collar and on the edge of your seat.

Samantha lives in Melbourne, Australia and when she's not plotting her next novel, she can be found travelling, drinking margaritas and enjoying a sunset or a stargaze somewhere.

To join in the conversation join Skye's The Limit Facebook group here;

https://www.facebook.com/groups/skyesthelimit books